Lost Angel

Lost Angel

MANDASUE HELLER

ISIS
LARGE PRINT
Oxford

First published in Great Britain 2012
by
Hodder & Stoughton Ltd.

Published in Large Print 2012 by ISIS Publishing Ltd.,
7 Centremead, Osney Mead, Oxford OX2 0ES
by arrangement with
Hodder & Stoughton Ltd.
An Hachette UK Company

British Library Cataloguing in Publication Data
Heller, Mandasue.
    Lost Angel.
    1. Large type books.
    I. Title
    823.9'2–dc23

ISBN 978–0–7531–9064–7 (hb)
ISBN 978–0–7531–9065–4 (pb)

Printed and bound in Great Britain by
T. J. International Ltd., Padstow, Cornwall

For Margaret Jobey
With joy to have known you,
and sorrow to have lost you

With much love to Wingrove, my mum Jean, Michael, Andrew, Azzura (and Michael), Marissa, Lariah, Antonio, Ava, Amber, Martin, Jade, Reece, Kyro, Diaz, Auntie Doreen, Peter, Lorna, Cliff, Chris, Glen — and the rest of my lovely family both here and abroad, past and present. Also Joseph & Mavis Ward, Jascinth, Donna, Valerie, Natalie, Dan, Toni, children, uncles & aunts.

Love to good friends, Liz, Norman, Betty and Ronnie, Martina, Kimberley and Wayne.

Special thanks to my editor, Carolyn Caughey, for her patience & advice; and to the rest of the guys at Hodder — Lucy, Emma, Phil, Francine etc . . .

Thanks, as always, to Cat Ledger and Nick Austin.

Also to Asda & Waterstones, and all of the other stores who have got behind me in such a great way — and, of course, you, the buyers & readers of my work.

And, lastly, thanks to my Facebook friends who played the game to find a title for my next book, especially Phil Martin and Alison Reeder, who both suggested the one that was ultimately chosen.

Oh, and not forgetting those who have been buying our and Azzura's music — thank you!

PROLOGUE

"I've missed you so much," Angel said softly.

"Missed you, too," said Ryan. "But we shouldn't be in here."

"I just want to be alone with you," she murmured.

He kissed her gently, but pulled back when she slid her hand down to his crotch. "Don't," he groaned.

"I love you," she told him huskily. "And you love me, too — don't you?"

"Yeah, course, baby girl. But you're only fifteen, and that's too —"

"Sshhh." She pressed a finger to his lips. "Don't say anything, just do it. Please . . . I really want you to."

She moved her hand back down and slowly unzipped his fly. Ryan closed his eyes. He knew it was wrong, but he'd been dreaming about this ever since he'd first met her, and he wasn't strong enough to resist.

"I haven't got anything on me," he gasped at the last minute.

"I don't care," Angel whispered, pulling him into her.

3

PART ONE

1995

CHAPTER
ONE

Johnny Conroy woke with a start to find Elvis standing over him.

"*Jeezus!*" he squawked, the sheet gathering in a roll beneath his heels as he scrabbled to sit up. "What's going on?"

"That's what I wanna know." The man's dark eyes scanned the messy room. "I take it you know why I'm here?"

Johnny swallowed nervously and shook his head. Frankie Hynes had the most unnatural shade of jet-black hair he'd ever seen, and his denim jeans and jacket — and shoestring tie complete with silver guitar clip — looked so ridiculous on a man of his age that Johnny would have pissed himself laughing if it had been anyone else wearing them.

But no one laughed at Frankie Hynes — not if they wanted to live.

"Is that perfume I can smell?" Frankie's nostrils twitched like those of a dog scenting drugs.

Johnny's blood froze when he remembered the girl he'd brought home from the club last night. He flicked a furtive glance at the other side of the bed — and thanked God when he saw that it was empty. He hadn't heard the girl leave, so she must have sneaked out while he was asleep — and he could only hope that she hadn't taken anything with her, like the contents of his wallet — or his weed.

Frankie's man-mountain of a mate, Big Pat O'Callaghan, had Johnny's flatmate Dave pinned up against the wall over by the door. He raised his head and gave a loud, exaggerated sniff.

"Yeah, I can smell perfume, an' all."

"It's aftershave," Johnny blurted out.

Frankie snapped his head around and peered down at him. "And why would you be needing aftershave, son? I know you wasn't with our Ruth last night, so who was you trying to impress?"

Johnny's mouth flapped open but nothing came out. Had someone seen him with the girl and reported him to Frankie? If so, he was already dead and Frankie was just toying with him.

"It was my birthday yesterday," Dave piped up — praying as he said it that Frankie wouldn't demand proof. "We just went out for a couple of pints with the lads, that's — *Aargh!*"

"Speak when you're spoken to, dickhead."

Johnny winced when Big pat punched Dave in the gut, but he had a feeling that worse was to come. He licked his lips nervously.

"Is — is something wrong, Frankie?"

"First off, it's Mr Hynes to you," Frankie said sharply. "And I'd say so, yeah. But I thought I'd hear what you had to say for yourself before I decide what to do about it."

8

Johnny was confused, and it showed on his face. Frankie leaned over him and bared his tobacco-stained teeth.

"Don't try and mug me off, son, 'cos you know *exactly* what I'm talking about. Your idea to get *her* to tell me, was it?"

Spittle dotted Johnny's face, but he didn't dare wipe it off. "I swear I don't know what you're talking about," he bleated truthfully.

"Let me spell it out for you, then," spat Frankie, his eyes flashing fire. "She's *pregnant* . . . you're gonna be a daddy."

"No way." Johnny's mouth had gone dry. "It's not mine."

The last words slipped out before he had a chance to stop them, and the punch landed like a sledgehammer, splitting his lip and sending a spray of blood up into the air. And then Frankie was on top of him, his hands around his throat.

"I didn't mean it!" Johnny squealed, choking as his lip ballooned and blood trickled down his throat. "I swear to God!"

Frankie tightened his grip, overcome by a sudden urge to put an end to this right here and now. Ruth deserved better than this piece of shit. But she was adamant that she loved Johnny, so what was a father to do?

"I trusted you," he snarled. "You came down to my yard and asked if you could take my girl out, and I thought, now *there's* a boy who knows the meaning of respect. And you swore you'd keep your dirty little hands to yourself. But I should've known you were lying, you little shit."

"I'm sorry," Johnny gasped, his face turning purple with the pressure. "Honest to God, Fra — Mr Hynes, I never meant for it to happen. It just —"

"If I had my way," Frankie cut him off, "I'd be slinging you off a bridge minus your fuckin' head right about now. But, lucky for you, Ruth's made me promise not to hurt you. So, here's what's going to happen . . . You're going to get your arse round to my place at seven tonight, and then you, me and her are going to sit down and work out where we go from here. Okay?"

"*Okay!*" Johnny squeaked.

Frankie let go and pushed himself up off the bed. "Seven o' clock," he repeated, wiping his hands on the quilt. "And just in case you get any stupid ideas about doing a runner — *don't*. 'Cos I'll hunt you down and skin you alive, and then I'll feed you to my dogs piece by fucking piece. Understand?"

"I'll b-be there," Johnny stuttered, his lip throbbing painfully.

Frankie gave him one last fierce look and then stalked out. Big Pat dropped Dave and followed, slamming the front door so hard that it sent the unopened mail wafting up the hall.

Dave untied his dressing gown and gingerly examined his ribs. The punch had hurt like hell, and he could have sworn he'd heard a crack, so he was surprised to see no obvious signs of damage. He covered himself backup and gave Johnny an accusing look.

"Hope you're pleased with yourself, you knob. You nearly got us fucking killed just then."

"Don't blame *me*," Johnny gasped, rubbing at his throat. "Blame Ruth. She's the one who —"

"Shut up!" Dave gestured frantically towards the door. "They might still be out there."

White as a sheet, Johnny cocked his head to one side and listened for sounds of movement. Hearing nothing after a moment, he eased the quilt off his legs and tiptoed to the window. A couple of minutes later, Frankie and Big Pat emerged from the stairwell and strolled towards the parking lot. Relieved when they climbed into Frankie's big red Cadillac and drove away, Johnny exhaled loudly and turned back to Dave.

"Don't ever do that to me again, man."

"*Me?*" Dave's eyebrows shot up. "What did *I* do?"

"You let them in," Johnny reminded him accusingly. "You must have known it'd be trouble when you saw who it was."

"Oh, yeah, 'cos they really gave me a chance to look. *You* might be able to sleep through a plane crash, but the sound of my front door getting booted in tends to put me in a bit of a fuckin' spin — know what I mean?"

Annoyed that Johnny was trying to make out like this was Dave's fault when he was the one who'd been shagging the man's daughter rigid for the last six months and got her up the duff, Dave kicked a path through the clothes littering the floor and snatched Johnny's cigarettes off the bedside table. About to light

11

up, he jumped when he heard a muffled cough from under the bed.

"Who the fuck's *that*?" He lifted the edge of the quilt and peeked in.

A naked girl was lying on top of the rubbish that had piled up under the bed. "Room service?" she quipped, grinning at him.

Already shocked, Dave's eyes widened further when she wriggled out, and his gaze slid like melting wax from her face to her tits to her pussy.

"I thought you'd gone!" Johnny gasped, dreading to think what would have happened if it had been Frankie who'd found her.

"Nah, I was hiding." The girl reached for her T-shirt and tugged it over her head. She pulled her hair free and grimaced at Johnny's split lip. "That looks nasty. You'd best put some ice on it before it splits even more."

"Never mind that," he snapped. "If you had time to hide you must have heard them coming in, so how come you didn't warn *me*?"

"I thought it was dibble, and my mum would go mental if I got arrested again, so I didn't stop to think. Sorry." She crawled across the bed and retrieved her knickers from beneath the pillow. "Haven't seen my bra, have you?"

"Never mind your fucking bra," Johnny said angrily. "This is your fault, this. If you'd warned me, I'd have had a chance to talk my way out of it."

The girl gave a derisive snort. "After what I just heard, I reckon you deserved everything you got, mate.

But while we're on that tip, how come *you* didn't warn *me* that you had a girlfriend before you ripped my knickers off last night? I don't do sloppy seconds. You could have given me a disease, for all I know."

"Best get yourself round to the clinic, then, hadn't you?" Johnny said nastily, wondering what had possessed him to bring a bitch like her back to the flat in the first place. He must have been even more bladdered than he'd thought last night.

The girl gave him a contemptuous look and pulled on her jeans before snatching her jacket off the floor.

"I won't say it was a pleasure, 'cos you were shit," she sniped, heading for the door. "And I hope the baby doesn't take after you or it'll be a right little mong."

"Fuck off!" Furious now, Johnny looked around for something to throw at her.

She stuck up two fingers and sauntered out, her hips swaying sexily.

"Wow, man, she's *hot*," Dave murmured, leaning back to watch.

"Go after her if you're that desperate," Johnny snapped.

"Aw, quite sulking," Dave chided, turning back to him when she'd gone. "It ain't her fault you've got yourself in Frankie's bad books. Anyhow, considering what he *could* have done, I reckon you got off pretty lightly."

"You what?" Johnny screwed up his face. "Ruth's pregnant, and she's pinning it on me. How's that getting off lightly?"

"I did warn you," Dave reminded him unsympathetically. "I told you to steer clear of her from the start."

"No, you didn't."

"Mate, I *so* did. There were tons of birds at the club that night, and you could have had your pick of 'em. But, no . . . you had to go and prove what a stud you are by bedding Frankie Hynes's girl."

"Yeah, well, it's not all me," Johnny grumbled. "She's like a leech. Frankie doesn't know the half of it."

"Neither do I by the sounds of it," Dave drawled. He lit his cigarette and blew out a smoke ring. "Never told me you went down to his yard and asked his permission to take her out. What kind of arse-licking bollocks is that?"

Embarrassed to be caught out as a creep, Johnny's cheeks reddened. "Just thought it was the right thing to do. It didn't mean anything."

"You were trying to get in with him through Ruth," Dave corrected him knowingly. "Don't try and shit a shitter, matey."

"Yeah, well, that was before I realised what she was like."

"So why didn't you finish with her before it got to this?"

"I've *tried*. But it's like she knows what I'm going to say and goes all emotional on me before I can get it out — crying, and going on about how she'll kill herself if she ever loses me. And who do you reckon Frankie'd blame if anything happened to her?"

Dave sighed. "Well, it's too late to get rid of her now. Looks like you're gonna be stuck with her for life."

14

"Don't be stupid." Johnny frowned. "They can't force me to stay with her."

"And you're gonna tell Frankie that, are you?" Dave raised an eyebrow. "You're gonna go round there tonight and say sorry, mate, but your Ruth was nowt but a shag, and I don't want a kid with her?"

"If that's what it takes, yeah."

Johnny turned his back, and Dave watched as he examined his lip in the dressing-table mirror with a self-pitying look on his face. He could talk big now that Frankie and Big Pat had gone, but they both knew he'd bottle it when he went round to the Hyneses' place later. Just like they both knew that Dave *had* warned him off Ruth. But, as usual, Johnny's ego had turned him deaf. As soon as he'd realised who her dad was, he'd gone all out to get off with her.

Well, he'd succeeded, but Dave doubted whether he'd bargained for any of this when he'd bagged his prize.

"What am I going to do?" Johnny moaned, dropping his head into his hands.

Dave took another drag on his smoke and shrugged.

"No point asking me, 'cos you never listen to anything I've got to say. If you did, you'd have worn a joey when you shagged her — like I told you. And I wouldn't even mind, but they're free at the clinic. You're just too lazy to get your arse round there."

Johnny mumbled something about being allergic to rubber but, in truth, he just didn't see why he should have to suffer numb-cock sex when it was the girl's responsibility to make sure she didn't get pregnant.

None of the others had ever been stupid enough to get caught. If they had, they'd obviously done the sensible thing and dealt with it without bothering him. They certainly hadn't sent their psycho dads round to tell him about it.

Dave knew he was struggling and felt sorry for him.

"Look, it's a bit late for shoulda woulda couldas," he said. "But if it was me — which it wouldn't be, 'cos I'm not that stupid — I'd act like a total twat when I went round there."

"How's that supposed to help?" Johnny frowned up at him.

"Well, we both know you're a waste of space," Dave explained. "So all you've got to do is convince Frankie of that and you'll be laughing."

"Waste of space?" Johnny's frown deepened.

"The way I see it," Dave went on, undeterred, "Ruth's way more into you than you are with her, so she's never going to give up on you if everything stays the same. But if you change, it'll throw her off balance."

"How am I supposed to change before seven?" Johnny asked. "Put on a load of weight so she thinks I'm too fat for her? Or how about I grow a beard? Yeah, she hates beards, that should do it."

"I'm not talking physical changes," Dave told him patiently. "I'm talking attitude. Mind you, you could start with a physical," he added, wrinkling his nose. "Go round there stinking like this and she'll boot you right back out."

"I don't stink," Johnny protested.

16

"Mate, you smell like a badger," Dave told him truthfully, picking up on the mingled odours of sweaty socks, unwashed sheets and sex. "But that's good if it stops Ruth from wanting to get too close. And you should turn up late so her folks think you're unreliable. And call her by the wrong name — that *proper* flips birds out, that." He gave Johnny a sly grin. "Do it my way, and I guarantee they won't want you anywhere near her *or* the kid."

Johnny thought about it. It would be a hell of a risk to act so disrespectfully in Frankie's house, but even if it earned him the beating of his life wasn't that better than being tied to Ruth for the next sixteen years or more?

"All right, I'll give it a shot," he said. Then, taking a surreptitious sniff of his armpit: "Do I really stink?"

The look Dave gave him was answer enough.

CHAPTER
TWO

Ruth was in her bedroom when Johnny arrived, but she didn't hear the bell because of the music blasting up through the floor from the parlour below. Her mum had hit the whisky straight after her dad had gone out this morning, and the more she drank, the louder she played her music. The Slim Whitman album had been on repeat-play for the last few hours, and it was at max volume now, so the house was literally rattling around them.

Ruth had escaped before the booze had had a chance to take control of her mum's tongue as well as her ears, because she was vicious when she got started, and Ruth always got the brunt of it — whether she deserved it or not. But while she usually didn't, she couldn't deny that she'd brought it on herself today. Her dad had been furious, and her mum still was.

But it was Johnny's reaction she was dreading the most.

He was going to be so pissed off at her for sending her dad round to tell him about the baby. But she'd been too scared to do it herself — terrified that he would tell her to get rid of it, and then finish with her to make sure it didn't happen again. That was why

18

she'd decided to tell her dad, because she'd known that once he got his head around it he would insist on telling Johnny "man to man", and then Johnny wouldn't dare turn his back on her.

It was one of the rare occasions when Ruth was glad to have Frankie Hynes for a father, but it hadn't always been such a blessing. The neighbours had banned their kids from playing with her when she was growing up, scared that she would taint them by association. And the local lads had given her a very wide berth, terrified of what her dad would do if he caught them sniffing around her. That was why she'd fallen so hard for Johnny when he'd approached her at that club. He'd said he didn't give a toss who her dad was, he liked *her* and wanted to get to know who *she* was. Those words had melted her heart — and it hadn't hurt that he was the most gorgeous lad she'd ever seen, with beautiful blue eyes, thick chocolate-brown hair, and a cheeky, sexy grin that still, six months down the line now, made her go weak at the knees.

Johnny was the first lad she'd ever gone all the way with, and she'd known as soon as it happened that he'd be her last, so it had almost killed her when her cousin Lisa had come to her a couple of weeks later and told her that he'd been seen with another girl. Ruth had cried her eyes out over that, heartbroken to think that her man would even think about cheating on her. And he *was* her man. She'd given herself to him heart and soul, and no bitch was ever going to steal him away from her.

She hadn't dared to confront him in case he admitted that it was true, so, instead, she'd convinced herself that Lisa was lying. And that was feasible enough, since it had been obvious from the start that Lisa had wanted Johnny for herself. She'd slept with his best mate, Dave, that night, but Ruth had seen the way she'd looked at Johnny when she thought no one was watching — like she was just dying to get her lips around his *thing*. And then there was all that stuff she'd said about him when they'd been walking back to hers the next morning; calling him a pretty boy, and a poser, and telling Ruth that she was fooling herself if she thought she was ever going to see him again, because boys like him were only after one thing — and now he'd got it he wouldn't want to know.

Well, Johnny had proved Lisa wrong about that. And now Ruth would prove her wrong about everything else. Whatever Johnny might or might not have done behind her back in the past, now that he knew she was carrying his baby he would put his partying ways behind him and step up to the mark and support her.

But she was still dreading having to face him, and she sighed now as she gazed at her reflection. She was a pretty girl, with thick black hair, Bambi brown eyes, and plump pink lips that would have been described as kissable if they weren't always pursed in disapproval. But, right now, she looked a mess from all the crying she'd done today. Her eyes were puffy, and her nose was an ugly, shiny red blob.

But she'd already reapplied her make-up several times over to no avail, so there was nothing more she could do. She just hoped that Johnny would be too wrapped up in thoughts of being a dad to notice.

Outside on the doorstep, Johnny rang the bell for a second time — although he didn't see how anyone on the inside expected to hear it over the God-awful country music they were blasting out.

This was the first time he'd ever been to the house. Ruth had invited him round loads of times, but always when Frankie was out of town. And since it was Frankie he'd been desperate to get in with, Johnny hadn't seen the point. Now that he was actually here, it was nothing like he'd imagined. He'd thought it would be some kind of mansion, with stone lions on the gateposts and a fancy fountain on the manicured lawn — because that was the kind of place *he'd* have bought if he was as loaded as Frankie was supposed to be. But this was just a semi — and a shabby one at that, even by Johnny's standards, which were pretty low considering the squalor of the flats he'd grown up in and now lived in by choice. There were chunks of plasterwork missing off the walls, and the fence was falling to pieces, while the garden was little more than a mud-pit dumping ground for all the knackered old motors that were parked up on it. The way Ruth acted, he wouldn't have been surprised to learn that the Hyneses were related to the queen. But now he knew that they were no better than him, he felt a bit easier about being here.

Johnny pushed the bell for a third time, and added a couple of sharp raps on the knocker for good measure.

That did the trick. The music stopped abruptly and, seconds later, the door opened and a gaunt-featured skinnier version of Ruth stared out at him. Guessing it to be her mother, he held out his hand and gave her one his most charming smiles.

"Mrs Hynes? Hi, I'm Johnny . . . Ruth's friend."

Rita Hynes's thin lips arched down in a contemptuous sneer.

"Is that what you call it these days? Not boyfriend, or lover? Or how about *father of the illegitimate child she shouldn't be carrying?*"

Engulfed by a waft of sour whisky-breath, Johnny drew his head back and stuffed his hands into his pockets. So much for the charm offensive. There was no need to guess how bad this was going to be, because Rita Hynes wasn't even bothering to pretend it would be pleasant.

"You might as well come in now you're here," Rita ordered, drink sloshing over the rim of the glass she was holding as she stepped aside to let him in. She slammed the door shut behind him. "Frankie's running late, so you'll have to make do with me till he gets here. And *her*," she added, glancing back when she heard footsteps on the staircase.

Ruth's cheeks were crimson when she reached the foot of the stairs.

"Why don't you go and sit down?" she suggested quietly to her mother. "I'll let you know when Dad gets home."

Rita stayed put stubbornly and raised the glass to her lips. She took a long, slow drink and raked her gaze from Johnny's face to his feet and back again. Then, sniffing as if she couldn't understand what all the fuss was about, she walked unsteadily down the hall and disappeared into her parlour.

Ruth turned to Johnny when she'd gone, all set to apologise. But the words died on her tongue when she saw his face.

"Oh, please don't tell me my dad did that? He *swore* he wouldn't hurt you."

"He didn't," Johnny lied, guessing that Frankie wouldn't be too happy if he told her the truth, considering *he* obviously hadn't. "I, er, got a bit roughed up playing footie with the lads."

"*Footie?*"

A frown of disapproval replaced the concern as Ruth wondered how he could even think about playing games after receiving such life-changing news. And then she noticed how dirty his clothes were, and saw a bit of sock peeping out through a hole in the toe of his scuffed trainers, and the frown deepened.

"You could have got changed before you came round," she scolded. "You must know how important it is to make a good impression — tonight of all nights."

"Didn't have time," Johnny replied, shrugging as if he didn't see the problem — although he was secretly pleased that Dave's plan seemed to be working already.

He'd been nowhere near a football pitch, as it happened, he just hadn't bothered washing today. He also hadn't brushed his teeth, and had spent the last few hours chain-smoking to ensure that his breath smelled rank. And, to complete the picture of shameless neglect, he'd pulled the dirtiest clothes he could find from the bottom of the pile on his bedroom floor.

Ruth wasn't impressed, but she bit her tongue, reminding herself that it maybe wasn't too smart to criticise him when she was the one who was trying to put their relationship on a firmer footing.

"Sorry." She dropped the scowl and gave him an apologetic smile. "Didn't mean to be so tetchy, but it's been a bit tense round here today. Anyway, let me get you a drink while we wait for my dad. Do you want a brew, or something stronger?"

"Tea," Johnny murmured, disappointed that she hadn't reacted more strongly, because he'd put a lot of effort into making it look like he'd made none. And he could have murdered a beer, but he had a feeling he was going to need a clear head for when Frankie got home.

Ruth led him into the kitchen and waved for him to take a seat at the table while she got on with preparing the drinks. If she'd been nervous before, she was even more so now. Johnny hadn't kissed her — although that was hardly surprising, because her mum's presence was enough to put anyone off. But he also hadn't hugged her. And his face was giving absolutely nothing away, so she had no clue how he was feeling.

When everything had been done that could be done, and all that was left was to wait for the kettle to boil, Ruth turned around and leaned back against the ledge. Even with his battered face and dirty clothes, Johnny was still heart-wrenchingly handsome, and she longed to feel his arms around her, to hear him say that

24

everything was going to be okay. But there was an invisible wall between them, and she wasn't brave enough to scale it on her own.

Johnny was looking around, taking in the fact that the inside of the house was every bit as shabby as the outside. The floor was covered in the same type of lino as his nan's — although this was way more scuffed and cracked; and the fridge and washing machine looked older than him, Ruth, and his nan combined. But it was pretty clean for all that, and somebody had tried to pretty it up by putting a vase of flowers in the middle of the table — although, if their sweet scent was supposed to mask the nasty smell that was hanging in the air, it wasn't working. He'd caught a whiff of it out in the hall, but it was far stronger in here, and he guessed it was coming from the drains — or maybe from the bulging bin-bags he'd just noticed heaped up against the back door.

The kettle switched itself off with a loud click. Glancing around, Johnny was unnerved to find Ruth staring at him with a strange intensity in her eyes.

"Are you all right?" he asked.

Shaken from her thoughts by the sound of his voice, she blushed and placed her hands over her stomach.

"Just feel a bit sick. It's been coming and going for the last few days, but I'm hoping it won't last as long as it did for my mum. She reckons it went on all the way through with me."

Wishing he hadn't asked, Johnny gave her a tight smile and gazed down at his hands. But Ruth wasn't about to let him lapse back into silence. Now that the subject had been broached, she was determined to keep him talking.

"I hope it wasn't too much of a shock, my dad coming round like that?" she asked. "I wanted to tell you myself but he insisted."

"It was a bit," Johnny admitted. "Can't say it's the best news I've ever heard."

Tears sprang into Ruth's eyes and she dug her nails into her palms to keep them at bay. She didn't know what she'd expected him to say, but she'd hoped it would be more positive than *that*.

"What's up now?" Johnny asked when he saw her glittering eyes. "Have I said something wrong?"

"No." She folded her arms tightly as her chin started wobbling. "I just thought you might be a bit happier about it, that's all."

"Are you kidding?" Johnny screwed up his face and stared at her in disbelief. "What lad in their right mind would want to be a dad at my age?"

A tear escaped and trickled slowly down her cheek. Groaning when he saw it, he said, "Oh, don't start, Ruth. That ain't gonna help."

"I'm *pregnant*," she whined. "And you don't care, so I think I've got a right to be upset."

"Course I care," he lied, wishing she'd keep it down before her mum heard her and came rushing in to see what was wrong. "But you must know this isn't going to work."

"Why not?"

26

"Because I'm only nineteen, and you've only just turned seventeen. How can we have a kid when we're still kids ourselves? We'd be shit parents."

"Other people manage. And so will we."

"Oh, get real," Johnny moaned, slumping back in his seat. "I'm doing my best here, but you're not making it easy."

"You think it's easy for *me*?" Ruth shot back tearfully. "I'm the one who's carrying it — the one who's being sick and getting fat." Her face crumpled now, and she wailed, "I'm going to be a big fat pig, and you won't w-want me any *moooore*."

I don't even want you now! thought Johnny, grimacing when he saw the snot bubbling out of her nose. He didn't know why girls thought that crying softened a man's heart; it just turned his stomach and made him want to tell them how ugly they looked.

Her sobs were getting louder by the second. Desperate to shut her up, Johnny sat forward and said quietly, "Look, you're not fat. But if it's upsetting you this much just *thinking* about it, don't you think that's a good reason to put a stop to it before it gets that far?"

Ruth inhaled sharply as if he'd just punched her in the stomach.

"You want me to kill our *baby*? Just to stop myself from getting *fat*?"

"You're the one who's getting worked up about it," Johnny reminded her. "I'm only saying it would be better if we —"

"Better if you what?"

Almost falling off his seat in shock, Johnny turned and gaped at Frankie standing behind him in the doorway.

"I said, better if you *what?*" Frankie repeated, walking fully into the room now and slamming his car keys down on the table. "Come on, big lad . . . you had enough to say when you thought it was just you and her."

"I — I was just saying I think we're too young for a baby," Johnny croaked. "And it might be better if we — you know — think about stopping it before it goes too far."

He cast a helpless look at Ruth, begging her with his eyes to help him out. But she raised her chin and shook her head.

"I wouldn't get rid of it even if I could," she said, a firmness in her voice that hadn't been there moments earlier. "I've wanted it from the second I knew about it. It's ours, and I already love it — just like I love you."

She and Frankie both stared at Johnny now, and he started to feel physically sick. That was obviously his cue to say it back, but he didn't feel that way, so he couldn't.

Frankie hissed in disgust and looked at Ruth. Shaking his head when he saw the desperation in her eyes, he said, "I don't know why you're bothering, love. He obviously don't feel the same. Know what he said when I told him about the baby? He said it ain't his."

"You *didn't?*" Ruth gaped at Johnny in disbelief. "Why would you say something so horrible? You know you're the only one I've ever been with."

Ashamed of how pathetic he sounded, Johnny muttered, "I didn't mean it like that. You know what I'm like. I don't think before I speak, and shit just —" He caught himself and gave Frankie a nervous look. "Sorry, *stuff* just jumps out of my mouth."

Frankie leaned forward and slammed his fist down on the table, knocking the vase over.

"It ain't the stuff coming out of your mouth I'm bothered about, it's the stuff you've been putting *in her*." He jabbed a finger in Ruth's direction. Then, straightening up, he rolled his head on his neck until a loud crack echoed through the kitchen and said, "But the doctor says it's too late to get rid, so we need to decide what we're gonna do about it."

Not daring to move as the spilled flower water poured down onto his trainers, Johnny cast a hooded glance of accusation at Ruth, silently cursing her for letting him go on about getting rid of the baby when she already knew it was too late.

"Am I talking to my fucking self here?" Frankie snapped. "I said what are we going to do about it?"

Johnny was well and truly trapped. He spread his palms in a gesture of surrender and said, "I'll do whatever you want, Mr Hynes. I know it won't be much after I've given my flatmate my share of the electric, and food, and that, but I'll give you whatever's left of my dole money. And I'll do my share of babysitting, and make —"

"Are you having a laugh?" Frankie interrupted. "You think I'm gonna let you walk away and leave her to do all the dirty work? Not a chance, sunshine! You both had the fun of making it, so you'll both have the grief of fetching it up."

"I've already said I'll do my bit," Johnny mumbled. "Any time you want me to have it, just tell me and I'll come and get it."

Frankie inhaled deeply and clenched his fists. The boy was winding him up, and he was struggling to keep his hands off him. But he'd promised Ruth, so he had to try.

"You still ain't getting it," he said through gritted teeth. "My girl ain't gonna be no single mother. And no grandchild of mine is coming into this world a bastard."

It took a few seconds for the meaning of his words to sink in. When it did, Johnny's eyes widened.

"You're not serious?"

Frankie's patience snapped and he seized Johnny by the collar, barking, "Do I look like I'm fucking joking?" as he slapped him hard around the face.

"Dad, stop it!" Ruth yelped, pushing herself away from the ledge and rushing over to drag him off. "Let go!" She tugged on his arm. "*Please*, Dad . . . you promised."

"Stay out of this." Frankie shrugged her off. "This is between me and him."

"But it's my baby," she protested.

"*And* his," said Frankie, as if he needed to remind her. "And he ain't worming his way out of it."

"I'm not trying to," Johnny spluttered, blood trickling from his nose. "And I swear to God I'll do my bit. But you can't seriously expect us to get *married*?"

30

"That's *exactly* what I expect," Frankie told him, his face so close that Johnny could almost taste the onions the man'd had on his lunchtime burger.

Ruth's mouth flapped open in shock. She'd known when she started this that her dad would force Johnny to come round, and she'd hoped that he would make him promise to stand by her. But she hadn't expected *this*. It was beyond her wildest dreams.

"That's what you want, isn't it?" Frankie glanced back at her. "'Cos if I've got it wrong, just say the word and I'll sort it."

All too aware that he meant he would sort *Johnny* out — once and for all — Ruth said, "Yes! Our baby needs him, and so do I."

Frankie's chest rose and fell as he battled to bring his temper under control. The boy didn't deserve his daughter, but Ruth would never forgive him if he didn't give her the chance to find that out for herself. Anyway, as he'd already said, she would be left holding the baby if he allowed the cunt to walk away — or, rather, *he and Rita* would, and there was no way he was having that.

"All right, you win," he conceded, releasing Johnny and holding up his hands. "I won't say I'm happy about it, 'cos I'm not. But if this is what you want, you've got my blessing."

"*Really?*" Ruth's eyes flooded with tears again, but of joy this time, not pain. "Oh, thank you, Daddy, thank you!"

"What's all the noise?" Rita demanded, lumbering through the door, glass in hand.

"I'm getting married!" Ruth announced, her face glowing with happiness.

"Well, halle-flamin'-lujah for that!" Rita muttered. "And there was me thinking we were going to have to hide the little bastard under the stairs when it pops out."

Frankie could smell the alcohol on his wife's breath from all the way across the room. Pushing his daughter aside, he said, "How much have you had?"

"Not nearly enough if I can still hear *you*," Rita drawled, giving him a dirty look as she lurched over to the table and flopped into a chair. "See how he talks to me?" She swivelled her glassy gaze onto Johnny. "Always trying to tell me what to do and when to do it, like I haven't got a mind of my own. You know what he is, Jimmy? He's a . . . a . . ." She trailed off and pushed out her lips in search of a cutting enough word to describe her husband.

Frankie had heard enough. He clicked his fingers at Ruth. "Get her upstairs and sort her out."

Rita snapped her head around and fixed her daughter with a fierce glare. "Touch me and I'll claw your bleedin' eyes out," she warned, her posh accent slipping momentarily into the gutter.

Ruth knew better than to mess with her mum when she was in this kind of mood, so she held up her hands and backed off.

Rita turned back to her husband. "And you ever dare talk to me like that in front of company again, Frankie Hynes, and so help me I'll . . ."

She didn't finish the sentence, but the unspoken words hung heavy in the air as she and Frankie locked stares across the table, and Johnny held his breath, waiting for all hell to break loose. To his relief, the phone started ringing out in the hall, and Frankie broke the stare to go and answer it.

"I've got to go," he said when he came back a couple of minutes later.

"Where to now?" Rita demanded.

"Never you mind," he muttered, snatching his keys off the table.

"That's right, you run out and leave us to do all the work, as usual," Rita snarled, her eyes flashing with fury. "In out, in out — that's you all over, that. And never mind that we've got a flaming wedding to arrange."

"That's your department, not mine," Frankie retorted smoothly. "Just send me the bill when you've finished. And don't leave it too late, 'cos I'm not having her walk up the aisle in a fuckin' tent and have people say that's why she's doing it. We'll wait till a few weeks after the wedding, then tell 'em she got caught first time."

"Don't you think they might get a bit suspicious when it arrives a few months early?" Rita pointed out.

"They can think what they like, so long as they keep their gobs shut around me," said Frankie. He turned to leave now, but hesitated when he saw Johnny's miserable expression. "You're not looking too happy there, son. Hope you haven't forgotten what I said about the dogs?"

Johnny shook his head and gazed down at his sodden feet. He felt like he was about to pass out — wished that he could. But he wasn't that lucky.

"What are you talking about?" Ruth asked, looking from Johnny to her dad.

"Nothing that concerns you," Frankie said sharply. Then, "But that reminds me . . . now we know what you've been getting up to behind our backs, you don't go near *him* again between now and the wedding unless me or your mam is with you. Got that?"

Ruth opened her mouth to argue, but quickly closed it again. It would be awful not being able to see Johnny but she knew better than to disobey her dad. And, anyway, it wouldn't be for long. When they were married, she'd be able to see him as often as she liked.

Frankie left at last. Waiting until she'd heard the front door close behind him, Ruth took a pack of tissues out of a drawer and carried them over to Johnny.

"Sorry that got so heavy," she apologised, wiping the drying blood from his nose. "He said he wanted to talk, but I had no idea he was going to spring that on you."

Her words brought Johnny's head up with a snap. Of course! This wedding was Frankie's idea, but he couldn't make it happen if they *both* refused to go along with it.

"Tell him you won't do it," he blurted out.

"I *can't!*" Ruth gasped, a look of horror leaping into her eyes.

"Please," Johnny pleaded, clutching at her hand. "I'm begging you."

34

"No," Ruth said firmly. "You heard him. He doesn't want the baby to be born a bastard. And neither do I."

"Over my dead body," Rita chipped in indignantly. "And have everyone looking down their noses at me? I don't think so. This wedding is *on*, and that's final!" She slapped her hand down on the table to emphasise her words, completely forgetting about the glass she was holding.

"Oh, Mum, look what you've done!" Ruth cried when it shattered and blood spilled onto the lino at her feet.

Johnny jumped up and backed away from the table. "Should I call an ambulance?"

"No!" Ruth shook her head and grabbed a tea towel to try and stem the flow. "She's had too much to drink; she'll only fight with them. But you can drive us, if you want. Take those keys." She nodded at a set hanging on a hook behind the door. "There's a Merc down the side of the house. Go and start it up."

Too anaesthetised by the whisky she'd consumed to feel the pain, Rita slapped her daughter's hands away.

"Stop fussing, stupid. It's only a scratch."

"It needs looking at," Ruth insisted.

"Your *head* needs looking at," Rita retorted nastily. "Little Miss Perfect's really gone and done it this time, hasn't she? Daddy's precious little girl ain't so special now he knows she's nothing but a common little slut."

Ruth dipped her head and let her hair fall over her face to hide her blushes. She was used to her mum's tongue, but it was humiliating to have Johnny witness it in action.

"Let me see your hand," she ordered through gritted teeth.

Rita gave her a dirty look, but did as she'd been told and thrust out her hand. Ruth dabbed at it with the tea towel. The bleeding seemed to be slowing down, and she decided that maybe it wasn't as bad as it had looked initially.

"Okay, I'll clean it up and put a bandage on it for now. But if it's not healed by morning I'm calling the doctor."

"Yakity yak," mocked Rita, making a chatterbox gesture with her uninjured hand as Ruth walked out into the hall to get the things she needed from the first-aid box.

She got up when Ruth had gone and lumbered across to the cupboard. Taking out a glass and a fresh bottle of whisky, she eyed Johnny as she poured herself a shot.

"Why are you still standing there like a spare part? We've got stuff to talk about, so you'd best just sit yourself back down."

Johnny didn't want to spend one more second with the obnoxious bitch. His head was already throbbing from the shrillness of her voice. And as pissed off as he was with Ruth for putting him in this position, now that he'd seen how badly she was treated he actually felt sorry for her.

"I should get going," he muttered. "I said I'd give someone a hand with —"

"Like dates," Rita spoke over him as she carried her drink back to the table. "The thirteenth of next month

36

is good for me, because that's when my dad passed away. But I might compromise if you've got a special date of your own in mind."

Johnny's head started to swim. She had to be fucking joking. That was less than three weeks away.

Rita looked up at him expectantly. When he didn't answer and made no move to sit, she narrowed her eyes and made a barking sound to remind him of her husband's warning. And when his face paled all over again, she let out a cackling laugh.

"What's the joke?" Ruth asked, returning with a bandage, some plasters, and a pair of scissors and laying them all on the table.

"*You* are," Rita sneered, swiping the items onto the floor with the back of her hand. Smirking when Ruth bent down to pick them up, she drained her glass and held it out to Johnny. "Here . . . make yourself useful and get me another one. Then piss off."

"Mum, don't be so rude!" Ruth protested. "And why are you sending him home when you've only just told him to stay?"

"I'm sick of looking at him," spat Rita, giving Johnny a dirty look as he went to refill her glass. "Anyhow, men are fucking useless when it comes to weddings. You only have to look at your toerag of a father to know that."

Ruth's heart sank. Her mum only ever swore like this when she'd reached the point of no return alcohol-wise. And, much as Ruth didn't want Johnny to leave — because she didn't know when she'd get the chance to see him again before the wedding — she knew that it would probably be safer if he did.

Johnny was already on it. Handing Rita's fresh drink to her, he said, "Right, I'll get out of your way. Nice meeting you, Mrs Hynes. I'll see myself out. Bye."

"Thanks," Ruth hissed, flashing her mum a sulky look before darting after him.

Johnny yanked the front door open and almost fell over the step in his haste to get out. Close on his heels, Ruth pulled the door to and gazed sadly up at him.

"I'm going to miss you so much," she said, shivering as the cold night air bit into her. "Are you going to miss me?"

"Mmm," Johnny murmured, taking a couple of backward steps onto the path.

"I'm sorry I won't be able to see you before the wedding," Ruth went on regretfully. "But it won't be for long. And I suppose we'll have plenty to keep us occupied till we're together again." Smiling now, she added, "I can't wait to tell Lisa. She's going to be *so* jealous. What do you think Dave will say?"

That I'm the biggest idiot walking, thought Johnny.

"I, er, don't know," he said, stumbling back towards the gate. "See you later."

Sighing wistfully when he turned and walked away, Ruth wrapped her arms around herself and watched until he'd faded into the darkness at the end of the avenue. When she could no longer see him, she went back into the house, picked up the phone and dialled a number.

"Hello, Lisa? You're not going to believe what's just happened . . ."

★   ★   ★

38

Dave was lying on the couch watching a video when Johnny walked in. He jumped up, switched the TV off and gave his flatmate a quizzical look.

"Well?"

"Not now." Johnny shrugged out of his jacket and tossed it over the back of the couch. "My head's mashed. I just need a spliff, then I'm hitting the sack."

Dave reached for his stash tin and started rolling, looking at Johnny out of the corner of his eye as he did it.

"Well, you haven't got any new bruises, so I'm guessing it didn't kick off. And you're back, so Frankie didn't lock you up and throw away the key. All pretty positive so far."

"You couldn't be more wrong if you tried," muttered Johnny, flopping into his chair.

"Why, what happened?" Dave pounced. "Come on, you might as well tell me now you've started. You know you want to."

Johnny groaned and ran a hand over his eyes. He really didn't want to discuss this until he'd got his own head around it, but he knew that Dave wouldn't let up until he'd heard every little detail. So, sighing, he said, "He wants us to get married."

Dave had finished rolling by now and was leaning forward to get his lighter off the coffee table. Pausing mid-stretch, he gaped at his friend.

"You're shitting me?"

"Wish I was." Johnny rested his head on the back of the chair and stared miserably up at the ceiling.

Dave lit the spliff and took a couple of quick tokes before handing it to his friend.

"You didn't agree to do it, did you?"

Johnny gave him a *what do you think?* look.

"Did he actually say the M word?" Dave persisted. "Or are you just assuming that's what he meant? No offence, mate, but I know what you're like for twisting things around and hearing what you want to hear — or should I say *don't* want to, in this case."

"Oh, he said it, all right," Johnny replied miserably. "And then he fucked off out and left me with Ruth and her alkie mother. Hope you're free on the thirteenth of next month, by the way, 'cos that's when Ruth's grandad died, and her mum seems to think that'd be a good . . ."

He trailed off when he felt a sudden breeze around his ankles, and looked up in time to see Dave heading out into the hall.

"I'm going to round up the lads," Dave called back over his shoulder. "This needs more heads. Won't be a minute."

"*No!*" Johnny shot up in his seat. "Frankie doesn't want anyone to know about the baby."

"Bit late for that," Dave retorted bluntly. "She could be showing any minute, depending how far on she is, then they'll all know anyway."

"Yeah, but he doesn't want them finding out *before* the wedding," Johnny told him. "And I'm in enough shit without you and your big mouth making it worse, so just get back in here and sit down."

40

Dave obeyed reluctantly. Putting his elbows on his knees, he pursed his lips thoughtfully and stared at the floor.

"Right," he said, looking up after a few minutes. "The way I see it, there's only one way out of this: you're going to have to do one. And before you say you're skint, *I've* got a bit of money saved. It's not much, but it should see you right for a few days. And —"

"I know you're trying to help," Johnny interrupted, passing the spliff back to him. "But you heard what Frankie said this morning about hunting me down if I try to do a runner."

"Aw, that was just talk." Dave was dismissive. "Anyway, he'll never find you if you get far enough away."

"Know anyone in Australia I can stay with, do you? 'Cos that's how far I'd need to go. And, even then, I reckon he'd find me."

Dave shrugged. "I don't know what else to suggest, mate."

"No point thinking about it, 'cos it ain't going to change anything," Johnny said philosophically. He gave a resigned sigh and got up. "See you in the morning."

"You can't go to bed," Dave protested. "We need to talk about this."

"I've got a headache," Johnny reminded him.

"More like you just don't want to hear what I've got to say, 'cos you know I'm right," Dave argued.

"Right about what?" Johnny paused in the doorway and looked back at him with a look of strained patience on his face.

"About not needing to be married to be a dad, for starters," said Dave. "Our mams and dads never got wed, and we did all right."

"This is different," Johnny told him. "The Hyneses are Catholics."

"So?" Dave shrugged again. "Anyhow, have you ever thought this might be a wind-up?"

"What are you talking about?" Johnny asked, resting his aching head against the door frame.

"I saw the way Frankie looked at you this morning, and there's no way he wants you with Ruth," Dave told him knowingly. "And I reckon he knows it's the last thing *you* want, an' all. My bet is he's doing this to punish you. Making you squirm before he kicks you out on your arse."

"Hope so," Johnny murmured. But he knew in his heart that it wasn't true. Ruth was pregnant, and she wanted him involved — and, good daddy that Frankie was, he was going to see to it that she got what she wanted.

CHAPTER
THREE

Johnny stayed in bed for the next three days, struggling to get his head around everything that had happened. He was glad that Frankie had banned Ruth from coming round because he didn't think he could handle seeing her just now. But he still had Dave to contend with, and his friend had been a proper pain, popping in and out every five minutes with spliffs and suggestions as to how Johnny could get out of the wedding — each of which was more implausible than the last, ranging from Johnny *accidentally-with-a-little-help-from-Dave* falling off the fifth-floor balcony and breaking every bone in his body so he couldn't get to the church to him declaring that he was a secret tranny, and wondered if Frankie would mind if he and Ruth wore matching dresses on the big day.

Dave was trying to help, but he was wrong if he thought that Frankie was joking about the wedding. Frankie wouldn't just get mad if Johnny tried to wriggle out of it, he'd get *murderous* — and Johnny didn't even want to think about the pain he would suffer along the way.

It wasn't that he disliked Ruth, or anything, because he actually thought she was quite sweet — in an overly adoring, *wipe your feet on me* kind of way. But if he'd been told to choose someone to spend the rest of his life with, it wouldn't have been her in a million years. He liked girls who were up for a laugh — and didn't need the joke to be explained word for word until it was no longer funny; girls who knew what they wanted in bed, and weren't too shy to say it — unlike Ruth, who hid under the duvet if he so much as mentioned turning the light on. And, sex aside, it pissed him off that Ruth never wanted to go out when she came round. She just wanted to stay in his room and pretend that they were the only two people in the world. And that drove him insane, because he was a party boy. He liked getting pissed with his mates and making a total tit of himself, smoking too much shit and having mad, spaced-out sex with whichever like-minded girl happened to be around.

But those days were well and truly over. And, loath as he was to admit it, Johnny kind of understood why Frankie was forcing him to do the right thing by Ruth. He was every bit as responsible for this baby as she was, after all — more so, if he was honest, because he'd known before he set foot in that club that he would have a girl on his arm by the time he left and should have gone prepared. Ruth, on the other hand, had been a virgin, so protection had been the furthest thing from her mind. And she wasn't to know that she would stray into Johnny the master-knicker-remover's sights. But he'd lined her up and picked her off, so now he was going to have to face the consequences like a man.

44

Either that, or run. And even if he'd had anywhere to run to, which he didn't, how could he go through life knowing that his child was out there somewhere — hating him for walking away, just like he'd hated *his* dad; pining for him as much as Johnny had pined for his.

By Sunday, Johnny had more or less resigned himself to the fact that he was getting married and was going to be a father. But one thing was still bugging him: whether or not to tell his mum.

He hadn't seen her since he'd bumped into her in town five months earlier, and he'd been too pissed to have a sensible conversation at the time. He didn't relish the thought of going round to her place now, because he hadn't been near the flat since she'd kicked him out on his sixteenth birthday. But she was still his mum, and he did still love her, so he supposed he should tell her before someone else did.

Anyway, the kid was going to need at least one good grandma to compensate for the other one being a disgusting lush with a venomous tongue.

His mind made up, he got out of bed, had a wash and got dressed. Dave was lying on the couch with headphones on, singing along tunelessly to a Bob Marley track and sucking on a spliff. Johnny leaned over the back of the couch and tapped him on the shoulder.

Almost jumping out of his skin, Dave shot up and pulled the headphones down, leaving them dangling around his neck.

"Fuckin' hell, man! You scared the shit out of me," he squawked. "What's got you up, anyhow?" he asked now, looking Johnny up and down. "Did you shit the pit, or summat?"

"I'm going to see my mum," Johnny told him, reaching for his jacket and slipping it on.

"Really?" Dave raised an eyebrow. "Why?"

"To tell her about the wedding and the baby."

Dave sucked in a breath through his teeth. "Good luck with that, mate." He took another drag on his spliff and squinted up through the smoke. "I take it you've decided to go through with it, then?"

"Looks like it."

"You're a dick," Dave said bluntly.

"Maybe so," Johnny conceded. "But there's no way out of it, so I figured I might as well stop fighting it. Anyhow, never mind cussing me, you need to start thinking about where you're going to get your hands on a suit in the next three weeks."

"In your dreams." Dave pulled a disgusted face. "I don't do suits. They make me look like the top wanker at a wanker convention."

"You're not coming in jeans or trackie bottoms," Johnny told him firmly as he pocketed his keys. "The best man's supposed to look as slick as the groom."

"Best man?" Dave cocked his head to one side.

"Who else am I gonna ask? You're my best mate, it's your job."

"Oh, wow, man, that's ace!" Objections seemingly forgotten, Dave grinned like a Cheshire cat. "I've never been a best man before. Shit, that means I get to organise the stag do, doesn't it? *And* I get first dibs on the bridesmaids. She *is* having bridesmaids, isn't she?"

"I think she mentioned something about it," Johnny murmured, wondering if now might be a good time to tell him that Lisa would probably be one of them. Dave hadn't talked about her in a while, but he'd been pretty scathing about her after they'd split so Johnny doubted he'd be overjoyed at the thought of seeing her again.

"Get in!" Dave punched the air. "Pussy on tap, *and* the best stag do ever!"

"Take it easy," Johnny cautioned. "We're skint, don't forget."

"You just leave all that to me," Dave said confidently. "You're forgetting I'm the bargain master. If it costs ten, I'll get it for five — four-fifty at a push."

"Good luck," Johnny chuckled. As crafty as Dave was, even *he* couldn't magic money out of thin air. Knowing him, the stag party would end up being a bring-your-own-drugs-and-booze bender right here at the flat. But that was cool — as long as he didn't do something stupid, like invite Frankie.

"I need to make a list." Dave dumped the headphones on the couch and jumped up. "All the lads will want to come, so I don't want to miss any of 'em out."

Johnny waved and headed out, leaving Dave rooting through the drawers in search of paper and a pen.

Johnny caught a bus to his mum's estate in Ardwick. It was only a fifteen-minute ride from the flats, but it was so different around there that it might as well have been on the other side of the moon. Hit by a bitter-sweet pang of nostalgia when he got off outside the old Methodist church, he traced the faded outlines of the graffiti that he and his gang had spray-painted on its wood-panelled wall. His stomach lurched when he looked further along the road and spied the high green railings that surrounded his old primary school. That place had felt like a prison when he'd been a kid, and he'd been terrified of the headmaster, Mr Jacobs, with his bushy nose-hair, booming voice and sticky-out eyes. He remembered bolting out at last bell every afternoon and running home as fast as his little legs would carry him, then pleading with his mum not to send him back again. But she'd never listened. She was always too busy fretting over the latest fight she'd had with his dad.

Johnny had been invisible in his own home back then, and it got worse after his dad pissed off with his bit on the side.

His mum had locked herself in her room for weeks, leaving Johnny to fend for himself. Things had improved when she'd finally come to terms with it and got herself a part-time job as a barmaid in the pub down the road. She'd started smiling again after that, and whenever she got good tips she'd treat Johnny with trips to the pictures and ice creams in the park.

But that had all stopped when Les moved in, at which point Johnny's life had turned to shit.

His mum had been nervous about introudcing him to Les, worried that he might resent a new man taking his dad's place. But Johnny hadn't been the one with the problem. Les had picked on him from the start, goading him about his dad abandoning him, and slapping him around for the slightest little thing — then laughing when he cried, and taking the piss because he was too small and weak to fight back. Johnny had only once made the mistake of trying to tell his mum where his bruises had really come from, but she hadn't believed him — and Les had been twice as vicious the next time he'd got him on his own.

Johnny had kept his mouth shut after that. But the resentment had grown like a cancer, turning him from a nice polite kid into a nightmare teenager who stole anything that wasn't nailed down, smoked and drank whatever he could get his hands on, and caused trouble wherever he went so the police were never too far from the door. All of which proved Les's point: that Johnny was a bad seed.

The beatings had lessened as Johnny got older, bigger and angrier. But Les must have sensed that revenge was just around the corner, so on Johnny's sixteenth birthday he made Johnny's mum choose between them.

It still hurt that she had chosen Les, but Johnny tried not to let it get to him, reminding himself that his mum had only had one side of the story to go on — Les's fictitious one. But now that he was actually here, back on the streets that he'd called home for most of his life, he wasn't so sure it had been such a good idea to come. His mum had hugged him and told him that she missed him when he'd bumped into her in town that night, but Les had been nowhere in sight at the time, so she'd been free to talk without him giving her the evil eye. If he was home when Johnny got there now, he wouldn't be too pleased. But so fucking what? Johnny wasn't a scared kid any more, and if the cunt tried to stick his oar in *he'd* be the one pissing his bed in fear by the time Johnny got through with him.

The lift wasn't working when he reached his mum's block a few minutes later, so he climbed the stairs to the third floor. Johnny knew she was home as soon as he turned the corner onto her landing, because he could hear Northern Soul music drifting down from her end. She'd always loved her tunes, and in his mind's eye he could still see her and her mates doing their crazy sliding dances and clumsy backdrops all over the living-room floor. But those impromptu parties of hers had been another casualty of Les's arrival. Les didn't like music. Or TV. Or conversation. In fact, the boring bastard would probably only be happy if he could force everyone to live in total silence — the way he'd tried to force little Johnny to do.

But that was then, and this was now, so Johnny swallowed his anger and knocked on the door. He would just tell his mum what he'd come to tell her, then get the hell out of there — and if Les didn't like it, fuck him.

Cathy Conroy was shocked when she answered the door and saw her son standing in front of her.

"What are *you* doing here?" she gasped, quickly adding, "Not that it isn't good to see you, but it's been ages since . . ." She trailed off and gave a sheepish, guilt-laden shrug. "Are you coming in? I was just about to put the kettle on."

"I'm not stopping," Johnny murmured, stuffing his hands into his pockets.

"Les isn't here," Cathy told him, sensing that might be the cause of his reluctance. "He went out a while ago, and I'm not sure when he'll be back."

Johnny gave a nonchalant shrug as if he didn't care one way or the other, but Cathy saw right through it. Smiling, she held out her arms.

"Oh, come here, you daft sod. Give us a hug."

Engulfed by the familiar scents of Head and Shoulders shampoo and Charlie perfume, Johnny closed his eyes, and for one sweet moment it was just the two of them again. No girls, no babies, no weddings — and, best of all, no cuntbag Les.

When Cathy let go at last, Johnny followed her down the short hall into the kitchen and gazed around. It felt weird being in there again after all that time; like he still belonged, and yet didn't at the same time. The stench of Les was all over it, as if the prick had cocked his leg and pissed on every surface to ward Johnny off. But so much for his big talk about turning it into a palace: it looked exactly the same as it had when Johnny had left. The clock on the wall above the cooker still wasn't working, its hands still at the 10 to 9 position they'd been in the last time he'd seen it; and the bin lid was still hanging askew, so he could see the packets of ready-cooked chicken korma — evidence that his mum still couldn't cook.

51

"Christ, I can't believe you've still got that," he said when he spotted the spider plant he'd given her when he was eight sitting on the windowsill, complete with a dust-covered pink rosette stuck to its side. "It looks like a dead weed. Why don't you chuck it?"

Cathy glanced around to see what he was looking at and smiled. "No way. You won that for me in the raffle. I remember how chuffed you were when you brought it home and gave it to me."

"Chuffed to get rid of it, more like," Johnny corrected her, moving over to the tiny table that was tucked away in the corner and sitting down. "When I told the teacher I was giving it to you, she bunged that pink shit on the side of it and my mates took the piss all the way home."

"Well, I thought it was lovely," Cathy said, casting another fond look at it as she stirred their coffees.

She carried the cups over to the table and handed Johnny's to him before squeezing through the gap between the radiator and the loaded washing maiden and sitting across from him.

"So, what's brought you round?" she asked, sliding two cigarettes out of her pack and passing one over. "Were you missing me?"

"Whatever," Johnny drawled as he leaned forward to take a light from her. Sitting back, he exhaled into the air above her head. "Actually, there's something I need to tell you."

A loud bang from out on the landing cut him off before he could say any more, and Cathy rolled her eyes with irritation.

52

"That flaming woman! I swear she does that on purpose. I'm going to bloody throttle her if she doesn't pack it in."

"Who, Lynne?" Johnny gave his mother a bemused look. "Don't tell me you two have fallen out? You've been best mates for ever."

"No, not Lynne." Cathy flapped her hand dismissively as if he'd been stupid for even thinking she'd fall out with Lynne. Then, "Oh, I forgot, you wouldn't know, would you? Lynne moved out a few months back to look after her mum, and *that* one got her flat."

"That one?"

"*Maureen.*" Cathy sneered. "Right stuck-up ugly bitch, she is. Reckons she's the same age as me, but there's *no* way she's still in her thirties. And she's a flaming nuisance, as well as a liar. You just heard how hard the door banged, didn't you? Well, that was going on at all hours after she first moved in, so I had a word — explained about how you've got to hold it till it shuts instead of just letting it go. She said it wasn't her, so I collared them lads from the other side. But they swore it wasn't them, either. But I knew it had to be one of them, so I stayed up one night — to catch them at it."

She paused and took a deep drag on her cigarette before continuing.

"Anyhow, it *was* her. Or should I say one of her fancy men. And I say *men*, 'cos after I saw the first one coming out of her place I started keeping an eye on her. And I swear to God she's got a different one every night — sometimes *two*, one straight after the other."

53

Johnny eased his cuff back and took a surreptitious peek at his watch. His mum had said she didn't know when Les would be back, but he could walk in at any time and Johnny wanted to be long gone by then.

"I wouldn't mind, but she's got a face like a bleedin' bulldog," Cathy rambled on. "So God only knows what kind of men they are, 'cos no decent bloke would pay to sleep with a boot like that. Anyhow, I was right, 'cos Diana told me. You remember Diana, don't you — lives round your nan's way? Well, she popped round for a brew the other week, and she bumped into that one on the stairs and —"

"Mum . . ." Johnny held up his hand to stop her. "I really haven't got time for this."

Cathy stopped talking and smiled. "Sorry, was I going on? I should have realised when your eyes started glazing over. You always did that, even when you were little. I'd be saying something, and you'd be pretending you were listening, but you wouldn't have heard a word."

Johnny's brow creased and he gave a weary sigh.

"Sorry." Cathy held up her hands. "Go on . . . you said you had something to tell me? It's not about that girl, is it?"

"Girl?" Johnny frowned, wondering if she'd already heard about Ruth and had just been waiting for him to come out with it.

"The one I saw you with in town that time. I didn't like to say anything at the time in case you thought I was interfering, but I didn't really like the look of her. You're not still seeing her, are you?"

Relieved, Johnny smiled and shook his head. "God, no, she was just a one-night stand. But, you're half right. This *is* about a girl."

"I knew it," Cathy crowed. "So, who is she? Do I know her?"

"No, but you will."

Cathy's eyebrows knitted together as she waited for her son to go on. When he didn't, she said, "I'm guessing it's serious, or you wouldn't have bothered coming round to tell me about her."

"Yeah, it's serious," Johnny affirmed. "She's pregnant. We're getting married."

"Wow." Stunned, Cathy flopped back in her seat. "Well, I wasn't expecting *that*."

"Join the club," Johnny murmured. "I was as shocked as you when I first heard about it."

A look of concern crept into Cathy's eyes as she gazed at him. They might not have seen each other for a while, but she knew her son better than anyone, and there was something he wasn't telling her.

"You don't seem very happy," she ventured. "Are you sure you're ready to take such a big step? How long have you been seeing her?"

"Six months."

"*Six months?*" Cathy squawked. "And you're even *thinking* about getting married? Are you stark raving mad?"

"I know it doesn't seem long," Johnny said lamely. "But it's happened, so I've got to do the right thing by her."

"I don't believe this." Cathy shook her head and tapped her cigarette agitatedly on the side of the ashtray. "Marriage isn't something you can do one day and undo the next, you know. It's a massive commitment. Don't you think it'd be better to get the baby out of the way and spend some time getting to know each other before you think about tying yourself down like that?"

Irritated that she was lecturing him as if he was a kid who didn't know his arse from his elbow — even if she *was* right — Johnny said, "Like you and my dad did? Oh, but you didn't bother going the whole hog, did you? Never mind what that made *me*."

A look of hurt leapt into Cathy's eyes and she raised her chin proudly. "I think you'll find that I wanted to get married," she told him. "It was your dad who couldn't be arsed. Too busy screwing that slag behind my back."

She took another drag on her cigarette, and Johnny could tell that she was struggling to hold the tears at bay. Feeling guilty, he said, "Sorry, I didn't mean that. You know I don't blame you."

"I did my best," she replied quietly. "And I thought you were happy."

"I was," Johnny told her.

Until you fetched Les home and ruined my life.

"I *was*," he repeated, more positively. He reached across the table and took his mother's hand in his. "I know how tough you had it after my dad walked out, and I've got tons of respect for the way you handled it."

56

Cathy peered down at their joined hands and bit her lip hard. It had been ages since she'd felt her son's flesh on hers, and it made her realise that she had missed him more than she'd allowed herself to admit.

"Are we all right?" Johnny tilted his head and gazed up at her. "Am I forgiven?"

Cathy swallowed the lump that had formed in her throat and pulled her hand free. "Yeah, course," she said, lighting a fresh cigarette and pushing the pack across the table for him to help himself. "Anyhow, whose idea was it to get married? Yours or hers?"

"Both," Johnny lied.

Cathy arched her eyebrows and gave him a disbelieving look. "You never could fool me, Jon-Jon, so don't bother trying now."

Caught out, Johnny said, "All right, so maybe she wants it more than me."

"So why are you going along with it if you don't want to do it?" Cathy demanded. "And don't say you're doing it for the baby, 'cos it's *her* you'll have to go to bed with every night and wake up next to every morning. And, believe me, that's hard enough when you love each other. But if you don't, it'll kill any feelings you *have* got stone dead. And you don't love her, do you?"

She asked the question, but then snorted softly and answered it herself.

"Course you don't. How could you after six months?"

Johnny groaned and ran his hands through his hair. His mother was right on all counts, but he couldn't tell her that. If she suspected he was being forced into it, she'd have him straight down to the police station screaming for Frankie to be arrested. But that was her world, where people played by the rules and respected authority. In his world, people like Frankie only followed the rules *they* had set — and anyone who grassed was a dead man walking.

"It's not too late," Cathy persisted. "Just tell her you've changed your mind and put it on hold. You can still be a dad to the kid. And you can even carry on seeing her — if that's what you want. Then, if you're still together a few years down the line, there'll be nothing to stop you giving it another go. But at least you'll know you're doing it for the right reasons by then, won't you?"

"I know you're trying to help," Johnny said wearily. "But I can't back out of it."

Cathy drew her head back and gave him a knowing look. "Oh, I see. She's one of *them*, is she? Thinks she's too special to have a baby if she hasn't got a big fat ring on her finger? Well, maybe *I'*d better have a word with her, 'cos I'm not having any little madam push *my* son around like that."

Johnny cursed himself for having made it so obvious that he wasn't happy about the wedding and the baby. His mum had always been able to see right through him. When he was a kid, no matter where he told her he'd been she'd always known exactly where he'd really been, who he'd seen, *and* what he'd done while he was there. But confessions weren't an option here. He had to convince her that she'd got it wrong.

"Look, I think we've got our wires crossed," he said, looking her straight in the eye. "I was shocked when she told me she was pregnant, I'm not going to deny that. But once I got my head around it, I was made up. I'm chuffed to bits now, and you will be, an' all — *nan*."

He grinned as he said that last word, knowing that it would knock her for six.

"God, don't call me that," Cathy moaned, rolling her eyes. "Have you any idea how old that makes me feel?"

"Yeah, well, you don't look it," Johnny said, using flattery to manoeuvre her away from the other subject. "You're still a babe."

"Shut up," she scolded, a hint of pinkness colouring her cheeks.

"It's true," Johnny insisted. "My mate went on about you for ages after he saw you that time. I had to tell him to pack it in, 'cos it was getting too freaky."

"You're such a liar," Cathy chuckled. Then, self-consciously flicking her bottle-blonde hair back, she said, "Was that the lad who let you move into his flat?"

"Yeah — Dave. He's a good mate."

"He's a nice-looking boy. And I'm glad it worked out all right, 'cos I *was* worried about you, you know."

Johnny sensed that she was on the verge of getting emotional, and said, "Forget it." Then, "So, about the wedding . . . do you want to come, or what? Only I'll need to tell Ruth and her mum, so they can send out a proper invite."

"Ruth?" Cathy raised an eyebrow. "Is that her name? Bit old-fashioned, isn't it?"

"Never really thought about it," Johnny answered. And it was true, he hadn't. But now that she'd brought it up, he supposed it was a bit dreary.

Dreary name for a dreary girl.

"Well?" He shoved Ruth out of his mind and gave his mum a questioning look.

"I'm not sure," she murmured, scraping her chair back and reaching for their empty cups. "Let's have another brew while I think about it."

"Not for me." He shook his head. "It's being booked for the thirteenth of November, so if you're coming I need to know asap."

"Let me talk to Les," Cathy said quietly. Sighing when Johnny rolled his eyes, she said, "Well, you can't invite me and not him. It wouldn't be right."

"I don't want him there," Johnny told her bluntly, unable to hold his tongue any longer. "And I can't believe you're still trying to force him down my throat after everything he did."

"Oh, Johnny, not this again," Cathy groaned. "I know you blamed him for your dad walking out, but he wasn't even around at the time. He's done nothing but try to support us."

"And beating the shit out of me was supporting us, was it?"

"Stop it," Cathy scolded. "He might have given you the occasional smack, but that's all. And you should think yourself lucky, 'cos anyone else would have snapped if you'd pushed them as far as you pushed him."

"Really?" Johnny raised an eyebrow and stared at her.

"Yes, *really*." Cathy held his gaze. "I'm the one who had all the neighbours looking down on me like I was the world's worst mother whenever the police dragged you home, so don't try and make out like you were some kind of angel."

"I never said I was," Johnny replied coolly. "But I was only nine when he moved in, and I'd never got into any kind of trouble before, so didn't it strike you as odd that I suddenly went off the rails?"

"You were twelve when you started playing up," Cathy reminded him. "All kids are little bastards at that age."

"Especially if they're getting the shit beat out of them day in, day out, eh?"

Cathy tutted. "Les never did anything of the sort, and you know it. You just said it to break us up, 'cos you'd had me all to yourself and you were jealous of him moving in. But it didn't work then and it won't work now. Les might not be perfect, but he's done his best by me — *and* you. It was't his fault you wouldn't let him near."

Johnny's cheek muscles twitched as the rage he'd tried so hard to suppress came bubbling to the surface.

"Oh, he got near, all right. Every time you went out, he was on me like a fucking dog. I remember how scared I used to get when he was standing over me with that evil look on his face. And he fucking *loved* it — seeing me cry, and knowing I'd end up pissing my bed and get into trouble with you."

Cathy gave him a pained look. "I can't keep doing this, Jon. I've lived with Les for near enough ten years,

61

and I know him inside out. If he was like that, I'd know."

"So all the bruises I started getting after he moved in just came out of thin air, did they?"

"Lads play rough. You were always getting scuffed up when you were out with your mates."

"Not when I was *nine*," Johnny reminded her. "You didn't let me play out till I was eleven, 'cos you always wanted me where you could see me after my dad left. Don't you remember?"

"Oh, so now I'm a bad mother because I tried to protect you?" Cathy shot back defensively. "The kids round here were a load of hooligans; I didn't want you ending up like them."

"I'm not saying you were a bad mother for keeping me in," Johnny replied coolly. "Just for leaving me with a man you didn't even know, then calling me a liar when I told you what he was doing to me. Any mother who cared about her kid would have kept an eye on the bloke if she heard something like that. But not you — you just fucked off out and left him to it."

"I had to work," Cathy reminded him.

"No, you *wanted* to work," Johnny corrected her. "You got a buzz from it. Used to come home boasting about you and Julie getting all the tips 'cos you had a 'special way of flirting with the punters'." He did speech marks in the air with his fingers.

Cathy's eyes sparked with anger and she gritted her teeth. "Don't you dare try and make out like I was some kind of tart."

62

"I'm not. I'm just saying if it was *me*, and *my* kid was covered in bruises every time I came home from work, I wouldn't care how much I liked my job, I'd jack it in and stay home to make sure it never happened again — even if I didn't really believe him."

"You can think what you like, but until you've been there you haven't got a clue what it's like bringing a kid up. A parent *knows* when their kid's lying. And you were a born liar — just like your dad."

They locked eyes across the table and glared at each other for several long moments, the silence broken only by the sound of their breathing. Inhaling deeply through his nostrils when he'd had enough, Johnny stabbed the butt of his burned-down cigarette into the ashtray, scraped his chair back and stood up.

"So, that's it?" Cathy peered up at him with a hint of victory in her eyes. "You're just going to piss off like this is all my fault?"

"No point staying if you still think I'm lying," Johnny replied. Calmer now, but no less angry, he added, "You're my mum, and I love you, but you're wrong about Les. *He*'s the one who caused this, not me. I just hope you can live with yourself when you realise I've been telling the truth all along."

"Won't happen." Cathy shrugged. "You're lying, and we both know it."

Johnny shook his head in disgust. He could understand why she might have believed Les rather than him when he'd been a trouble-making teenager, but not when he'd been a scared little boy crying out for protection. But if the bruises hadn't alerted her, and she hadn't thought it strange that a nine-year-old who hadn't wet the bed in years would suddenly start again for no reason, then nothing was ever going to convince her.

"I'll see myself out." He headed for the door.

"You'll let me know about the baby, won't you?" Cathy called after him. "I'm going to be its grandma, so I've got a right to see it. I'll take you to court if I have to."

"Whatever," Johnny called back, slamming the front door firmly shut behind him.

He trotted down the stairs, walked out into the crisp air and breathed in deeply. It had been going so well to start with, but he should have known it would end like that. As long as his mum insisted on making out like he was the devil and Les was some kind of saint they were never going to rebuild that shattered bridge. Which left him with two choices: wallow in self-pity for the rest of his life — or put the past to bed once and for all and concentrate on the future.

Opting for the latter, Johnny set off back to the bus stop with a new resolve in his heart. The thought of being responsible for a tiny baby absolutely terrified him, but if he was going to be a parent he'd rather be one like Frankie than like his mum. Frankie might be an evil bastard but no one could question the strength of his love for and loyalty to his own. He worked his arse off to provide for Ruth and her mum and, despite his frequent absences, he'd instilled a real sense of family, respect and decency into Ruth.

64

Johnny still wasn't looking forward to being tied to her for the rest of his life, but now that he'd started to think about the child as being his he was determined to give it a better upbringing than the one he'd had. It hadn't asked to be conceived, and it deserved to feel safe and loved. Whatever other failings Ruth might have, he had no doubt that she would do her damnedest to be a good mum — and he, in turn, would try to be a great dad.

CHAPTER
FOUR

Johnny woke up on the morning of the wedding with the stench of piss in his nostrils, a foul taste in his mouth, a banging head — and absolutely no recollection of the events of the night before. He didn't even know where he was when he opened his eyes, and it took a few moments before he realised that he was in his own room.

As he lay there waiting for the bed to stop lurching beneath him, he had a vague recollection of Dave and the lads dragging him out for his stag party. But he had no clue where they had gone, what had happened when they got there, how he'd got home, or who had undressed him and put him to bed.

Feeling sick, he rolled onto his side and groaned when he felt a telltale damp patch beneath his thigh. He peeped at the other side of the bed through half-closed eyes, and was flooded with relief to see that he was alone. That would have been all he needed — some girl telling everyone that he'd pissed the bed.

He got up, yanked the shameful sheet off and stuffed it into a plastic bag to take to the launderette. He was pulling on his dressing gown when Dave burst through the door a couple of minutes later.

"My alarm didn't go off! We've got less than half an hour till the car gets here."

"*Sshhh*," Johnny begged, holding his aching head in his hands.

"Never mind sshhh." Dave shoved him out into the hall. "Get washed — and hurry up, for fuck's sake. Frankie'll kill me if I don't get you to the church on time."

"Oh, no," Johnny moaned, feeling nauseous again at the mention of that name and the thought of what lay ahead.

"Oh, yes." Dave pushed him into the bathroom. "Hurry up!"

Johnny closed the door and took a piss. Then, sitting on the edge of the bath, he filled the sink with cold water and sank his face into it until he felt more awake.

Dave was dressed and waiting for him in the hall when he came back out.

"Drink that and take them," he ordered, shoving a fizzing glass of Alka-Seltzer and two paracetamol tablets into his hand. "Then get your suit on. You've got fifteen minutes."

Johnny did as he was told, and was almost ready when a car horn tooted down below. Dave looked out of the window and waved to let the driver know they were coming.

"Ready?" he asked, turning back to Johnny.

"No." Johnny shook his head miserably.

"Ah, you'll be fine," Dave said, shoving his friend's hands aside and doing his tie for him before straightening the blood-red carnation in his buttonhole.

That done, he picked up his keys and cigarettes and patted his pocket to check that he had the rings before hustling Johnny out of the door.

Johnny felt as sick as a dog as he numbly followed Dave down to the car park. It was a freezing cold day, and a dark grey cloud hovered above them as they climbed into the back of the E-type Mercedes that Frankie had sent. Shivering, he hunched in the corner and felt sorry for himself. This was all happening too fast. He hadn't had a chance to wake up properly yet, and he desperately needed a coffee. His head felt like it was stuffed with wet cotton wool, and he could barely remember his own name so he had no idea how he was going to remember what he was supposed to say when he got to the church.

"Come on, mate, shake yourself out of it," Dave said with forced cheeriness. "Soon be done." He lit two cigarettes and passed one over.

"Easy for you to say," Johnny grunted, winding the window down an inch. "And how come you're so lively when I feel like shit?"

"'Cos I paced myself last night," Dave told him, glancing at his watch. "Frankie warned me not to let you get in a state, so I had to keep a clear head."

"Didn't do a very good job, did you?" Johnny grumbled. "I can't remember a fucking thing. What happened?"

"Later," Dave said offhandedly. Then, to the driver, "Any time you're ready, mate."

They set off with a lurch, and Johnny swallowed down a mouthful of bile. Stomach churning all the way, he felt like his bowels were going to give when they reached the church and he saw his mates having a smoke on a pile of old flat gravestones round the side. Their women were already inside — no doubt fighting over the aisle seats, from where they could best see and bitch about the bride when she arrived.

If she arrived.

Please, God, don't let her come.

"Where's Mikey and Andy?" he asked. As the car came to a stop outside the gates he clocked that those two weren't with the others.

"I don't think they'll be coming," Dave told him quietly.

"Why not?"

Dave cast a furtive glance at the driver and lowered his voice to say, "There was a bit of bother at the club last night and I haven't heard from either of them since, so I'm guessing they might have got arrested."

"Why, what happened?" Johnny demanded. "And what club?"

"Not now," Dave whispered. "Just concentrate on what you're doing. And don't look so worried. That priest looked like a right little pisshead when we came for the rehearsal, so I'm betting he'll race through the service like a bat out of hell so he can get to the bar."

"Hope so." Johnny ran a sweaty hand over his clammy face.

Frankie came out through the church door just then. Dave chuckled, and nudged Johnny.

"Jeezus, cop a load of that. We must have took a wrong turn and ended up in Vegas."

Johnny glanced out at his soon-to-be Elvis-in-law and groaned. Frankie's face was practically orange, and there was so much gel in his slicked-back hair that it looked like he'd just stepped out of an oil shower. But his suit was surprisingly nice compared to the shit he'd got Johnny and Dave trussed up in. He'd taken them to a tailor and had them fitted out to make sure they looked the part, but the suits that had been delivered yesterday bore no resemblance to the ones Johnny and Dave had spent an hour describing to the tailor. They'd wanted chino-type pants and fitted jackets, but they'd ended up in suits that only a Teddy boy would rave about, with lapels like pieces of string and trousers to match.

"Bastard," he muttered, guessing that Frankie had done it to punish him.

"He don't look too happy," Dave murmured as Frankie spotted the car and came striding towards them with a thunderous look on his face. "You'd best try and look a bit more enthusiastic, or he'll think you're having second thoughts."

"Try third, fourth and fifth," said Johnny.

Frankie yanked the car door open and glared in at them.

"What fuckin' time do you call this? Ruth got here ten minutes ago and I had to tell the driver to do another lap. Do you know how much shit I'm going to get off her mam when she finds out I had to send her away?"

"Sorry," Johnny apologised, forcing his wobbly legs to carry him out of the car. "My stomach's been a bit dodgy."

70

Frankie snapped his glare onto Dave who was climbing out the other side. "He'd best not have a hangover! I warned you what'd happen if you let him get in a state."

"He hardly drank anything," Dave lied, peeling the crotch of his ultra-tight trousers away from his nuts. "He was as good as gold. Went home early, and everything."

Frankie glowered at him, and then turned his attention back to Johnny. "Right, you — inside." He shoved him up the path. "And no fuck-ups. Just say what you've got to say, swap rings and kiss her, and then we can all get the fuck out of here." Casting a glance at the graves as they passed, he shuddered. "I fuckin' hate churches."

"Me, too," Johnny murmured, wishing they could have just gone for the registry office instead. But, like everything else to do with this wedding, he'd had no say.

"She's back," one of the smokers hissed, pointing towards the gate.

Frankie glanced back and saw the nose of the Roller turning in. "Quick! Get in," he ordered, shoving Johnny so hard he stumbled over the step.

"I need the loo," Johnny bleated.

"Too late." Frankie pushed him on through the door.

It was packed to the rafters inside the church, and Johnny's cheeks flamed when all eyes turned his way. He felt like turning and running, but Frankie propelled him up the aisle with a firm hand on his back and left him at the alter before rushing back outside to collect his daughter. Dave quickly caught up and tipped him a wink that was meant to be reassuring but only made him feel worse.

Johnny glanced back over his shoulder and swallowed loudly when his gaze met Rita's in the pew immediately behind. He gave her a sick smile, but wasn't surprised when she didn't return it. She'd made it quite clear in the run-up to today that she didn't think he was good enough for her daughter. But he didn't give a toss what she thought. She was a miserable little pisshead with a face like a slapped arse, and he'd be keeping well away from her after today was over.

Somebody signalled to the organist from the door, and she stabbed her fingers down on the keys, flooding the church with music. A tremendous rustling went up behind Johnny as all the women in the congregation turned to watch the bride's entrance. Johnny's throat closed, and he ran a finger around the inside of his collar to loosen it. Squeezing his eyes shut, he made one last silent plea to God to make Ruth change her mind and stay in the car. Or, better still, drop dead. Something — anything — to stop her from making it up the aisle.

But Ruth had no intention of changing her mind. She'd wanted Johnny from the first moment she'd laid eyes on him, and there was no way she was letting him get away now. She walked slowly in and raised her chin as she glided up the aisle on her father's arm, smiling proudly to herself beneath her veil as she glimpsed the envy in the eyes of every girl she passed.

Johnny's eyes widened when Frankie handed her over, but he swallowed the shock and forced out a smile. He'd guessed from the way she'd gone on about the dress that it wouldn't be as conservative as the stuff she wore on a day-to-day basis, but this was over the top to the max. Like something you'd expect to see on stage at a pantomime, it was full-on crinoline style, and the skirt was so wide that it touched both sets of pews at once. The snow-white satin underbody was topped with layer upon layer of frothy white lace, every visible inch of which was saturated with sequins and pearls, while the veil was held in place by a tiara of sparkling diamante.

At least, Johnny presumed it was diamante, but he wouldn't have put it past Frankie to have splashed out on the real deal. Nothing like a flash wedding for your daughter to remind everyone how loaded you were, and all that.

In startling contrast, the bridesmaids were clad in shocking pink, and Johnny's eyes hurt when he glanced at them. The little ones looked quite sweet, but the same couldn't be said for Lisa, and he almost choked when he saw how low her neckline was. One wrong move and both of those babies would be coming out to play.

"Johnny," Ruth hissed, nudging him with her elbow. "The Father's talking to you."

Snapping his gaze away from Lisa's tits, Johnny looked up at the little priest.

"Sorry?"

"I asked if you're ready?" Father Dougherty arched a bushy white eyebrow.

Johnny nodded, his eyes drawn now to the man's bulbous nose with its busy map of red lines criss-crossing it.

"And are all of *you* lovely people ready?" The priest gazed out over Johnny's head and addressed the congregation. "No last-minute trips to the toilet needed, or arguments to settle?" He looked directly down into Ruth's eyes now, and added, "No risk of untimely arrivals?"

If looks could kill, the man would have fallen down stone dead under the weight of the poisonous glare that Rita aimed his way. But Frankie guffawed like he'd said something hilarious, and turned to look at the congregation as if to say *what a joker, eh?*

As Dave had predicted, once Father Dougherty got going the service raced along at a fair old pace, and before Johnny knew it he was being ordered to kiss his bride.

"But no tongues now," the old priest cautioned with a leery grin. "Got to save *something* for the honeymoon, eh?"

Numbed by the pressure of the gold band that Ruth had crammed onto his finger, Johnny pecked her on the lips. Then he went into the vestry to sign his life away in ink, before heading back out into the chill daylight, with Ruth clutching possessively at his arm all the way.

"Let's have the family lined up on the steps for the photos," Frankie ordered, pushing and prodding everybody into place. "The rest of you over there." He

74

gestured for non-family — namely, Johnny's mates — to stand out of the way on the grass.

Lisa elbowed her way in on Johnny's free side and pressed her breasts up against his arm, whispering, "Saw you looking back there. Like what you see, do you?"

Johnny blanched and looked the other way.

Ruth narrowed her eyes. She hadn't heard what Lisa had said but she didn't appreciate her standing so close to Johnny. He was her husband now, and no woman — family or not — had better try and muscle in on him.

"Move," she hissed. "My mum and dad are supposed to stand there, not you."

"I can stand here if I want," Lisa replied, casually slipping her hand behind Johnny and pinching his bum.

"I'm not going to tell you again," Ruth growled, fixing her with a fierce warning glare. "*Move.*"

"Who d'ya think you're talking to?" spat Lisa, putting her hands on her hips.

"It's my wedding day."

"So? That doesn't give you the right to treat me like shit in front of everyone."

Before Ruth could reply to this, Dave rushed over. He didn't know what was going on but it was obvious from the way the girls were glaring at each other that they were about to kick off, and Johnny was having a hard enough time today without having to deal with that.

"You're supposed to stand with the best man for the piccies," he said, taking Lisa's arm and pulling her firmly down the steps. "And if you're good, I might even let you have the first dance."

"As if I'd dance with *you*," she snorted, snatching her arm away and stomping over to stand with the other bridesmaids.

Johnny put on his best happy-groom smile and determinedly held it in place while the photographer snapped and snapped and snapped. What felt like an hour and ten thousand photos later, he smiled again when all of the men filed past and shook his hand and the women kissed his cheek. Done at last, he jumped gratefully into the back of the Rolls that had brought Ruth, looking forward to a few minutes of peace before they reached the hotel and he had to face them all again at the reception.

It took several minutes for Ruth to manoeuvre her massive dress through the door, but when she was finally in she tried to snuggle up to Johnny, only to find that the rigid hoops in her skirt prevented her from getting close. Reaching for his hand instead, she smiled.

"Happy?"

"Mmm."

"Me too." She sighed and raised her left hand to examine her rings in the light. "I can't believe we're really married. It feels like a dream. Is it like a dream for you?"

"Mmm."

"God, I'm so glad it's over," Ruth went on, as if a weight had been lifted from her shoulders. "It's been murder not being able to see you on our own. But no one can stop us now, can they?" A gloating little smile curled her lips as she added, "Did you see Lisa's face when I told her to move away from you just now on the steps? I knew she was going to be funny, 'cos she was a right bitch last night. She's been weird ever since I told her we were getting married, actually, but she's just jealous. She always has been — right from when we were kids. Whatever I had, she wanted it. But she's got no chance of getting *you*, Mr Conroy, 'cos you're all mine. Mine, mine, mine."

Unable to contain the groan that bubbled up into his throat, Johnny flopped his head back and rubbed at his eyes.

"What's wrong?" Ruth was instantly concerned. "You're not feeling sick, are you? Do you want me to tell the driver to stop?"

"I'm okay," he lied. "Probably just nerves."

"Ah, was my new husband nervous?" she teased. Then, giggling, she said, "God, it feels so weird saying that. My *husband*. You say it. Say, *my wife*."

"Ruth, please . . ."

"Aw, come on, I just want to hear what it'll sound like to other people when you talk about me. It's not that hard, is it? *Please*?"

"My wife," Johnny said dully, figuring that it was easier just to do as she asked. "Now, can we have a bit of quiet while I try to shake this headache?"

"Sorry," Ruth cooed, almost breaking her neck in an effort to lay her head on his shoulder. "I suppose I'd best get used to doing as I'm told, hadn't I?" she went on happily, instantly forgetting his plea for quiet. "I did promise to love, honour and obey you, after all. Not that I'll be the kind of wife who lets herself get pushed around," she added quickly, as if to warn him that he'd better not even try it. "But it's traditional for a wife to listen to her husband. And traditions are really important, aren't they? That's how I want to raise our children when we start a family — the old way."

"What do you mean, *when* we start?" Johnny picked up on what she'd said and gazed down at her.

"I mean when we start trying for the next one," Ruth corrected herself, cradling her stomach with her hand as if to reassure *this* baby that she wasn't dismissing it. "You can't just have one child and call yourself a family, can you?"

"You're an only child," he reminded her. "So am I, come to that."

"Yes, which is why I want *us* to have loads — because we both know how lonely it is to be the only one. You haven't got a problem with that, have you?"

Johnny frowned. It had taken him ages to get used to the idea of having *this* one, and here she was planning the next God only knew how many.

"What are you thinking?" Ruth asked. Shaking his arm when he didn't answer, she said, "Johnny, don't ignore me. We're nearly there, and my dad will wonder what's wrong if you're quiet."

Johnny rolled his eyes. He wished she would just shut the fuck up and leave him alone for two minutes. But she was right: Frankie *would* think something funny was going on if they turned up like this. So, smiling, he said, "I'm fine. Stop worrying about me and enjoy your day, eh?"

78

"My day," Ruth repeated, sighing as she laid her head on his arm again. Mercifully, she stayed quiet for the rest of the journey.

The other guests had already made their way inside by the time they reached the hotel, but Frankie was pacing around at the foot of the steps and he rushed forward to open the door when the car stopped.

"Thought you'd changed your minds and gone straight off on honeymoon," he joked, offering his hand to Ruth to help her out.

"As if," she grunted, puffing for breath as she struggled to drag her skirts out behind her. She gave Johnny a disapproving look when he strolled around from the other side. "You should have helped me out. You're my husband. It's *your* job, not my dad's."

"Well, that's you told," chuckled Frankie, nudging Johnny with his elbow. "Lesson one — don't argue with a Hynes woman, 'cos you'll never win."

"I'm a Conroy now," Ruth reminded him.

"Only in name," said Frankie, still smiling.

As Ruth gathered up her skirts and started hauling herself up the steps, Frankie clapped a hand down on Johnny's shoulder.

"I want to talk to you later, so don't get too happy with the fizz."

"Don't worry, he won't," Ruth called back. "I'm not having my new husband too drunk to remember our wedding night." She glanced back over her shoulder now and flicked Johnny a conspiratorial little smile.

Grimacing, Frankie hurried inside and marched across the foyer to a set of double doors outside which a sign stood on an easel, directing people to the reception of "Mr and Mrs Johnny Conroy".

Ruth bit her lip when she saw it and traced the embossed lettering with her fingertips. "That's us," she told Johnny quietly. "Doesn't it look beautiful?" She reached for his hand now and squeezed it, whispering, "I think I'll make my excuses after dinner and go up to the room to get changed. You can come with me."

"You're going nowhere," Frankie informed her sternly. "And you definitely ain't getting changed. I paid thousands for that dress, so you'll bloody well get some wear out of it."

"I already have, when I got married," Ruth reminded him, a sulky little pout appearing on her lips. "Now I want to put my other dress on."

"No."

"But, Dad . . ."

"Don't make me say it again."

Ruth tutted, put her hands on her hips and looked at Johnny as if to say *tell him*. But Johnny wasn't stupid enough to think he would get away with disagreeing with Frankie, so he just shrugged, and said, "Your dad's right. And at least everyone knows who the bride is if you keep it on. If you get changed, you'll look like the rest of them, won't you?"

Ruth sighed. The wedding dress was ridiculously heavy, and her shoulders were aching where the straps were digging in. She'd spent ages finding the perfect dress for the reception, and she'd been really looking forward to showing it off. But she supposed Johnny was right.

"You're so clever," she murmured, giving him an adoring smile.

Frankie pushed open the doors and stepped into the reception room.

"All rise to welcome the happy couple."

Embarrassed when everybody stood up and started clapping, Johnny kept his head down and followed Ruth across the floor to the top table. Holding out her chair, he waited until she was seated before sitting down beside her.

The next couple of hours passed in a blur of food, alcohol, speeches, and more alcohol. Buffered by the triple vodka Dave had slipped into the Coke that Ruth had ordered him to stick to, Johnny got through the first dance without making too much of a fool of himself. But he'd barely sat down again before Frankie summoned him to one of the hotel's public bars for a chat.

"So, you're officially part of the family," Frankie said when they were seated and had ordered their drinks. "How's it feel?"

"Fine," Johnny answered cautiously, wondering where this was leading.

"Hope you got all the bachelor shit out of your system last night?" Frankie gave him a knowing look. "I won't say I'm happy about it, 'cos I'm not, but I've decided to let it pass under the circumstances. Just don't do it again. Okay?"

"Okay," Johnny murmured, feeling sick all over again. Frankie obviously knew more about what had happened last night than he did, and that wasn't a comfortable position to be in.

"Good lad." Frankie gave him a half-smile. "Anyhow, forget about the slags — we need to talk about your future."

Slags?

"First things first: we need to set you up with a job."

"A job?" Johnny repeated numbly. He didn't want a job. Jobs were for losers.

"Yes, a job," said Frankie patiently. "How else are you going to take care of my girl and pay me back for that fucking great rock I put on her finger?"

Johnny gave a miserable little shrug. He hadn't thought about it. Hadn't really thought about *anything* beyond getting through today, if he was honest.

"Hope you didn't think that was a freebie," said Frankie. "'Cos I haven't got this far by being a fucking mug. And Ruth's got expensive tastes, so you're going to have your work cut out keeping her happy. That's why you're coming to work for me," he announced. "You can start down at the yard in two weeks. At the bottom, obviously, 'cos I don't want the other lads to think you're getting preferential treatment. I'll start you off washing the motors, and shit like that. But we'll reassess after a few weeks — depending how you get on." He paused and gave Johnny a piercing look. "You do *want* to get on, don't you, son? You ain't gonna disappoint me?"

"Yeah, course I want to get on," Johnny lied. "I just didn't expect you to take me on, that's all. I've not had much luck with jobs."

"You're family now," Frankie reminded him. "And family takes care of its own. Loyalty is everything in my book — do you understand what I mean by that?"

Johnny nodded and smiled up at the waitress who had just brought their drinks over.

"It means never letting anyone come between you and yours, and never, ever betraying them," Frankie told him.

"Like that bird." He nodded at the waitress's back as she made her way back to the bar. "You can look, but if you so much as think about touching I'll chop your fucking hands off."

"I wasn't looking," Johnny spluttered. "I was just thanking her for the drink."

"You're a bloke, it's in the genes," said Frankie. "But Ruth's your number-one priority now." His gaze was steely as he stared Johnny in the eye. "Like I said before, I'll let last night slip. But if I ever find out you've put your cock near another tart now that you're married to my girl, you'll be eating it. *Capiche?*"

Johnny nodded and reached for his drink, but his hand was shaking so badly that he spilled some of it down his shirt. What the hell had he done last night? And how the hell did Frankie know about it — whatever *it* was? Had he sent someone to follow them, or been there himself, watching?

Frankie saw the questions flickering through his eyes and smiled slyly.

"I've got eyes everywhere, Johnny boy, and don't you ever forget it. Your mates are lucky they ain't looking at life right now," he went on seriously. "I only stepped in to keep you out of the shit, but I won't be doing it again, so steer clear of them from now on."

"Okay," Johnny agreed, wondering what the hell had happened — and what Frankie had meant about stepping in. Dave had acted weird when he'd asked him about it, and now this. It sounded heavy, and he hoped Andy and Mikey were all right.

Satisfied that the boy understood the rules, Frankie raised his glass and clinked it against Johnny's.

"Family first — and fuck everyone else."

Frankie took a swig of his drink now and wiped his mouth on the back of his hand.

"Right, about the job . . . You're starting low, so your wages will be shit. But you'll be stopping with me and Rita to start with, so it won't be too hard on you."

"Sorry?" Johnny frowned. "I thought we'd be staying at the flat?"

"Are you having a laugh?" Frankie screwed up his face. "You think I'm letting my grandchild live in a shithole like that?"

"But . . ."

Johnny said the word, but nothing came after it, and he just sat there looking and feeling helpless. It was bad enough that Frankie was going to force him to work, but making him move out of the flat was way worse. Dave was his best mate, and he was the perfect flatmate, never nagging him to clean up, or stressing out when he wasted his money on weed instead of buying food. And they liked all the same stuff — the partying, the birds, the clubbing. Johnny didn't want to leave him *or* the flat — and definitely not to move in with a bitch like Rita.

"It's time to grow up," Frankie told him. "You're a married man now, and you're going to be a dad in a few months. You've got responsibilities, and you need to start thinking about the future. And that starts now — today."

"I know," Johnny agreed. "I just hadn't really thought about where we'd live. It'll take a bit of time to sort everything out, though, 'cos I've got loads of stuff to pack," he added, hoping that he'd be able to buy himself a bit of time by dragging out the actual moving for as long as possible.

"It's all sorted," Frankie assured him. "Your mate Dave is going to pack it up for you when he gets home, and one of my lads will be picking it up in the morning, so it'll all be waiting when you and Ruth get home."

"Thanks." Johnny blinked back the tears as the lead weight that had been constricting his heart all day sank into his stomach. They reckoned this was supposed to be the happiest day of your life, but it had been the worst one of his by far — and he couldn't see it getting any better.

Frankie downed his scotch and waved for the waitress to bring another one.

"You can go now," he said, dismissing Johnny. "Just do as you're told and look after my girl, and you and me will get along just fine. Oh, and remember what I said about staying away from them so-called mates of yours," he added warningly. "Trouble and stupid is a dangerous combination, and I don't want that kind of shit around my family. You got that?"

Johnny nodded and rose miserably to his feet. Passing the waitress as she carried Frankie's fresh drink to the table, he dropped his gaze and rushed on out of the bar.

He hadn't taken two steps into the reception hall before Lisa ambushed him.

"There you are," she purred, brushing up against him. "I've been looking everywhere for you."

"Leave it out," he muttered, pushing her away.

"Don't act like you're not interested," she persisted. "I saw you checking me out at the church, and we both know what you were thinking."

"I was thinking that I was just about to get married to your cousin," he told her coolly.

"Yeah, whatever," Lisa drawled, pushing him further into the corner. "Ruth's not good enough for a gorgeous man like you. You need someone who knows how to keep a man happy."

"Go and find someone else to bother," Johnny hissed, pushing her away again. "If Ruth sees you, she'll think there's something going on."

"And she'd be right," Lisa said huskily. "We both know it's going to happen, so don't try to resist it."

"What are you playing at?" Johnny demanded. "You've hardly said two words to me in all the time I've known you, so where's all this coming from?"

Lisa shrugged. "I've always been too pissed or stoned to really notice you before. But after our Ruth told me you'd proposed, it made me look at you in a whole new light. And I've got to say, you're not half bad."

Johnny took a step back and glanced nervously around. "Has Frankie put you up to this? Is it some sort of test to see if I'm stupid enough to cheat on Ruth?"

"Frankie?" Lisa frowned. "Are you crazy? Do you think I'd be saying any of this if I thought he was going to find out? He'd kill me."

"Yeah, well, maybe you should back off and save yourself the trouble," Johnny said firmly.

He sidestepped her now, and was about to walk away when she grabbed his arm.

"I don't kiss and tell, Johnny. You can trust me."

"Yeah, and I bet Ruth thinks *she* can as well," Johnny shot back, yanking his arm free. "I know what you Hyneses are like when it comes to family, so I wonder what she'd say if she knew her cousin was coming on to her husband like this."

Lisa's eyes widened with fear. "If you tell her, I'll deny it. I'll say it was all you."

"And who do you reckon she'd believe?" Johnny asked. Smirking when her lips tightened, he said, "Just leave me alone, Lisa. Go and find Dave if you're looking for fun. You might have pissed him off, but I'm sure he won't turn you down if you're offering."

"Get stuffed," spat Lisa.

"Gladly." Johnny turned his back and walked away.

Lisa folded her arms and, through narrowed eyes, watched him go. Ruth had been dead right about her being jealous. She was absolutely seething with it. Like

Ruth, she'd been born and raised in England with few, if any, of the restrictions that their female relatives in Ireland were expected to abide by. But like any girl who had so much as a single drop of gypsy blood running through her veins, she had been planning her own big day ever since her hands were strong enough to hold a wedding-dress catalogue, and she just couldn't believe that her divvy cousin had beaten her up the aisle. Lisa was the one all the lads went for when they hit the clubs; the blonde sexy one with the big boobs and the tiny waist, who made an effort with her appearance and spent a fortune making sure she was always up to date. So how the hell Ruth, whose idea of dressing up meant covering herself from neck to toe, had managed to bag herself a gorgeous man like Johnny Conroy while Lisa didn't even have a steady boyfriend, she didn't know. It was so unfair.

Johnny walked across the dance floor without looking back, even though he could feel Lisa's stare burning holes into his back with every step. Now that she'd made her move, he would have to be careful around her — careful around *every* girl he came into contact with, in fact, since Frankie had made it clear that he would be watching him.

Ruth was sitting with her mum at the top table, her arms tightly folded, a sulky look on her face. There were dozens of empties in front of them, and it was clear from the glassiness of Rita's eyes when she glared at Johnny that she'd drunk most of their contents.

"Where've you been?" Rita demanded churlishly. "Have you any idea how stupid she looks sitting here on her tod on her wedding day? You're supposed to stay with her, not waltz off with your mates. It's a good job she's got her mother to look after her, that's all I can say. And where's *yours*, while we're on the subject? Too busy to come to her own son's wedding, was she? Thinks she's too good for the likes of us, does she?"

"They're not talking," Ruth reminded her, wishing that she would butt out. She looked at Johnny now, and asked, "Where have you been? You've been gone for ages."

"Sorry." He came around the table and kissed her on the cheek before sitting down. "Your dad wanted a word."

She gave him a tart smile. "Oh, and you thought you'd just stop for a little chat with Lisa on your way back, did you?"

Johnny gritted his teeth, wondering if he was ever going to be able to move again without someone from this damn family spying on him.

"I bumped into her," he admitted. "But we weren't chatting. She nearly fell over and I was just checking she was all right, that's all. I think she's had too much to drink."

"She's a big girl," Ruth sniped. "She doesn't need you looking out for her."

"She's your cousin," Johnny reminded her calmly. "And your dad was just lecturing me about family loyalties, so I thought I'd best do my bit."

"Well, in future, just leave her to it."

"Yeah, she's part of *our* family, not yours," Rita chipped in. "Not that the little slut deserves to be classed as family, letting it all hang out like that. She needs a bloody good slap, if you ask me."

Ruth had heard enough from her mother for one day. This was between her and her husband, and she would deal with it on her own.

"I'm going up to the room." She pushed her chair back and rose to her feet. "Come on, Johnny."

"We can't," he told her, staying put. "Your dad said we've got to —"

"It's *my* wedding, not his." Ruth cut him off shrilly. "I'm a married woman, and I can do what the hell I want. And I want to go to the room, so we're going — *now*."

"Quit mouthing off and park your arse," Rita ordered sternly. "No one's going anywhere. Your dad's shelled out a fortune for this party, and I'm not having him giving me grief because you feel like flouncing off like a spoiled little brat."

Ruth's lips tightened, but she did as she'd been told and flopped back down into her seat.

"This is your fault, this," Rita hissed at Johnny.

Johnny didn't see why she was blaming him for her daughter being in a mood. But it was pointless arguing, so he gazed wistfully out across the room, wishing that he could go and join his mates who were happily filling their boots at the free bar and cutting loose on the dance floor.

Time dragged slowly on, and Johnny was almost asleep with boredom when Dave came over at 2a.m. to inform him that he was leaving. Smirking at Rita, who had given up the ghost some time back and was slumped over with her head in an ashtray, Dave gave Ruth a polite goodbye peck on the cheek before giving Johnny a back-slapping hug.

"Don't tell me you're in trouble already?" he whispered into his ear. "Talk about if looks could kill. What've you done?"

"I'll tell you tomorrow," Johnny whispered back. "And cheers for leaving me on my own with them all night, by the way. You're supposed to be my best man."

"Sorry, mate, I've been a bit tied up." Dave smiled secretively. "Hope Frankie's boy don't come round too early tomorrow, 'cos I don't reckon I'll get too much packing done tonight."

"On a promise?" Johnny asked, glad that at least one of them was ending the night on a high. "Who's the lucky girl?"

"Lisa." Dave gave him a sheepish look. "And before you ask, *I* didn't do the chasing. She came on to me. And you know what they say . . . if it's on a plate, and you're hungry — eat."

"God, you must be starving if you're going there again," Johnny chuckled. "Hope you don't regret it in the morning."

"Me too," Dave said. Then, flicking a glance at Ruth who was scowling up at them, he gave Johnny a sympathetic look and whispered, "Good luck, mate," before going off to scrape the drunken Lisa out of the chair he'd left her on.

"What was all that about?" Ruth demanded when he'd gone.

"Nothing," Johnny lied. "He was just congratulating me again."

Ruth gave him a disbelieving look. "Well, I hope he doesn't think you're going to keep on having secret conversations now we're married. I'm your wife, and he's just going to have to respect that. If he wants to talk to you, he can include me or get lost."

Johnny drew his head back and frowned at her. She was really pushing it now. He was already pissed off about the way she'd been talking to him tonight, and now she was trying to dictate who he could and couldn't talk to.

Before he could pull her up about it, Frankie strolled over.

"Looks like people are getting ready to leave, so you'd best come out into the foyer to say goodbye and thank them for coming."

"About time," Ruth grumbled, gathering her skirts together and standing up. "And then we're going to our room, so don't try and stop us."

"You can do what you want," Frankie conceded. "After you've helped me get your mam into the car." He cast a disapproving look at his wife, shook his head in disgust and walked away.

"Let's get this over with," Ruth said, jerking her head at Johnny before following her dad.

After the last guest had gone, and he'd helped Frankie to manhandle Rita into the back of the Rolls and waved them off, Johnny followed Ruth up to the room Frankie had booked for them. He'd never stayed in a hotel before, and he was knocked for six when he walked in and saw how luxurious it was. There was a massive four-poster bed with satin drapes at each corner, and matching curtains hanging from the floor-to-ceiling picture window which overlooked the hotel's immaculately landscaped gardens. There was also an en-suite bathroom with a bidet and a walk-in shower, a TV, a telephone, and a minibar. And somebody had placed a huge vase of red roses on the breakfast table in the window alcove, alongside a bottle of champagne in a bucket of ice.

It was incredible, and if Johnny had been there with any other girl he would already have been getting stuck in to the champagne and bouncing around on the bed. But he didn't hold out much hope of having a fun-packed night with Ruth if the moody look on her face was anything to go by.

"Can you help me with this?" She stood in front of him and looked back expectantly over her shoulder.

"What do you want me to do?" he asked.

"Unhook me," she said, with a sarcastic edge to her tone, as if he should have known without needing to be told.

There seemed to be a million tiny little hooks and eyes, and Johnny fumbled with them for ages before he finally managed to get a rhythm going.

When the back of the dress was undone at last, Ruth waddled off into the bathroom to complete the job in private. Johnny opened the champagne and poured out a couple of glasses. Adding a miniature bottle of Jack Daniel's from the minibar to his, he drank it in one and refilled it before getting undressed and climbing into the bed.

When Ruth came back a short time later, she laid her dress carefully over the back of one of the chairs before slipping into bed beside Johnny and pulling the quilt up around her throat. She'd changed into a red satin nightie and, in the brief moment that he'd had a chance to see it, Johnny couldn't help but notice how good it looked on her. Although he wasn't sure why she'd bothered if she was just going to cover herself up like that.

"It's lovely here, isn't it?" Ruth said after a moment, snaking her hand out and reaching for the glass he'd placed on her bedside table.

"Oh, so you're talking to me now, are you?" Johnny muttered, taking another hefty swig of his own drink.

Ruth gazed at him and gave a guilty little smile.

"Sorry I've been such a bitch, but I wasn't enjoying myself down there. I've been dying to be alone with you since we left the church, but then you took off and left me with my mum, and everyone else was ignoring me. It was like they all forgot it was my day, or something. They just wanted to get at the food and booze."

"That's what people do at parties," Johnny replied coolly, adding under his breath, "Wish I'd been a bleedin' guest."

Ruth caught it and blinked back the tears that immediately sprang into her eyes.

"I ruined it for you, didn't I?"

The words *Too right!* sprang to the tip of Johnny's tongue, but when he looked at her and saw how forlorn she looked, he couldn't bring himself to say it. It had been a stressful enough day for *him*, so God only knew how hard it must have been for her — especially since she'd had to spend most of it with her mother.

"You didn't ruin it," he lied. "We're both wiped, and we've probably both said things we didn't mean today."

"You haven't," she simpered. "You've been lovely. It's me. I've been horrible. Do you hate me?"

"Don't be stupid." He sighed.

Ruth swallowed the rest of her drink and held out her empty glass. Looking up at him through her lashes, she said, "Pour me another one and let me make it up to you. And hurry up and drink yours. This is supposed to be the best night of our lives."

God help me if this is the best I've got to look forward to, thought Johnny. But he did as she'd asked.

In desperate need of Dutch courage, Ruth downed her second drink without pausing for breath before snuggling up to him. Johnny put his arm around her and closed his eyes. Almost immediately, a hazy vision of a naked woman crept into his mind, followed by an image of himself standing in a pitch-dark room with his back against the wall and his cock in the woman's mouth.

The quilt started to rise. Ruth noticed and bit her lip.

"Is that for me?" she purred, gazing up at him.

"Ugh?" Johnny opened his eyes and looked at her. Smiling slyly when he realised how hard he was, he said, "What do you think?"

It might not have been the best of days, but she was here, and so was the hard-on. So, closing his eyes again to recapture the horny visions, he pulled her towards him and pushed his tongue between her teeth.

Ruth kissed him back for a moment, then pulled away and whispered, "Turn the light off. And be quiet. I don't want next door to hear us, or they'll know what we're doing."

"We've just got married," Johnny reminded her amusedly. "I'm sure they'll be expecting a bit of noise."

"I don't care," she insisted. "We might pass them in the corridor in the morning, and I won't know where to put my face."

"Fine." Sighing, Johnny threw the quilt aside and got up.

"Shhh," Ruth hissed when he flicked the wall switch.

Johnny's hard-on went out with the light. Cock drooping, he came back to the bed.

"Where were we?" Ruth rolled towards him.

Johnny's heart was no longer in it. He tried, but now, when he closed his eyes, disturbing images crept in alongside the sexy ones: visions of men fighting, girls screaming, and Dave dragging him into the back of a taxi and telling the driver to put his foot down.

Ruth pushed herself up onto her elbow. "What's wrong?"

"Nothing." Johnny felt sick. Something bad had happened last night, and it must have been pretty serious to make Mikey and Andy miss his wedding because, after Dave, they were two of his best mates. And what had Frankie meant about stepping in? He obviously knew about the woman, so he must have been there — wherever there was.

"Is it me?" Ruth asked plaintively. "Have I done something wrong?"

"Course not," Johnny lied. "I'm just tired, that's all. And I think I've probably had too much to drink. Sorry, babe."

He'd never called her that before, and Ruth's stomach flipped with happiness. Laying her head on his chest, she played with the fine hairs.

"This is lovely, isn't it? Just you and me, all alone at last."

"Mmm." Johnny peered around the dark room, wondering if Frankie had eyes even in here. He wouldn't put it past him.

"Do you know what I'm looking forward to?" Ruth went on sleepily. "Shopping for stuff for our house."

"We haven't got a house."

"Not yet, but we soon will have now you're going to work for my dad," said Ruth. "I think it's great that he wants to take you on, because he wouldn't have bothered if he didn't like you. And I know you don't think my mum likes you, but she's really looking forward to you coming to live with us. She acts tough, but she wouldn't have let us get married if she didn't like you. My dad thinks he's the boss, but you've probably guessed by now that she is really. I just wish she didn't drink so much," she added wistfully. "I know she gets lonely, but I'm sure my dad would stay home more if she stopped getting so drunk."

Johnny clamped his eyes shut and willed her to shut up. Sex was off the agenda, so now she was obviously intent on talking him to death.

"She's not been too bad this week," Ruth went on obliviously. "This was supposed to be a surprise, but I might as well tell you — they've given us the room at the back. It's twice the size of mine, and they usually only use it when relatives come over. But it's ours now, and we can do it up any way we like. Mum's been helping me to paint it this week, and it's a kind of lemony yellow. Sounds yucky, but I think you'll like it."

She paused when Johnny didn't respond, and lifted her head to look at him. His eyes were tightly closed, and his breathing had become deep and heavy. He looked so beautiful she thought her heart might burst. But she didn't want to wake him, so she placed a little kiss on his lips and then lay back down.

Relieved when she started softly snoring some time later, Johnny eased his arm out from under her and got up quietly. He eased the minibar open and took out a handful of miniatures. Then, tiptoeing over to the table by the window, he filled his glass and lit a fag.

A feeling of loneliness settled over him as he gazed out at the tarry silhouettes of the trees down below, and he felt tears stinging at the back of his eyes. He had so much shit going through his mind right now, and he couldn't get a firm grip on any of it. Everything seemed so cold and final, and he longed to be back at home, chilling with Dave, smoking some spliffs and listening to some good music to clear these horrible doom-laden thoughts out of his head.

But this was his life from here on in and, like it or not, he was just going to have to deal with it.

CHAPTER
FIVE

Life in the Hyneses' house was even worse than Johnny had imagined. Frankie was hardly ever home, so Johnny was stuck with Ruth and Rita 24/7. Determined to project the image of wedded bliss, Ruth was all over him like a rash from the minute they stepped out of their disgusting yellow bedroom of a morning until they went back of a night. But Rita was the one who was really making his life a misery, since she'd decided to transfer all of the venom she'd previously heaped on her daughter onto him instead. She looked at him like he was a piece of shit that was still steaming, and delighted in criticising every little thing he said or did. And, infuriatingly, she wouldn't stop calling him Jimmy.

The days were horrible, what with Ruth smothering him and Rita using him as a target for her verbal bullets. But the nights were a major headache. After the aborted attempt at having sex in the hotel on their wedding night, Johnny just couldn't get it up — at least not when he was supposed to. He was still getting hard-ons left, right and centre, brought on by anything from a glimpse of a fit bird on TV to the whiff of perfume when he walked past a girl in the supermarket whenever Ruth dragged him out grocery shopping.

Even just the sound of a girly giggle could bring it rearing to life. But come bedtime, forget it — his cock would shrivel up and hide. And the longer it went on, the more upset Ruth was getting about it.

"You don't love me any more, do you?" she asked as they lay in bed on the night before he was due to start working for her dad. "You regret marrying me, don't you?"

Yes on both counts, thought Johnny. But he knew better than to say it out loud, so he trotted out the "It's not you, it's me" line that he'd used on so many one-night stands who'd wanted to take things further in the past. And, knowing how freaky *she* was about anyone hearing them at it, he added, "It doesn't feel right with your mum and dad in the next room."

But she was obviously more desperate than he'd thought, because she said, "They won't hear us if we're careful."

So Johnny was forced to play his trump card, telling her, "I'm worried about hurting the baby."

"You can't hurt it," Ruth assured him, touched that he was being so protective. "It's perfectly safe."

"I don't want to risk it," he insisted. "Talk to the doctor. If he says it's all right, I'll think about it."

Ruth couldn't argue with that, not when he was showing genuine concern for their unborn child. So, off the hook — for now, at least — Johnny was able to go to sleep.

Honeymoon officially over, Johnny was up and out of bed before the alarm went off the next morning, and he was dressed and waiting by the door by the time Frankie came downstairs.

It was only half-seven, and he hadn't been up that early on a weekday since he'd been at school. But this was the first chance he'd had to escape from Ruth, her mum, and this prison of a house since the wedding, and he couldn't wait to get out of there.

Frankie's car lot was situated at the end of a little industrial estate on a cul-de-sac off Great Ancoats Street. It was surrounded by six-foot-high metal railings and had two gates, both of which were closed when Frankie pulled up outside, secured by a thick steel chain and a massive padlock.

Frankie beeped the horn, and Big Pat came to let them in.

"We've got a bit of a problem with that thing you sent the lads to do last night, boss," he said, casting a cautious look at Johnny.

"What kind of problem?" Frankie demanded, not giving a shit if Johnny heard or not. He was part of the family now, and if he forgot the loyalty rule and opened his gob about anything he saw or heard here he'd only have himself to blame for the consequences.

"You'd best come and take a look." Pat relocked the gates and walked back the way he'd come.

Johnny gazed out of the window as Frankie drove through the front part of the lot. There were loads of cars parked haphazardly around, and they looked in even worse shape than the shit-heaps back at the house. Some had windows missing, most were minus at least one wheel, and they were all battered, with dents and scratches on their bodywork. If these were the ones that Frankie expected him to clean, he'd be here from now till the next blue moon.

A low prefab-type building sat around the corner, its windows protected by thick wire meshing, its roof edged with deadly-looking rolls of barbed wire. Two vicious-looking dogs were chained up at the side, and when they saw the car they started barking and straining to get free.

The prefab door opened as Frankie drew up, and two lads stepped out onto the top step.

"What happened?" Frankie demanded, hopping out of the car.

The lads exchanged nervous glances and came down the steps.

"It wasn't our fault, boss," one of them said. "We got chased, so I had to squeeze through some bollards and go over a field."

"You fucking what?" Frankie roared. "What've I told you about going off-road?"

"I had no choice," the lad insisted. "It was either that, or get nicked. And I didn't think you'd want them getting hold of me and risk having them come sniffing round here."

"You'd best not have messed it up too bad," Frankie warned as he marched over to the garage. "Shut the fuck up," he yelled at the dogs as he rolled up the metal shutter. They both lay down immediately and gazed sulkily up at him.

Johnny climbed out of the car. Shivering when the dogs locked their stares onto him and started growling deep in their throats, he gave them a wide berth and followed Frankie into a big, dark workshop. The combined stench of grease, oil, petrol and sweat hit him smack in the face, and he wrinkled his nose as he gazed around. There were tools strewn all over the floor and worktops, and an oldish BMW was up on a ramp at the far side. But it was the car that was parked up in the middle of the garage floor that caught his attention. It was a black Sierra Cosworth, with low-profile tyres, and a great big fin on the back. If it hadn't been for the deep scrapes gouged into both wings, the headlight hanging out of its socket at the front, the massive dent in the bumper, and both of the back light panels being smashed to pieces, it would have been his dream car.

"How the fuck did you manage to do all this on one set of bollards?" Frankie demanded, anger glinting in his eyes as he strolled around the car and looked it over in disbelief.

"The coppers rammed us," the lad told him. "It weren't my fault."

"Stop fucking saying that!" Frankie roared, punching him in the side of the head. "Have you got any idea how much you've just cost me, you stupid twat? The buyer's waiting, but I can't send it over in this state."

"Me and Del can fix it up," the lad bleated. "We looked it over while we were waiting for you, and we reckon it won't take that much to get it back up to spec."

"You mean apart from knocking out the dents, fixing brand new light units, and giving it a complete fucking respray?" Frankie bellowed, grabbing him by the front of his jumper now and shaking him like a rag doll. "That'd cost more than I'm fucking getting for it, you knob. And you two work like a pair of fucking snails so, by the time you've finished the buyer would have gone somewhere else."

"It weren't my fault," the lad protested. "It was the coppers. They proper wanted to stop us."

"How did they spot you in the first place? What did you do, set off the fucking alarm or something?"

"No, the pickup went sweet, but the sneaky cunts were parked out of sight in a lay-by when we turned off the motorway on the way back, and they pulled out behind us."

"So you thought you'd be a dick and put your foot down, did you?"

"No, I carried on like there was nothing wrong for ages. But then he shoved his blues on, so what was I supposed to do? It was either run or get nabbed. And at least we got it back here in . . ."

The lad trailed off and swallowed loudly when Frankie bared his teeth and glared at him as if he was contemplating ripping his face off.

"Get rid of it," Frankie growled, tossing him aside. "It's fucking useless to me now you've been clocked in it." When the lad immediately darted around to the driver's door, Frankie screwed up his face. "What you doing now?"

"Getting rid — like you said."

Losing patience, Frankie kicked him in his back and sent him sprawling across the greasy floor.

"Not in broad fucking daylight, you cretin! Wait till it gets dark, then dump it and torch it. And keep the fuck out of my way for the rest of the day, or I won't be responsible. D'ya get me?"

Johnny winced when Frankie aimed one last kick into the boy's ribs. But Big Pat and the other lad looked on impassively, as if violence was par for the course if you screwed up around here.

Frankie turned to Big Pat now and said, "Give them something to do" before jerking his head at Johnny and striding back outside.

Johnny made a mental note to stay on Frankie's good side as he followed him back out into the yard and around to the front. Frankie opened a door in the garage sidewall and flicked on a light.

"This is where we keep all the cleaning shit," he explained, waving Johnny into the storeroom. "It's a mess, so you can sort it out before you get started. Then I want all the motors washed — and use the proper shampoo, 'cos I don't want you scratching the paintwork."

Johnny wondered how anyone would notice a new scratch on any of the cars when they were all covered in them already.

"When you've finished washing the outsides, hoover them out and give them a polish," Frankie went on. "There's a box of plastic covers somewhere. Find them and cover all the front seats, then make a list of all the plates, and detail what damage each one's got: dents, bald tyres, knackered wiper blades, ripped seats and carpets — that kind of shit. Give it to Big Pat when

106

you're done." He paused now and gave Johnny a questioning look. "Got all that?"

"Yeah." Johnny nodded.

Frankie glanced at his watch. "Right, I've got some calls to make, so find yourself some overalls and get started. You can take a fifteen-minute break at half-ten, and an hour for lunch at one. There's a butty shop across the road. I'll be in the office if you need me."

When he'd gone, Johnny gazed around and scratched his head. It would take hours to sort this mess out, and then he had the cars to deal with. It was going to be a mammoth task, and he just hoped that Frankie wasn't expecting him to get it all done today.

Already knackered just *thinking* about what lay ahead, Johnny chose the least dirty, least smelly pair of overalls off the hook on the back of the door and pulled them on over his jeans.

There were numerous bottles of shampoo, tins of polish, sponges, and various other stuff that he didn't recognise crammed together on the shelves and heaps of unmarked boxes all over the floor. Starting on the shelves, he took every item off one by one and put them into groups on the ledge.

He'd cleared one shelf and was halfway through putting it all back when one of the lads he'd seen in the garage suddenly emerged from the shadows in the far corner of the room.

"Jeezus!" he gasped, jumping at the sight of him. "Have you been there the whole time?"

"Nah, there's a connecting door," the lad told him, jerking his head back towards it. "What you doing?"

Johnny used the back of his hand to push his sweaty hair out of his eyes.

"Frankie told me to sort this lot out, but it's a fucking nightmare. I don't even know what half of it is."

"Me neither," the lad snorted. He leaned against a ledge and took a pack of rolling tobacco out of his pocket. "Want one?"

"God, yeah," Johnny said gratefully. He'd been dying for a fag, but he'd run out last night and had no money to buy any more.

The lad rolled two and passed one over. Lighting his own, he squinted at Johnny through the smoke.

"So, you're the new son-in-law, are you? How's that going?"

"All right." Johnny leaned forward to get a light. "Johnny." He held out his hand.

"Del." The lad shook it.

"Is your mate all right?" Johnny asked. "He didn't look too good back there."

Del shrugged. "Our Robbie's a tough bastard, he can take it."

"Oh, you're related?"

"Brothers," Del told him. "We do the pickups," he added — as if he thought that Johnny would know what that meant.

Johnny didn't have a clue, but he was curious to know who was supposed to do what around here. As far as he could tell nobody had touched the cars before he'd arrived, and that made him wonder how Frankie could possibly be making any money out of them. He sure as hell couldn't see anyone being mug enough to pay for them in the state they were in now.

"Del . . .?" Big Pat shouted just then. "Where are you?"

"Shit, best go," Del muttered, dropping his rollie and grinding it into the floor with his heel. "See you later."

"Yeah, see you." Waving as the lad rushed back out the way he'd come in, Johnny finished his smoke and got back to work.

Once he got into the swing of it, it went pretty smoothly, and he finished the storeroom well before he'd expected to. He was dying for a brew by then, so he wandered round to the prefab to ask if there was a kettle.

Frankie was inside. About to knock, Johnny decided against it when he heard him yell, "Quit fucking me about, Phil. I told you I'd get it, and I have, so you'd best get your arse round here with the dosh. And don't make me come looking for you, or I'll make you shit yourself and eat it."

Reluctant to disturb Frankie when he was obviously still pissed off, Johnny started backing down the steps. But he hadn't reached the bottom when the door was yanked open.

"What you doing?" Frankie demanded.

"I've finished cleaning the storeroom," Johnny told him nervously. "And I was just wondering if there was anywhere to make a brew before I start on the cars. But I'll wait till lunch if it's a problem."

"Get yourself a fucking brew and quit acting like you've shit your kecks," Frankie snapped. "The kettle's in there." He jerked his thumb back through the prefab door. "Don't use all the milk," he warned, coming down the steps and striding towards the garage.

Johnny went into the prefab and looked around. It was every bit as messy as the storeroom had been before he'd sorted it out, with a desk at the far end upon which sat a phone and several untidy heaps of paper. A couple of fold-down chairs were leaning against the window wall, and a kettle, coffee, tea bags, sugar and milk sat on a table opposite the door. He contemplated asking if anybody else wanted one. But Frankie was already in a foul mood and he didn't want to piss him off by getting in his face again, so he made himself a coffee and scuttled back to the solitude of his storeroom.

When he'd finished the drink, he filled a bucket with hot water and got cracking on the cars. By lunchtime his stomach was grumbling loudly. He'd been so eager to get out of the house that morning that he hadn't bothered with breakfast. But the gates were still locked and he didn't want to ask Big Pat to let him out. Anyway, nobody else seemed to be thinking about food, so he pushed the hunger to the back of his mind.

The day had started off cold, but it got progressively worse as it went on. By four in the afternoon there was a glittering of frost on the scrubby grass edging the fence, and Johnny's hands and feet were frozen by the time Big Pat strolled around the corner. Frankie was right behind him in his car. Stopping, he leaned his

110

elbow on the open window and gazed at Johnny's handiwork.

"You've done a bloody good job on that, son." He nodded at the gleaming bonnet of the Escort that Johnny had just finished cleaning. "Don't even look like the same motor."

"Thanks," Johnny replied, trying to sound modest despite feeling ridiculously pleased with himself. He'd worked harder today than he'd ever worked in his life before but, surprisingly, he'd enjoyed it. There was something hypnotic about the repetition of washing, polishing and hoovering. And considering what a heap of shit the cars had looked when he'd arrived that morning, the ones he'd done now looked almost good enough to sell.

"You can pack up for the day," Frankie said, taking a tenner out of his pocket and holding it out. "Get a cab back. And tell Rita not to wait up, 'cos I don't know how late I'm going to be."

When Frankie had gone, Johnny gathered his cleaning equipment together and carried it into the storeroom. He shrugged out of the overalls and reached for his jacket. Then, taking one last proud look around, he switched off the light and went home.

Ruth ran out from the kitchen when she heard Johnny coming in and threw herself into his arms.

"I've missed you so much," she gushed. "Have you missed me?"

"Yeah, course." Johnny eased her away. "Don't get too close. I stink."

"I don't care," she insisted. "Anyway, I'm used to my dad coming home filthy, so it doesn't bother me."

"*I'm* not used to it," he said firmly. "Is it all right if I get a bath?"

"I can't believe you're still asking." She giggled. "Darling, you live here. You can do whatever you want."

That was the first time she'd ever called him that, and it made Johnny feel weird because it sounded contrived, as if she'd spent the day practising it in front of the mirror.

"That you, Frankie?" Rita's voice drifted out from the parlour.

"No, it's Johnny," Ruth told her.

"Isn't your dad with him?"

"He, er, said he had something to do," Johnny called to her. "And he said not to bother waiting up 'cos he might be late."

"No change there, then," Ruth whispered, giving him a conspiratorial smile. "Anyway, I hope you're hungry. I've made something special to celebrate your first day at work."

"Starving," he admitted.

"Thought you would be." She smiled and pushed him towards the stairs. "Go and get your bath. I'll have it on the table when you come back down — like a good little wife."

True to her word, there was a steaming plateful of food and some bread and butter waiting on the table when Johnny came back downstairs a short time later.

"What is it?" he asked, sitting down and reaching for his fork.

"Chicken chasseur," Ruth told him, perching on the edge of the chair opposite his and clasping her hands together under her chin.

Johnny got started, but glanced up after a couple of mouthfuls. "Where's yours?"

"I'll get it in a minute," she said. "I just want to see what you think of it first. I've never made it before. I got the recipe from a book at the library."

"It's great," he told her. "Really tasty."

"Oh, good." Ruth exhaled as if she'd been on a knife's edge, and fetched her own dinner to the table. But instead of tucking in like Johnny, she just pushed the food around.

"Something wrong?" he asked, wishing she'd just get on with it because she was making him feel uncomfortable.

"No." She shook her head. "Just been feeling a bit sick today. But don't worry about me. Tell me about your day."

"It was all right, actually," Johnny said, reaching for a piece of bread. "Your dad seemed pretty pleased with me, anyway."

"Oh, that's brilliant." Ruth smiled. "The last lad was terrible, so he had to sack him. But if he's already pleased with you, you won't have anything to worry about."

"I met some of his other lads," Johnny told her, mopping up the last of the juice off his plate. "One of them mentioned something about doing pickups, but I didn't know what he meant. Do you?"

"No point asking me about dad's business." Ruth laughed. "I don't get involved in man stuff."

Johnny's stomach groaned when she whisked his plate away and replaced it with a steaming bowl of rice pudding, but he dutifully reached for his spoon. She'd cooked his dinner every night since the wedding but she'd gone overboard tonight, as if she thought that he would need twice as much now that he was a working man.

"Cake?" she asked when he'd finished his dessert.

"No!" Johnny held up his hands. "Seriously, I couldn't eat another thing. I just need some water and a lie-down."

"It's not even seven o'clock," Ruth pointed out. "You can't go to bed this early. Anyway, that film's on in a bit. I thought we could snuggle up together on the sofa."

With your mum giving us dirty looks all the way through? thought Johnny.

"Nah, I think I'll give it a miss." He scraped his chair back and stood up. "I'm absolutely knackered. And it's going to be the same again tomorrow, so I'll need an early night. Don't want your dad to think I'm not taking the job seriously."

"I suppose not," Ruth conceded, sighing her disappointment. "I promised my mum I'd watch the film with her. You don't mind, do you?"

"Course not. Don't worry about me."

Barely able to suppress his grin of delight, Johnny ran upstairs, threw off his clothes, jumped into bed, and spread his arms and legs, revelling in the space and

114

freedom. He hadn't felt this relaxed since he'd been in his own bed back at the flat.

God, he missed it.

The bed, the flat . . .

Dave.

Unexpected tears flooded his eyes. Blinking rapidly, he bit down hard on his lip and told himself to get a grip. Men didn't cry — especially not over other men. But he couldn't help it. Ruth hadn't let him out of her sight since the wedding, and whenever he mentioned going to see Dave she made excuses to stop him. Johnny knew he should take a stand and tell her that he was going to see him, whether she liked it or not, but it just wasn't that easy.

So don't tell her, dickhead.

The thought came from nowhere, but it was so obvious that Johnny didn't know why he hadn't thought of it before. It had been easy for Ruth to keep control of him when she'd been with him day and night, but she couldn't keep tabs on him now he was working, so she'd be none the wiser if he took a detour on the way home. And none of his mates liked her, so even if she bumped into any of them they'd never drop him in it by telling her that they'd seen him.

Happier now that he'd figured out a way to claw back a bit of freedom, Johnny rolled over and closed his eyes — willing sleep to come before the film finished and Ruth came up.

It was gone eleven before Rita had sunk enough whisky for Ruth to be able to sneak away without waking her.

She tiptoed out of the room, ran lightly up the stairs, got undressed and climbed into bed.

Johnny had his back turned, but he wasn't yet snoring, so she leaned over him and whispered into his ear, "Are you awake, Johnny? Mum's asleep, and dad's not back yet, so we're safe if you want to do it." Getting no response, she shook him gently. "Johnny . . . can you hear me? *Johnny?*"

Her breath tickled his ear and he jerked his head away from her.

"Are you awake?" Ruth whispered again.

I am now, Johnny thought grumpily.

"What's up?" he asked, gazing sleepily back at her over his shoulder.

"I was just saying mum's asleep and dad's still out, so we can make love without anyone hearing us. If you want to?" she added shyly. "I know you're tired, but it's been ages."

Johnny was surprised when Ruth slid her arm over him and started stroking his cock through his pyjamas. She'd never been this forward before; she'd always been more of a lie-back-and-let-him-get-on-with-it kind of girl. But if she thought her newfound forwardness was going to reignite his passion, she was wrong.

"Ruth, I'm tired," he said, gently moving her hand.

"You've gone off me, haven't you?"

She had a plaintive edge to her voice that signalled impending tears, and Johnny squeezed his eyes shut.

"Don't be daft. I've just told you, I'm tired. It'll be better when I get used to the routine."

"Promise?"

116

"Yeah."

"I love you, Mr Conroy." Ruth wriggled closer and pressed her body against his.

"Great," he murmured. "Now, let's go to sleep, eh?"

Ruth sighed and tried to relax, but it wasn't easy. She didn't just want him to make love to her, she *needed* him to — and if it didn't happen soon, things were going to get very tricky.

CHAPTER
SIX

Johnny was up and out of bed before the alarm went off again the next morning. And, again, he was ready and waiting at the door by the time Frankie came downstairs. But this time he'd eaten breakfast and had made himself a sandwich in case he couldn't get out for lunch.

"You're keen, ain't you?" Frankie remarked as they set off. "I thought I was going to have to drag you out of bed of a morning, but this is two days on the trot you've been up before me. I'm impressed."

"Thanks." Johnny grinned, chuffed that Frankie was pleased with him. "I know it probably sounds stupid to you, seeing as you've been at it so long, but it gave me a right buzz seeing how good the cars looked after I'd finished polishing them yesterday, and I just want to get back to it."

"I vaguely remember the feeling," said Frankie, amusedly. "But I don't get it no more myself. They're just chunks of metal to me now."

Reminded of one of the questions that had been flitting through his mind, Johnny said, "I meant to ask, how come none of them have got prices on them?"

"No point trying to flog them till they look the part," Frankie explained. "And I had to sack the lad before you, so there's been no one to sort them out till now."

"Couldn't Del or Robbie have done it?" Johnny ventured, thinking that Frankie must have lost a whole heap of money leaving the cars sitting there in that state for so long.

"They've got other things to do," Frankie said evasively. "Anyhow, whats with all the questions? You an undercover cop, or what?"

"Sorry," Johnny apologised. "I just figured you'd make a lot more money if the yard looked more . . . customer-friendly, I guess."

"That right?" Frankie glanced at him out of the corner of his eye. "And how do you suggest we do that?"

His tone was mocking, but Johnny thought he had a valid point, so he shrugged and said, "I just reckon people would be more interested in having a look around if they knew how much everything was. And it might help if you opened the gates."

"Reckon I need to start attracting passing trade, do you?"

Encouraged by his responsiveness, Johnny nodded. "Yeah. And maybe we could line the motors up along the fence so they don't look like they've just been dumped all over the place."

"We could, could we?"

"Look, I know I don't really know anything about it, so you probably think I'm talking through my arse," Johnny went on. "But if I was looking to buy a motor,

119

I'd take one look at your yard and go to the one down the road instead." He caught himself, and cast a nervous glance at his father-in-law. "Sorry, I probably shouldn't have said that last bit."

"No harm in voicing your opinion, so long as you've actually got something to say." Frankie shrugged. "And I suppose you've got a point. It *is* a bit of a tip. But that's what I've got you for, isn't it?"

Johnny nodded, but he still had loads of questions. As far as he could tell, nobody seemed to be in charge of the sales side of things. Big Pat stayed in the garage all day, only venturing out to let people in and out. Del and Robbie usually only worked at night — although doing what, Johnny still had no clue. And Frankie stayed in his office.

"What's going to happen after I've finished cleaning them?" he asked. "Only, I was thinking that I wouldn't mind having a go at selling them. But only if you think I could do it," he added quickly, not wanting to appear too pushy.

Frankie sighed, and said, "I'll think about it. But belt up now, eh? You're giving me a fuckin' headache."

Johnny went into his storeroom when they reached the yard, and switched on the light. Compared to the mess that had greeted him yesterday, everything was clean and orderly, and it gave him a real sense of achievement to know that he'd done it all by himself. It was a weird feeling, because he'd never really cared about anything before. But then, he'd never had anything to prove before and now he did. Frankie tolerated him because he was married to Ruth, but he wanted the man to like him for himself. More than that, he wanted Frankie to respect him. And the only way that was going to happen was if he proved that he was willing to do whatever was asked of him in order to provide for his new family — the way that Frankie worked to provide for his. So he pulled on his overalls, filled his bucket, and got to work.

Several men called in to see Frankie throughout the day but, just like yesterday, none of them so much as looked at the cars on their way in or out, leaving Johnny to wonder — again — what kind of business Frankie was running here.

The rest of the day passed quickly and before Johnny knew it, it was four o'clock. But this time, when Frankie drove around and gave him a tenner to make his own way home, Johnny wasted no time. He threw the bucket and sponge into the storeroom, shrugged out of his overalls, snatched his jacket off the hook, and made it to the gates before Big Pat had a chance to relock them behind Frankie.

Dave was sitting cross-legged on the couch, sucking on a bong. Eyes narrowing when he heard a scraping sound coming from the front door, he slid his baseball bat out from under the cushion and rushed out into the hall with it raised above his head — at the exact moment Johnny walked in.

"Fuckin' hell, man, it's me!" Johnny squawked, stumbling back when Dave took a wild swing and the bat whizzed past his face.

"Jeezus!" Dave croaked, realising how close he'd come to caving his friend's head in. "What are you doing here?"

"Nice to see you, too." Johnny laughed, then tipped his head back and inhaled deeply. "God, it's good to be home," he murmured, savouring all the old familiar smells.

"Home?" Dave gave him a quizzical look. "Don't tell me you've gone and left her already?"

"Like I'd dare," Johnny snorted.

"So, what's up?" Dave put the bat down and wiped his sweaty palms on his pants.

"Nothing." Johnny shrugged. "Just thought I'd show my face before you forget about me."

"You've only been gone two weeks," Dave reminded him amusedly.

"Feels more like two years," Johnny moaned. Then, grinning, he pounced on his friend and gave him a big bear hug. "Have you missed me?"

"Not that much, you big poof." Dave pulled a face and shoved him off.

"Yeah, you have," Johnny teased, throwing a mock punch at his arm.

"Pack it in," Dave complained, rubbing at the spot where it had landed. "I need that arm for bong-lifting."

"Oh, yes, count me in for some of that," Johnny said longingly. "Go and get it loaded up, I'll be with you in a minute."

"Yo, don't go in there," Dave warned when he headed for his old bedroom. "Wazza's got a bird in."

122

"Wazza?" Johnny stopped with his hand on the door handle. "What's he doing here? And why'd you let him use *my* bed? He'll have my quilt stinking of cheesy feet and BO."

Dave gave him a sheepish look. "He ain't actually using your quilt, mate. He brought his own when he moved in. Yours is on top of my wardrobe."

"Moved in?" A wounded look leapt into Johnny's eyes. "Christ, you didn't let the grass grow, did you? Would you have rented my grave out as fast?"

"Mate, you don't live here no more," Dave reminded him. "What was I supposed to do, keep it like a shrine to you?"

Johnny couldn't speak. He knew he had no right to complain, but he still didn't like it. It was horrible living at Ruth's, but at least he'd had this place to escape to when he closed his eyes. Now he had nothing. His room was gone, and his best mate had replaced him with a lad who'd never met a can of deodorant in his life.

"You can still come round whenever you want," Dave told him guiltily. "And the couch is yours any time you need it."

"Yeah, I know." Johnny sighed and turned away from the door. "Come on, man, get me stoned."

Dave headed back into the living room and loaded up the bong. Handing it to Johnny, he said, "So how's it feel being a respectable married man, an' all that?"

"Aw, don't go and spoil it," Johnny groaned, reaching for the lighter. "This is all I've been thinking about for weeks. Soon as I finished work, I —"

"Er, stop right there." Dave held up his hand. "Run that by me again, 'cos I'm sure I heard you say the dirty W word."

Johnny grinned. "Yeah, I'm working for Frankie."

"Since when, and doing what?" Dave demanded.

"Since yesterday, and washing cars," Johnny told him. "But I'll be moving on to sales before too long," he added proudly, even though Frankie hadn't said anything of the sort.

Dave's brow was creasing more by the second. "And you look happy about this *because* . . .?"

"I like it," Johnny admitted. "It totally wipes you out, but you feel dead good after you've finished. You should try it. You might surprise yourself."

"Er, nah, I don't think so," Dave muttered, looking at him as if he'd gone completely doolally. Then, nodding at the bong, he said, "Are you smoking that, or what?"

Johnny lit up and took a deep suck on it before handing it back to Dave and flopping back in his seat. Exhaling a thick plume of smoke a few seconds later, he said, "Man, I needed that. It's the first hit I've had since the wedding, and I was getting serious withdrawals."

"Yeah, right." Dave gave him a disbelieving look as he put a fresh bud of weed into the bowl and tamped it down with his thumb. "You couldn't go two *days* without, never mind two weeks."

"Honest, I haven't," Johnny insisted. "Ruth hasn't let me out of her sight since I moved to hers. I've been going totally stir-crazy."

"You make it sound like a prison." Dave chuckled. "You're only a mile away — you should have just come round if you wanted a smoke."

"Don't think I haven't wanted to," Johnny told him. "But every time I mention it, she's like, '*Oh, we can't go out, my aunt so-and-so's coming round.*' Or, '*No, Johnny, we can't go out, I've got to keep an eye on the pisshead I call a mother.*'"

His tone was scathing as he mimicked Ruth, and Dave's eyebrows bunched together over his nose.

"Is it that bad?"

"Worse," said Johnny. Then, grinning slyly as the stone started to creep up on him, he said, "But let's not talk about it now. I just want to enjoy my freedom while I can."

A couple more bongs later, when they were both slumped back in their seats with their half-closed eyes a matching shade of scarlet, Dave said, "Does shagging feel different now you've got a ring on your finger? My brother reckoned it turned to total shit after him and his missus tied the knot."

"I wouldn't know," Johnny admitted.

"You what?" Dave flopped his head to one side and peered at him.

"We haven't done it yet."

"Why not?"

"Haven't felt like it."

"Nah, man . . ." Dave shook his head and sat up straighter. "Let me get this right . . . you're telling me you can have it any time you want, but you're turning your nose up?"

125

Johnny shrugged.

"Have you lost your mind?" Dave demanded. "Do you know what I'd give to be in your shoes? I spend half my life trawling round the clubs looking for birds who are pissed enough to say yes, and there's you, got it on tap."

"You've got Lisa," Johnny reminded him.

"Nah, I fucked her off," Dave told him. "We shagged each other stupid after your reception, and I thought we might be able to make a go of it. But all she ever wanted to do was talk about you and Ruth, and I couldn't be arsed. Anyhow, never mind me, I wanna know what's up with *you*. You're not *impotent*, are you?" He pulled a horrified face.

"Don't be daft," Johnny scoffed. "I get about fifty hard-ons a day. Just not over her."

"I don't get it." Dave shook his head confusedly. "I know you weren't crazy about her, but she ain't that bad-looking. And pussy's pussy, at the end of the day — so what's going on?"

"I don't know?" Johnny ran his hands through his hair. "I've tried, but the more desperate she gets, the more it turns me off. It doesn't help having her mam and dad in the next room. And then there's the baby."

"What about it?"

"Don't laugh, but I keep thinking I'm going to hit it with my dick and give it brain damage, or something."

"Brain damage?" Dave spluttered. "You don't think you're that big, do you? Jeezus, I knew you were vain, but that takes the whole packet of biscuits and half a cake, that."

126

"Well, I don't know, do I?" Johnny muttered, wishing he hadn't told him.

"Mate, if that's your problem, forget it," Dave said with certainty. "Believe me, your little dick ain't gonna get anywhere near it. Women's bodies are designed to protect it, aren't they?"

"Suppose so." Johnny sighed. "I've told her I'll try again if she gets the okay from the doctor, so I'll wait to see what he's saying."

"And what you going to do till then?" Dave asked. "Wanking's all right as a stopgap, but it ain't as good as the real thing."

"I haven't been wanking," Johnny admitted. "The lock's fucked on the bathroom door, and I'd be scared one of them was going to burst in on me."

Dave sucked in an ominous breath through his teeth.

"Man, that's not good. You can't keep it in for that long. It'll fester in your bollocks and give you knob-rot."

"Do you have to?" Johnny shifted uncomfortably in his seat.

"It's a medical fact," Dave intoned. "It'll start dripping pus if you leave it much longer, and your balls will explode."

"All right, that's enough," Johnny muttered, grimacing at the thought.

"Well, that's sobered me up," Dave said, sitting up and reaching for the bong. "Let's get re-wrecked and pretend that last conversation never happened."

Johnny glanced at his watch and shook his head.

"Best not. Ruth'll be wondering where I am."

"Have you heard yourself?" Dave teased. "Has she got you on an invisible lead, or what? Hey . . . are you sure that's not the real reason you can't get it up?" he mused. "'Cos she's yanking your chain too tight?"

Dave was joking, but his words struck an uncomfortable chord with Johnny. He'd been concealing it, but the resentment had been simmering like a pool of lava beneath the surface. He was still pissed off about the way Frankie had collared him at the reception and announced that he'd organised for Dave to pack up his stuff. And he really hated how much control Ruth'd had over him since he'd moved in with her and her folks: always finding excuses to keep him at her heel, knowing that he had to be on his best behaviour around her dad and her bitch of a mother. They might have taken control of his life but they couldn't control his body, so was it possible that he was subconsciously using that as a means to punish her — withholding the one thing that she desperately wanted: sex?

The problem was definitely mental, not physical. But Dave was right — he couldn't let it go on for too much longer. Whatever was holding him back, he had to get over it and do the deed before it affected his health — *and* his sanity.

Ruth was sitting at the kitchen table having a cup of tea when Johnny got home, and one glimpse of her miserable expression was enough to make him want to turn and walk straight back out. But he reminded himself that he'd vowed to make an effort and forced out a smile.

"All right, love?" He slipped his jacket off and looped it over the back of the chair.

"You're late," she replied tersely. "I was getting worried."

"Sorry," he apologised, sitting down and trying not to look her in the eye in case she saw how red his own were. "It's been mad busy down at the yard today, so I got a bit held up."

"Oh, well, I suppose it couldn't be helped," Ruth conceded. "Your dinner's in the oven, but it's probably dried out by now."

Johnny's stomach rumbled loudly at the mention of food. That was the problem with weed: it always gave him the raving munchies. And he hadn't been stoned for so long that it was worse than usual today. He was so ravenous right now he reckoned he could happily eat a scabby horse.

"It's shepherd's pie," she told him, using oven gloves to carry the hot plate over. "I hope you like it. It's another new recipe."

"It smells ace," he said, reaching for his fork. "Pass us the ketchup."

Ruth took the bottle out of the cupboard and handed it to him. She wanted to maintain the martyred act, to let him know how unfair it was to come home so late without letting her know what was happening. But she couldn't help smiling as she watched him squeeze a huge dollop of sauce onto his mash before tucking in like a starving man.

"All that hard work has certainly given you an appetite. It must suit you."

"It does," Johnny agreed, his words muffled by the huge mouthful of mince, mash and carrots he'd just shovelled in. "I like it."

"I'm surprised," Ruth admitted. "I thought you'd really hate it."

But you still made me go ahead and do it, though, didn't you? thought Johnny, a twinge of resentment momentarily resurfacing.

"Is my dad treating you all right?" she went on, reaching for her tea. It was cold now, but she took a sip anyway.

"Don't really see that much of him, to be honest," Johnny told her, swallowing the negative thoughts along with the food in his mouth. "He pretty much stays in the office all day, and Big Pat's always in the garage, so it's just me and the cars for the most part. Which is cool, 'cos I can just get on with it at my own pace."

Ruth smiled again, delighted that he'd come home not only with an appetite for food but also for conversation. That was an unexpected and very welcome surprise, because he'd barely spoken two words to her since the wedding. She'd known it would take time for him to adjust to the idea of being a husband and father, but lately she'd started to think he was never going to settle. Now, finally, she could see a glimmer of light at the end of the tunnel — and she couldn't have been happier.

"That was great," Johnny said when he'd finished his shepherd's pie. "But you'd best ease off on the

130

portions, 'cos I'm going to be a right fat bastard if you carry on piling my plate up like that."

"Rubbish," Ruth scoffed, whisking his plate away and replacing it with a bowl of sponge pudding and custard.

Rita wandered in just as he was finishing the last spoonful, and a nasty glint sparked in her eye as she watched Ruth take his empty bowl over to the sink.

"Got her running round after you like a proper little slave, haven't you, Jimmy?"

"For God's sake!" Ruth banged the bowl down hard on the ledge. "His name is *Johnny*. How many times do I have to tell you?"

"I prefer Jimmy," Rita replied dismissively, pulling out a chair. "So where's Frankie disappeared to this time?" she asked, peering at Johnny.

"I don't know." He gazed coolly back at her. "He didn't say."

"Oh, I see." Rita narrowed her eyes slyly. "Well, that didn't take long, did it? This time last month he was all set to slit your throat, but now look at you. Frankie's little puppet. Yes, sir, no, sir, three bags full, sir."

"Mum, stop it," Ruth scolded as she wiped her hands on the tea towel. "It's not Johnny's fault Dad doesn't tell you where he's going."

"*He's* no better," Rita sneered, jerking her thumb at Johnny. "He might come home when he's supposed to, but I guarantee he doesn't do it for your sake. It's because he knows what your dad'd do to him if he upset you. Isn't that right, *Jimmy*?"

Johnny didn't bother answering. She'd more or less hit the nail on the head, but there was nothing to gain by admitting it, so he stood up and smiled at Ruth.

"Thanks for dinner. I'm going for a bath."

"Don't use all the hot water," Rita called after him. "This is *my* house, not yours, and I might want a bath myself."

"You don't even like baths," Ruth reminded her when Johnny had gone. "You're just being funny. And I don't see why, 'cos he's been really respectful to you."

Rita slammed her palms down on the table and snapped, "Who the hell do you think you're talking to like that? You might be married, but that doesn't make you queen of this hive, lady. *I'm* the only queen around here, and don't you ever flaming well forget it."

Cheeks reddening as she fell quickly back into her place, Ruth said, "I was only saying you could be a bit nicer to Johnny. It hasn't been easy for him, having to move in with us when he's used to having his own place."

"Don't make me laugh," Rita sneered. "He's never owned a thing in his life. He was bumming off that mate of his before he started freeloading off us, so don't try and make out like he's good for anything, 'cos he's nowt but a scrounger. Now, quit talking rubbish and get me a drink." She snapped her fingers in the direction of the cupboard where she kept her supplies.

Ruth did as she was told without saying another word, but her lips were as taut as two elastic bands tied in a double knot. She usually just got upset when her mum had a go, but this time she was furious. Her mum had no right to talk about Johnny like that when she didn't even know him. He had made a real effort with her, but she hadn't even pretended to welcome him into the family. So now he just tiptoed around her, afraid of attracting her attention, because the tiniest meeting of eyes was all it took to unleash the devil in her mouth.

Well, her mum could say what she liked about Johnny's reasons for coming home on time, but she'd be better off thinking about why *her* husband didn't do the same, in Ruth's opinion. Although it wasn't hard to figure that one out, because no man in his right mind would be in a hurry to rush home if he knew a bitch like *her* was waiting for him.

"What are you staring at me like that for?" Rita demanded when Ruth handed her the glass of whisky.

"Didn't realise I was," Ruth muttered, folding her arms. Then, glancing at the clock, she said, "I think I'll go up in a minute. Johnny's got another early start in the morning, and it isn't fair to make him go to bed on his own again."

"He won't thank you for it," Rita sniped. "If you ask me, he goes up early to avoid you."

"He does not," Ruth shot back, raising her chin proudly. "He just doesn't want YOU to think he's taking me away from you, 'cos he knows you like me to watch TV with you at night. Any other man would have told you to get stuffed by now, but he's too nice."

"Nice, my backside," Rita snorted. "I bet he'll already be in bed pretending to be asleep when you get up there. That's what he usually does, isn't it? And don't say no, 'cos I have got ears." Mimicking Ruth now, she put her hand on her heart and simpered, "'*Don't you love me any more, Johnny? Oh, Johnny, please do it to me, I just need to know you care.*'" She gave her daughter a dirty look when she'd finished and said, "Pathetic."

"Oh, my God, you've been listening," Ruth gasped. "Johnny was right."

"No, Johnny was *wrong*," Rita retorted. "That squeaky little voice of yours carries all over the flaming house, so I suggest you keep your gob shut if you don't want us knowing your business in future."

"Don't worry, I will," Ruth muttered, her cheeks flaming.

Rita took a sip of her drink and looked at her daughter's stomach through narrowed eyes.

"How far on did you say you were supposed to be? Four or five months? Weird you're still not showing, isn't it? If you ask me, you're losing weight, not putting it on."

"I've been sick."

"I haven't heard you. In fact, I'm starting to wonder if you're really pregnant at all."

Ruth inhaled sharply and said, "Don't be stupid. You know I am."

"You forget I've been there, so I know what it looks like," Rita reminded her. "And you don't look pregnant to me."

"You're drunk," said Ruth, clasping her hands together to hide how badly they were shaking. "You always talk rubbish when you're drunk."

"I'm not so drunk that I can't see what's in front of me nose," Rita persisted. "Did you lose it? Is that why you've been moping about these last few weeks? Did you drop it down the loo and flush it away by mistake? 'Cos that can happen, you know."

Chin wobbling, tears burning her eyes, Ruth said, "I'm not listening to this. I'm going to bed."

"You don't fool me," Rita called after her as she headed out of the door. "And if I'm right, you'd best tell that stupid husband of yours before he cottons on. *And* your dad, before he goes and tells the family and they all start fetching presents round for it."

Ruth closed the door on her mother and ran upstairs. Johnny was still in the bath, so she sat on the bed and stroked the indentation in his pillow. The tears came now, dripping down onto the quilt like big soft raindrops, turning the light green satin ten shades darker. She swiped at her eyes with the back of her hand and pinched herself hard on the leg to snap herself out of it. But it was useless. She'd been an emotional mess for weeks, right as rain one minute, sobbing her heart out the next. She loved Johnny so much and couldn't bear the thought of losing him, but that was exactly what was going to happen when he found out what she'd done. And if her mum had already guessed that something wasn't right, it wouldn't be long before he did too.

She was still sitting there when Johnny crept in a few minutes later with a tiny towel wrapped around his waist. He jumped when he saw her and said, "Christ, you scared me. I didn't hear you coming up. How long have you been here?"

Ruth turned her head away without answering, and he heard a little sniffling noise.

"Are you crying?"

She shook her head, but Johnny knew she was lying. He sat next to her and put his arm around her.

"It's me, isn't it?" he asked guiltily. "I've upset you."

When Ruth sobbed and buried her face in his chest, he guessed he must be right, and that made him feel terrible. She'd been trying so hard to be a good wife but he'd been a selfish bastard, too wrapped up in his own misery to notice how miserable he was making her.

"Don't cry," he said soothingly. "Talk to me."

"It's not you," Ruth told him when she'd got herself under control. "It's me."

"No, it's not," Johnny argued. "You've done nothing wrong. It's me. I've been neglecting you, and you don't deserve it."

He brushed her dark hair back off her face as he spoke. It felt silky, and his dick twitched to life as the sweet scent that he'd forgotten drifted up to him.

"Look," he said, nudging her when it pushed its way out through the gap in the towel.

Ruth gazed down and gave a little gasp. "Is that for me?"

"What do you think?" Johnny raised her chin with his finger, kissed her softly, and then pushed her down onto the bed and peeled her panties down over her thighs.

136

And, for a change, she didn't stop him and tell him to turn off the light, or freeze and tell him to quieten down when he pushed himself into her and set the headboard banging against the wall.

CHAPTER
SEVEN

Ruth felt as if she'd been given a reprieve, and she floated around in a little bubble of bliss for the next couple of weeks, relieved to have found a way out of the hole that she'd dug for herself.

It had seemed like such a good idea to tell her dad that she was pregnant, a sure-fire way of making Johnny stay with her. At the time, marriage hadn't even entered her mind, but once her dad had told Johnny that he had to make an honest woman of her it had been too late to admit that she'd been lying. She'd thought naively that no one would ever find out and had convinced herself that she would get pregnant really quickly once they were sleeping together regularly. So when Johnny hadn't been able to do it, she'd panicked. Then her mum had sussed her out and she'd known that the game was up. But just as she'd been about to confess, Johnny had made love to her at long last.

And they had done it every night since, so, when Ruth realised that her period was three days late, she truly thought that her prayers had been answered.

She had been walking around in a daze ever since, cradling her stomach, convinced that she could feel a tiny heartbeat flickering to life in there. They said that women instinctively knew when they were expecting, and she had never been more certain of anything in her life. She even *knew* that it was a girl, and she was mentally compiling a list of names as Johnny made love to her tonight. But her fantasy crashed and burned when he pulled out of her and looked down in horror.

"Oh, Jeezus — you're bleeding!"

"What?" Ruth sat up and peered down in dismay at the red stain on the sheet between her legs.

"I told you I was going to hurt it," Johnny said guiltily, leaping off the bed and snatching his underpants off the floor. "I'm going to call an ambulance."

"No!" Ruth blurted out as he shoved a leg into his jeans and hopped towards the door. "Don't."

"You need to get checked out," he insisted. "Even *I* know you're not supposed to bleed when you're pregnant. And it's my baby as well as yours, so no arguments."

Ruth burst into tears. She couldn't go to hospital and risk them telling him that it was just a slightly late period and not a miscarriage. And that was what it was, she knew.

"I know you're upset," Johnny said supportively. "But you have to go to hospital. So I'm going to get your mum, then I'm calling an ambulance."

"Please don't," Ruth sobbed, clutching at his hand. "Just sit down for a minute. There's something I need to tell you."

"We haven't got time."

"Yes, we have." Gazing forlornly up at him, Ruth took a deep breath. "I didn't want to tell you, because I didn't want to upset you, but I've already lost it."

"*What?*" Johnny's face creased into a confused question mark.

"It slipped out last week when I was on the toilet," she lied, using her mum's words. "I didn't know what it was at first — I just saw blood and panicked."

"Why didn't you tell me?"

"You were at work. I didn't want to disturb you."

"I wouldn't have minded," Johnny said quietly, knowing as he said it that he probably would have. "Anyway, it might not have been the baby," he went on reassuringly. "It could have just been a clot, or something."

Silently begging God's forgiveness for her wickedness, Ruth shook her head. "It was the baby. I saw it."

"Oh, God." Johnny flopped down beside her and ran his hands through his hair. He hadn't even wanted to be a dad, but since he'd accepted that it was actually happening he'd begun to look forward to it. He'd had big plans for his boy. He was going to take him fishing, and teach him how to play footie. And when he was older he was going to take him to all the home games at Old Trafford and let the kid sit on his shoulders with his Man U scarf round his little neck. But none of that was going to happen now, and he felt like a part of him had been torn out.

Ruth was overcome with guilt when she saw how upset he was.

140

"I'm so sorry," she cried. "I know I should have told you, but I didn't even want to admit it to myself."

"Don't blame yourself." Johnny pulled her into his arms. "It's not your fault."

Unable to look at him, because she knew that it was, albeit not in the way he meant, Ruth buried her face in his chest.

"Don't cry," Johnny said softly. "We might have lost this one, but we can still try for another."

"Really?" Ruth's heart skipped a beat and she gazed up at him through her tears. "You're not going to leave me?"

"Don't be stupid." Johnny frowned. Then, sighing, he said, "Do you want me to tell your mum and dad?"

"No. It was our baby, so we'll tell them together." Ruth wiped her nose on the back of her hand and looked up guiltily at him. "I am sorry, you know — for everything. I know you didn't really want to get married, and my mum's been horrible so it can't have been easy for you, having to live here. And now this has happened. I wouldn't blame you if you wanted to get away."

"I'm not going anywhere," Johnny assured her, pulling her closer so that she couldn't see his eyes. She was right: he *hadn't* wanted to get married, and living here had been pure hell. But Frankie would never allow him to leave, so there was nothing to gain by allowing himself to go down the if-only-it-hadn't-happened route again.

"Are you sure you don't want to go to hospital?" he asked after a while. "Just to make sure the bleeding isn't serious."

"The doctor said it's normal," Ruth lied. "It should stop by the end of the week."

"Oh, I didn't realise you'd already seen him, but I suppose it must be all right if he says it is." Johnny eased her away from him now and gave her a small smile. "Why don't you get yourself cleaned up while I change the bed? And can I get you anything? Painkillers, or a brew, or something?"

Ruth shook her head and sloped off to the bathroom with her eyes downcast in shame. Johnny was being so lovely, but kindness was the last thing she deserved. And she was bound to get more of the same from her dad when they told him.

But the guilt was her punishment, and she was just going to have to suffer it if she was to keep them from finding out how wicked she'd been.

Johnny and Ruth called her mum and dad into the kitchen the following morning, and sat them down to deliver the news — and it was every bit as distressing as Ruth had known it would be.

Frankie didn't say a lot but Ruth could tell that he was upset, and that made her feel ten times worse, because she hadn't even stopped to think how it might affect him when she'd started this whole charade. Like Johnny, he hadn't been happy about it to start with, but he'd obviously come around to the idea, because she saw the disappointment flash through his eyes.

"I'm so sorry," she murmured, clutching at Johnny's hand.

"Sorry for what?" Rita demanded.

142

Already pissed off about being dragged out of bed at such an early hour, she was in no mood for bullshit — and this was a great big bucketful of the stuff, if she was any judge. It had only been a few hours since she'd asked Ruth if she'd lost the baby down the loo, and the girl had not only denied it, she'd made out like Rita had committed a sin for even *thinking* it. But now here she was, saying that it had happened exactly like that — and she actually expected Rita to swallow it.

"You've got absolutely nothing to apologise for," Frankie said, jumping in and saving Ruth from having to answer her mother. "It's just one of them things, darlin'. Nowt you can do about it."

"That's what I said," Johnny agreed, putting his arm around Ruth when she started to cry again. "It's sad, but we'll get through it. And there'll be other babies."

Frankie pursed his lips when he noticed how gently Johnny was holding Ruth, and the way that he was stroking her hair. The boy would never have married her if he hadn't been forced to, but Frankie had to give him his due for the way he'd handled it so far. Johnny had been polite to Rita, despite her constant nit-picking; and he was respectful down at the yard, doing whatever was asked of him without question or argument. Frankie knew the lad had sneaked round to see that mate of his a few times, but he'd decided to let it slide since no girls had been involved. And at least Johnny didn't take the piss and crawl home in the middle of the night — which was more than could be said for Frankie himself. And, rather than looking relieved right now, Johnny actually looked upset about losing the baby, which made Frankie wonder if he hadn't misjudged him.

The sudden ringing of his mobile phone broke the silence that had fallen over the kitchen. Frankie snatched it up off the table.

"I'm on my way, Pat. Just give us ten." He ended the call and sighed. "Sorry, love, I've got to go. Will you be all right?"

"Yeah, course." Ruth sniffed back her tears and gave Johnny a little push. "Go on, I'll be fine."

"No, he can stop here." Frankie scraped his chair back and stood. "Oh, and here . . ." he said, taking a key out of his pocket and tossing it down on the table. "I wasn't going to tell youse just yet, but I reckon you could both do with a lift."

"What's that for?" Ruth asked. She took a tissue out of her dressing-gown pocket and blew her nose.

"Your new house," Frankie told her.

"I beg your pardon?" Rita snapped her head around and stared at him.

"You heard," Frankie said offhandedly.

"You can't just go around buying houses without asking me first," Rita screeched, incensed that he'd gone behind her back.

"It's my money, I can buy what the fuck I want."

"I'm your *wife*."

"And she's our daughter." Frankie pointed at Ruth. "And she's just lost our grandchild, but you're more bothered about the fucking money, so why don't you

144

just crawl back to your bed and your bottle, and keep your nose out, you cold bitch!"

Rita's face went purple and she pursed her lips so tightly that Johnny thought she was going to burst. But she got up after a moment and, casting a glare of pure undisguised hatred at Ruth, flounced out, slamming the door behind her.

Ruth shivered. "You shouldn't have done that, Dad. She's really mad."

"Do I look like I care?" Frankie scoffed. "Anyhow, I'm not as generous as she thinks, 'cos there's a mortgage — and you'll be paying it." He aimed this last at Johnny.

Johnny's heart sank as he wondered how the hell he was supposed to afford a mortgage on his wages. He hadn't even received his first pay packet yet.

"In a year," Frankie added with a grin. "I'll pay till the end of next March to give you a leg-up. After that, it's down to you."

"Oh, Dad, thank you so much," Ruth sobbed, bursting into tears all over again. She'd been dreaming about having a home of her own since it had first been decided that she and Johnny were getting married, but she hadn't dared to hope that it would ever actually happen. Now, after seventeen years under the guillotine of her mother's tongue, she was finally going to be free.

Frankie gave Johnny a mock-pained look. "For fuck's sake, get her back up to bed before she drowns the lot of us."

"Thanks, Frankie," Johnny said, helping her to her feet. "I'll pay you back every penny — that's a promise."

"Too right you will," Frankie chuckled, winking at him. "Make sure she's ready when I get home and I'll take youse round to see it."

CHAPTER
EIGHT

The house was in the middle of a run-down little terrace on the outskirts of Hulme. It had two windows, one up, one down, and the brown front door still bore the scars of where it had been kicked in by the police after the foul smell had been reported by the neighbours some months earlier.

"It doesn't look much, but it's better inside," Frankie said. He double-checked that he'd locked the car as Johnny used the key he'd given them to open up the house. Casting a hooded glance around, to make sure there were no shady fuckers watching, Frankie followed the kids inside.

The living room was immediately behind the front door, and it was dark, even though there was only an old grey net curtain covering the narrow, filthy window. The walls were covered in wallpaper that had probably once been bright and cheerful but was now the colour of a heavy smoker's lungs and teeth. An ancient dust-coated corporation gas fire hung at an angle off the wall, and the floorboards were heavily stained. But one big patch under the window was particularly ominous, because that was where the previous owner's fluids had leaked through his chair before his badly decomposed body had been found a month after he'd died.

That was why the place had been so cheap — because nobody had wanted to touch it, knowing its history. But Frankie wasn't superstitious about the death of a stranger. As far as he was concerned, the old man's loss was Ruth and Johnny's gain, and a lick of paint and a couple of bottles of bleach would soon shift the smell.

"What do you think?" He squeezed in behind Johnny and walked into the centre of the room.

"I love it," Ruth said quietly as she gazed around, already picturing where she would put the furniture, and what colour she would paint the walls.

Frankie exchanged a surprised glance with Johnny. That wasn't the reaction he'd expected. The house was poky and dirty, and he'd thought that she would turn her nose right up at it.

Johnny was thinking pretty much the same, and all he could see as he gazed around in despair was the mould in the corners of the ceiling, the numerous cobwebs, and the clusters of dog and cat hairs coating every visible surface. It was going to take months to bring it up to being anything like liveable.

"Is that the kitchen?" Ruth headed for the door at the rear of the room. She stepped through it, stopped and grinned back at Johnny. "We've got a dining room!"

Johnny smiled, but there was no joy in his expression. He already hated the house and was thinking back wistfully to his days in the flat, with its

148

big windows, spacious rooms, fantastic central heating, and totally chilled atmosphere. This was a little shit-pit, and he didn't want to live here. Hell, even the Hyneses' house was preferable — Rita and all.

The kitchen was little bigger than a cupboard, and whoever had removed all of the old tenant's junk from the other rooms had stopped short of coming in here: it was crammed with rubbish. The sink was hidden beneath a mound of mouldy plates, cups, and pans, and the ledges and floor were littered with pizza boxes, chip wrappers, newspapers, and empty cans of dog and cat food that stank to high heaven. And, amongst it all, every spare inch of space contained empty cider bottles, fag ends, and little dried heaps of what looked to Johnny like shit — and it was anybody's guess as to whether it was human or animal.

"I know it's a tip," Frankie said brightly. "That's why I wasn't going to tell you about it just yet. I was going to send some of the lads over to clear it out first. Even bought some paint so they could give it a quick lick." He gestured towards some cans heaped in the corner of the dining room behind them. "I know how much you like your yellows, Ruthie, so I played safe and went for lemon, and that magnolia shite."

Johnny's hopes had soared at the thought of someone else doing the dirty work, but they quickly fell again when Frankie went on: "Now you've seen it, you might as well crack on with it yourselves, eh?"

"When can we move in?" Ruth asked, already itching to get at it.

"Soon as it's ready," Frankie told her. "Then I'll sort a van to move your stuff over."

"Can you get it tonight?"

"Tonight?" Frankie pulled a face that almost matched Johnny's look of horror.

"Yes, tonight," said Ruth. "I can clean around us."

Frankie laughed, and Johnny was so sure he was going to say yes that his heart dropped into his feet and on through the shit-caked lino beneath. But Frankie shook his head.

"I know you're keen, love, but it ain't fit for a dog to live in right now, so I'm definitely not letting you move in in your condition."

"But I want to move in *now*," Ruth complained.

"No." Frankie put his arm around her and led her back out into the living room. "You can start cleaning any time you want — so long as you promise to take it easy. But you're not stopping here till it's done. Now, come and have a quick look upstairs, then I'll drop you back off at home."

Ruth didn't want to stay at home for one more second, never mind one more night, or week — or however long it was going to take to clean the filthy new house. But her dad was adamant, so she had no choice but to stay put until it was done.

Barely able to sleep for excitement, she was up at the crack of dawn the following morning. Kissing her dad and Johnny goodbye, she took a load of cleaning stuff out of the cupboard under the sink and sneaked out

150

before her mum surfaced and demanded to go with her.

At the new house, she put on her rubber gloves and got cracking — and she was still hard at it when Johnny joined her later that afternoon.

Expecting her to have made barely a dent, he was shocked to see how much she had done. The living room was still dark, the wallpaper still a depressing reminder of the old tenant's poor state of health, but the cobwebs were gone, as was the horrible net curtain, and Ruth had cleaned the window so it was now as sparkling as the gas fire — which she'd somehow managed to right so that it was no longer listing dangeroulsy. And while the floorboards were still stained, the unpleasant smell that had been emanating from them had been replaced with the fresh scent of bleach from the numerous moppings she'd given them.

She'd done the same in the tiny dining room, and she'd not only scrubbed the minuscule kitchen, she'd also cleared most of the rubbish out into the back yard, so there was only the ancient cooker and fridge left for Johnny to remove.

"You should have waited for me," he said guiltily. "You're not supposed to be straining yourself, and you definitely shouldn't have done all this by yourself."

"My mum's still in a mood, so I didn't want to ask her to help me," Ruth told him, refilling the mop bucket as she spoke and pouring in a hefty slug of bleach. "And I didn't want to just sit in the bedroom all day waiting for you, so I thought I might as well get on with it. Don't worry, I paced myself."

151

Johnny gave her a disbelieving look and went upstairs, only to find that she'd blitzed those rooms as well.

"Leave it," he said when she carried the mop bucket into the bathroom behind him.

"Won't take me a minute," she insisted, pushing up her sleeves to give the lino its third scrubbing of the day.

"I said leave it," Johnny ordered, taking her firmly by the arm and walking her out onto the landing. "You're going home and putting your feet up."

"But I need to carry on," Ruth complained. "There's not much left to do, and the sooner it's done, the sooner we can move in."

"Leave the rest to me." He ushered her down the stairs ahead of him. "I'll come back after tea and make a start on stripping the wallpaper."

"I'll come with you," she said. "Four hands are better than two."

"No." Johnny gave her a stern look. "Your dad will go mad if he finds out you've been at it on your own all day. I'll do it."

"But, Johnny . . ."

"Don't argue." He snatched her coat off the back of the dining-room door and pushed it into her hands before herding her out of the front door.

Now that most of the mess had been cleaned up and it didn't smell quite so much like an abattoir, Johnny didn't mind going back. So, staying home just long enough to take a quick shower and eat the fish and chips they'd stopped off for on the way back, he tucked

152

Ruth up in bed — and gave her strict orders to stay put. Then he took a bus back to Hulme, calling in at the flat on the way to enlist Dave's help.

Several lines of speed and a few spliffs later, they whizzed through the wallpaper removal, and soon every wall in the house was bare and crying out for paint. It was one in the morning by then, and Johnny was starting to flag, having worked all day. But Dave wasn't ready to call it a night just yet.

"We might as well finish it now we've started," he insisted, using a screwdriver to pop the lid off a can of emulsion. "Won't take long to slap a few coats on. But baggsy I do the walls, 'cos I can't be arsed with all the fiddly woodwork shit."

It was gone four by the time Johnny got home, and slashes of daylight were already breaking through the darkness of the sky. Conscious of Frankie's car being parked on the path, he crept in and tiptoed up the stairs.

Ruth was still awake. She and Johnny might not have been married for overly long, but she was already used to the warmth of his back against hers and the soft sound of his snores, so the bed had felt too big and empty without him. She had fallen asleep for a short time at around eleven but her mum had soon woken her up again. Rita usually stayed in her parlour after sundown, only venturing out to get a fresh bottle if her alcohol ran out before she conked out. But tonight she'd decided to come upstairs and have another go at Ruth while they were alone.

"Think you're smart, don't you?" She'd hissed after bursting into the room and shaking her daughter awake. "Not good enough that you've got those idiots feeling sorry for you, you thought you'd dip your thieving hands into my retirement fund an' all, didn't you? Well, nothing good'll come of it, I'll tell you that for nowt. You got that house by dishonest means, and it'll bring you nothing but tears and heartache. *God* knows what you've done, and He'll punish you in kind — you watch if he doesn't."

Ruth had been terrified after her mum had staggered back down to her lair, and she'd tearfully begged God's forgiveness, praying that He might understand her reasons for doing what she'd done and take pity on her. Taking comfort from the thought that at least she hadn't killed a *real* baby, because that really would have been a sin too far, she'd eventually stopped crying. But her eyes were still raw and swollen when Johnny crept in.

"I thought you'd be asleep," he whispered. "Did I wake you up?"

"No, I couldn't sleep," she told him, cuddling up to him when he climbed into bed. "I missed you too much."

"Sorry," he murmured, praying that she wasn't expecting a shag, because there was no way he was going to get it up after the graft he'd done today.

"Did you get much done?"

"Finished it."

"Really?" Ruth raised up onto her elbow and gazed down at him. "Everything?"

154

"The whole lot," he affirmed with a grin. "You won't believe it when you see it. It looks like a brand new house."

"How did you manage to do all of that on your own?"

"Dave gave me a hand."

"What was he doing there?" Ruth demanded.

"I asked him to come," Johnny told her, having decided that he'd had enough of tiptoeing around the subject of his best mate. They'd had a right laugh tonight, and he felt a little bit like his old self again, so there was no way he was letting her criticise him back into submission.

"That was nice of him," Ruth said tersely.

"Yeah, it was," Johnny agreed. "But you can thank him when you see him, 'cos he's coming round for dinner on Monday."

"You can't just invite him round like that," Ruth blurted out. "You know how funny my mum is about anyone from outside the family coming to the house. And we've got the baby's wake on Sunday, so she won't want to see anyone straight after that."

"Don't worry about it," Johnny replied smoothly. "Your mum's got no say in who we invite round to *our* house."

"Eh?" Ruth frowned. "How am I supposed to make dinner over there without a cooker? And where are we supposed to sit? On the floor?"

"I thought I told you not to worry about it," Johnny said, grinning slyly. "Me and your dad have got it sorted."

"Meaning what?"

"Wait and see. It's a surprise."

"I don't like surprises," Ruth snapped, desperate to know what was going on. "Tell me, Johnny. Or I'll go and wake my dad up and ask him."

Johnny's good humour began to fade. He shouldn't have said anything, but it was too late now. He doubted that she'd carry out her threat to wake her dad, but now that she knew he was hiding something from her she would nag him until he told her, and he was too tired for playing games.

"Your dad's mate owns a furniture warehouse down Cheetham Hill," he told her. "And we went over there this lunchtime and picked out a load of stuff. It was supposed to be a surprise but you've ruined it, so you can tell your dad why you're not shocked when he tells you."

"You'd better be joking!" Ruth spluttered. "That's *my* house, and *I* wanted to choose what went into it."

"It's ours, actually."

"You know what I mean. The woman looks after the house, so she gets to decide how to furnish it. It's traditional."

"Yeah, well, we've created a new tradition," Johnny replied coolly. "It's called taking the strain off the woman when she's too ill to do it for herself."

"I'm not ill," Ruth moaned. "And it's going to be horrible if my dad's chosen what *he* thinks I'll like. And you're no better," she added accusingly. "Your room at Dave's was disgusting. Nothing matched, and that

156

bedside table wasn't even proper furniture; it was just a dirty old box you'd found in a skip."

"It did what it was supposed to," Johnny informed her.

"That's not the point," she cried. "I wanted my house to be really nice and classy."

Johnny had heard enough. He'd worked his arse off all day and night, and he was exhausted. But, more than that, he was pissed off that Ruth was being so ungrateful when he and Frankie had tried to do something nice for her. She might be feeling under the weather, but that didn't give her the right to act like a spoiled little bitch.

"Don't turn your back on me," Ruth said when he did exactly that. "I'm talking to you."

When Johnny pulled the quilt up around his head, making it clear that she was getting nothing more from him, she balled her hands into fists and gave a strangled cry of frustration. It wasn't fair, and she felt like telling him to go back to the warehouse first thing tomorrow and cancel whatever he'd ordered.

But she knew she couldn't do that, because it would offend her dad. And that would be unforgivable after he'd been generous enough to buy the house for her. So, however disgusting the furniture turned out to be, she would just have to smile and say thank you — and then replace everything bit by bit.

And at least she'd be free of her mother, at long last — and that was worth any amount of discomfort.

CHAPTER
NINE

Lisa's eyes were brown, but they were shining a deep envy-green as she entered her cousin's new house on Monday evening.

She hadn't seen much of Ruth since the wedding and would happily have kept it that way if she hadn't been forced to attend the so-called wake for the baby that Ruth had lost — the baby none of them had even known about until then. Well, not for sure, anyway, although Lisa had suspected all along that Ruth was pregnant, because that was the only reason she could think of for a gorgeous man like Johnny to have agreed to marry her.

Lisa had never seen the point of mourning something that probably hadn't even had arms and legs yet, never mind a face or a brain. An old person, yes. Even a kid that you'd at least had the chance to smile at before it snuffed it. But there hadn't even been a coffin at this one, which just made it all the more ridiculous.

But that was the Hyneses' way. If the baby had lived it would have been one of their own, so that made it worthy of grieving over as you would have done for a real person. And since her Uncle Frankie was one of only a few Hynes men who'd had the balls to break

158

away from the poverty and come to England to make his fortune, while the rest had stayed firmly in their ruts back home in Ireland, it was important to him that the relatives who had followed him over came together on these occasions. Nothing short of being on your own deathbed was excuse enough to miss one.

So Lisa had dutifully donned her wailing weeds and gone along to pay her respects. Then she'd parked herself in a corner of Rita's parlour and watched in disgust as her mum, aunts and cousins swilled their drinks and pretended to be sad. Her mum had been play-acting to the max but she'd never have admitted it in a million years, because she was Frankie's sister and he as good as kept them — and God knew they needed whatever he threw their way, because they'd have been destitute if it had been left to Lisa's useless father.

But that was another Hynes tradition: the men looked after their womenfolk, even after they got married. And their husbands — unless their families were from the same village — were classed as outsiders. Hence Lisa's dad not being invited to the wake, despite having been married to her mum for twenty-odd years. But it was his own fault for being such a pathetic loser.

It hadn't escaped Lisa's notice, however, that Johnny already seemed to have done a pretty good job of getting his feet under the Hyneses' table. Frankie might have started out by treating him as dismissively as he treated all the other outsider men, but he'd taken him into his business *and* brought him to live in his family home since then, so something had obviously clicked.

Still smarting about the way Johnny had humiliated her at the wedding reception, Lisa had been relieved when Ruth had decided not to talk to her afterwards: it would have tortured her to have had to visit their place and see them playing happy families. But that didn't mean she'd given up on Johnny.

Quite the contrary.

He was the first and only lad who had ever knocked her back, and she refused to believe that he found Ruth more attractive than her. So she'd done some digging, determined to find out what made him tick, and it seemed that Ruth wasn't even his usual type. According to his mates, Johnny usually went for sexy blonde girls with big tits and sassy mouths — girls just like Lisa, in fact. Which led her to believe that he probably *was* interested but was just too scared to do anything about it in case Frankie found out.

Aware that she must have scared him off by coming on too strong at the reception, she'd played it cool at the wake and had focused all her attention on Ruth instead; hugging her, and telling her how sorry she was to hear of her loss — even though she was secretly glad that her cousin's rosy little world wasn't so picture perfect after all. And the charm offensive had worked, because Ruth had invited her round to her new house for dinner — which had been a bit of a shock, because Lisa hadn't even known that they were moving.

Foster Street was in the old, dirty, undeveloped part of Hulme, and Lisa had been praying that it would be some kind of decrepit fleapit, so she was disappointed to walk in now and find that — yellow walls aside — it

160

was actually really nice. The warm glow from the lamp in the corner gave the living room a cosy feel, and Johnny and Dave looked right at home on the beige leather settee, watching football on a big colour TV with their beer cans on the glass coffee table in front of them. A mirror with an ornate gold frame was hanging on the wall above the fire, and a fluffy cream rug lay on the floor below it. And there was a shelf unit in the corner, already crammed with brass ornaments and crystal knick-knacks — most of which Lisa recognised from her Aunt Rita's display cupboard back at the old house.

"What do you think?" Ruth asked, looking as pleased as Punch.

"Nice," Lisa murmured, forcing out a smile.

"Come through here while I turn the meat over, then I'll show you round the rest of it," Ruth said, leading her through the dining room and into the kitchen.

Lisa stood in the doorway and gazed around as Ruth pulled on a pair of oven gloves and lifted a tray out of the oven. There was everything here that a woman could possibly need, and it sickened Lisa that Ruth'd had it all handed to her on a plate — and even more so that she was acting so cool about it, as if it were nothing less than she deserved. Spoilt bitch.

Ruth had her back turned to Lisa as she flipped the lamb over and basted it, but she could feel the envy coming off her cousin in waves, and that tickled her. She'd had no intention of inviting her round, and if her dad hadn't pulled her to one side yesterday and told her to kiss and make up, Lisa would never have set foot through that door.

"She's blood," her dad had said. "And there's not many of us left, so we've got to keep those who *are* still here close, especially at a time like this. So forget whatever shit went on between youse at the wedding and put it right — that's an order."

Ruth had sulked to start with, because she didn't want to let Lisa back into her and Johnny's life. But when she'd thought about it, she'd realised that she could turn it to her own advantage and had made a big show of apologising to Lisa before inviting her round to dinner. Not because she wanted to put things right with her — just so she could rub it in her face that she had everything that Lisa had ever wanted and would probably never get.

It had also been deliberate to invite her round on the same night that Dave would be here. Ruth knew they had split on bad terms again, and was looking forward to watching them squirm as they were forced to eat at the same table and make polite conversation. And they would *have* to make the effort, because it would be unforgivable to ruin her special night by arguing after she'd been gracious enough to invite them round — and so soon after losing her baby.

With any luck, Dave would feel so uncomfortable that he would eat and run — and never darken their door again. And Lisa's jealousy would stop *her* from wanting to come back again, so that would be two birds slain with one crafty well-aimed shot.

162

"Right, that's almost done," Ruth said, turning back to Lisa when she'd put the tray back into the oven. "Can I get you a drink? Tea, coffee . . .?"

"Got any wine?"

"Red or white?" Ruth opened the fridge wide to display how well-stocked it already was despite the fact that they had only moved in a few hours earlier.

"White," said Lisa, taking her cigarettes out of her pocket — desperate for a blast of nicotine to calm the sickening churning in her stomach.

"Sorry, no smoking in here," Ruth told her before she had a chance to light up. "I'd have preferred everyone to go outside, but Johnny insisted on having a place to smoke so we've agreed that he can do it in the living room. But let me show you round first."

A tiny smirk lifting her lips at the thought that Ruth and Johnny had already had a disagreement, Lisa followed her cousin upstairs.

"This is the spare room," Ruth told her, waving her into the smallest of the three bedrooms, which contained a single bed and a chair — which was just about all she'd managed to cram in.

"And this is going to be the nursery," she went on, leading Lisa to the second, marginally bigger room. "It's empty, but that's because I didn't want to tempt fate by getting any baby stuff before the four-month mark."

"You've not got caught again already, have you?" Lisa asked.

"Not yet, but we're trying."

"Is that safe? So soon after miscarrying, I mean?"

"The doctor says it's all right, so it must be," Ruth lied. "Just as well," she added with a secretive smile, "because Johnny can't keep his hands off me."

"Really?" A look of disbelief came over Lisa's face, but she quickly removed it. "Well, that's how it's supposed to be when you're still in the honeymoon period, isn't it?"

"Yeah, and it's great. Really, really great," Ruth said wistfully.

It wasn't easy to keep up the pretence of bliss when you knew it was a lie. After the shock of seeing the blood, and thinking that he'd been responsible for her losing the baby, Johnny had gone a bit funny about sleeping with her again. They still did it, but nowhere near as much as she wanted to. And she always felt like she was begging, which wasn't very nice.

But there was no way she was giving Lisa the satisfaction of knowing that things were so strained between them. So, moving on to the next room, she opened the door and stood back.

"This is our room."

Lisa's envy deepened. The king-size bed had fancy wrought-iron head and footboards, and a dusky pink satin quilt, dotted with little clusters of sequin flowers. Two plump pillows with matching cases sat side by side, and a mushy heart-shaped cushion nestled between them.

Opposite the bed there was a tiny white vanity table, the top of which already contained all Ruth's perfumes and crap — all neatly lined up in true pernickety Ruth style, Lisa noticed. A dark oak wardrobe hulked in the alcove, and an old wicker chair on which a heap of teddies had been carefully arranged in height order sat beneath the window.

"I see you couldn't bring yourself to leave your friends behind?" Lisa teased, remembering how Ruth had always taken the stupid things to bed with her and told them all her secrets as she was growing up — like they'd have been interested if they could actually hear her. "Bet Johnny won't be too pleased to have them staring at him when youse are at it?" she added with a dirty chuckle. "It'll put him right off, that."

"I'm going to move them into the nursery as soon as the time's right," Ruth told her snippily, annoyed that Lisa thought she was entitled to talk about Johnny in a sexual manner. Ruth could do it, because she was his wife, but no other woman should even be *thinking* about him in that way. "We'd best go back down," she said, hustling Lisa out onto the landing. "Don't want the meat to burn."

"I'll just have a quick fag with the lads, then I'll come and help you," Lisa said, following her down the stairs.

"No, don't disturb them," said Ruth, pushing her bossily on through to the kitchen before she had a chance to sit down. "You can open the back door and smoke it there while I'm plating up."

"My feet are killing me," Lisa complained. "And it's bloody freezing outside."

Shouldn't have worn high heels and such a short skirt, then, should you? Ruth thought meanly.

Ruth had been warming the plates at the bottom of the oven, and she took them out now and lined them up on the ledge, dishing up while Lisa shivered with her cigarette in the doorway. When Lisa had finished her smoke, Ruth handed two of the plates to her.

"The table's already laid — take these through."

"Who's sitting where?" Lisa asked.

"Me and Johnny at the heads, you and Dave opposite each other," Ruth said, bustling in with the other two plates. "Johnny, Dave . . . you can come through now," she called.

"Just a minute," Johnny called back.

"*Now,*" Ruth insisted, going back into the kitchen and snatching a bottle of wine out of the fridge. "I've spent all day on this, and I don't want it to go cold."

The lads traipsed in miserably. Dave sat where Ruth told him to, but he shuffled his chair back and tipped it onto its back legs in an effort to carry on watching the match. It was 0-0, but there were still eight minutes to go, and their boys had just put a spurt on, so there was still time for a lucky one.

"No telly while we're eating," Ruth ordered, marching into the living room and switching the set off.

A look of despair passed between Johnny and Dave as the screen went blank. Catching it, Lisa whispered, "Bet you wish you'd gone to the pub, eh, lads?"

"Tell me about it," Johnny muttered.

"Everyone comfortable?" Ruth asked, coming back in and taking her seat.

Johnny and Dave sighed their resignation and reached for their forks. Quickly recovering from his

166

disappointment at missing the end of the match as the scents rose to his nostrils, Dave said, "Smells great, Ruth. Didn't realise you were such a good cook."

"Our Ruth's always been the homely one," Lisa told him, smiling so that Ruth couldn't accuse her of having a dig — even though she was. "I remember when we were kids. Me and our mates would be all dolled up for the disco, but she'd still be in the kitchen when we went round to get her, with her apron on and another bloody cake in the oven."

"Don't tell me you can make cakes, an' all?" Dave groaned. "You're a right jammy bastard, Johnny. No wonder you couldn't wait to get out of my place."

When Ruth beamed, Lisa looked down at her plate. That wasn't quite the reaction she'd expected, but at least Johnny hadn't joined in with the flattery.

Dave gazed over at her with a streak of gravy dribbling out of his stuffed mouth. "Not staying, Lisa?"

"You've still got your coat on," Johnny explained when she frowned as if to say *what are you talking about?*

"Oh, yeah, silly me." Lisa giggled. "Totally forgot."

Ruth nearly choked on a roast potato when her cousin unzipped her jacket and hung it over the back of her chair. Her T-shirt was so tight that it made her breasts look even bigger than usual, and her nipples were standing out like coat-hooks because of the cold.

Dave's eyes widened. "You look nice."

Heart pounding, lips tightly pursed, Ruth stared at Johnny from under her lashes, daring him to look — praying that he wouldn't.

Johnny could feel her staring and sensibly kept his eyes on his plate, before turning his head deliberately towards Dave.

"Wonder if anyone's scored yet?"

"Who's playing?" asked Lisa, both of her little fingers sticking out as she used her knife to push a piece of broccoli onto her fork. Well, Ruth wasn't the only one who could act like a lady. If Johnny wanted posh, Johnny would get posh.

"United, Chelsea," Dave told her, remembering that this was one of the things he'd liked about her — that she was one of those rare birds who didn't mind a bit of footie banter.

"Oh, yeah, I think Mikey mentioned it when I saw him at the market this morning," she said.

"Mikey?" Johnny's head shot up. "I haven't seen him in ages. How is he?"

"Yeah, he's okay." Aware that Ruth was watching them like a hawk, Lisa kept her eyes on her food. "He's over in Levenshulme now, but he's trying to get a swap with someone up in Hyde."

"Eh?" Johnny frowned. "I didn't even know he'd moved."

"Oh, yeah, I forgot you haven't seen him since all that shit on your stag night," said Dave, cramming another loaded forkful of lamb into his mouth. "They got a lift home after we left, and they were warned to keep their heads down for a few weeks. But you know what Mikey's like, he went on a total para and did a runner in case they came looking for him."

168

"What's this?" Ruth looked from Dave to Johnny. Johnny hadn't mentioned the stag do, and she'd been too wrapped up in the wedding and all of the problems that came after it to remember to ask. But she didn't like the sound of this.

"Oh, something and nothing," Dave said offhandedly, flicking a hooded glance of apology at Johnny.

"It can't be nothing," Ruth said sharply. "Otherwise no one would have had to keep their heads down or do a runner."

"Honest, it was nothing," Dave assured her. "Just Mikey and Andy getting into a barney with some blokes at the pub, that's all. But I dragged your man home before it kicked off, so he didn't know anything about it."

Ruth pounced. "Why would they need to get a lift if you were only at the pub?"

Dave shifted in his seat and wished he'd kept his big mouth shut. "We, er, weren't at the local," he backtracked. "We'd gone to The Whalley to watch the footie 'cos they've got a bigger screen."

"So you took Johnny to watch a football match on his stag night?" Ruth's eyes were bright with disbelief.

"Well, it was either that or a club," Dave shot back with a cheeky grin. "And I didn't think you'd be too happy if we took him to see a stripper. Anyhow, *he* wouldn't have gone even if me and the lads had wanted to," he added, rolling his eyes as if Johnny was a proper killjoy. "Footie comes first with this one — stag night or not."

Ruth flicked her suspicious gaze at Johnny, trying to read his eyes to see if there was any guilt there.

"It was the derby," he lied, fronting it out and looking straight back at her. "United and City — most important match of the season."

"You're wasting your time trying to explain football to our Ruth," Lisa laughed, giving her cousin a fond look. "Too rough for you, isn't it, babe?"

Ruth stabbed her fork into a piece of lamb and chewed on it angrily. She was sure that Dave and Johnny were lying, and she didn't know why Lisa was being so nice, but it felt like they were all in on something and had closed ranks to keep her out of it. And that wasn't right. Not when they were sitting in her house, eating her food and drinking her wine.

Dave and Lisa ate the rest of their meals in silence, afraid of opening their mouths in case they dropped Johnny in it again. After dessert, Dave glanced at his watch.

"Shit, I didn't know it was that late. I'd best get moving."

"Already?" Johnny gave him a *please don't go yet, mate* look.

"Sorry, but I promised Jeff I'd pop round and have a look at that motor." Dave shrugged and finished his wine in a gulp. "Cheers for dinner, Ruth, it was ace," he said as he stood up and went into the living room for his jacket.

"You're welcome," Ruth muttered, gathering the pudding bowls together.

170

Dave came back into the doorway and raised an eyebrow at Lisa. "Want me to walk you home?"

"No, thanks," she replied coolly. "I'm staying to help Ruth clear up."

"No need," Ruth said quickly. "I can manage."

"I insist," Lisa told her firmly. "Uncle Frankie would kill me if he thought I wasn't pulling my weight — especially while you're not well. So you just go and sit down and leave it to me."

Dave sighed as he watched Lisa take the dishes off her cousin and wiggle her way into the kitchen. They'd had sex a few times, but it was obvious they were never going to be anything serious because they always ended up wanting to kill each other. But she was still one of the best shags he'd ever had, and he'd been fantasising about giving her a good old seeing-to ever since she'd taken her jacket off tonight.

Johnny showed Dave out as Ruth slumped down sulkily on the couch and Lisa busied herself with the washing-up.

"Cheers for fucking off and leaving me on my own," he hissed, pulling the door to behind him so that Ruth couldn't hear — or complain that he was letting the heat out.

"Sorry, mate, but it was doing my head in," Dave apologised, pulling his collar up. "She's like the fucking Gestapo when she gets going, isn't she?" he added in a whisper, flicking a glance through the window to make sure that Ruth hadn't crept up behind the door to eavesdrop.

"You're all right, you don't have to live with her," Johnny muttered.

He'd been made up to escape from Rita and her house that morning, but it seemed like Ruth had dragged her right along with them in spirit, because she'd been acting like Lady Muck ever since she stepped foot in the new house. She'd already cluttered the house up with Rita's cast-offs, *and* tried to lay down the law about him smoking inside. But she could fuck right off with that one, because this was his home as well as hers and he would do whatever he damn well liked in it.

"Do us a favour," Dave said quietly, bringing Johnny out of his mutinous thoughts. "Word Lisa up and see if she fancies coming round to mine when she leaves here."

"You what?" Johnny drew his head back. "Haven't you learned your lesson yet?"

"I know we're never gonna be a proper couple or anything," Dave conceded. "But there's no harm in the occasional shag, is there? And she's looking well fit tonight. I thought Ruth was gonna blow a gasket when she took her coat off and her tits popped out like that."

"Tell me about it," Johnny snorted. "Why do you think I spent half the night with my head twisted towards you like a fucking retard, so she couldn't accuse me of looking."

Dave grinned and shook his head. "Glad I ain't in your shoes, mate." As he walked backwards down the pavement he said, "I've got some top gear coming in

172

tomorrow. Why don't you pop round — if she hasn't chained you to the bed by then?"

"Fuck off," Johnny laughed, waving him off.

Ruth had her arms and her legs crossed when Johnny went back into the house, and she was agitatedly jiggling her foot up and down.

"What were you two whispering about?" she demanded.

"We were talking, not whispering," Johnny informed her irritably.

"Excuse me?" Ruth drew her head back. "Who do you think you're talking to like that?"

Johnny's patience snapped. Gritting his teeth, he hissed, "We're not at your dad's house now so you can quit treating me like a dickhead, 'cos I'm sick of it. I'm the man of this house, and I'm not having you or anyone else push me around in it. Got that?"

Astonished that he'd stood up to her after doing as he was told for so long, Ruth felt her jaw drop. But just as she'd recovered enough to tear him off a strip, Lisa strolled in from the kitchen.

"Everything all right?" she asked, looking from Johnny to Ruth and sensing from their strained expressions that they'd been having words.

"I've got a headache," Ruth lied, her eyes still flashing with anger. "It's been a long day."

Aware that she was being given her marching orders, Lisa said, "Sorry, didn't mean to outstay my welcome; just didn't want you wearing yourself out. I'll get moving and let you get to bed." She went back into the dining room and pulled her jacket on.

"Do you want me to pop round in the morning and give the place a going-over with the Hoover?" she offered when she came back. "And it'll probably need going over with a mop as well," she added with a chuckle. "Dave's left a right mess under his chair — sloppy bastard."

"No, thank you," Ruth said haughtily, getting up to show her out. "I'm going shopping with my mum tomorrow, so I'll be out."

Lisa shrugged, as if to say *well, you can't say I didn't offer*. Then, after saying goodbye to Johnny, she stepped outside and turned back to hug Ruth.

"Cheers for dinner, babe, it was lovely. You know where I am if you need me. Just give us a ring."

Ruth didn't reply to this. She just smiled tartly and closed the door.

"Thank God for that," she sighed. "I thought they were never going to go."

"It's not even ten o'clock yet," Johnny pointed out grumpily, wishing that he could have gone with Dave. This was the start of most normal people's nights, not the end.

"I'm exhausted," Ruth complained. "It's been a really hard day for me, what with moving and then having to play hostess."

"Shouldn't have invited Lisa round if you weren't up to it," Johnny replied unsympathetically. "Me and Dave would have been fine with a chippy dinner."

Ruth flashed him a dirty look and marched into the kitchen to inspect the plates that Lisa had washed. Tutting loudly when she saw a streak of bubbles on the edge of one, she said, "I might have known she'd make a mess of it. I'm going to have to do them all again."

"I thought you were knackered?" Johnny called back sarcastically. "Can't be washing dishes if you're knackered, you might drop one."

"Fine, I'll do them in the morning," Ruth conceded, coming back into the living room. She frowned when she saw that he'd switched the TV back on. "What are you doing? It's bedtime."

"I'm not tired," Johnny told her. "You go. I'm going to see if I can find the scores."

"I wanted us to go together," Ruth whined. "It's our first night in our new house."

"I'll be up in a bit." Johnny pulled a cigarette out of his pack and lit up.

"Why are you being so horrible?" Ruth demanded, feeling sorry for herself.

"*Me?*" Johnny gave her an incredulous look. "I'm not the one who invited people round, then spent the whole night acting like I couldn't wait for them to go."

"I'm *tired*," Ruth wailed, as if that excused her behaviour.

"So go to bed," said Johnny.

Ruth gritted her teeth when he turned back to the TV. She stomped upstairs and got undressed. She'd folded her clothes and was on her way to the bathroom when she heard a knock on the front door.

"Who's that?" she asked, peering down the stairs as Johnny headed towards the door.

He looked through the spyhole. "Lisa."

"Don't answer it," she hissed.

Ignoring her, Johnny opened the door.

"Sorry for disturbing you again," Lisa said, giving him an apologetic smile as she shivered on the step.

"You're all right," he said, frowning when he noticed the scared look in her eyes. "Has something happened?"

"Not really." She glanced nervously back over her shoulder. "There were some lads hanging round at the corner when I was going for the bus, and they started following me and saying stuff. It freaked me out 'cos I didn't know if they were going to jump me, or something."

Johnny stepped outside and looked down the deserted road. "They're not there now, but you'd best wait inside for a few minutes — make sure they've really gone."

"What's going on?" Ruth demanded, rushing downstairs as Lisa stepped in. "Why have you come back?"

"Some lads were trying it on with her," Johnny explained. "And she's a bit shook up, so I've said she can wait here till they've gone."

"I'm still shaking." Lisa perched on the edge of the chair he'd just vacated and held out her hand to show them. "Don't suppose you've got any of that wine left, have you?"

Ruth tightened her dressing-gown belt when Johnny went off to get Lisa a drink, and sat down on the couch with a sour expression on her face.

"I know you're pissed off with me for coming back," Lisa said apologetically. "I would have gone to Dave's, but then I would have had to go through the park and that would have been worse 'cos there were loads of them."

"Dave reckons the Salford crew have been sniffing around over the last few days," Johnny called out from the kitchen. "He reckons they're getting geared up for another war in the Moss."

"Trust Dave to know something like that." Ruth gave a disapproving tut. "And you wonder why I don't like you hanging around with him."

Johnny ground his teeth as he poured the wine and got himself a can of beer out of the fridge.

"Just because he knows about it doesn't mean he's involved," he said, coming back and handing the wine to Lisa. "Anyway, you need to know about these things when you live around here, so you know when to keep your head down."

"He's right," Lisa confirmed, nodding sagely. "You've never lived round here before, so you don't know what it's like."

"You don't live round here, either," Ruth reminded her tartly.

"No, but I've spent a lot more time here than you," Lisa countered. "You only ever saw the inside of Johnny's bedroom, so you don't know what it's like out on the street. It can be dead rough, can't it, Johnny?"

"Really rough," he agreed, peeling back the tab on his can. "But it's cool if you keep yourself to yourself. I've had some of the best times of my life round here."

"Me too," Lisa cooed.

Sickened by the way they were smiling at each other, like they were exclusive members of the Hulme Appreciation Club, or something, Ruth sniffed and said, "You'd best hurry up with that, Lisa. The bus comes in ten minutes — wouldn't want you to miss it."

Lisa flicked her a cold glance from under her lashes and took a swig of her wine. The bitch had a spare bed sitting empty upstairs, and any other relative would be insisting right about now that she stay the night. But not Ruth. She couldn't wait to shove Lisa back out into the war zone.

Johnny was thinking much the same thing. But he couldn't be arsed with the argument he'd get if he suggested letting Lisa stay the night, so instead he said, "I'll walk you to the bus stop."

"We're going to bed," Ruth reminded him icily.

"No one's asking you to come," Johnny replied irritably. "But I'm not having your dad blame me if she goes by herself and gets attacked."

Ruth was furious but she couldn't argue with what he'd said, because her dad *would* go mad if he heard that her cousin had been in potential danger and she'd refused to help her out.

"Don't worry about it," Lisa insisted. "I'll be all right. I've got a big gob. I'll just scream my head off if anything happens."

"I'm walking you," Johnny said firmly.

Ruth's eyes were blazing when she saw them out a few minutes later. "Don't wait with her," she hissed at

178

Johnny through gritted teeth. "Just see her to the bus stop, then come straight back."

Lisa folded her arms as she and Johnny set off with Ruth's glare dogging their every step.

"Sorry about that. If I'd known it was going to upset her this much I wouldn't have come back. I hope you're not going to get into trouble?"

"Probably," Johnny muttered. "But it's not your fault, so don't worry about it."

"It is, though, isn't it?" Lisa said guiltily. "None of this would be happening if I wasn't here. You'd have had a nice dinner with Dave, and everything would still be lovely."

"You reckon?" Johnny snorted softly.

Lisa glanced at him out of the corner of her eye as they walked on in silence. His version of married life sounded very different to Ruth's — and she knew which one she believed.

When they reached the bus stop, she said, "Thanks for walking me, but you'd best not wait. Don't want to get you in any more trouble."

"I'd be in trouble whether I went straight back or stayed out till morning," Johnny told her. Then, sighing, he said, "Sorry, don't mean to be such a miserable git. I'm just tired."

"I'm not surprised," Lisa said knowingly. "Uncle Frankie was singing your praises to my mum the other day, going on about how hard you've been working. *And* you've done up the house on top of all that," she went on approvingly. "Ruth's doesn't know how lucky she is, 'cos there's not many men who'd knock themselves out for their wives like that."

Johnny shrugged. "She's had a rough few weeks."

"So have you," Lisa reminded him softly as she pulled her cigarettes out of her pocket. She offered him one and lit one for herself. Shivering, she pulled her collar a little higher around her throat. "Thought Ruth said that bus would be here soon."

"Should be."

Johnny leaned back against the shelter and took a deep drag on his fag, squinting at her through the smoke. After the way she'd come on to him at the wedding he'd been dreading seeing her today. But she'd been cool. She hadn't reacted badly to any of Ruth's snipes, which must have been hard; and she'd even been nice to Dave, which couldn't have been easy considering it was the first time they'd seen each other since their latest split. And she looked good, too, in her tight T-shirt and equally tight miniskirt — which was more than could be said for Ruth, in her frumpy ankle-length dress. Ruth was only seventeen but she was rapidly turning into a duplicate of her mother — and that was a real passion-killer, both in and out of bed.

"Can I say something?" Lisa asked quietly. "About what happened at the wedding."

"What about it?" Johnny snapped out of his thoughts and took another drag on his cigarette.

"I just wanted to say I'm sorry." She gave him a repentant smile. "I drank too much, and I was well out of order for saying all that stuff to you."

180

"Forget it." Johnny shrugged. "I have."

"It still shouldn't have happened," Lisa murmured. "My mum reckons I need gagging when I've been drinking."

Johnny grinned, but before he could say anything else the bus trundled into view. As it drew alongside, Lisa smiled and said, "See you, then. And tell our Ruth I'm sorry."

Johnny nodded and watched as she hopped aboard, paid her fare and made her way to the back seat.

Lisa turned her head and waved goodbye through the window — just a little flick of a wave, though, nothing too obvious. Then, turning to face the front as the bus drove on, she clenched her fist and pumped the air in a gesture of victory.

Oh, yes! She was *so* going to have him. But this time she would wait for him to come to her.

Ruth was standing on the doorstep when Johnny got home, her arms tightly folded, the same pissy scowl on her face.

"Don't tell me you've been there the whole time I've been gone?" he asked, waiting for her to move so that he could get in.

"Thought you were only supposed to be walking her there and coming straight back," she said accusingly. "But I see you stayed long enough to have a smoke. And don't lie, 'cos I can smell it."

"So, we had a fag," Johnny admitted, pushing past her. "Anyone would think we'd been shagging in the bushes, the way you're going on about it."

"Don't swear at me," Ruth snapped, closing the door.

"Well, don't make out like I've been up to something when I haven't," he snapped back as he took off his jacket and threw it onto the couch.

"I wasn't," she lied, her chin wobbling as tears flooded her eyes. "I've just lost a baby, but none of you even cares. You all just sat there ignoring me all night."

"No, we didn't," Johnny said wearily, wondering where the hell *that* had come from. "We were just trying to enjoy our dinner, that's all."

"So you're saying *I* ruined it?"

"No, I'm saying you were tired, and everyone was walking on eggshells trying not to upset you. But it's over now, so you might as well stop worrying about it."

Ruth gazed up at him like a badly treated puppy in need of reassurance.

"You hate me, don't you?"

Oh, Jeezus, not this again, thought Johnny, turning his back on her and switching off the lamp. He inhaled deeply. He hated the wheedling tone of voice she used when she'd been called to account. It made him feel physically sick.

"I'm sorry," Ruth whimpered. "I tried really hard to be nice, but no one understands what it feels like to lose a baby. I'm trying to pretend that everything's okay, but it's not that easy."

"Let's just go to bed," Johnny said, waving her towards the stairs. "You'll feel better in the morning."

182

CHAPTER
TEN

Spring was in the air when Johnny stepped out of the door, and his spirits rose briefly when he felt the warmth of the first real sunshine of the year caressing the top of his head.

"You forgot this," Ruth said, casting shadows as she came into the doorway behind him and held out his butty box. "And don't forget my mum's coming round, so make sure you're not late home 'cos she'll be staying for dinner."

"Can't wait," he muttered.

Rita turned up not long after he'd gone. It was the first time she'd clapped eyes on the house since Frankie had announced that he'd bought it, because she'd stubbornly refused to come anywhere near the place when they'd been doing it up. But curiosity had finally got the better of her.

The way Ruth had jabbered on about it she'd expected it to be some kind of little palace, so she was pleasantly surprised to walk in and see how poky and dark it actually was. But it especially amused her to notice her influence stamped all over it. Ruth made out like she was a big independent woman, with a mind and taste of her own, but she'd done up the living room like an almost exact replica of Rita's parlour. The curtains were the same colour, the nets had the same pattern, and the ornaments were actually Rita's own, from the little crystal bell to the horseshoe nailed above the front door.

Independent woman, my backside, Rita scoffed to herself.

Ruth might go by the name of Conroy these days, but she was her mother's daughter through and through — and that stupid husband of hers was wrong if he thought he was going to keep them apart.

It was easy to see which was Johnny's chair because it was the only one that had an ashtray on the table beside it. So that was where Rita parked herself after she and Ruth got back from their shopping trip into town a few hours later.

And she was still there when Johnny got home from work that evening; slipper-clad feet up on the footstool, TV remote in one hand, glass of whisky and Coke in the other.

"Remembered where you lived, then, did you?" she sniped, looking pointedly at the clock.

Furious, Johnny walked straight into the kitchen without answering.

Ruth smiled when she saw him and raised up onto her tiptoes to kiss him.

"Dinner's nearly ready," she told him. "I got some nice steak while we were in town. Oh, and the phone got switched on while we were out," she added, reaching for the kettle to make him a cup of tea. "I've already rung dad to give him the number. Which reminds me . . . he's got a late meeting tonight, so I said Mum might as well stay the night. Don't mind, do you?"

"What do you think?" Johnny asked.

"I could hardly say no, could I?" Ruth said quietly. "And it's only for one night."

"Make sure it is," he said, snatching an ashtray off the drainer. "I'm going for a bath."

One night quickly became two, and then three, until Rita was turning up with her whisky and her nightie whenever Frankie went off on one of his "late meetings". Which pissed Johnny off no end, especially since he'd begun to suspect that there were no meetings — not business ones, anyway. He had no proof, but he'd heard enough of Frankie's phone calls by now to know the difference between him talking business and talking sweet.

Ruth knew that he hated finding her mum there when he got home, but it seemed stupid for them to be lonely in separate houses while their men were at work for such long hours. And, if she was honest, she was enjoying having her mum back in her life. She'd been dying to escape from her for as long as she could remember, but the reality of living apart had been much harder than she'd expected.

Content now that life was pretty much back to normal, Ruth got a shock when she checked her diary one morning a few weeks later and realised that she'd missed a period. It was what she had been praying for, and she was ecstatic to think that those prayers had been answered. But she was also terrified, so she kept it to herself and made an appointment at the doctor's for the following week.

Determined not to put any unnecessary strain on her body, she took it easy for the next few days, only doing the bare minimum of cleaning and washing, and even making excuses when Johnny climbed into bed on the Friday night expecting sex.

Ruth was so tightly wound up by the time she finally saw the doctor on Monday morning that she burst into tears when he confirmed that she was pregnant.

"Is there a problem?" he asked, looking at her with concern. "Because there are options that you might like to consider."

"No!" she cried, smiling through her tears. "There's no problem. It's a gift from God."

And that was genuinely how she saw it: that God had forgiven her for her wicked lies, and blessed her with the one thing that she needed to bring her and Johnny closer together. And she was determined to repay His kindness by being the best wife and mother that she could possibly be.

Desperate to tell somebody now that it was official, she rushed straight over to her mum's house.

"Are you sure this time?" Rita asked when she told her.

"Positive." Ruth beamed as she sat down at the kitchen table. "I can't wait to tell Johnny. He'll be made up."

"You reckon?" Rita muttered under her breath as she reached into the cupboard for a glass.

186

"You'll have to cut down on that now you're going to be a grandma," Ruth said disapprovingly when her mum opened the whisky and poured her first shot of the day.

"Why, what difference will it make?" Rita demanded. "You weren't so bothered last time. Or is that because you weren't really pregnant last time?"

Ruth blushed. It was the truth — and they both knew it. But she hadn't admitted it yet, and she wasn't about to now.

"Don't start all that again," she said sharply. "Anyway, I only popped in to tell you, so I'd better get going."

"You've only just got here," Rita protested. "You can stop for a cuppa, at least."

"I've got someone coming round to look at that drippy tap," Ruth lied, standing up. She was too excited to sit here arguing. She wanted to go shopping. Alone.

"Wait while I get dressed, and I'll come with you." Rita said, swigging at her drink.

"I haven't got time," Ruth insisted as she headed for the door. "See you later."

She rushed out, caught a cab into town and wandered around Mothercare for a couple of hours, looking at prams and cots and Moses baskets. She just hoped it was a girl, because you could really go to town when you were dressing up little girls. Boys' clothes were so boring, but there were so many pretty little dresses to choose from. And then there were all the special-occasion dresses that she would have to have specially made, for parties and weddings and the all-important first communion. She couldn't wait.

187

CHAPTER
ELEVEN

"Johnny! *Johhnnnnny . . .!* "

Johnny was watching *EastEnders*, but he jumped up when he heard Ruth screaming his name and raced up the stairs.

"Are you all right?" he asked, rushing to her when he saw her slumped on the bathroom floor. "What's wrong?"

It was a month since she'd told him about the baby, and she'd been floating on air ever since. They both had. But a couple of days ago he'd noticed that she was looking a bit pale and didn't seem to have the same spring in her step. Concerned, he'd told her to go back to the doctor and get checked out. Ruth had insisted that everything was fine so he hadn't pressed her. But he wished that he had now, because something was obviously wrong.

One glance at the towel she was holding confirmed his suspicions. Almost throwing up at the sight of all the blood, he pushed himself back up to his feet and staggered out onto the landing.

"Stay there. I'll call an ambulance."

Sobbing, Ruth held the towel to her breast and rocked to and fro. The pain in her stomach was excruciating, but it was nothing to the pain in her heart. Johnny couldn't have looked properly or he'd have realised that she was holding their baby in her arms. It was so tiny that she had almost mistaken it for a clot when she'd felt it slipping out. But when she'd really looked, she'd seen the little black blobs where its unformed eyes lay beneath the protective cover of its skin, and the stubby little balls of flesh that would soon have formed into recognisable hands and feet.

She had frantically tried to revive it but it had been futile — because there wasn't even a proper mouth to try and breathe life into.

The doctor who examined Ruth at the hospital had a kindly face.

"These things happen, I'm afraid," he said as he peeled off his gloves when he'd examined her. He sighed as he dropped them into the bin. "But you're young so there's no reason why you shouldn't go on to have a perfectly normal, healthy pregnancy in the future."

"There's got to be a reason why it keeps happening," Johnny said worriedly. "If it was the first one, I might be able to understand it. But this is the second one, so there's got to be something wrong."

"The second?" The doctor frowned and looked down at his notes. "There's no mention of another pregnancy here. When was this?"

"About . . ." Johnny started. Then he trailed off, unable to think straight. "When was it, Ruth?" he asked, looking down at her.

She was sobbing too hard to answer, so he tried to calculate when it must have been. But he couldn't even remember how long they had been married, never mind how long into it they'd been before she'd lost that baby.

"I don't know," he admitted, shrugging helplessly. "A few months at most."

"And she was seen here?" The doctor looked through the notes again.

"I think she only saw the doctor back at the local surgery," Johnny told him.

"Yes, but she would have been referred to us from there," the doctor replied. "The procedure I'm about to send her for now should really have been done then as well, you see," he explained, trying to keep it simple because he could see how confused Johnny already was. "We have to be sure that there's nothing left inside that could cause infections or complications."

"Right," Johnny murmured, running a hand through his hair and swallowing loudly. The hospital smell was really starting to get to him, and he felt sick.

"How far along was she at that last termination?" the doctor asked. He pursed his lips when Johnny shrugged and said, "Okay, well, what's the name of your GP? I'll give the surgery a ring and have them check their records."

"Do you have to?" Ruth squawked, desperation helping her to find her voice.

"Well, yes, I rather think I do," the doctor told her. "I'm not saying for one moment that your GP was negligent during your last pregnancy. But if you weren't

190

properly cleaned out afterwards, that may in part be responsible for the loss of this one."

"You're joking!" Johnny gasped. "You're telling me that he should have sent her to hospital?" Gritting his teeth in anger when the doctor raised an eyebrow in reply, he looked down at Ruth. "I *told* you to let me get an ambulance, but you said the doctor had told you it was normal to bleed like that."

"I'm sorry," Ruth whimpered, sinking back into the pillow as fresh tears streamed down her cheeks.

"Now, now, no point blaming yourselves," the doctor said, patting her on the shoulder. "Let me go and see what I can find out, and we'll take it from there."

"I need a drink," Ruth blurted out. "Johnny, can you go and get me some water, please?"

Glad of an excuse to leave the cubicle and take in some fresh air, Johnny did as he'd been asked.

When he'd gone, Ruth looked up tearfully at the doctor and whispered, "There was no baby before this one. I — I thought there was, but then I had a period and realised I wasn't pregnant."

"But your husband —"

"Doesn't know anything about it," Ruth cut in. "He was so happy when he thought he was going to be a dad, I didn't have the heart to tell him."

The doctor's frown deepened. "You thought it was kinder to let him believe that it had died rather than just tell him that it hadn't even been there in the first place?"

"I know it was wrong," Ruth croaked, keeping half an eye on the curtain in case Johnny came back. "But it was too late to put it right after I'd done it, so I had to keep it up. And he can't find out now or he'll never forgive me. Please don't tell him."

The doctor sighed deeply. In his opinion, fathers had as much right to know what was going on with their babies as the mothers did. But she was his patient, and he had to respect her right to confidentiality.

"I'll book you in for the D and C," he told her.

"Will — will it stop me from having another one?" Ruth asked as he started to leave.

"Unlikely," he said as he went on his way.

Left alone, Ruth squeezed her eyes shut and let the tears flow. The doctor had looked at her as though she was scum, and he was right. This was her comeuppance for tricking Johnny into getting married. God hadn't blessed her with this baby, he'd used it to punish her for her wicked lies; dangling it in front of her, and then snatching it away again, to let her know that He didn't think her fit to be its mother.

Ruth stayed in hospital that night, but Johnny was worried about her when he brought her home the next morning. She wouldn't talk to him or her mum, and she just cried when Frankie sat with her on the bed and held her in his arms.

"It'll take time, but she'll get through it," the GP reassured them when he visited in the afternoon. "Just make sure she has plenty of fluids, and try to persuade her to eat a little something to keep the painkillers and sleeping tablets from aggravating her stomach. There's enough here for a week, but I'll pop back in a couple of days to check on her. And if you're concerned about anything in the meantime, don't hesitate to ring."

"Too late to act like you care now," Johnny snarled, glaring at the man as he snatched the prescription from his hand.

"Sorry?" The GP was confused.

"He's just tired," Frankie said, stepping between them and showing the doctor out. "Thanks for coming round, Doc. Much appreciated."

Turning to Johnny when he'd closed the door behind the doctor, Frankie frowned. "Have you got no respect? You can't go around talking to medical men like that. What's up with you?"

Johnny opened his mouth to explain but clamped it shut again when he realised that he couldn't, because he didn't fully understand it himself. The doctor at the hospital had made out like the GP was to blame for Ruth losing this baby and had been all up for ringing the surgery to find out why they hadn't sent her in to get properly checked out after she'd lost the first one. But then he'd done a complete U-turn and said it wasn't necessary, after all. So Johnny still didn't know whose fault it was.

"Son, I know you're upset," Frankie said. He fetched two cans of beer from the fridge and shoved one into Johnny's hand. "But you can't go round taking it out on everyone else. Ruth's the one who needs looking after, not you, so you're just going to have to get a grip and sort yourself out. I know it ain't gonna be easy, so that's why we've decided that Rita's going to move in for a bit."

"No!" Johnny blurted out. Quickly tempering his tone, he said, "Sorry, but I don't want to impose on Rita. I can look after Ruth."

Frankie looked at him and nodded slowly. "You know, when she first told me what you'd done I wanted to kill you with my bare hands," he said quietly. "And there were plenty of times leading up to the wedding when I came proper close to sending you off a cliff with my boot up your arse. But you've been good to my girl, and a father can't ask for better than that."

"I try," Johnny murmured, feeling guilty about the thousands of times he'd wished that he'd never laid eyes on Ruth — and the numerous times he could happily have shoved her under a bus and walked away without looking back.

"The tough times make you stronger," Frankie went on sagely. "And you'll cope with this just like you coped with the last one. But don't try to rush it. Just take it one step at a time. Oh, and don't worry about work. We'll manage without you till you're ready to come back."

Rita didn't want to leave, mainly because she knew that Frankie would just dump her at the house and then take off again. But he was adamant that Johnny and Ruth needed some time alone, so she had no choice but to get into the car.

Johnny waved them off and then nipped upstairs to tell Ruth that he was taking her prescription to the chemist's. She was fast asleep.

Lisa was on the step when he opened the front door a few seconds later, her hand raised, about to knock.

"Jeezus, you scared me," he said.

"Sorry," she apologised, giving him a small sad smile. "I've just heard. How are you?"

"I'm all right. But Ruth's not too good. I'm just off to get her script while she's asleep."

"Do you want me to come with you?"

"Actually, I'd rather you stayed here in case she wakes up while I'm gone," Johnny said, relieved to have a helping hand. He'd told Frankie he could cope, but he wasn't so sure that he was equipped to deal with Ruth if she woke up and started crying again. Rita would have driven him crazy within two minutes flat, but he and Lisa had been getting on fine, so it wouldn't be too bad having her here. And at least she'd have a better understanding than him of what Ruth was going through, with them both being girls.

"I'll make myself a brew and listen out for her," Lisa said, stepping inside and slipping off her jacket. "You look like you could do with a break, so why don't you pop round to Dave's while you're over that side?" she suggested, smiling as she added, "Bring me a little smoke back and I might even cook your dinner."

Johnny could have kissed her. Getting wasted was exactly what he needed right now, but there was no way Ruth would have suggested it.

Immediately feeling guilty for thinking about himself when his wife was lying upstairs with an empty womb and a ripped-up heart, Johnny said, "Won't be long."

"Take as long as you like," said Lisa. "I'm here now, and I'll stay as long as you need me."

Dave held out his arms when he opened the door and pulled Johnny into a hug.

"Aw, man, I'm so sorry. How are you feeling — or is that a stupid question?"

"How did you know?" Johnny asked, wondering who could have told him — or Lisa, come to that.

"Pauline from upstairs works nights at the hospital," Dave said. "She saw you and Ruth coming in with the ambulance last night, and she came round on her way home to tell me. How's Ruth doing?"

"She's a mess."

"I bet." Dave tutted and shook his head. "I can't believe it, mate. It's shocking. Totally shocking. Do they know why it happened?"

"No, they reckon it's just one of them things," Johnny said as he followed him into the living room and flopped down on the couch. He hadn't lived here for months, but it still felt like home — even with Wazza's shit instead of his cluttering the place up.

"Ah, well, I suppose you've just got to pick yourselves up and move on," Dave said philosophically. "Bet you could do with a smoke, couldn't you?"

"Why else would I be here?" Johnny grinned. "And hurry up, 'cos I've left Lisa babysitting."

"Oh, is she round at yours?" Dave's eyebrows lifted as he loaded up the bong. "I might walk round with you when you go back."

196

"Probably best if you don't," Johnny told him. "Ruth's asleep, but I'm betting she'll start crying again as soon as she wakes up, and I don't think she'll appreciate anyone being there. I even had to send her mum home."

"That must have been hard!" Dave chuckled. "I know how much you love having her around."

"Like a hole in the fuckin' head," Johnny moaned. "Still, Frankie gave me a nice little speech about how much he appreciates me being there for Ruth, so with any luck he'll tell her to give us a bit of space."

"Wouldn't bank on it," Dave said dryly. Bong loaded, he passed it over. "There you go — get your gob around that."

A lot lighter at heart by the time he left Dave's flat and floated home a little while later, Johnny smiled when he walked in and found Lisa scrubbing the kitchen sink.

"Sorry," she apologised. "I'm not implying that our Ruth's dirty or anything, but I was looking through the freezer for something to cook for your dinner and I noticed everything could do with a bit of a going-over."

"She's been taking it easy for the past few weeks for the baby's sake," Johnny told her. "Didn't work, though," he added with a sigh. Then, rubbing his hands together, he said, "Anyhow, what was that about dinner?"

"I take it you've been to Dave's, then?" Lisa laughed, guessing that he had the munchies. "I hope you remembered to go to the chemist before you got blasted?"

"Check." Johnny patted his jacket pocket. "And I didn't forget your smoke," he added, taking a tiny plastic packet out of a back pocket of his jeans and handing it to her.

"Cool," she said, slipping it inside her bra. "I'll have some of that after I've got you sorted."

"Cheers." Johnny grinned. "Has Ruth woken up yet?"

"No." Lisa shook her head and moved him out of the way so that she could take a pan out of the cupboard. "But I was thinking I should probably put a plate out for her, just in case."

"Doubt she'll eat it," Johnny said. "But the doctor said to try and persuade her. Something to do with the tablets and her stomach."

"What's he given her?" Lisa asked as she took three chops out of the microwave and tested them with her finger to make sure they had defrosted all the way through.

Johnny took the chemist's bag out of his pocket and pulled out the tablets. After staring at the label for several moments, he shrugged and said, "No idea."

"Give it here," Lisa said amusedly.

"Hang on a minute." Johnny swerved to the side as she reached for the tablets. "I don't give up that easy."

"Stop messing about and let me see," Lisa scolded, going for the packet again. But this time she stumbled and fell against him. They both held their breath — then, suddenly, their lips were locked together, and Johnny's tongue was moving into her mouth.

198

"Oh, Jeezus," he moaned, pulling away. "I'm really sorry, that was well out of order. You must think I'm a right bastard."

"Don't be daft," Lisa murmured. "We're both to blame."

"I was the one who made the move," Johnny said quietly. "You didn't do anything."

"Let's just put it down to stress and call it quits," Lisa said as she turned to put the chops in the oven. "Don't worry, I won't tell anyone."

"Thanks," Johnny said gratefully.

"Right, why don't you go and check on Ruth while I do the veg?" Lisa suggested, back to her practical self. "And have a bath while you're up there, 'cos you stink," she added with a cheeky smile.

"Do I?" He frowned and sniffed at his armpit.

"You have been up all night," Lisa reminded him. "But you're still nowhere near as bad as that Wazza," she added, wrinkling her nose as if she could actually smell the man. "Now he *does* reek."

"You're not wrong there." Johnny grinned. "Don't know why Dave let him move in."

Lisa raised her hand and rubbed her fingers together. "Dosh. Who do you think's been paying for all the gear Dave's been buying? He's taking him for a right mug, if you ask me. But if Wazza's stupid enough to fall for it, that's his business. And don't you go telling Dave I told you," she warned, giving him a mock-stern look. "I only found out 'cos I overheard Dave tapping him up."

"My lips are sealed," Johnny assured her. "Subject of Dave," he added. "He wanted to come back with me when I told him you were here."

"I hope you said no," Lisa squawked, a look of horror on her face. Rolling her eyes with relief when he shook his head, she said, "I know he's your best mate, but he's proper doing my head in. I've told him I'm not interested but he keeps phoning me, and turning up at the pub when he knows I'm working."

"He's got it bad." Johnny laughed. "But how come you're so dead set against him all of a sudden? I thought you didn't mind the occasional get-together?"

Only 'cos I couldn't have you, thought Lisa.

"It's complicated," she said. "I know everyone thinks I'm a slag, and I won't lie and say I haven't had my fair share of boyfriends. But that's all in the past. I've grown up since then and realised most of them weren't even worth it." Shrugging, she added, "If our Ruth can find her Mr Right, I'm damn sure mine can't be too far behind."

"Too right," Johnny assured her. "Anyhow, I'll go and check on her."

"Yeah, and give me some bloody space," Lisa laughed, pushing him towards the door.

When he'd gone, she closed her eyes and touched her fingertips to her lips. She could still feel the ghost of the kiss, still taste the sweetness of his tongue. This had started out as a game, but it had gone way beyond that now. All of her life, Ruth had only had to click her fingers for Frankie's wallet to fall open at her feet, and she'd used that to try and make Lisa jealous, rubbing it in her face that they were rich and she was poor. But Lisa had got her own back by nicking out from under her nose any lad that Ruth showed interest in — even the ones that she hadn't fancied in the slightest.

Johnny had been a tough nut to crack but that had just made Lisa all the more determined. And now, at last, she'd made a breakthrough. But the victory wasn't as sweet as she'd expected. When she'd started this she'd just wanted to have him so that she could feel superior to Ruth. But now that love had reared its painful head she didn't just want a part of him, she wanted all of him — for keeps. But that could never happen, because Frankie would never allow it.

Still, at least she had the memory of that kiss to see her through the heartache that was sure to come. And as long as she stayed on the right side of Ruth, she would be able to come round and see Johnny from time to time, which was better than nothing.

Upstairs, Johnny had run himself a bath and he was lying in it now, cursing himself as the steam swirled up around his face. It had been stupid and dangerous to kiss Lisa like that, and all hell would have broken loose if Ruth had caught them. And it was totally his fault, because Lisa had done nothing to encourage him. She'd only shown concern for her cousin by trying to see what medication the doctor had given her, and he'd totally taken advantage.

But it wouldn't happen again. No matter how frustrated he was, how sexy Lisa looked, or how good she smelled, she was a no-go zone, and he'd be steering well clear from now on.

CHAPTER
TWELVE

It was two weeks since Ruth had lost the baby and Johnny had done his best to be supportive. But the constant crying had done his head in, so he was more than ready when Frankie said he needed him to come back to work.

It felt great to be back out in the open with his bucket and sponge, but the fun didn't last long. At lunchtime Frankie called him into the office.

"I need you to do the pickup tonight," he told him. "That idiot Del's gone and got himself nicked, and Robbie's bust his foot. So are you up for it, or what?"

"I don't know," Johnny murmured. "I've never done anything like that before. What if I screw it up?"

"If two gormless pricks like Del and Robbie can pull it off, I'm fucking sure you and your mate can," Frankie assured him.

"*Dave?*" Johnny frowned.

"If that's his name, yeah. You trust him, don't you?"

"Yeah, course, but . . ."

"Good enough for me," said Frankie. "Tell him there's fifty in it for him, and all he's got to do is drive you there and hang around to make sure nothing goes wrong. Which it won't," he added quickly. "You just go in, get the keys, and get back out of there — quick as, no fucking about."

"Go in where?"

"The house, where d'ya fucking think?" Frankie gave an irritated sigh.

"You want me to burgle a house?" Johnny gasped, praying that he would say no.

"No, I just want you to break in and take a set of fucking keys off a hook," said Frankie. "It'll be a doddle, or I wouldn't ask you to do it. And there won't be no one there, 'cos the family's gone on a cruise."

"What if there's an alarm?"

"There is. But it won't make no odds 'cos the gaff's out in the middle of nowhere. No one'll hear it, and by the time anyone cottons on the car will be long gone."

"I don't know," Johnny said uncertainly. "What about Ruth?"

"Isn't she still on them sleepers the doc gave her?" Frankie asked. Shrugging when Johnny nodded, he said, "There you go, then. She won't even know you've been out."

"I don't know," Johnny said again.

"Son, I wouldn't ask if there was anyone else I could trust to do it," Frankie told him, changing tack and making it sound like Johnny would be doing him a massive favour. "This needs doing tonight or I'm going to miss it, and there's a load of money riding on it."

"All right," Johnny agreed reluctantly. "But I can't speak for Dave. I'll call round on my way home and see if he's up for it."

204

"Go now," said Frankie, tossing a twenty onto the desk. "Take a cab. Just make sure you're back here by twelve. There'll be a motor parked across from the gates, and I'll leave the key under the bush."

Johnny picked up the money and turned to leave. Hesitating at the door, he said, "What about the address?"

"You're holding it." Frankie grinned.

Johnny turned the twenty over and frowned when he saw a Post-It note stuck to the back with an address scrawled on it. Not doing the pickup had never been an option; Frankie had known that he would do it from the start.

"Memorise it, then get rid," Frankie ordered. "And don't fuck this up, son. I'm counting on you."

Johnny nodded and went on his way.

"Fifty quid?" Dave spluttered when Johnny told him about the job. "Just for driving out to Altrincham and back? Count me in, matey!"

"You'll have to hang around while I find the key and get the other motor," Johnny told him.

"No skin off my nose." Dave shrugged. "What time do we go?"

"We've got to be at the yard at twelve," Johnny told him. "So I'll come and get you in a cab at twenty to. And make sure you're ready."

"Don't you worry about me," Dave scoffed, reaching for his bong. "Me and that fifty quid have got a date — and I'm never late for dates."

They spent the next few hours smoking and listening to music. At six, Johnny tore himself away and headed home as if returning from a normal day's work. He was surprised to find Lisa waiting for him in the living room.

"What are you doing here?" he asked, looking around. "Where's Ruth?"

"In bed," Lisa said quietly. "I knew you were going back to work today, so I thought I'd pop round for a brew — make sure she was all right on her own."

"And was she?"

"Not really. She was out on the street when I got here, screaming abuse at the old woman from a few doors down."

"You're joking!" Johnny's brow crinkled. "Why? What was going on?"

"She was drunk." Lisa folded her arms in a defensive *don't shoot the messenger* gesture. "Still is, a bit. I pulled her inside and made her a black coffee, but she still had half a bottle of whisky so she wouldn't drink it. I tried to take the bottle off her but she wouldn't give it up, and the mood she was in, I thought I'd best leave it or we'd have ended up scrapping."

"Where did she get whisky from?" Johnny asked. "We've only got a bit of wine and some beers." He drew his head back as a thought occurred to him and looked around with narrowed eyes. "Has Rita been?"

"Not while I've been here," said Lisa. "But I think Ruth went to the shop, 'cos she still had her shoes and coat on when I found her."

"What's she playing at? She's supposed to be resting."

"That's what I thought. But I'm more worried about her drinking while she's still on her tablets. They're really strong — you're not supposed to have alcohol with them."

"Jeezus." Johnny exhaled loudly and ran his hands through his hair. "It's bad enough having to put up with her crying all the fucking time, but if she's going to start messing about with her tabs an' all . . ." He gave Lisa a helpless look. "What am I supposed to do? I can't watch her all the time. I've only just gone back to work — what's Frankie going to say if I tell him I can't come in tomorrow?"

"She's his daughter, he'll want whatever's best for her," Lisa assured him. "But you don't have to do that. I can stay with her."

"No." Johnny shook his head. "It's not your problem."

"I don't mind," she insisted.

A crash from the bedroom interrupted them. Exchanging nervous glances, they both darted for the stairs. Embarrassed when they collided and his arm brushed across her breasts, Johnny muttered, "Sorry," and ran on up.

Ruth was on the floor. She giggled when Johnny came in and said, "I fell out of bed."

"Are you hurt?" he asked, rushing to help her up.

"Nothing a bit of loving wouldn't cure," she purred, wrapping her arms around his neck. "Kiss me, Johnny. It's been ages since you kissed me."

"Not now," he murmured, conscious that Lisa was standing right behind them. "Just get back into bed."

"Only if you come with me," she wheedled. "Come on, let's make another baby."

"Shall I put the kettle on?" Lisa asked, feeling awkward.

Ruth's head snapped around at the sound of her cousin's voice. "You still here? I thought I told you to go!"

"She was worried about you," Johnny told her, pulling her to her feet and pushing her gently onto the bed. "You're not supposed to be drinking — *or* walking to the shops — when you're taking those tablets."

"I had to get out," Ruth complained, sliding back obediently beneath the quilt. She flashed another glare at Lisa. "You can go now. Me and my husband want some *private* time."

"You need to sober up," Johnny muttered. "So Lisa's going to make you a coffee while I get you sorted."

"I don't want coffee," Ruth argued, reaching for the whisky bottle. "This is all I need."

"No!" Johnny snatched it out of her hand. "You've had enough."

"Give it back," she demanded, pawing at his arm. "It makes me feel better."

He put it out of reach on the dressing table and pushed her down onto the pillows. "If you don't want coffee, you can sleep it off instead."

"Stop treating me like a baby. I'm a grown woman, I can do what I want."

"Not while you're still taking your tablets, you can't."

208

Aware that she wasn't going to get her own way, Ruth's eyes flooded with tears and she gave Johnny a pitiful look.

"You're angry with me, aren't you?"

"A bit," he admitted, pulling the quilt up to her throat. "We're both upset about the baby, but I'm trying to get on with things and this isn't helping."

"You don't understand," she whimpered, her chin wobbling now. "I just want my baby back."

"I know." Sighing, Johnny sat down on the edge of the bed and stroked her hair off her face. It felt wet, and he hoped to God that it wasn't vomit. "Just try to get some sleep. You'll feel better when you wake up."

"I won't," she said plaintively. "I'll never feel better again. I've lost my baby, and you don't love me any more."

"Don't be stupid," Johnny said patiently. "I just want you to get better. That's all any of us want. Me, your mum, your dad, Lisa — we're all worried about you."

"Will you lie down with me?" Ruth sounded like a lost little girl. "I'll go to sleep if you hold me, I promise."

Johnny climbed onto the bed beside her and lifted his arm. She snuggled into it and laid her head on his chest.

"Sorry. I won't do it again."

A few minutes later she was fast asleep. Sliding his arm out from under her, Johnny tiptoed out of the room and closed the door quietly behind him.

Lisa was in the kitchen.

"Is she okay?" she asked, passing a coffee to him when he joined her.

"Flat out," he told her, sitting down.

She took in the strained look on his face, and said, "You look wiped. Have you eaten anything?"

"Not yet. But I'll go to the chippy in a bit."

"What's the point of wasting money when I can do it for you?"

"No, you've done enough."

"We're family," Lisa reminded him. "And family takes care of its own."

"You can't half tell you're related to Frankie," Johnny said amusedly. "He's always banging on about that, an' all."

"Yeah, well, he's been more like my dad than my uncle," Lisa explained as she rolled up her sleeves. "I worshipped him when I was little. Just wish he'd let me sort his clothes out," she added with a grin. "He's been wearing the same shit ever since I can remember, and it's embarrassing."

"Yeah, what's with the Elvis thing?" Johnny asked. "I've always wondered, but I didn't like to ask Ruth."

"No, don't mention it to her." Lisa pulled a face as if that would be the worst mistake he could ever make. "Frankie's God in her eyes."

"And she's a princess in his," said Johnny.

"Tell me about it." Lisa turned and pulled the freezer door open. "Burger and chips do you?"

"Anything," Johnny said gratefully. "So . . . the Elvis thing? Is he just like a massive fan, or something?"

210

"I don't think so." Lisa switched the grill on. "I've never heard him playing his music, or anything. I think it's just that he used to look so much like him when he was younger, and he cottoned on that women went crazy when he dressed like him. They used to fight over him, and everything."

"You're kidding me!" Johnny laughed, unable to picture that.

"No, he was proper handsome," Lisa said quite seriously. "Before my nan got too ill to travel, he used to throw these massive family parties, and my other uncles and their wives and kids would come over from Ireland. All the blokes would go down to the pub and get pissed, while the women caught up on the gossip back at home. Then the men'd come back singing and telling jokes, and they'd have a big old knees-up. But you could guarantee there'd be a massive argument before the end of the night. And it was usually about Uncle Frankie and one of the brothers' wives."

"Why, was he was shagging them?"

"They *wished*. But nah, he'd never do the dirty on his brothers. They'd be so pissed by then that they'd accuse him of it, anyway. So he'd kick off and tell them to piss off back to Ireland if they didn't trust him. And then the women would start scrapping, 'cos they were jealous of the one he was *supposed* to be sleeping with. It was a right laugh."

"Sounds it," Johnny agreed, wishing he'd been there to see it. "But why does he still dress like that? No offence, but he's a bit old now, isn't he?"

"He's Frankie Hynes," Lisa replied simply. "Would *you* tell him he looks stupid?"

"No way."

"There you go, then." Lisa put the burgers under the grill and dropped a handful of chips into the chip pan. "Don't suppose you've got a fag?"

Johnny passed one to her and gave her a light before lighting his own.

Lisa noticed him glancing at the clock on the wall and said, "That's the third time I've seen you do that since you came in. Have you got somewhere to go?"

"Frankie asked me to pick something up for him later on," Johnny told her. "But I'm thinking I'd best ring him and tell him I can't make it. There's no way I can leave Ruth on her own again tonight."

"I told you I'd stay if you need to work," Lisa reminded him.

"I know. But you've been here all day as it is, and I wouldn't be back till really late."

"So? I've got nothing else to do."

Johnny pursed his lips. Frankie had said that he would miss out on the car if they didn't get it tonight, so he supposed he should do it if he could. It just pissed him off that Ruth was making everything so difficult. He was sure she couldn't still be this upset over the baby, and suspected she was putting it on for the attention. But he couldn't stay home and look after her for ever. Frankie had a business to run, and if Johnny couldn't do his bit it wouldn't be long before he was out on his arse.

CHAPTER
THIRTEEN

Dave was hiding in the shadows when Johnny arrived at the flats later that night, and he glanced around furtively before darting out and climbing into the back of the cab.

"Dude." He touched fists with Johnny.

Amused, Johnny said, "What's up with you?"

"Just keeping it cool," Dave told him quietly, flicking a suspicious glance at the back of the driver's head. "Can't be too careful. Talk later, yeah?"

Guessing that he was being told to zip it, Johnny shook his head and gazed out of the window as the cab set off. When they reached Great Ancoats Street, Dave leaned forward and tapped the back of the driver's seat.

"You can stop here, mate."

"What did you do that for?" Johnny complained when he'd paid and they were standing on the pavement. "Now we'll have to walk the rest of the way."

"You're a shit criminal, you," Dave scoffed. "Rule one: never let people know where you're going, so then they can't put two and two together and make five when they see it on the news."

"On the news?" Johnny chuckled. "Jeezus, man, what kind of job do you think we're pulling here? We're not robbing a fucking bank."

"Better safe than sorry," Dave insisted.

As Frankie had promised, there was a small car parked opposite the yard gates. Johnny found the key in the shrubs and tossed it to Dave. Then, after climbing quickly into the passenger seat when Dave unlocked the doors, he hunched down and pulled his collar up around his ears.

"You can pack that right in," Dave ordered, lighting two cigarettes and passing one to him before setting off coolly as if they were just two mates heading out for a night on the town. "It's all about front in this game. Pigs zone in on fuckers like you who sit there looking like they've shit their kecks, so you've just got to chill."

"Check you acting like *Mr I've Done This A Thousand Times*, when I didn't even know you could drive," Johnny muttered. But he sat up and made an effort to look more relaxed nevertheless.

"I've had a few motors away in my time," Dave admitted. "Used to be a bit of a bad lad back in the day."

"Could have fooled me," Johnny snorted. "You've hardly moved off the sofa since I've known you."

"That's 'cos the weed turns you lazy," Dave explained. "Anyhow, shut up and let me concentrate. I haven't been down that end in years, and I don't want to get lost when we get there."

Half an hour later they found the road they were looking for. As Frankie had said, it was out in the middle of nowhere, and there were no street lamps so it was pitch dark. All they could see on both sides were inky fields, bordered by tarry hedges.

"How the fuck are we supposed to find the house when we can't see anything?" Johnny complained, his forehead pressed up against the cold glass of the windscreen as he peered out. "This is worse than being blind." He jerked back when something flew right past his nose. "What the fuck was *that*?"

"Probably an owl. Or a bat."

"Jeezus, I can't wait to get back to civilisation. This is like a horror film."

"There!" Dave slammed on the brakes.

"What did you do that for?" Johnny yelped, using his hands to stop his head from smashing into the dash.

"I saw a house." Dave reversed back to a gap in the hedges where an old stone gatepost was standing at an angle. Squinting at the name carved in its head, he read, "Hillgate . . . is that the one?"

Johnny nodded and peered past him. In the distance he could just about make out the faint outline of a roof.

"It's miles away," he complained.

"Stop moaning and get moving," Dave ordered.

Johnny took a deep breath, unbuckled his seat belt, and reached for the jemmy that Frankie had left on the floor behind his seat. This was it. He was about to break into a house for the first time in his life — and it didn't feel good. In fact, it felt fucking horrible, and his legs were shaking so badly that he doubted they were going to support him.

"Are you all right?" Dave asked. "Do you want me to do it?"

Johnny wished that he could pass the job over. But Frankie had asked him to do it, not Dave, so he shook his head.

"I'll be okay. Just go and park up somewhere out of sight."

"Out of *whose* sight?" Dave chuckled, looking around. "There's no one around for miles, mate. I could run stark bollock naked down the road and no one would ever know."

"*I* would," Johnny muttered, grimacing at the thought. "Right, here goes." He pulled his gloves on. "Wish me luck."

"Fuck off, you poof," Dave grunted, pushing him towards the door. "And if you're not out of there in ten, I'm coming in after you."

Johnny gave him a nervous smile and opened the door. But just as he'd dropped one foot out, Dave yelled, "*WATCH OUT!*"

"What?" he squawked, slamming the door shut again. "What is it? Is something out there?"

Dave burst out laughing and clutched at his stomach. "Man, you should have seen your face! I thought you were gonna drop a load!"

Johnny tutted, climbed out, and edged his way up the path with the jemmy held out in front of him like a sword. He was relieved to find the house in darkness and the curtains parted, which told him that Frankie had been right and nobody was home. He gave the front door a push, just in case. It didn't budge, so he moved on to the windows and tried to prise one open with his gloved fingers before walking around to the garage that was built on to the side of the house.

He squatted down and jammed the end of the jemmy into the hasp of the padlock, and his heart started thumping like a jackhammer when the lock fell off at his feet. He grabbed the bottom of the roller door and pushed it up quickly, desperate to do what he had to do and get the fuck out of there.

The car was in the garage and Johnny ran his hands over the bonnet. It was icy cold, so he moved to the connecting door and rammed the flat edge of the jemmy into the crack between the lock and the frame, wrenching it backwards and forwards until the wood gave and the door flew open.

Dim moonlight was filtering in through the uncovered window and he saw that he was in a kitchen. Still nervous of being caught, he tiptoed in and looked around for the keys. After several minutes he came across a small metal box that had a key-shaped cut-out in its door and was attached to the side of one of the units. It had a tiny padlock, like the kind that little girls used to keep their diaries from prying eyes. Johnny popped it off easily, grabbed the keys that were hanging inside and ran back out to the garage.

Dave had reversed into the hedge directly opposite the drive. He was listening to the radio and smoking a spliff when Johnny come tearing out as if he had a pack of wolves chasing him. He flashed his lights to make him stop and pulled alongside, gesturing at Johnny to roll down his window.

"Quit panicking, or you'll get nicked," he ordered. "And keep an eye on your speed, an' all."

Johnny nodded and took a deep breath. But he still managed to stall — twice — before he got going properly again.

Big Pat was waiting at the yard. He opened the gates when he saw their headlights approaching and waved them in, directing Dave to park out on the lot and Johnny round to the garage, where another man Johnny had never seen before was waiting.

When Johnny climbed out shakily, Big Pat handed him a wad of money. Then he passed another slightly slimmer one to Dave before showing them both out — all without uttering a single word.

"That was fucking *ace*," Dave exclaimed as they walked back out onto the main road and headed over to the taxi rank. "I haven't been that psyched up in years. D'ya reckon Frankie'll ask us to do it again?"

"I hope not," Johnny said, wishing that his heart would slow down. "I nearly shit myself when we passed them coppers."

"I told you, it's all about front," said Dave, pushing the taxi-rank door open and stepping into the filthy customer area. "We're going to Moss Side," he told the woman behind the counter.

"Hulme," Johnny corrected him. Wincing when Dave back-kicked him in the ankle, he clamped his mouth shut and hobbled back out.

"What did I tell you?" Dave hissed when he followed a few seconds later. "Don't let 'em know where you're going — there or back."

A car arrived a couple of minutes later and Dave told the driver to drop them at Moss Side market. After walking the rest of the way into Hulme, he said, "Your place or mine?"

"I've got work in the morning," Johnny told him. "Best give it a miss or I'll never get up."

"A couple of spliffs ain't gonna hurt," Dave insisted, too wired to think about sleeping just yet. "Tell you what, we'll go to yours, then at least you'll be next to your bed if you fall asleep. I'll kip on the couch."

It was a reasonable expectation, and usually Johnny wouldn't have hesitated. But Lisa was back at the house, and after what she'd said about trying to shake Dave off Johnny didn't think she'd be too happy to see him.

"Sorry, mate, but Ruth's not too good at the moment," he told him.

"What's up with her now?" Dave asked. Like Johnny, he considered two weeks ample time for a girl to get over losing a baby, and anything beyond that was just self-pity — for which he had no patience.

"She was drunk when I got back from yours earlier," Johnny told him. "And she's still on them tabs, so it sent her a bit loopy. I just want to keep everything calm."

Dave gave a disappointed sigh and shrugged. "Oh, well, you've got to do what you think best. You know where I am if you change your mind."

Johnny said goodbye and headed home, but he felt guilty all the way. Dave had been brilliant after his mum had kicked him out. He hadn't known Johnny from Adam when he'd come across him sleeping rough in the garages under the flats, but he hadn't thought twice about taking him in. And he'd been the best mate anyone could have asked for since, so it felt wrong to have knocked him back like that. Especially when Ruth would most likely still be sleeping — and Lisa might well have gone home.

Even as he thought it, Johnny knew instinctively that Lisa would still be there. And he was right. She was curled up on his chair with a blanket over her knees, and her face looked soft and relaxed in the warm glow of the lamp.

As he gazed at her, Johnny realised that she was the real reason he had knocked Dave back just now. Not because he'd thought that she would be uncomfortable if Dave was there but because he hadn't wanted to risk them getting friendly again. That was the shameful truth of it.

Disappointed with himself, he went into the kitchen to get a beer. He didn't know where this sudden interest in Lisa had come from but he wished it would go away, because he was a married man. And just because Ruth was going through a rough patch that didn't give him the right to revert back to his doggish ways — albeit only in his head.

"Johnny . . .?" Lisa came padding into the kitchen. She smiled when he turned around, and rubbed her

220

eyes sleepily. "I thought I was dreaming when I heard a noise in here. When did you get back?"

"Just now," he told her, gripping his beer can tightly and trying to keep his eyes on her face. She'd taken off her jeans and was wearing an old T-shirt of his which just about covered her thighs.

"Hope you don't mind?" she asked. "I was uncomfortable, and I thought if I'm staying the night I might as well get changed."

"It's fine," Johnny assured her, desperately trying to ignore the stirring sensation in his pants.

Lisa noticed his cheek muscles jumping and frowned. "Is everything okay?"

He nodded and turned to the sink to conceal the fact that he now had a full-blown hard-on.

"Something's wrong," Lisa said perceptively. She moved closer and touched his back. "If you're still worried about Ruth, don't be, 'cos she's fine. She woke up a couple of hours ago with a headache, so I made her a cup of cocoa. She took one of her sleeping tablets and dropped straight off."

"Thanks," Johnny murmured, unable to move while Lisa was still standing there. "Why don't you go and sleep in the spare room?" he suggested. "You must be knackered. I'll just do a quick tidy-up down here."

"I'm awake now," she said. "Might as well have a drink with you if you're staying up for a bit. Unless you'd rather be alone . . .?"

Johnny groaned. "Just go to bed, Lisa — *please*."

"Have I done something wrong?"

"No."

"Well, what's wrong, then?" She pulled him round to face her. "Johnny, please tell me what I've done. I thought we were getting on okay."

"We are," he assured her, swallowing deeply. "Probably a bit *too* well."

Confused, Lisa shook her head. Then a light came on and her gaze slid from his face. "Oh."

"So *now* will you go to bed?" Johnny begged.

She bit her lip and shook her head. Then she took a step towards him, reached up and put her hand behind his head, bringing his face down to hers. And this time Johnny didn't pull away.

They were on the floor in an instant, their lips locked together as Johnny unzipped his fly, tugged Lisa's panties to one side and pushed himself into her, groaning. She wrapped her legs around him and held him tight as he rode her hard. It was wild and raw, and Johnny wanted it to go on and on. But when she sank her teeth into his neck, he had to bite down hard on his lip to keep from crying out and waking Ruth as he exploded into her.

"Sorry," he murmured, when his heart had stopped racing and he was able to breathe again. "I'm not usually that fast."

"Neither am I," Lisa told him, giving him a shy smile.

Johnny gave her a questioning look.

"Do I have to spell it out?" she giggled, rolling her eyes.

"Really?"

"Yes, really." Sighing now, she said, "I suppose we'd best get up."

"Yeah, we should," Johnny agreed, casting a nervous glance out through the door as he slid out of her and zipped himself up.

"You don't regret it, do you?" Lisa asked softly as she stood up and pulled the T-shirt down to cover herself.

"I don't know." Johnny shrugged. "Do you?"

"Only if you do," she said.

"I don't think so," Johnny told her, sensing that she would probably go on a guilt trip if he didn't reassure her — and he suspected that he'd be on a big enough one for both of them come the morning.

"Me neither," said Lisa. "But we probably shouldn't do it again."

"No, definitely not," Johnny agreed.

"Not here, anyway."

"Where, then?"

CHAPTER
FOURTEEN

Five months after losing the baby, Ruth found out that she was pregnant again. Johnny was working regular days and most nights by then, and he came home just long enough to eat, shower and get changed before going out again. Ruth would invariably be asleep by the time he got home in the early hours, so lovemaking had been a real hit-and-miss affair. And it was especially difficult to get time alone when her mum was here — which seemed to be most of the time lately.

But one of their snatched moments had paid dividends — and this time she was determined not to let anything go wrong. So the first thing she did was to ban her mum from drinking in the house.

"Don't be ridiculous," Rita scoffed, already twisting the top off the bottle of whisky she'd brought with her that day.

"I'm serious," Ruth told her. "I'm pregnant, and I want everything to go right this time, so I'm cutting out all the negative energies in my life."

"Negative energies?" Rita repeated scornfully. "You sound like you've been reading one of them stupid Chinese books. Next you'll be telling me you're taking up bleedin' yoga."

"Don't swear," Ruth chided, covering her stomach with her hands as if to protect the baby's innocent little ears.

"Sod this for a game of soldiers," Rita snorted as she took a glass out of the cupboard. "You can do what you want, but you ain't telling me what I can and can't drink."

"I'm not saying you can't drink," said Ruth. She pulled the glass out of her mother's hand and put it back where she'd got it from. "Just not here."

"Why? Don't you trust yourself not to join me?" Rita gave a knowing smirk. "I can see right through you, lady. You're dying for one, aren't you?"

"No." Ruth shook her head. "I don't want to hurt the baby, and my doctor said —"

"Your doctor's about twelve," Rita interrupted dismissively. "What does *he* know?"

"More than you," Ruth retorted defensively. "He's trained."

"You can't learn about life from a book," Rita told her. "I've been there and done it, and I'm telling you it's a load of bollocks when they say you can't drink when you're pregnant. Your nan drank all the way through with me, and it didn't do me any harm."

"Are you serious?" Ruth gasped. "You've been drunk for as long as I can remember, and now I know why."

"Don't you dare bad-mouth my mother." Rita's jowls wobbled with fury. "And you can get off that flaming high horse, 'cos you've been happy enough sharing my whisky for the past few months, so you ain't no better than me."

"I was depressed — you should have helped me," Ruth muttered, tearful now because she was ashamed she'd been so weak. She *had* been drinking too much, but she'd needed something to ease the loneliness between Johnny's flying visits. And her mum had done nothing to discourage her, because she'd been only too happy to have a drinking buddy.

"Don't try and make out like it's my fault you can't control yourself," Rita snapped, jabbing a finger against Ruth's chest. "I brought you into this world, you snotty little bitch, and if you ever dare look down your nose at me like this again, I'll take you right back out of it — d'ya hear me?"

Ruth raised her chin. "Right, that's it. Get out. This is my house, and I don't want you coming round if you're going to talk to me like this."

"You what?" Rita screwed up her face. "All your life I've been running round after you, picking up the pieces when you fucked up, and wiping your shitty little arse — and you've got the nerve to try and kick me out? And I wouldn't mind, but it's not even your house — me and your dad are paying for it."

"No, you're not," Ruth told her. "Me and Johnny have been paying the mortgage for weeks."

She'd never spoken to her mother like this before, and her stomach was churning like a washing machine. But the baby was her priority now and if her mum didn't like it then she'd have to stay away.

"Go to hell," Rita snarled, pushing past her daughter and stomping back onto the living room. She snatched her bag up off the couch, stuffed her whisky bottle into it and marched out, slamming the front door so hard behind her that it dislodged the horseshoe that was nailed above it, leaving it hanging at an angle.

Superstitious about losing the good luck it had been collecting on her behalf, Ruth grabbed a hammer and put it back where it was supposed to be. Then she tidied the house, and waited for Johnny to come home.

Johnny was thrilled when he heard the news, but felt concerned when Ruth told him about the argument.

"Don't you think you'd best go round and sort it out?" he suggested. "We're rushed off our feet down at the yard, so I won't be able to take any time off to look after you."

"I don't need looking after," Ruth assured him. "And I don't want her here if she's just going to be horrible about it. She didn't even say congratulations when I told her; all she was interested in was getting a drink."

"She's still your mum," Johnny reminded her.

"And I'm this little one's mum," said Ruth, stroking her stomach. "And I'll manage just fine on my own."

It was lonely with nothing but the TV to keep her company, but pride prevented Ruth from calling her mum. And Lisa had got herself a mysterious new boyfriend, so she hardly ever came round any more. And there was no point trying to chat with the neighbours, because they still weren't speaking to her after her drunken verbal attack on old Mrs Dobbs from a few doors down.

So Ruth enrolled herself in an exercise class for expectant mums. And then she borrowed some healthy recipe and Feng Shui books from the library and set about creating the kind of atmosphere in the house that was conducive to a happy, healthy pregnancy and a complication-free birth.

Relieved when she reached and then passed the dreaded four-month milestone, she finally felt brave enough to start buying things for the baby and it wasn't long before the nursery was packed with pretty neutral-coloured stuff.

But just as she'd begun to allow herself to believe that nothing could possibly go wrong, she woke up one morning to find blood on the sheets, and her stomach gripped by the same agonising cramps that she'd felt when the last baby had slipped out.

Back home from the hospital with her womb once again scraped clean, Ruth fell straight back into the pit of despair that she'd not long climbed out of. But this time everybody seemed to think that she would bounce back pretty fast, given that she'd already gone through it twice before. So they carried on as normal, leaving her to deal with the overwhelming grief on her own.

Unable to do that, she started mixing the booze and tablets again, craving the numbness that would rise up through her body when they joined forces and the merciful release when it reached her head, freezing her thoughts and silencing the screaming agony. But it never lasted long enough and, as Ruth's tolerance grew, she was forced to take more and more pills and alcohol to gain the same effect.

When the hallucinations began, there were whole days when she would stay locked in her bedroom, terrified of the insects that she could see crawling all over the floor; petrified by the sound of footsteps pounding up and down the stairs, and the tapping noises on the windows and doors.

She tried to tell Johnny what was happening but, instead of reassuring her like he'd done in the past, he got angry and told her she was imagining things. But Ruth *knew* that the things she was seeing and hearing were real, and Johnny's denials just made her wonder if he was behind it. Maybe he was trying to drive her crazy so that he could get her locked up and be free of her?

It all came to a head when she woke up in a cold sweat one night. Convinced that she could hear whispering coming from the living room below, Ruth slipped out of bed and crept down the stairs, sure that she was going to catch Johnny with another woman. But the house was in darkness, and the curtains were still open — which they wouldn't have been if Johnny had been home, because that was the first thing he always did when he came in: closed the curtains to prevent any passers-by from looking in and seeing him smoking his drugs.

Confused, Ruth switched on the light and reached for the phone.

"Mum . . .?"

"What do you want?" Rita demanded sleepily. "And what do you think you're playing at, waking me up at three o'clock in the flaming morning?"

"I'm scared," Ruth sobbed, swiping at the tears that had started to fall. "Can you come round?"

"Stop being such a baby," Rita barked. "You've had me and your dad running round after you for years, but we've had enough, so get lost!"

Crying hysterically when the phone went dead in her hand, Ruth dropped the receiver onto the floor and dragged herself to her feet. If nobody cared, and they all just wanted to wash their hands of her, she might as well do them all a favour and kill herself.

Dave was pissed off when he turned off Chester Road and walked up Foster Street at 3.30 a.m. It was freezing cold, and his legs were aching. And tonight's pickup had been a complete fuck-up from start to finish, so he hadn't even got paid.

The householder had heard Johnny rooting around for the keys and had come charging downstairs wielding a baseball bat. Luckily, Dave had been parked close enough to the house to see what was happening through the window, so he'd been able to rush in and tackle the cunt before he did any serious damage. But he hadn't gone down without a fight, and they'd been forced to gag him and tie him up before locking him in a cupboard and making their escape with the Jag he'd fought so hard to protect — only for Big Pat to tell them that they could whistle for their money, because

230

there was no way Frankie would pay them for a red-hot motor that he'd now have to get rid of.

To add insult to injury, Johnny had pleaded poverty when Dave had asked him for a loan to pay for a cab home — even though it was Johnny's fault they'd come away empty-handed. And then he'd gone swanning off in the opposite direction, claiming that he'd arranged to meet some bloke — like he thought that Dave was too stupid to have guessed that he was going to see the bird he'd been shagging for the past few months.

Johnny genuinely thought that no one knew about her, but Dave had sussed him from the off. He just didn't know who it was, or why Johnny was being so secretive about it, so he could only assume that his friend didn't trust him any more — which pissed him off almost as much as being forced to walk home after a long, fruitless night.

About to pass Johnny's house now, Dave hesitated when he saw a light on in the living room. He knew there was no way that Ruth would be awake at this time, and Johnny couldn't have beaten him back on foot.

Unless the crafty bastard *had* had the money for a cab, after all?

Furious at the thought that Johnny might have pulled a fast one, Dave shielded his eyes with his hands and peered in through the window. He frowned when he saw Ruth lying on the floor beside the couch and moved to the door. He shouted through the letter box, "Ruth, are you all right? Can you hear me? *Ruth . . .?*"

Getting no response, he pulled out the mobile phone that Frankie had given him when he'd set them on regular nights and tried to call Johnny. But his friend had switched his phone off. Spitting curses through gritted teeth, Dave raced around to the back yard, climbed over the locked gate and pulled the spare key out from under the plant pot below the kitchen window.

"Oh, what have you done, you stupid cow?" he moaned when he ran in and saw the empty tablet bottle lying next to the empty whisky bottle on the floor beside Ruth. "Don't fucking do this to me." He shook her roughly. "*WAKE UP!*"

Ruth groaned and tried to pull away.

"Oh, thank God!" Dave gasped, slipping his hands under her arms and pulling her to her feet. "Come on, let's get you sorted." He dropped Ruth onto the couch and dragged her into a sitting position. "Stay there while I make you a coffee. Then we're going for a walk."

Luckily, there had only been two tablets and less than half a bottle of whisky left, which wasn't enough to do any serious damage, so Ruth came round fairly quickly. But Dave still couldn't leave because he didn't know if she had anything else stashed around the house. And if he left her and she did something stupid he'd never forgive himself. Resigned to having to stay with her until she fell asleep or Johnny came back — whichever happened first — he did what he always did in times of crisis, and rolled a couple of spliffs.

"Here, have some of this." He lit them both and pushed one into Ruth's hand.

"I don't smoke," she murmured, trying to pass it back.

"One spliff ain't gonna hurt you," he insisted. "And, trust me, it'll make you feel better."

In desperate need of *something* to relieve the pain, Ruth took a tentative drag. And then another, and another, until, finally, she relaxed and laid her head on Dave's arm.

"Why are you being so nice?" she asked. "You don't even like me."

"Don't be daft," he lied, taking another drag on his own smoke. "Who told you that?"

"No one needed to tell me," Ruth murmured. "It's obvious. And I don't blame you, 'cos I'm a horrible person."

"Course you're not," he lied again. "You're a very pretty girl."

"But I'm not sexy, though, am I? I can't be, or Johnny wouldn't have gone off me. He hasn't slept with me for ages."

"He's just knackered from all the work your dad's had him doing lately," Dave assured her. "And he's been dead worried about you, so he's probably just waiting for you to get better."

"How am I supposed to get better if I never see him?" Ruth asked. "And where is he, anyway? You work together at night so if you're back, why isn't he?"

"Your, er, dad sent him to see some bloke about something," Dave told her evasively. "Anyhow, never mind that, let's just concentrate on making you feel better, eh?" He flicked the lighter and held it in front of her face until she relit her spliff.

"Do you really think I'm pretty?" Ruth asked after a few more puffs.

"Yeah, course," said Dave, grinning down at her. "Wouldn't have said it if I didn't."

"What about sexy?"

"Yeah, that too."

"Prove it."

"Eh?"

"I said prove it."

Dave resisted when she reached up and tried to pull his face down to hers.

"Aw, now, come on, Ruth, you can't be doing this. I know you're feeling a bit low, but this ain't the answer."

"It is for me," she insisted, her other hand creeping up his thigh.

"What about Johnny?" Dave spluttered, jumping when her nails scraped his crotch. "He's the one you want, not me."

"He doesn't care about me, so why should I care about him?" Ruth murmured, pressing her lips against his.

"Don't." Dave twisted his head to the side. "Johnny's my best mate."

"You want me," Ruth said huskily as she rubbed her hand over the bulge in the front of his pants.

"That's not the point," Dave argued.

"It is for me," whispered Ruth.

234

"Well, it's not for me," he repeated, taking her wrists in his hands to hold her at bay.

Ruth burst into tears. "You hate me, don't you?"

"Don't be daft," he murmured. "Come on, you're knackered — let's get you up to bed."

"Don't leave me," she sobbed, clinging on to him as he helped her to her feet.

"I won't," he promised. "I'll stay right here on the couch till Johnny gets home."

"I'm sorry," Ruth sniffled as she let him lead her upstairs.

"Stop apologising," he chuckled. "Someone might get the wrong idea and think we're mates, or something."

Tucking her in when she slipped under the quilt, he said, "I'll be downstairs, so just shout if you need me."

"Stay with me till I'm asleep," she begged, clutching at his hand. "*Please*."

Sighing, Dave sat down.

CHAPTER
FIFTEEN

Frankie had been feeling rough for a while. Not rough enough to stay off work, but enough to go straight home afterwards for the first time in years. He felt so drained tonight that he could happily have gone to bed and slept for a week. But that wasn't an option, because it was Ruth's birthday and she had invited him and Rita round for dinner.

It had been months since his wife and daughter had spoken to each other and without Ruth to distract her, Rita had been driving Frankie absolutely crazy. She'd taken to ringing him a thousand times a day to ask where he was, what he was doing, and when he was coming home. And the constant interruptions were starting to piss off his mistress, so he was getting earache from her as well as from Rita — all of which he could do without.

Determined to get them back on course tonight if it killed him, Frankie took a shower and climbed into the clothes that Rita had laid out on the bed for him. Then, after throwing a couple of painkillers down his throat, he hustled Rita into the car and set off.

★   ★   ★

Over at the Conroys' house, as he got ready for the dinner Johnny was equally as eager for Ruth and her mum to settle their differences — and for almost the same reason as Frankie.

He liked Lisa, and the sex was fantastic, but it was becoming increasingly difficult to keep up the double life now that Ruth was back on her feet and he no longer had an excuse not to have sex with her. And while shagging two women had never been a problem before he'd got married, now he had the added worry not only of Ruth and Frankie finding out, but Dave as well.

Dave wasn't stupid. He knew there was another girl on the scene and was constantly asking Johnny who she was. But Johnny couldn't tell him, because mates weren't supposed to shag each other's exes — especially not when they knew that their mate still had feelings for the girl. Lisa might have made it clear to Dave that they were never going to get back together but that didn't stop Dave from hoping, and he was always banging on about her to Johnny. If he found out that his mate was the real reason why Lisa wouldn't entertain him, all hell would break loose — and Johnny was scared that he might even be pissed off enough to tell Frankie out of spite.

And, since she'd decided to tell Johnny that she loved him, Lisa was just as much of a threat. As Johnny knew only too well from bitter past experience, love-struck women were more than capable of doing something stupid to get revenge if a man tried to break up with them. So he was stuck with her. And that was why it was so important for Ruth and her mum to kiss and make up tonight: because then Rita might start staying over again, and that would cut down his and Ruth's "alone time".

He hoped.

Ruth had spent the whole day cooking. She'd made her dad's favourite honey-basted lamb, crispy roast potatoes, carrots, peas, and gravy; and sherry trifle for dessert. And, to keep her mum happy, she'd bought a bottle of her favourite whisky.

Excited now when she heard the distinctive roar of her dad's car pulling up outside, she lit the candles on the dining table and switched off the overhead light before rushing to the door.

"Thanks for coming." She stepped out and gave her mum a hug. "It's good to see you."

"You'd have seen me months ago if you weren't too stubborn to apologise," Rita sniped. "And now I'm here, I'm not sure I want to come in," she added huffily. "We all know what a moody little so-and-so you are these days, and I don't want to come in if you're just going to tell me to get straight back out again."

"Shut up," Frankie ordered as he climbed wearily out of the car. He slammed the door shut and gave Ruth a kiss. "Happy birthday, love."

"Thanks," she said, waving them inside. "Dinner's ready, so go straight through to the dining room."

"Dining room," Rita repeated scathingly under her breath. "And I suppose we'll be having canapes in the conservatory an' all, will we?"

238

"Pack it in," Frankie warned her when Ruth went through to the kitchen. "This is our daughter's night, and you'd best not ruin it after she's gone to all this effort."

Rita sniffed and sat down without saying another word.

"All right, son?" Frankie held out his hand when Johnny walked in.

"Yeah, fine." Johnny shook it. Then, nodding at Rita, he said, "Good to see you, Mrs H. How are you doing?"

"I'd be better if I hadn't been bullied into coming round here," Rita replied huffily. "And I wouldn't mind, but I haven't even been offered a drink yet."

"It's behind you. Help yourself," said Ruth as she carried the lamb in on a tray, nodding at the whisky bottle that was standing on the bookshelf. "Will you carve, Dad?"

Frankie glanced at Johnny. "Shouldn't the man of the house be doing it?"

"You *always* do the lamb," Ruth said coquettishly. "Anyway, I need Johnny to help me with the veg."

"Got him running round after you like a right little sap, haven't you?" Rita scoffed, pouring herself a half-glass of neat Scotch.

It shot to the tip of Ruth's tongue to say that men who loved their wives were supposed to help, and not just sit there and let them do everything. But she kept her mouth shut and smiled. This was a special night, and she wasn't about to let her mother spoil it.

When everything was on the table, Ruth handed a bottle of wine to Johnny and asked him to fill all their glasses. Then, sitting down, she reached for hers and said, "Thanks for coming, Mum and Dad. But I didn't just invite you because it's my birthday. I've got something to share with you."

"Don't tell us you're getting divorced?" Rita blurted out gleefully.

"Don't be ridiculous," said Ruth, flashing Johnny an *as if* smile.

"Just shut up and let her talk," Frankie groaned.

His voice sounded weird and Johnny frowned when he noticed how pale his face was. "Are you all right, Frankie?" he asked.

"Fine," his father-in-law murmured.

But he clearly wasn't, and Ruth forgot what she'd been about to say. "What's the matter, Dad? Don't you feel well?"

"He's got a bug," Rita informed her, adding accusingly, "I told him not to come, 'cos I know you'd get uppity about him passing his germs around. But you insisted, so it's your own fault if you catch it."

"There's nothing wrong with me," Frankie insisted, scraping his chair back. "Just need to —"

"Oh my God!" Ruth yelped, jumping up when he keeled over and fell heavily to the floor. "Dad! *Dad!*"

Johnny rushed to Frankie and pressed a hand to his forehead. Frankie looked as though he was burning up, but his skin was cold and clammy and his breathing sounded laboured.

240

"I'm calling an ambulance," Johnny said as he ran into the living room.

Unconcerned, Rita reached for her glass and said, "Stop being so melodramatic. He's only fainted. He'll come round in a minute."

"You really are a *bitch*," Ruth hissed, kneeling beside her father and glaring up at her mother.

Rita glared right back. "Watch your mouth, lady. You're not too big to get knocked right back down off that pedestal you've put yourself up on."

"It's coming," Johnny said, running back in. "Any change?"

"No," said Ruth, still angrily eyeballing her mother. "No change at all."

By the time the paramedics arrived, Rita had finished her first drink and was halfway through her second. Too drunk to care by then, she switched on the TV and settled down in Johnny's chair to watch it, leaving her daughter and son-in-law to go along to the hospital in her place.

Ruth cried all the way, as scared by the fact that they had the full flashing lights and sirens going as by the fact that her dad still hadn't come round. She wanted to stay by his side when they rushed him into the emergency department, but a nurse blocked her path and ushered her gently but firmly back out into the reception area. She told Ruth that she needed to go and give her father's details in at the desk, and assured her that somebody would come out to see her as soon as they had assessed him.

Ruth complained bitterly but she did as she'd been told. Then she paced the waiting-room floor, biting her nails and staring at the door every time anybody went in or came out.

Johnny was already tired but Ruth's pacing and the stressful vibes she was throwing off exhausted him, so he took himself off into a quiet corner, put his feet up and closed his eyes. But no sooner had he dropped off than a doctor came out to tell them what was going on.

"Your father's had a heart attack," he told Ruth gravely but simply. "And we think he may have suffered a stroke as well, although we'll need to do some more tests to confirm this. In the meantime, I'm having him transferred to the ICU where he'll be closely monitored."

"Can I see him?" Ruth asked, a fresh flood of tears streaming down her cheeks.

"For a couple of minutes," the doctor agreed. "He's conscious, but only just. And please try not to upset him; we need to keep him as calm as possible."

Frankie was surrounded by machinery when Ruth and Johnny entered the resuscitation room. There were wires trailing all over him, and pads stuck to his grey-haired chest. Johnny looked at him as Ruth sat on the chair beside the bed and clutched her father's hand. Frankie looked a good twenty or thirty years older than when he'd arrived at the house a few short hours earlier, and that made Johnny wonder just how ill he really was. The doctor had

242

kept it light, but he had to be worried if he was sending Frankie to intensive care.

"Trust you to go and ruin my birthday," Ruth scolded her dad softly. "All day I've been cooking that flaming lamb, but you couldn't just say you didn't fancy it, could you? No, you had to go and make a big scene and get yourself rushed into hospital. But don't think you've got away with it, 'cos I'll be putting it in the freezer when I get back, and I'll be serving it up again when you come home. Do you hear me?"

Frankie made a noise and gave her hand a weak squeeze.

"Oh, Dad," she gulped, getting teary all over again.

"Hey, you can pack that right in," said Johnny, coming up behind her and resting his hand on her shoulder. He grinned down at Frankie and shook his head. "What's she like, eh? I've just heard the doc telling her that you're fine — now here she is going on like you're on your deathbed, or something."

"*Johnny!*" Ruth gasped, appalled that he'd mentioned the D word. She winced when he dug his fingers into her shoulder. Then she realised what he was doing and forced a smile onto her lips. "Sorry, Dad, didn't mean to sound so gloomy, but you know what I'm like. You say it's a spot of rain, I call it a thunderstorm."

A nurse came into the room and smiled apologetically. "Sorry, folks, you'll have to say your goodbyes. We're ready to take him up to ICU."

"Come on." Johnny reached for Ruth's hand and pulled her to her feet. Winking at Frankie, he said, "Don't be taking the mick and stopping in here any longer than you have to, 'cos there's no way I can handle the pair of them for more than two days. Okay?"

Frankie gave a slow blink in reply.

A porter came to move the bed.

"Just a minute." Ruth pulled her hand free of Johnny's and leaned over her dad. "I didn't tell you my news."

"Can't it wait?" Johnny asked, conscious that the nurse was keen to get things moving.

"No." Ruth shook her head. She grasped her dad's hand again and smiled through her tears. "I'm pregnant," she told him. "You're going to be a grandad."

"You what?" Johnny gave her a questioning look. "Really?"

Ruth nodded.

"Wow, that's great," he said, hugging her. "Do you feel okay?"

"Fantastic," she told him truthfully.

Frankie made a noise and Johnny saw his hand move weakly. Realising that his father-in-law was gesturing for him to come closer, he leaned down.

Frankie swallowed loudly and tried to say something. A frustrated look came into his eyes when he couldn't get it out, but he didn't give up.

"Look after them for me," he managed after a moment.

"Course I will," Johnny promised. Then he added quietly, "But you'll be home before you know it. Then you can do it yourself."

Frankie held his gaze for several long seconds, then gave a feeble wave of his hand. Aware that they were being dismissed, Johnny put his arm around Ruth and took her home.

CHAPTER
SIXTEEN

Frankie suffered another stroke during the night and the family were called back to the hospital in the early hours to say their goodbyes. Against the odds, he pulled through — but not without losing the use of the entire left side of his body. His speech was also affected, but his mind was clearly intact, and the frustration at not being able to make himself understood blazed from his eyes as he tried to grunt his wishes to Johnny.

When Big Pat turned up later in the morning, he greeted Rita and Ruth and then pulled Johnny to one side to ask how the boss was really doing.

"Not too good," Johnny told him honestly, thinking that there was no point trying to put a positive gloss on it. "But he got through the worst of it, so he's obviously stronger than he looks. Don't worry, we'll look after him," he added, giving the big man's arm a reassuring squeeze. Pat and Frankie had been friends for a long time, and this had to be hard for him.

They both glanced back at Frankie. Ruth was sitting beside the bed holding his hand, a forced brightness in her voice as she chattered to him. But Rita had taken herself into a corner, and was clearly more interested in whatever she was doing with her mobile phone than she was in her husband. Frankie's gaze, however, was fixed firmly on Big Pat, and when their eyes met Pat gave a slight nod before turning back to Johnny.

"Come out here for a minute," he said quietly. "We need to talk."

Johnny followed him out and closed the door. "What's up?" he asked, folding his arms.

"The boss hasn't been feeling right for a while," Big Pat told him. "He didn't say anything to you lot 'cos he didn't know if it was serious or not. But he's been making plans — just in case. And he's just given me the go-ahead."

"Go-ahead for what?" Johnny asked, wondering how Frankie could have told him anything when he couldn't even talk.

"Handing over the reins," said Big Pat. "To you."

"Eh?" Shocked, Johnny drew his head back and gave him a disbelieving look. "What are you talking about?"

"He wants you to take over." Big Pat spelled it out. "Just until he's up and running again. If that don't happen . . ." He shrugged. "Well, we'll just have to take it from there."

Johnny exhaled loudly. This was completely unexpected, and he wasn't sure how he felt about it. He and Frankie had been rubbing along all right, but he'd had no clue that his father-in-law saw him as anything more than a capable car-valeter and picker-upper, so he was stunned to realise that Frankie considered him worthy of stepping into his shoes.

"How come he didn't ask you to do it?" he mused. Johnny was sure that Big Pat would make a much better job of it, given that he'd been involved in the business from the off and knew everything there was to know about it.

"I'm not family," Big Pat replied — sounding almost regretful, Johnny thought. "But I'm the next best thing," he added loyally, "and if you take it on, I'll have your back just like I've had his all these years."

Johnny glanced back through the window. Frankie was staring back intently at him, waiting for an answer. Johnny breathed in deeply and nodded.

"Okay, I'll do it. But only till he's back on his feet."

"Good lad." Big Pat gave Johnny approving slap on the shoulder before pushing his cuff back and checking the time. "Right, I'd best get over to the yard. Let me know when you're ready and I'll call everyone together for a meet."

"Everyone?" Johnny frowned. As far as he knew, the business consisted of Frankie, Big Pat and the guy who helped him to prep the cars, Johnny and Dave, and — when they weren't locked up or injured — Del and Robbie.

"Not here." Big Pat glanced around warily. "I'll gen you up later." He extended his hand now. "Call me if there's any change."

Johnny promised that he would and waved him off before going back into the room. He looked down at Frankie and, seeing what looked like relief in his eyes, squeezed his useless hand.

"I'll do my best by you," he said quietly. "You've got my word on that."

"What are you saying?" Rita demanded. "And what were you and Big Pat whispering about out there?"

Johnny glanced down at Frankie again. If he was to prove that he was capable of running things in his father-in-law's absence, he guessed he should start as he meant to go on.

"Nothing for you to worry about," he said, using the words that he'd heard Frankie use so many times when she had been questioning him.

Ruth snapped her head around and gaped up at Johnny in amazement. But she didn't censure him, he noticed.

"How dare you!" Rita bristled. "Don't think you can get away with talking to me like that just because Frankie's out of action. I'm the head of this family now, and you'd better remember your place or you'll be out on your arse like *that*." She snapped her fingers in Johnny's face.

"No, he won't," said Ruth, standing up to show that she was on her husband's side. "Johnny's his son-in-law, so that makes him next in line."

"And I'm his wife," Rita reminded her furiously. "And everything's mine if he dies. Not yours, and definitely not his. *Mine*. And now he's lost his mind," she went on, as if Frankie had lost the power of hearing as well as speech, "I'm going to get a court order putting *me* in charge of the business, the bank accounts, the house — everything."

Frankie made a loud grunting noise, and they all turned to look at him. Rita tutted after a second and carried on with the argument.

"I've already phoned the solicitor, and —"

"Shut up!" Ruth barked at her. "I'm trying to hear what my dad's saying."

"Sounds like *gagaga* to me," sneered Rita.

"Shut your mouth, or I'll shut it for you," Ruth warned her.

Rita's mouth flapped open, but she wisely held back the retort that had jumped to the tip of her tongue when she saw the look in her daughter's eyes. There was anger there, and hatred — both of which she'd seen many times before. But there was also an unfamiliar strength, as if a volcano had been building inside Ruth for a lifetime and was a hairsbreadth away from erupting.

"I'm not staying here to be spoken to like this," Rita muttered, raising her chin proudly and snatching her handbag off the chair. "I'm going home."

"I'll see you later, then," Ruth called after her as she marched to the door. "And you'd best clear all that junk out of our room, 'cos we're moving back in."

Rita stopped in her tracks. "Over my dead body."

"I'm not arguing about it," Ruth told her firmly. "Dad needs looking after, and you obviously can't be trusted seeing as you've already as good as written him off, so it'll have to be me."

"We'll talk about this later," Johnny murmured, in total agreement with Rita — over *his* dead body would he live with that bitch again.

"I'm sorry, I know I should have discussed it with you first," Ruth apologised quietly. "But I can't leave him with *her*. It's not permanent, just until he's better.

And you *will* get better," she said with conviction, turning back to her father. "'Cos we need you."

"He'll be fine," said Johnny, putting his arms around her when her tears began to fall.

"I need to do this," Ruth sobbed. "But our house is too small, so it's got to be there. Please don't say no."

Johnny sighed and looked down at Frankie. "Is that what you want?"

"What are you asking him for?" squawked Rita. "I'm the one you should be asking, and I say no."

Ignoring her when he read the affirmative in Frankie's eyes, Johnny turned back to Ruth and said, "I'll sort it out."

"Thank you," she murmured, as if it could never have gone ahead without his say-so.

It was strange for Johnny to know that he was in control, and he needed to get out of there so that he could get his head around it in peace.

"I'm going to pop down to the yard and sort some stuff out," he told Ruth. "Will you be all right making your own way home?"

"I'll stay with Dad for a bit," she said, dabbing at her nose with a tissue. Then, reaching up, she kissed Johnny on the lips and whispered, "I love you."

Johnny nodded and made his way off the ward and out into the bright morning sunlight.

It had been a long night, and it was starting to catch up on him. His eyes were burning, and his legs felt heavy. He just wanted to go home, climb into bed, and stay there for the rest of the day.

But that was what the old Johnny would have done, and he had responsibilities now. Frankie had entrusted the business and the family to him, and he had to step up to the mark like the man that Frankie obviously believed he could be.

CHAPTER
SEVENTEEN

When Frankie was discharged from hospital a few weeks later, he was brought home to an invalid-friendly house. In his absence, Johnny, Big Pat and Dave had transformed the front room which had previously been used as a dining room into a bedroom, and the large hall closet into a wheelchair-accessible toilet cum wet room. They had also redecorated all over to cheer the place up, and had laid new laminate flooring in the hall to make it easier for Frankie's chair to be wheeled around.

Still sulking, having found out that Frankie had visited his solicitor a few weeks before falling ill and had put Johnny in control of everything, Rita had refused to lift a finger while the alterations were going on and had stayed locked in the parlour with her booze.

Which suited Ruth just fine, because it gave her free rein to look after her dad without interference when he came home, and get the house just so for when the baby arrived.

Big Pat, in the meantime, had brought Johnny up to speed on the true nature and extent of Frankie's business dealings — and Johnny had been shocked by what he'd learned.

He'd always known that the car lot was a front for the stolen motors, but he'd had no clue that Frankie was also dealing drugs and running a protection racket from there. All the men he'd seen traipsing in and out when he'd been a lowly car-washer — the ones he'd always wondered about, because they never even looked at the cars — they were dealers coming to drop off money and pick up their next batch, or heavies come to deliver the takings from whichever clubs and pubs they had collected from the night before. And on top of all that, Frankie had stakes in two massage parlours — both of which were actually brothels.

Johnny couldn't understand why Frankie had taken the risk of doing all this from the yard — or how he'd been getting away with it for so long. Money was pouring in hand over fist, but with so many people involved it would only take one of them to open their mouths and the whole thing would explode. And while Frankie's reputation had most likely been the zip that had so far kept everyone's mouths shut, once they realised that he was no longer a threat who knew what could happen?

Johnny's most pressing concern was the large quantities of cannabis that seemed to be routinely stored at the yard. He'd seen enough busts while living on the estate to know how the police operated, and one of the major flag-ups was a continuous stream of people going in and out of a place. And while it was perfectly normal for a business to have a large volume of visitors on any given day, it *wasn't* normal that none of those visitors ever actually bought anything.

"We need a total clear-out," he told Big Pat decisively. "The yard is the only legitimate thing Frankie's got going for him, so it needs to be squeaky clean and operating properly."

"It works fine the way it is," Big Pat argued, afraid that this boy was going to fuck everything up if he was left to his own inexperienced devices.

"If Frankie wants to turn everything around when he's back on his feet, that's his business," Johnny said firmly. "But while I'm in charge, things are going to be done my way. And if you don't like it, maybe you should think about bowing out till he's back at the helm."

There were several long moments of silence after he said that when Johnny felt sure that Big Pat was going to jump up and kick the shit out of him to put him back in his place. So he was relieved when the man nodded, and said, "Okay, you're the boss. Tell me what you want me to do."

Once Johnny had the bit between his teeth, things moved pretty quickly. He shifted the drug operation into a nearby flat, and set up one of Frankie's most trusted dealers to run it. And then he rented a dingy little backstreet garage so that Big Pat and his mechanic mate, Jeff, could deal with the stolen motors away from the legit ones. Then he hired a couple of lads from the estate who Dave had known and trusted since they were kids and put them on the pickups, while he and Dave got the yard properly up and running.

It was ambitious and expensive putting his plans into action, but Johnny was so deeply immersed in his new role by then that he decided to just go for it — and deal with the fallout when or *if* Frankie ever recovered enough to take over again.

CHAPTER
EIGHTEEN

Johnny was at work when he got the call to say that Ruth's waters had broken.

"Give her my love," Dave called as Johnny rushed out and jumped into his car. "And good luck!"

Johnny waved and tore out of the yard.

Nine hours of screaming and shouting later, his ears were ringing and his nerves were completely shredded. But it was all forgotten in an instant when the midwife placed his daughter in his arms. And when she opened her eyes and gazed blurrily up into his, he fell head over heels in love.

"Is she okay?" Ruth asked sleepily.

"Absolutely perfect," the midwife assured her with a smile. "What are you going to call her?"

"Rebecca," said Ruth — at exactly the same time as Johnny said, "Angel."

"I thought we agreed it was going to be Rebecca," Ruth reminded him.

"That was before I saw her," Johnny said, stroking a fingertip down the soft, peachy little cheek. "She looks like an angel, so that's what she should be called."

Too tired to argue, Ruth waved her hand in a gesture of surrender.

"Hello, Angel Conroy," Johnny cooed. "I'm your daddy."

A bitter wave of jealousy washed over Ruth when she saw the way he was looking at the baby. They had been married for almost three years, and she loved him more with every passing day. But even in their most intimate moments he had never looked at *her* like that. There was a pure, soul-deep love shining from his eyes, and in that moment Ruth realised that, even if she were with him from now till kingdom come, Johnny's feelings for her would never come close to what he already felt for his daughter.

PART TWO

CHAPTER
NINETEEN

Angel was an exceptionally pretty baby, and Ruth couldn't take her out without somebody stopping to peek into the pram and comment on her white-blonde hair and enormous sapphire-blue eyes. And it was even worse at home.

Johnny was still so busy at work that Ruth was lucky if she saw him from one day to the next, but when he *did* come home she didn't get a look-in because he only had eyes for Angel. And it was already becoming obvious that Angel adored him every bit as much. Ruth was the one who fed her, bathed her, changed her nappies and made sure that her little bottom didn't get sore. But Angel didn't appreciate any of that. All she cared about was Johnny: she would twist her head whenever she heard his voice, and her eyes would light up with delight whenever he went near her.

Ruth hated her. She couldn't help it. She'd thought that a baby would bring her and Johnny closer together but, instead, it had just driven an even bigger wedge between them. And she wasn't the only one who had noticed.

"Still think he's ever going to love you?" Rita gloated as Ruth sat in the parlour one day, watching enviously as Johnny played with the baby in the back garden. "You can't even compete with a snivelling little brat. But, like they say, what goes around comes around. You destroyed my marriage making goo-goo eyes at your father, and now you're getting a taste of your own medicine."

"What are you talking about?" Ruth glowered at her. "I never made goo-goo eyes at my dad."

"You still do it now," spat Rita. "Always in there, messing about with him. God only knows what the pair of you get up to behind my back."

"You're disgusting."

"And you're stupid. You tricked your precious husband into getting wed 'cos you thought he'd learn to love you. But take a good long look at the pair of them, 'cos they're the only two people he's ever going to love — himself and *her*."

Ruth got up and marched into the kitchen. She felt sick. Her mother had wrecked her own marriage by being a foul-mouthed alcoholic, but Ruth hadn't put a foot wrong in hers. She'd tried to be the perfect wife, giving Johnny everything his heart could possibly desire, and yet still he didn't love her. Now here he was, doting on a baby who had given him absolutely nothing. It wasn't fair.

Johnny came in a short time later.

"I think she needs changing," he said, handing Angel over to Ruth.

"You know where the nappies are," she replied, holding the baby at arm's length.

"You what?" Johnny frowned as if she'd just suggested that he should go and wipe her dad's arse, or something.

"Nothing," Ruth muttered.

"Shit, I didn't realise it was that late," Johnny said when he clocked the time. "Is my bath run?"

"No, I forgot," said Ruth, dumping Angel in her pram and wiping her hands on her skirt.

"I told you I was going out," he complained. "What've you been doing?"

"Looking after my dad. Sorry, I'll do it now."

"Forget it, I'll do it myself."

Ruth gritted her teeth when Johnny left the kitchen and snatched a nappy out from under the pram. Angel's chin wobbled when Ruth yanked her tights off roughly, and she started bawling.

"Oh, for God's sake," Ruth hissed, bouncing the pram up and down. "Just shut up, you little bitch!"

When Angel's crying got louder, Ruth reached into the pram and pinched her leg. Angel sucked in a sharp breath and momentarily stopped crying. But when she started up again, she was more hysterical than ever.

Johnny had forgotten his mobile phone. He came back down to get it, and frowned when he walked in to find Angel screaming.

"What's wrong with her?" he asked as he walked over to the pram.

"I don't know," Ruth lied, letting her hair fall over her face so that he wouldn't see her guilty blush.

"Hey, what's all this noise?" Johnny cooed, leaning over and tickling Angel's tummy. He hesitated when he saw the red spot on her leg, and peered at it closely. "What's that?"

"What?" Ruth asked innocently.

"This." Johnny traced his fingertip over the welt.

"No idea." Ruth shrugged and looked down at it with a frown of concern. "Looks like an insect bite. Did you put her on the grass?"

"Yeah, but not for long," Johnny admitted guiltily. He picked Angel out of the pram and held her against his chest to comfort her. "Don't cry, baby," he soothed, kissing her hot wet cheek. "Daddy's sorry."

Angel's crying gradually quietened, and she relaxed against him, sniffling softly.

"She's wiped," he told Ruth. "Maybe you should feed her and put her down."

"I'll get a bottle," Ruth said, sidestepping him when he tried to hand Angel back to her.

"Bottle?" Johnny frowned. "I thought *you* were feeding her."

Which just shows how much attention you really pay to what's going on around here, thought Ruth peevishly. She'd stopped giving Angel the breast weeks ago.

"I was having trouble getting her to latch on," she told him. "So the health visitor told me to switch her to the bottle in case she wasn't getting enough."

"Oh, well, I suppose she knows best," Johnny conceded. He placed Angel gently back in the pram, took his phone out of his jacket pocket and went back up to his bath.

264

Ruth changed Angel's nappy, made the bottle and pulled a chair up to the pram. Lifting the baby out, she held her in her arms and slid the teat into her mouth. A wave of guilt washed over her as she gazed down into the teary eyes, and a tear slid down her own cheek.

"I'm sorry," she whispered. "I didn't mean to hurt you."

And she meant it. But it didn't stop her from doing it again.

"That baby's doing my flaming head in," Rita complained a few weeks later. "It's that idiot husband of yours's fault 'cos he's spoiling her bloody rotten. You need to put a stop to it, or you're going to regret it in the long run. It's not natural."

"I can't tell him not to play with her," Ruth replied defensively, all too aware of why Angel cried whenever Johnny left: because he was the only one who was ever nice to her. But the more the child gravitated towards him, the more Ruth resented her, so it was a vicious circle.

Rita reached for the remote and turned the volume of the TV up to a deafening level. Drumming her fingernails on the arm of her chair, she stared at the screen for several seconds, then snapped, "Oh, for God's sake! I've had enough of this. I can't get any peace in my own flaming house."

"I'll sort it," Ruth told her, getting up.

"Make sure you do," Rita warned as Ruth made her way to the door. "'Cos if you don't, I will."

Ruth's nostrils were flaring with irritation as she stomped up the stairs. As usual, Angel had started crying as soon as Johnny had tired of playing with her and put her down, and Ruth had tried everything to shut her up. She'd given her a bottle and bathed her, but that hadn't worked, so she'd dumped her in her cot and shut the door on her. But her high-pitched wailing still filtered out and echoed all over the house.

She walked into Angel's room now and gripped the cot rail. Angel's face was scarlet, her toothless mouth wide and quivering, her eyes a watery mess.

"Shut up," Ruth hissed, glaring down at her. But the sound of her voice just seemed to make Angel cry all the more, so she put her hand over her daughter's mouth — and held it there for several long seconds.

The child stopped squirming. Snapping to her senses, Ruth gaped down at Angel in terror.

"Oh, God, what have I done?" she gasped, snatching her out of the cot and shaking her. "Wake up, Angel, please wake up!"

Angel gulped in a quivering breath and started crying again. Her whole body shaking with relief, Ruth held the child against her chest and patted her on the back, whispering, "Ssshh, baby . . . ssshh, ssshh, ssshh."

Exhausted, Angel eventually fell asleep. Terrified to think that she had almost killed her, Ruth laid her gently back in the cot. The sheet felt damp, so she took another one out of the drawer and covered her with it. Then she sat down on the chair and cried.

Anyone who came into this nursery would think that Angel was the luckiest baby alive. The drawers were neatly stacked with freshly washed sheets and baby clothes, and the walls were painted in pretty pastel shades, and decorated with jolly murals of nursery-rhyme characters. And Ruth had done it all — like a good mother was supposed to. So why couldn't she actually *be* a good mother?

I'm going to change, she vowed for the hundredth time. *This stops now.*

CHAPTER
TWENTY

Frankie passed away a week before Angel turned six but the funeral was held on her actual birthday, so the child was pretty much overlooked while Johnny and Ruth concentrated on giving her grandfather a lavish send-off.

As befitted the big man Frankie had once been, they had spared no expense. Four black stretch limousines were booked to ferry the relatives from the house to the church to the cemetery and back, and an ornate glass-sided carriage and four black horses were lined up to parade Frankie through the streets in his super-expensive black-ash coffin.

Every living member of the Hynes family had come from all over to pay their respects, and the house was bursting at the seams by the time the wake kicked off on the night before the funeral — with Frankie in his open coffin taking centre stage in the front room.

First thing in the morning, Ruth cleared the whisky and Guinness bottles out of the coffin and wiped the lipstick marks off her dad's waxy cheeks, before rooting around for the cigar that an uncle had placed between Frankie's unresponsive lips the night before and which had mysteriously disappeared. Finding it underneath him, as if he'd concealed it to smoke in peace when the dust had settled, she brushed the ash off his suit and then carefully applied some make-up to give him the glow that he'd favoured in life. Then, as a final touch, she arranged his freshly dyed hair back into the quiff he'd always worn and kissed him goodbye before tearfully allowing the undertakers to secure the lid.

All of which should really have fallen to Rita but she was already half-cut, having started drinking even before she donned her widow's weeds, so Ruth had gladly taken on the task.

The parade kicked off once the rest of the mourners had arrived. After a slow walk through the local streets, followed by a full Catholic service at the church where Ruth and Johnny had been married, the cortege escorted Frankie on his final ride to the cemetery before making their way back to the house to continue the party in his honour.

Angel didn't understand any of it.

She hadn't really known her grandpa, because she'd been forbidden from going into his room on her own when he'd been alive. Not that she'd have gone in even if she had been allowed to, because she'd been scared of him on the occasions when she'd been forced to see him — usually on his birthday or at Christmas. He was old and grey, and he smelled bad. But it was the horrible noises he made when he tried to talk that had really frightened her.

Although nobody else seemed to have been frightened of him. Her mum, dad, and the big bear man used to smile and act as if they understood what he was saying, while her nan tended to shout at him — and everyone knew that you didn't shout at people you were scared of. You kept your mouth shut and stayed out of their way — like Angel had long ago learned to do with her mum and her nan.

Her nan wasn't crying today, but everybody else was, and it confused Angel to see so many strangers wailing, and going on about how much they were going to miss her grandpa. She couldn't help but wonder why they had never come to see him when he was alive if they loved him as much as they claimed to. But her mum really *was* upset, so she couldn't ask her about it. And she couldn't ask her dad, either, because he was too busy running around making sure that everybody's glass stayed full — even though Angel thought that they'd all had more than enough already. She'd seen her mum and her nan drunk often enough to know what it looked like, and it was never good, because they always ended up arguing and crying.

Angel was sitting quietly in a corner of the front room when Dave arrived later that afternoon. As a mark of respect, Johnny had closed the yard for the day. But only to the public, so Dave had still had to go in and do all his usual paperwork. He glanced around when he walked in now, and nodded hello to Ruth, Rita and Lisa who were across the room chatting to some female relatives while a clearly distraught Big Pat was being consoled by some elderly ladies in another corner. The men were standing around in groups, drinking and loudly reminiscing, while Johnny flitted between them topping up their glasses.

270

When he spotted Angel sitting by herself, Dave went over and squatted down in front of her.

"Hello, birthday girl. How you doing?"

"Fine, thank you," she replied, pulling her skirt demurely down over her knees.

Dave felt the same tug of sadness that he always felt when he looked into her huge, sombre eyes. His sister's kid, Kayleigh, wasn't half as pretty, but she was as vain as a little peacock as a result of all the compliments she received. And that was the way it should be if you were one of the lucky ones who'd been blessed with beauty. But Angel was the quietest, most unassuming kid he'd ever met, and that didn't seem right somehow.

Still, she was Johnny's kid not his, and he had no right to judge his friend's parenting skills — not when he knew that Angel would probably be as loud and as rude as his sister's lot if she had been his.

"Food looks good," Dave said, eyeing the loaded table. "Have you had anything to eat yet?"

When Angel shook her head, he said, "Wait there," and pushed himself back up to his feet. He took a couple of paper plates off the pile and walked from one end of the table to the other, loading one with savouries, the other with stuff that he thought a six-year-old girl would like — mainly cakes and biscuits, with a couple of mini sausage rolls for good measure.

"Thank you," Angel said when Dave came back and passed her plate to her.

"You're welcome," he said, sitting beside her and tucking in. A couple of sandwiches later, when he glanced at her and noticed that she hadn't even touched her food, he nudged her. "You are supposed to eat it, not just look at it, you know."

Angel smiled politely and nibbled on a fairy cake. She liked her Uncle Dave. He was funny, and he always made a point of talking to her when everybody else was too busy. But her mum and her nan didn't really approve of him, so she hoped he would move away before they noticed them sitting together and got mad at her.

Johnny only realised that Dave was here when he was on his way out to the kitchen to get some more alcohol.

"All right, mate," he said. "Didn't see you come in. How long have you been here?"

"Not long," Dave told him, putting his plate down and wiping his palms on his trousers before shaking Johnny's hand. "You were busy, so I thought I'd have a little chat with the birthday girl."

Johnny looked down at Angel and gave her a regretful smile. "Not been much of a birthday so far, has it, darlin'? But you know I'll make it up to you, don't you?"

Angel nodded, her eyes lighting up for the first time all day.

"Don't worry, I've been keeping her company," Dave assured him. "We've been having a little picnic."

"Cheers, mate." Johnny clapped him gratefully on the back. "I should have checked on her but I've been run off my feet all day. Anyhow, come and give us a hand getting some more booze for these greedy

272

dickheads," he went on quietly. "And I've got a bit of white, if you're up for it?"

"Cool." Forgetting all about Angel and their so-called picnic, Dave abandoned his plate and followed Johnny out.

Angel felt sad as she watched them go. Her dad was her sun, her moon, and all the stars in between, and she wished that he wasn't always so busy. But her mum was always reminding her that his work was more important than she was, so she had to stop being selfish and just be grateful that at least he'd been home today.

Her Aunt Lisa came over.

"Hey, babe, you okay?" she asked as she sat down on Dave's vacated chair.

Angel smiled and nodded. Lisa wasn't her real aunt — she was actually her second cousin. But it was respectful to call older people aunt or uncle, so that was what Angel had always known her as.

"God, my feet are killing me after all that walking," Lisa complained, slipping off her shoes and rubbing at her soles. "But I suppose it's my own fault for wearing heels. Should have been sensible like your mum and worn flats."

"They're pretty," Angel murmured, glancing down at the strappy black sandals.

"Yeah, but the better they look, the more they hurt you," said Lisa, gazing wistfully at the door through which Johnny had left and thinking that that went double for men.

Johnny still hadn't been to see her since her Uncle Frankie had died, even though he must have known how upset she'd be. And while she understood that it must have been difficult for him to get away, given that he'd had to arrange the funeral and everything, it had cut her up to think that he'd been here, giving comfort to that fat bitch cousin of hers instead.

"Mine hurt as well," Angel said quietly.

"Sorry?" Lisa snapped her head around. "What hurts, babe?"

"My shoes." Angel lifted her foot.

Wincing when she saw the blister on the back of the child's heel, Lisa said, "Ooh, that looks painful. You need a plaster on that. Does your mummy still keep them in the kitchen cupboard?" When Angel nodded, Lisa said, "Stay there, I'll go and get one."

Across the room, Ruth jumped to her feet when she noticed her cousin heading for the door. Johnny had just gone out there, and she didn't want the sneaky tart cosying up to him. Not that it would get her anywhere, because Johnny had always said that he wouldn't go near Lisa if she was the last woman on Earth. But that wouldn't stop her from trying, and Ruth wasn't having that.

Lisa was already on her way back from the kitchen when Ruth marched out into the hall. "Are you all right?" she asked when she saw the angry look on Ruth's face.

"I'm looking for Johnny," Ruth told her. "Have you seen him?"

"He wasn't in the kitchen." Lisa gave an innocent shrug. "Probably nipped out with Dave to have a fag. I just went to get this." She held up the Elastoplast. "Angel's got a massive blister on the back of her foot."

"Oh," Ruth murmured, a little ashamed that she hadn't noticed it herself. But it wasn't easy to think about the small stuff when you'd just buried your father. Anyway, Angel had a mouth. If it was that bad, she should have said something.

"How are you bearing up?" Lisa asked now, giving her cousin a concerned look. "We haven't had much of a chance to talk, what with the aunts rabbiting on, but I'm in bits, so it must be ten times worse for you."

Ruth gritted her teeth. She didn't want Lisa's fake sympathy. They might have been close once upon a time, but there was no way they were ever going to be that way again. And she didn't want Lisa to think that there was a chance that they could be or she'd go back to popping round whenever she felt like it, which would be totally unbearable.

"I won't say it's been the easiest day of my life," she replied coolly." Then, "Excuse me, I need to go and find my husband."

Lisa watched as her cousin walked away. When the doorbell rang almost immediately she turned to answer it, but Rita came hurtling out of the front room and shoved her out of the way.

It was Frankie's solicitor, Trevor Dean.

"Come in," Rita ordered, eyeing his briefcase. "Hope that's the will?"

Ruth heard her mother's voice and came back into the kitchen doorway. "Who is it?"

"Solicitor," said Rita, slamming the door shut behind him. She glared at Lisa as she pushed the man up the hall. "What are you standing there catching flies for? This is none of your business, so pull your big nose in and bugger off."

Before they had reached the parlour, Frankie's brother strode out of the front room. "What was that about a will? Is it here?"

Irritated, Rita waved her hand at him in a dismissive gesture. "This is nothing to do with you, Mickey. Go back in there."

"Actually, Mr Hynes ought to be present at the reading," the solicitor informed her. "Along with his brother William, Ruth and her husband, Lisa, and Mr O'Callaghan."

"Mr O'Callaghan?" Rita repeated blankly.

"Big Pat," Trevor Dean explained.

Rita drew her head back and pushed her lips out. "You must have brought the wrong will if them wasters are mentioned in it." She flashed Mickey a dirty look to let him know that she was including him in that. "I don't know about Big Pat, but I know for a fact he wouldn't have left his brothers anything, 'cos they haven't bothered with him in years."

"Shows how much you know, you hoity-toity bitch," spat Mickey. "I might not have had a chance to come over to see him in a while, but me and him still talked on the phone."

"I don't see how, considering he hasn't been able to talk for years," Rita sneered.

276

"Ask our Ruthie if you don't believe me," Mickey said angrily.

"I can assure you that this is the correct will," Trevor Dean piped up loudly. "And the faster we proceed, the sooner you'll all know what's what."

"If he's left him and that brother of theirs anything that's mine by right, you'd better believe I'll be contesting it," Rita told him spikily.

"Just let him read the damn thing," Ruth hissed at her mother impatiently. Then, smiling, she waved the solicitor into the parlour, calling back to Lisa, "Go and get Uncle Billy and Big Pat."

"What's going on?" Johnny asked as he came in from the back garden while the group was making its way into the parlour.

"Thought this was supposed to be a party?" Dave added cheerily when he saw all the solemn faces. Self-consciously wiping his nose when Ruth glared at him, he muttered, "Sorry. I'll go and get a drink." Then, lowering his head he walked quickly down the corridor and disappeared into the front room.

Trevor Dean waited until everybody was settled before he took the paperwork out of his briefcase. After reading quickly through the preliminary testaments of Frankie's name, and his assertion that he had been of sound mind when he had made the will, Dean at last got to the bit that they were all waiting for:

"To my brother Mickey, I leave the sum of twenty thousand pounds," he read. "On the strict understanding that he looks after our Mam until her death — or his. If he goes first, the money passes to our brother

277

Billy — on the understanding that he takes her on. And to Billy himself, I leave the sum of ten thousand pounds."

"That ain't fair," Mickey objected. "Our Billy gets to take his money and run, but I'm lumbered with me ma."

"She's already been living with you and Maria for years, so what's the fecking difference?" Billy argued.

"That ain't the point," Mickey grumbled.

"Just shut up and think yourselves lucky you're getting anything," snapped Rita, relieved that Frankie hadn't left them anything substantial, like a share in the business or something similar.

"To Lisa, who's been more like a second daughter to me than a niece," Trevor Dean continued, "I leave the sum of five thousand pounds, and the house known as number 23 Foster Street."

"I don't think so," Ruth blurted out, already upset that her dad had used his last words to place her cousin in the same category as her. "That's mine and Johnny's house. We've been paying that mortgage for years."

"That may be so, but your father never actually transferred the deeds into either of your names, so, therefore, it remained his property," the solicitor informed her. "And he has bequeathed it to Lisa."

"Wow," Lisa murmured, sitting back in her seat with a look of bewilderment on her face.

"That's getting contested, for starters," Rita asserted huffily.

278

After assuring her that it was all quite legal and above board, the solicitor shifted in his seat and looked at Big Pat.

"To Big Pat, I leave my Cadillac and fifty thousand pounds," he read. Then, blushing, he cleared his throat and said, "He, um, also asked me to pass on the following message: 'We had a fuck of a good run, old man, but it's time to retire, so go rent yourself a cottage in the country, or buy a caravan, or whatever the fuck you want to do, and let the young 'uns take over.'"

Big Pat nodded slowly, but his eyes were as unreadable as ever, so Johnny didn't know if he was relieved or devastated. But it was exactly the right decision, in his opinion. As Frankie had said, Big Pat was getting old, and that made him resistant to change. Johnny had spent the last couple of years banging his head against a brick wall, trying to make the man see the sense in getting rid of some of the more unprofitable arms of the business. The protection racket, for example, had turned out to be way more hassle than it was worth. Also, the stolen motors: Johnny had wanted to move into the luxury-car market for ages now, but Big Pat had insisted on sticking to the easy stuff. And he definitely hadn't liked the idea of Johnny branching out into powders, even though it made total sense — because it was a hell of a lot more profit, was way easier to shift, and required much less storage space. So, yeah, Frankie had hit the nail on the head, as far as Johnny was concerned. It was time for Big Pat to bow out and leave Johnny to get on with it in his own way.

"*Fifty thousand?*" squawked Rita. "There'll be nothing left at this rate. What's he flaming well playing at?"

"How come he gets so much more than us?" Billy was furious. "We're his feckin' family."

"Yeah, and youse have had sod all to do with him in years," Rita reminded him angrily. "At least Big Pat's been there for him. But that still don't mean he deserves fifty grand."

"Ssshh," Ruth scolded, eager to hear what her dad had left for her. "Please go on, Mr Dean."

"To my wife Rita," the solicitor continued, "I leave the jewellery I've invested in over the years."

"It's all bloody well mine anyway," Rita said indignantly.

"Including the items that are stored in my safety deposit box," added the solicitor.

"*What* safety deposit box?" Rita's brow furrowed deeply.

"I'll give you the details after we've finished," the solicitor told her. Then, turning to Ruth, he smiled and said, "To my daughter Ruth, who has been the light of my life and the apple of my eye since the day she was born, despite being as stubborn as a mule and as mean as a wasp, I leave my house and —"

"You what?" Rita cut in furiously. "He thinks he can leave *me* some poxy jewellery and give my house to *her?* No flaming chance! I'm his wife, and everything's mine now he's dead."

"Unfortunately, none of his properties, bank accounts or businesses were actually listed in joint

280

names, so I'm afraid you have no legal claim to any of them," the solicitor informed her. "He did, however, state that Ruth is to allow you to continue to live here, and provide for you in a monetary sense."

"Get stuffed!" Rita blurted out furiously. "He's got no right. Twenty-odd years I supported that swine, and he thinks he's doing this to me from the grave? I'm getting my solicitor onto this."

"As you wish." Trevor Dean inclined his head. "Although I would advise you to employ extreme caution, as any action you take will result in the contested assets being frozen with immediate effect. And these cases tend to take a considerable length of time to come to court, by which time both parties will have accrued sizeable bills for legal services."

"So you're telling me I'll lose either way?" Rita gasped.

The solicitor gave the slightest of shrugs.

"What about Johnny?" Ruth asked. "You said he needed to be here, but you still haven't mentioned him."

"I was getting to that," Trevor Dean told her. "Your father has left the house to you solely, but the business known as Hynes Autos — and several subsidiary concerns — will be co-owned by yourself and his son-in-law, at a rate of fifty-one per cent to yourself and forty-nine to Johnny.

"Johnny is to be allowed, without interference, to continue running everything exactly as he has so far been doing. He will also retain control of all monies related to and arising from said businesses.

281

"However," Dean continued, "if Johnny wishes to accept these shares he will be required to sign a contract to the effect that, should he and Ruth separate or divorce, he will relinquish all claim on the businesses, and will accept a lump-sum payment of fifty thousand pounds in final and absolute settlement."

Finished, he inhaled deeply and looked from one to the other of them.

"Is that all clear?"

"So we both own the businesses," Ruth murmured. "But Johnny stays in control. Unless we split up, then it's all mine."

"Not quite." Trevor Dean smiled. "Should Johnny relinquish his shares, they will pass over to Frankie's granddaughter, Angel, and be held in trust until she reaches the age of twenty-one."

"Hah!" Rita scoffed, flashing Johnny a triumphant sneer. "Bet you thought he was just going to hand everything over to you, didn't you, you little chancer? But he wasn't quite as stupid as you thought, was he?"

"No, that's why he didn't leave *you* anything," Lisa reminded her, feeling sick for Johnny — and herself. Bang went her dreams of him dumping Ruth and walking away with half. If they split, he'd lose everything. Well, almost everything, but fifty grand wouldn't get them very far.

Johnny was thinking the exact same thing. He'd worked his bollocks off turning Frankie's crappy little car lot into a respectable, lucrative business, and fifty grand was an absolute insult. But he knew exactly why Frankie had done it like this. The crafty bastard had known all along that Johnny didn't love Ruth, and this was his way of ensuring that he stayed tied to her for life.

Ruth glanced at her husband and saw that he wasn't happy. "This isn't right," she said guiltily. "Johnny's the head of the family now — it should be his name on all this stuff, not mine. I want to sign my half over too him."

"I'm afraid that isn't possible." Trevor Dean gathered the paperwork together and slotted it back into the briefcase. "Your father specifically stated that you should not be allowed to sign away your rights. But if you insist, alternative arrangements have been made."

"Like what?" Rita challenged, hoping that control would pass to her instead — as it should have from the start.

"In the event that Ruth relinquishes control, everything will be signed over to Angel, and administered on her behalf by an independent party," the solicitor explained. "Now, unless anybody has any further questions, I would like to speak with Mrs Hynes and Mrs Conroy in private."

When Johnny stood up and walked out of the room, Lisa jumped up and rushed after him.

"Johnny, wait," she hissed, catching up with him by the front door.

"Leave me alone," he muttered. "I need some air."

"I'll come with you."

"No. I want to be on my own."

"Please don't push me away," Lisa begged. "I know fifty grand's not a lot, but we're smart enough to make it work for us if we're careful. He's gone now, so there's nothing to stop you from leaving her. And the house is mine, so she can't do anything if you move in with me."

"Are you stupid?" Johnny spat. "I'm not walking away and letting her have it all. *I'm* the one who's made it what it is, and no one's taking it away from me."

"But we could be together," said Lisa. "*Properly* together."

"You think I'm going back to living on peanuts just so I can have sex with you?" Johnny shot back coldly. "I can get sex anywhere, darlin'."

He turned his back when tears flooded her eyes, and yanked the door open. But Angel's voice stopped him in his tracks.

"What's wrong, Daddy?"

Johnny spun on his heel, and felt sick when he saw his daughter standing in the front-room doorway, a worried look on her beautiful little face.

"Nothing, darlin'." He forced out a smile. "How long have you been there?"

"I just came out. I need the toilet."

"Did you hear any of what me and Aunt Lisa were talking about?" Exhaling shakily when Angel shook her head, Johnny picked her up and stroked her hair. "Sorry for being so snappy, cupcake. I'm just a bit tired. Take no notice."

"It's all right," Angel murmured, resting her head on his shoulder. She'd already figured out that something bad must have happened, because Uncle Mickey and Uncle Billy had been arguing when they'd come back from the parlour, and all the aunts and cousins had had to hold them apart to stop them from fighting.

"Go on up to the bathroom, babe," Lisa urged, wanting rid of Angel so that she could talk to Johnny.

But Ruth walked out of the parlour before anybody could move. She had offered to make the solicitor a cup of tea, but she stopped and stared when she saw the three of them standing there.

"What's going on?" she demanded, immediately suspicious.

Lisa stared defiantly back at her. She was tempted to tell the bitch exactly what she should have been told ages ago: that Johnny was *her* man now, and that they were going to be together whether Ruth liked it or not. But Johnny was in such a foul mood, she decided that it was probably wiser to keep her mouth shut. For now.

"I'm going home," Lisa said, raising her chin and heading back into the front room to get her coat and handbag.

Ruth glowered at Angel when her cousin had gone and said, "Stop pawing your father and go to your room."

"Don't take it out on her," Johnny snapped, keeping a tight hold on his daughter.

"She's six, not six months," Ruth reminded him. "And it's not healthy you always treating her like a baby."

Johnny glared coldly back at her, determined to stand his ground. But Angel knew who would get the blame when he'd gone, so she wriggled in his arms.

"Please, Daddy. I need the toilet."

Johnny relented and put her back on her feet. When she ran up the stairs, he turned and opened the door.

"Where are you going?" Ruth asked.

"Out," he said.

"You can't leave me on my own at a time like this," she protested, rushing to stop him. "Please, Johnny . . . I've only just buried my dad. And I can't deal with *them* on my own." She nodded towards the front-room door, from behind which the raised voices of her uncles could clearly be heard as they continued their argument.

"They're your family, not mine," Johnny reminded her.

"Don't be angry with me," Ruth begged. "None of this is my fault. I didn't know my dad was going to do this. I don't even *want* it. You heard what I said to Mr Dean."

"Yeah, I heard, but I bet you only said it 'cos you knew it couldn't happen."

"I had no idea."

"Yeah, right," Johnny muttered. "All that time you spent locked in there with Frankie before he died . . . you and him must have had the whole thing planned from the start."

"I swear to God," Ruth insisted, making the sign of the cross over her heart as a tear trickled down her cheek.

Johnny sucked his teeth and walked out, slamming the door behind him.

"Where's that tea?" Rita demanded, popping her head out of the parlour. "Me and Trevor are spitting feathers in here."

"Coming," Ruth said, sniffing back her tears and wiping her eyes on the back of her hand.

Johnny went straight to the nearest bar and stayed there for the rest of the day and most of the night, snorting coke and drinking.

Somewhere along the way, he picked up a girl and ended up back at her place, where he attempted to fuck away the stresses of the day. But it didn't work. The combination of booze, coke and rage made it impossible for him to come, and the girl had stopped enjoying herself long before he flipped her onto her stomach.

"You're hurting me," she complained. "Can you just stop now, please?"

Johnny gripped her hips firmly and carried on banging away at her.

"I've had *enough!*" she yelped, trying to crawl away from him. "Just get off me. You're *hurting* me!"

She was crying by now, and that was what finally brought Johnny to his senses. He had never before in his life forced himself on a woman, but that was what he had effectively been doing for the last half-hour or so, and he was disgusted with himself.

"Jeezus, I'm sorry," he croaked, sliding out of her and off the bed. "Are you all right?" he asked as he reached for his clothes.

The girl gathered up the sheet to cover herself and stared at him with terror in her eyes. "Will you just go, please?" she whimpered.

"I'm so sorry," he said again. "Here . . ." He took a handful of notes out of his wallet and offered them to her.

"I don't want your money," she sobbed, mortified that he obviously thought she was a prostitute. "I just want you to go."

Sick with self-loathing, Johnny put the money on the bedside table and walked out.

Ruth was still awake when Johnny got home. She was sitting at the kitchen table, with a bottle of whisky and a pack of cigarettes in front of her. She didn't even smoke, but this had been one of the longest, most stressful days of her entire life and she'd needed something to dull the pain, having spent most of the time in tears. Her eyes were so puffy now that she could barely see out of them, and her nose was so blocked that she sounded like she had a terrible cold when she asked Johnny if he was all right.

"Why wouldn't I be?" he replied coldly as he took a glass out of the cupboard and snatched the bottle.

Ruth picked up the strong scent of alcohol on him and guessed that he'd already had more than a few. But her heart constricted in her chest when she also smelled perfume.

"Where have you been?" she asked him quietly.

Johnny poured himself a drink and leaned back against the ledge. "Do you really want me to tell you?"

Ruth held his gaze for a few seconds. Then she shook her head and looked down at the glass in her hands. She wasn't stupid; she knew he'd had other women throughout their marriage. But she'd chosen to ignore it, afraid to confront him for fear that he might admit it. And as much as it hurt to think about him sleeping with another woman, the thought of him leaving and setting up home with one of them if it all came out in the open was unbearable.

"I was worried about you," she said, trying to bring him back to the subject at hand. "I thought you might still be upset about my dad's will."

"It was his business," Johnny replied, as if he didn't give a toss. "He was entitled to do whatever he liked with it."

"I know, but you've worked really hard to build it up."

"Yeah, well, it makes no odds to me now."

"You're not going to leave me, are you?" Ruth gazed up at him with fear in her eyes.

"Dunno." He shrugged. "Haven't decided yet."

"Please don't," she begged. "Nothing's changed. It's just names on a piece of paper — it doesn't mean anything. You're still the boss."

"We'll see," Johnny said. He swallowed the drink and put his glass in the sink. "I'm going to bed."

When he had gone Ruth lowered her face into her hands and sobbed. She knew that her dad must have done it like this to make Johnny stay with her, but he hadn't taken into account what a blow it would be to

Johnny's pride. And if Johnny decided that he couldn't live with it, she would lose him for ever.

Johnny slept on it and decided to stay. Like Ruth had said, nothing had really changed. She might have the majority share, but he was still in control, and forty-nine per cent of a booming business was infinitely better than a fifty grand pay-off. He still had his cars and his money, and now that Ruth had as good as given him the green light to screw around he didn't even have to make excuses for staying out late, so it was a total win-win situation as far as he was concerned.

Ruth was so relieved when Johnny said goodbye and went off to work as normal that morning that she burst into tears all over again. She hadn't slept a wink all night for worrying and had convinced herself that he would get up, pack his bags and leave. But it looked like everything was going to be all right.

She still wasn't happy about him seeing other women, but now that he knew that she knew she had no choice but to accept it. Either that, or confront him and risk losing him — and she would rather die than let some other woman get her claws into him. She wore his ring and shared his name, and it was her bed that he slept in most nights, her house that he called home, shirts washed and ironed by her that he wore on his back, and her womb that had provided his first child. Any woman could give him sex, but none could ever give him any of that — and that was the important stuff.

CHAPTER
TWENTY-ONE

Angel was excited. Her dad had been away on a week-long business trip, but he was coming home today and she couldn't wait for school to end so that she could see him.

Her last lesson was double English, and it had been dragging on and on. But when the bell rang at last, she jumped up, rammed her book and pen into her bag and made a dash for the door.

"Back to your seat, Miss Conroy," the teacher ordered. "I haven't given you permission to leave yet."

"Sorry, sir, can't wait." She backed out into the corridor. "Desperate for the loo. Women's problems," she added, grinning slyly when his cheeks flared.

"Wait for me," her friend Vicky called after her. But Angel just waved over her shoulder and ran.

She burst out through the main door and carried on running all the way up the path, out of the gate, and on down the road to the bus stop, with her long blonde hair streaming out behind her like a sheet in the wind.

Her dad's BMW was nowhere in sight when she reached the car lot a short time later. Disappointed, she waved hello to Tony, the salesman, who was busy giving a couple the hard sell on a Vauxhall Corsa, and made her way around to the office.

Angel didn't remember what the yard had been like back in her grandad Frankie's day, but it was really posh now, with a proper showroom for the more expensive cars and a glass-fronted office and reception area where the prefab had once stood.

Dave was sitting behind the desk inside, his head bowed as he dealt with some paperwork. Just like the yard, he had changed beyond all recognition over the past few years and was now a very different man from the stone-head that Johnny had first invited to help him get the business up to scratch. Back then it had been a laugh: a means of hanging out with his best mate while lining his pockets with easy money. Now it was his career, and he was proud to tell people that he managed a reputable business like this.

And it wasn't just his business life that had changed. Since cleaning up his act, Dave had met and married Hannah, a lovely woman who was everything that Ruth and her mother *thought* they were: classy, intelligent, kind, funny. Life was great, and Dave wouldn't change a thing. Apart from, maybe, kids. Hannah couldn't have them, and that was a great source of sadness for them both. But he had his sister's kids and his honorary niece to spoil, so he couldn't complain.

He glanced up and smiled when Angel walked in now. "Hello, sweetheart, what are you doing here?"

"I thought my dad might be here," she said. "Didn't he say he was coming back today?"

"He must have got held up," Dave told her, mentally cursing his friend.

Johnny had rung that morning to say that he was on his way back, but he still hadn't shown and Dave could only assume that he'd dropped in on one of his tarts en route. And while he wouldn't ordinarily begrudge him — because God knew it must be hell having to go home to Ruth and that devil in a dress that called itself a mother-in-law — Johnny must have known that Angel would be dying to see him, so he should have let her know if he was going to be late.

"Fancy a Coke?" Dave asked, reaching into his drawer for the keys to the soft-drinks machine.

"Yeah, thanks." Angel sighed and flopped into a chair to gaze longingly out of the window.

Dave took a can out of the machine and handed it to her before going back to his seat. "Does your mum know you're here?" he asked as he took a bottle of Scotch and a glass out of his drawer.

"She doesn't tell me anything, so why should I tell her?" Angel replied coolly, peeling back the tab of her can.

"She's still your mum," Dave reminded her, pouring himself a shot.

Angel didn't bother answering this, but she did cast a disapproving glance at his drink.

"Don't look at me like that," he groaned. "It's been a hard day. I need to relax."

"Yeah, that's what my mum and nan always say."

Dave raised the glass to his lips but lowered it again without drinking a drop. Angel always had this effect on him. Even when she'd been tiny, she'd had a way of looking at him that made him feel guilty. There was nothing snotty about her — she wasn't like her mum had been when Ruth, Johnny and Dave had been younger. It was more a kind of knowingness, as if she could see past whatever came out of your mouth and read the truth behind the lies. Hannah had described her as an "old soul" when Dave had introduced her to the family, and he thought she was spot on.

Angel took a sip of her drink and swivelled the chair back to the window in time to see a group of lads turn the corner and come strolling towards the office.

"They're early," Dave murmured, glancing at his watch. "Sorry, sweetheart." He stood up and came around the desk. "You're going to have to wait outside for a few minutes while I run through the schedule with them."

"Do I have to?" Angel moaned. "I'll be quiet — you won't even know I'm here."

"It's business," he said firmly. "And girls and business don't mix."

She tutted and gave him a disapproving look as she got reluctantly to her feet. "Don't *you* start. I get enough of that rubbish off my dad."

"Well, then you should know not to bother arguing about it, shouldn't you?" Dave teased, ushering her toward the door. "Go and sit in the showroom. I'll come and get you when I've finished."

Almost as soon as he'd said this, Angel heard the crunch of tyres and turned to see her dad's car pulling

294

up outside. She squealed with delight and ran to the door, just as the lads reached it.

"Ladies first," one of them said, winking at her as he held it open for her.

"Thanks," she said, waving to her dad as he climbed out of the car. She brushed against one of the others on her way out, and called back "Sorry!" over her shoulder.

"'S' all right," Ryan Johnson murmured, gazing after Angel as she ran to her dad. This was the first time he'd ever seen the boss's daughter, and she was nothing like he'd expected. The way his mate Tommy had described her, he'd thought she would be a spoilt bitch with her nose in the air and a silver spoon hanging out of her mouth. But she looked totally unaffected — and absolutely gorgeous, with her long blonde hair and sparkly blue eyes.

"You're late!" Angel threw herself into her dad's arms and hugged him tightly.

"Yeah, and so are you," he replied with a grin. "I've had about twenty messages off your mother in the last ten minutes, panicking about you not going straight home from school. Did you tell her you were coming here?"

"I think so." Angel shrugged.

"That's not good enough," Johnny scolded. "You know she gets worried. And I don't like the idea of you running around if no one knows where you are. What if something happened?"

"Dad, I'm nearly sixteen," she reminded him. "And I haven't seen you all week, so I don't see the problem. It's not like I'm always taking off, or anything."

"You still should have let her know."

"Fine, I'll tell her next time." Angel sighed. Then, giving him a cheeky grin, she said, "I'm going to say you were waiting for me outside school, then *you'll* get the blame."

"The earache, more like." Johnny chuckled. "And I suppose you'll be expecting a lift home, an' all?"

"Of course. Unless you want me to take the bus . . . in the dark . . . on my own."

"It's not even dark."

"No, but it will be in a bit. Anyway, I don't see why you're complaining. Anyone would think you didn't want to spend time with me."

"All right, you win," Johnny conceded. "Just let me have a quick word with Dave first."

"Can we go for a Maccy D on the way home?" Angel wheedled. She didn't even want a burger, but it was the only thing she could think of to snatch herself a bit of time alone with her dad before they got home. Once there, her mum would want him all to herself and she wouldn't get a look-in.

"We'll see." Johnny tossed his keys to her. "Wait in the car."

Smiling, because she knew that she would get her own way — like she always did with her dad — Angel climbed into the car and watched as he and Dave shook hands. She got the sudden feeling that somebody was staring at her and turned her gaze towards the lads who were standing in a group in the reception area. A little tingle ran through her stomach when her eyes met those of the lad she'd bumped into. All the others were

296

white, but he was mixed-race. He had a diamond stud in his ear, a lightning flash shaved into the side of his close-cropped hair, and he was wearing the baggy kind of jeans that were so low on his hips they looked like they were about to fall right down. Her friend Vicky would have called him a bad boy, but Angel thought he was gorgeous.

"Who were they?" she asked her dad casually when he came back to the car a few minutes later.

"Who?" He twisted his head to look back over his shoulder as he reversed around to the gate.

"Those lads in the office."

"They work for me," Johnny told her as he set off. "Why are you so interested?"

"No reason," she lied, grinning slyly as she added, "Just keeping tabs on the business — seeing as it'll all be mine when you snuff it."

"Jeezus, talk about bouncing on my coffin," Johnny snorted, shaking his head as they pulled up for a red light at the end of the road. "Anything happened while I've been away?" he asked when it turned green and they set off again.

"Not really," Angel said, seeing no point in mentioning her mum and nan's nightly drinking and arguing sessions, because they were hardly news. "How was London?" she asked instead.

"Boring," Johnny told her.

"Should have taken me." She grinned. "I'd have livened it up for you."

"Maybe next time."

"You always say that."

"I know, darlin', but I only found out I was going at the last minute, so there was nothing I could do about it. Anyway, I don't go down there for fun. It's business. You'd be bored stupid."

"Not if I was your PA." Angel gave him a hopeful look. She tutted when he shook his head and said, "What's the point of making me go to a posh school if I'm never going to be allowed to use any of what they've taught me?"

"How do you think it'd make me look if I let my girl work?" Johnny asked, unknowingly echoing exactly what Frankie had said to Ruth when she'd been Angel's age and had mooted the idea of getting a job after leaving school. "I'm your dad — it's my responsibility to look after you."

"Oh, and locking me away with *them* for the rest of my life is looking after me, is it?" Angel complained.

"Drop the attitude," Johnny told her. "And don't talk about your mother like that."

"Sorry." Angel sighed and gazed out of the window. It was all right for him; he hardly ever came home, so he didn't get it in the neck 24/7 like she did.

"What's up with you now?" Johnny asked, frowning as he drove into the McDonald's parking lot.

"Nothing," she muttered. Then, making an effort to shake off the mood before he changed his mind and took her back home instead, she tipped her head to one side and gave him a massive smile. "There . . . is that better?"

"Much," Johnny said approvingly. She was stunningly beautiful, and he was as proud as punch of her.

But he wished she wasn't growing up so fast, because the older girls got, the more adept they became at manipulating you — and if you didn't give them what they wanted, they piled on the guilt with their pouting and sniffling.

His mobile started to ring as he was parking up. He took it out of his pocket and rolled his eyes at Angel when he saw Ruth's name on the screen.

"She's with me, and she's fine," he said when he answered it. "I was passing her school and saw her coming out, so I picked her up."

"*Liar*," Angel whispered, her eyes twinkling with amusement.

"No, I couldn't text you back, 'cos I was driving," Johnny went on, giving Angel a mock-warning look. "No, she couldn't do it, either, 'cos the phone was in my pocket." He held the phone away from his ear when Ruth squawked that she'd been worried sick, but cut back in after a moment and said, "I've got to go, there's a pig car behind me. See you in a bit."

"You're bad," Angel teased when he'd disconnected the call.

"I'm an adult — I'm allowed," he said, grinning as he unbuckled his seat belt.

Back at the yard, the lads had received their instructions for the night and were making their way home. Ryan and his friend Tommy both lived in Hulme, so they walked down to the main road together to catch the bus back.

"I'm looking forward to this one," Tommy said, rubbing his hands together as they boarded the bus. "Baggsy I drive it back."

"Go for it," Ryan agreed as he made his way to the back seat.

Tommy had been working for Johnny for a couple of years longer than Ryan, and still buzzed off it. To his way of thinking, the world was made up of cunts and people like him. Cunts had shit, and stamped on people like him who *didn't* have shit to make sure they never *got* shit. So if they lost some of their shit every now and then — *tough* shit.

Ryan didn't see it quite like that. In his eyes, anyone who earned the money to buy a luxury motor was entitled to park it up at night without worrying that some little scrote like him or Tommy was going to come along and nick it. But principles didn't put food on the table, and with no qualifications to his name, a black face and a ghetto postcode, he'd had zero luck with all the legitimate employers he'd approached after leaving school. Fortunately, Johnny Conroy came from the same place, so it made no odds to him if you were black, blue, purple or green. As long as you showed loyalty and gave respect he would give you a fair crack of the whip, and Ryan was grateful for that because his wages were the only thing that was keeping his mam from having to sell herself to keep his deadbeat dad in beer and fags.

When the bus reached Hulme, Ryan and Tommy touched fists before going their separate ways. As Ryan darted through the heavy traffic on Chester Road and

300

made his way through the estate, his mind drifted back to Johnny's daughter. She was absolutely gorgeous, and if he saw her in a nightclub he wouldn't hesitate to ask her out. But it was easy to approach a girl when you didn't know anything about her. Not so easy, however, when you both already knew that she was out of your league. And Angel Conroy was way out of his. She'd grown up surrounded by money and power, and went to a posh school where loads of rich boys were probably drooling over her every day, so there was no way she would ever look twice at an uneducated scumbag like him.

Still, there was nothing wrong with dreaming, and Ryan was smiling to himself as he walked up the path a few minutes later and slotted his key into the lock. But his smile soon vanished when he opened the door and heard the sound of screaming coming from the living room at the back of the house.

He raced up the short hall and burst in to find his mother on the floor with blood trickling from her nose and one of her eyes already black and swollen. His dad was kneeling over her, one hand around her throat, the other bunched into a fist and raised above her face. In the playpen in the corner his baby brother was screaming hysterically, which told Ryan that it must have been going on for quite some time already.

"Get off her!" he yelled, rushing across the room and shoving his dad in the back.

Gary Johnson fell heavily onto his side, and a hissing sound came out of his mouth as the wind was temporarily knocked out of him. But he recovered fast and kicked out, knocking Ryan's legs from under him. He jumped up when Ryan went down, then booted him in the ribs.

"Think you're big enough to take me on, do you, you little cunt? Come on, then, let's have it! Here, I'll even give you the first shot . . ." He backed up a step and thrust his bristly chin out in a challenging gesture, inviting Ryan to take a swing.

Ryan stood no chance, and they both knew it. His dad had been a bare-knuckle fighter back in the day, and even though his muscle had long ago turned to fat and his lungs were fucked from smoking, he still had a punch like a sack of concrete. But Ryan knew from experience that his dad wouldn't stop until he'd had his fun when he was in this kind of mood, so he swallowed the bile that had risen into his throat and stood up to take whatever was coming.

As soon as he was up, Gary lamped him. Ryan's legs already felt like jelly, but they buckled like broken matchsticks when the punch landed and he went straight back down.

"Get up, you fuckin' pussy," Gary ordered. "Get up and fight like the man you reckon you are."

"Stop it!" Zeta Johnson sobbed when her husband started kicking her son all round the room. "Gary, *please* . . . you're going to kill him!"

"Shut your gob," he roared, backhanding her across the face and sending her sprawling across the floor.

He gave Ryan one last vicious boot in the ribs, then went back to his chair and flopped down. He was wheezing by now, his heavy chest heaving, so he took a couple of puffs on his inhaler before lighting a cigarette.

"Fuckin' little faggot," he sneered as Ryan dragged himself painfully to his feet. "What y' got for me?"

"I ain't got *shit* for you," Ryan replied defiantly, aware that his dad was asking for money, because that was all he ever wanted. The cunt thought the world owed him a living and sat in his chair from morning till night, watching telly and swigging the beer that he'd bullied Ryan's mam into buying, borrowing or stealing for him. And so what if there was never any food in the house, or the baby's arse was covered in sores because there were no clean nappies — so long as *he* was all right, the rest of them could rot.

"Like that, is it?" Gary smirked. "No problem, I'll just send your mam out to earn me some."

"Here . . . fucking have it." Ryan took a twenty out of his pocket and threw it at him. "Just leave me mam alone."

"Or what?" Gary snorted, pocketing the money. "She's my wife, I'll do what the fuck I want to her."

Ryan's eyes blazed with loathing as he glared at him. "One of these days you're gonna get what's coming to you, you fat bastard."

"Leave it," Zeta urged, scooping the baby out of the playpen as Gary burst out laughing. "You're just making it worse."

Ryan kissed his teeth with disgust and strode out, slamming the door behind him. He was nineteen and earning good money, so he could easily get a place of his own. But he couldn't walk out on his mam, because his dad would have her back on the game in no time. And he had his little sister and baby brother to think about, as well — both of whom had already witnessed more violence than any kid should ever have to see.

But you could only kick a dog so many times before it bit you and, one of these days, something was going to snap. And when it did, either Ryan or his dad was going to wind up dead.

CHAPTER
TWENTY-TWO

Three weeks after Johnny got back from London, Angel's school closed for the Easter holidays. She woke up on her first morning of so-called freedom and opened the curtains to see the sun blazing outside. But it didn't make her happy; it just made her think about all the fun she was going to miss out on. Her friends had arranged to meet up and go to the cinema today, and after a whole load of creeping, Angel had managed to persuade her dad to let her go with them. But last night her mum had complained that her stomach was playing up, so he'd told Angel that she had to stay home to look after her instead.

She was convinced that her mum was putting it on to stop her from going out, and had spent most of last night sulking in her room. But she knew there was no point arguing about it because it would probably only result in her getting grounded for life, so she pushed the thought of her friends having fun to the back of her mind and went out into the garden to try and get a tan.

Angel laid her towel out on the grass and lay down on it with her eyes closed and her arms and legs stretched out. But she hadn't been there ten minutes before she heard someone banging on the window.

Shielding her eyes, she looked up to see her nan gesturing frantically from the back bedroom window.

She went inside and called "Yeah?" up the stairs, expecting that the old bat would probably demand a cup of tea, or some toast — or something else that she was too lazy to get for herself.

"Call the doctor," her nan shouted down, sounding unusually panicked. "Your mum's taken a turn, and I don't like the look of her."

"Why, what's wrong?"

"She's bleeding. So never mind standing there asking stupid questions, just do it!"

Angel didn't understand why her nan hadn't already made the call if she was that worried, but she kept her thoughts to herself and did as she'd been told before going upstairs to see her mum.

Ruth was clutching at her stomach and writhing around in the bed. She'd been having pains on and off for a few weeks but she'd ignored them, telling herself that it was probably the onset of early menopause. But it had been getting progressively worse, and today it was unbearable.

Shocked when she saw how pale her mum was, and how clammy her skin looked, Angel felt immediately guilty for thinking that she'd been putting it on.

"Are you all right?" she asked. "Do you want me to get you anything?"

"Get her some water, and fetch me a couple of thick towels," Rita ordered, pushing her back out onto the landing. "How long did that doctor say he was going to be?"

"They said he'll try and come round after morning surgery," Angel told her, already halfway down the stairs.

"What do you mean, *try?*" Rita leaned over the banister and glared down at her. "Get back on that phone and tell him he'd better get his arse round here right now, or he'll have me to answer to."

"Don't you think we should just call an ambulance?" Angel suggested.

"And make me look a fool if there's nothing wrong with her?" snapped Rita. "Just do as you're flaming well told."

Angel rang the surgery again, only to be told that the doctor was with a patient and that she should call an ambulance if her mother was as ill as she was making out.

"All right, phone one, then," Rita snapped when Angel handed her the towels and relayed the message. "And tell 'em to hurry, 'cos it won't just be the sheets that are ruined in a minute, it'll be the mattress an' all."

The paramedics rushed Ruth straight to A&E. Angel rang her dad on the way and he reached the hospital twenty minutes later, just as the doctor finished examining Ruth and came out to tell them what was going on.

"It's cancer, isn't it?" Rita blurted out when she saw the grim expression on the doctor's face. "I knew it."

"The ultrasound has revealed a mass in Mrs Conroy's womb," the doctor explained. "We're concerned that there may have been some kind of rupture, but we'll need to operate as soon as possible to find out exactly what we're dealing with. Unfortunately, she's unable to sign the consent form, so her next of kin will have to —"

"That's me," Rita cut in, pushing herself forward. "I'm her mother. I'll do it."

"*I'll* do it," Johnny told the doctor, snatching the form.

Angel stood back and wrapped her arms around herself. She hadn't understood what the doctor had said, but she'd never seen her dad look so serious before and that scared her even more than the doctor's air of urgency.

"You can pop in and see her," the doctor told them when Johnny handed the signed form back. "But you'll need to be quick because she's about to be sedated."

Johnny turned to go into the room but hesitated when Rita plonked herself down on a chair and folded her arms.

"Aren't you coming in?"

"I'll wait my turn," she replied childishly. "You're obviously more important than me."

"Oh, just grow up," Angel snapped. "This isn't about you. My mum's about to have an operation."

"I've had loads," Rita informed her. "But you don't hear me complaining."

"You never *stop*," Angel retorted incredulously.

"Don't," Johnny said quietly. "Let's just go and say bye to your mum, then I'll drop you both home."

"I'm not going anywhere with *her*," Angel said defiantly.

"You'll do as you're bloody well told," Rita informed her angrily. "And if your father was any kind of man, he'd kick your backside from here to hell and back for being so disrespectful."

Johnny narrowed his eyes and peered down at his mother-in-law. "You're right," he said, bringing an immediate smirk of satisfaction to her lips. "But respect has to be earned — and you haven't earned it."

"It's no wonder she's turned out so bad with a no-mark like you for a father," spat Rita, her eyes flashing with hate. "Frankie should have cut your balls off the first time you ever went near our Ruth."

Angel burst into tears.

"Ignore her," Johnny said, putting his arm around her. "I do."

"No, I can't take it," Angel cried. "Not today. My mum's really ill, and all she wants to do is argue."

"Stop crying," Johnny said quietly. "Your mum doesn't need to see you like this, so pull yourself together. We'll go and say bye to her, then I'll drop you round at Lisa's. You can stay there till I've finished down at the yard. Okay?"

Angel nodded, and wiped her nose on the back of her hand.

Furious that he was rewarding the girl for defying her, Rita said, "Don't think you're bringing her back to my house if you take her round there, 'cos I'm not having it."

"It's not your house," Johnny reminded her coldly.

"It's more mine than yours," Rita shot back sharply. "But that's you all over, isn't it, Jimmy Conroy? You've been scrounging your way through this family from day one, and now you think you're king of the castle. But you're not. And you're not fooling me, neither, 'cos I know your game. You're gonna dump her on that slut, then take off with one of your whores while my Ruth's too sick to stop you."

"Stop it," Angel cried, covering her ears with her hands.

"You're the one who needs to stop it," Rita turned on her. "You need to stop mooning over him like he's some kind of god when you don't know the half of what he's put your poor mother through over the years. Why don't you ask him about all the other women he's had behind her back?"

Johnny had heard more than enough. Steely gaze fixed on Rita, he jerked his head at Angel. "Go and say bye to your mum."

Icy fear trickled down Angel's spine when she heard the tone of his voice. Her nan had pushed him too far, and she was scared that he might do something stupid and get himself arrested if she left them alone.

"Come with me," she begged, tugging on his arm. "Please, Dad . . . you heard what the doctor said. She's not going to be awake for much longer."

Johnny inhaled deeply and fought to bring his temper under control. Rita had been riding him like a dog from the very first time they'd met, and it was high time she got her comeuppance. But he didn't want to upset Angel any more than she already was so, nodding, he turned his back on Rita and ushered Angel in to see Ruth.

It was too late. She was already asleep, and the porter was preparing to wheel her up to the operating theatre.

Rita had gone by the time they came back out into the corridor. Concerned that he might have gone too far and scared the old bitch, Johnny said, "Maybe you'd best go home, cupcake. There's no telling what she'll do if she gets bladdered while she's in a state."

"No, I'm going to Aunt Lisa's." Angel dug her heels in. "Sorry, Dad, but she's already being nasty, and she'll only get worse if she's drunk."

"Okay," Johnny conceded. "I suppose she's old enough to look after herself. But I've really got to go now, or I'm going to be late for my meeting."

Angel gave him a probing look. "It's not with a woman, is it?"

"Behave," Johnny snorted, putting his arm around her. "Since when have I done business with women?"

"So my nan was lying?

"What do you think?" Johnny gazed down sincerely into her eyes.

"Sorry," Angel murmured, cuddling up to him as they walked out to the car.

CHAPTER
TWENTY-THREE

Lisa was surprised when she opened her door to find both Johnny *and* Angel on the step. Not so much Johnny, because he still came round quite regularly. But it had been ages since Angel had been here, and she looked upset, which made Lisa wonder if something had happened.

"Is everything all right?" She gave Johnny a questioning look as he ushered Angel inside.

"Ruth's in hospital," he told her. "And Rita was playing funny buggers, so Angel didn't want to go home with her. Can she stop with you till I've finished work?"

"Course she can." Lisa agreed without hesitation.

"Cheers. I don't know how late I'll be back, 'cos I've got loads on today, but I'll ring you when I'm on my way."

"Why don't you just let her stay the night?" Lisa suggested. "Then you won't have to rush."

"Can I?" Angel gave Johnny a hopeful look.

"I suppose so," he agreed, figuring that under the circumstances she'd be better off here than with her nan. At least he could trust Lisa to keep her mouth shut.

Lisa smiled at Angel. "Go and get yourself a drink while me and your dad have a quick word, babe. And there's some cake in the cupboard if you fancy it."

She closed the door when Angel had gone and went to Johnny for a hug.

"Leave it out," he muttered. "She might walk in on us."

"Sorry, didn't think." Lisa folded her arms. "So, is our Ruth bad, or what?"

"Didn't look too good. They were taking her for an operation when we left."

"Why, what's happened? She's not had an accident, has she?"

"No, it's her stomach. The doctor mentioned something about a rupture, but I wasn't really taking it in, to be honest."

Lisa winced and sucked in a breath through her teeth. "Sounds painful."

"Yeah, well, at least they're on it, so hopefully they'll get it sorted," said Johnny. "They're going to ring when they're finished, so I'll let you know what's going on. Hope it's nothing serious," he added concernedly. "Angel's trying not to show it, but she's worried sick."

"Don't worry," Lisa said reassuringly. "I'll keep her occupied to take her mind off it."

"Take her out," said Johnny, peeling some notes out of his wallet and handing them to her. "Go shopping, or whatever you girls like doing."

Lisa slotted the money into her pocket and gazed up at him through her lashes. "Are you coming round later?"

"Don't think that's a very good idea, do you?" Johnny nodded at the door.

"She'll be fast asleep by ten," Lisa whispered. "And I've got something special to show you."

Johnny's eyes tracked her finger as she trailed it slowly down between her breasts. "All right," he murmured. "I'll see what I can do."

"I'll be waiting," she purred, confident that he would come.

Johnny popped his head round the door and shouted goodbye to Angel. Lisa showed him out and watched until he'd driven away before going back to the kitchen.

"Find everything you wanted?" she asked.

Mouth too full of cake to answer in words, Angel nodded and watched as Lisa switched on the kettle and reached into the cupboard for a cup. Wiping her mouth on the back of her hand when she'd swallowed, she said, "Have you had your hair cut, Aunt Lisa?"

"Trust you to notice." Lisa smiled and touched it self-consciously. "I had it done a few days ago, but nobody else has said anything. I thought it might be a bit short."

"No, it really suits you," Angel told her. "And you look like you've lost weight as well."

"Oh, you're so good for my ego." Lisa laughed softly. "Never mind staying the night, I think you should move in."

I wish, thought Angel. Her mum and nan hated Lisa and were always talking about her behind her back, but Angel really liked her. She was pretty and easygoing, and she had great taste in clothes. Angel couldn't imagine her mum wearing any kind of jeans, never mind the sexy hipster ones that Lisa wore. And Lisa always wore heels, which made her legs look great, while Angel's mum slopped around in flats that looked stretched and baggy on her fat feet.

Disloyal as she felt for thinking it, Angel sometimes wondered how her mum had managed to bag a handsome man like her dad. Wherever he went, women fell over themselves to get near him. And he obviously enjoyed the attention because he was always flirting with them.

But while flirting might be harmless, playing around definitely wasn't, and it brought back to mind what her nan had said at the hospital. Angel hoped she'd been lying, because all her friends' parents had either split up or divorced — and Angel never wanted that to happen to hers. But why would her nan have said it if there was no truth to it? And why hadn't her dad denied it outright when she'd mentioned it?

"You're quiet." Lisa glanced back over her shoulder as she stirred a sugar into her tea. "You're not worrying about your mum, are you? 'Cos I'm sure she'll be fine."

"I was thinking about my dad," Angel told her quietly. "My nan said something at the hospital and it got me thinking."

Lisa rolled her eyes and carried her cup over to the table. "What's the old boot said now?"

"That my dad was only leaving me here with you so he could go out whoring," Angel murmured, blushing as she said the last word because it sounded so horrible. "But he wouldn't cheat on my mum, would he? He must love her or they wouldn't have been married for so long, would they?"

Lisa gripped her cup hard. Angel was pretty, and clever, but she was way too innocent for this world if she hadn't sussed out what her father was really like by now. *Ruth* knew, but she'd chosen to pretend that she didn't. And Lisa was no better, because she was still entertaining Johnny, despite the fact that he'd had almost twenty years to choose between her and Ruth. She'd known he couldn't leave while her Uncle Frankie was still alive, but when it still hadn't happened after Frankie died she'd tried to finish it, only for Johnny to talk her round and promise that he would do it when Angel was old enough.

So here she was — still waiting, and hoping, and taking whatever she could get of him in the meantime.

But there was no point hurting Angel with the truth so Lisa smiled, shook her head, and said, "Course he wouldn't cheat on her, babe." Then, "Anyway, we'd best go and get you a toothbrush if you're stopping the night. Your dad's given me some money, so where do you want to go — Arndale or Trafford Centre?"

"I don't mind," said Angel, her worried frown disappearing at the thought of going out — even if it was only for a toothbrush.

CHAPTER
TWENTY-FOUR

Johnny was in the office with Dave and a client when the call came from the hospital at six that evening. He excused himself and went out to the car to take it in private.

Dismayed when he heard that Ruth had haemorrhaged during surgery, and that the surgeon had made the decision to perform a hysterectomy, he said, "Is she all right?"

"She's still quite poorly," the nurse told him. "But we've moved her to ICU, and she'll be closely monitored for the next twenty-four hours, so there's no need to worry."

"Any idea when she'll be able to come home?" Johnny asked, already wondering how he was going to manage to balance work and looking after Angel.

"The operation was quite traumatic, so, depending how quickly she heals, she might be with us for a couple of weeks," the nurse replied. "You can visit whenever you like while she's in ICU, but she's still pretty heavily sedated, so you might want to leave it for tonight. If you do decide to come we'd advise you not to bring any children with you, because it can be upsetting for them to see all the tubes and breathing apparatus."

Johnny thanked her, and then called Lisa. He could hear noise in the background and guessed that they were out shopping. Angel sounded so happy when she came on the line that he decided it would be cruel to worry her all over again, so he lied and said that the operation had gone really well, and that her mum was already sitting up and complaining about the food they'd given her for dinner.

Angel laughed, and said, "Typical!" But Johnny heard the relief in her voice and knew that he'd made the right decision.

He wasn't about to spare Rita the worry, though. After her little tantrum at the hospital earlier, he thought it would do her good to know how serious it actually was. But when she didn't answer either the house or the mobile phone, Johnny hissed through his teeth with exasperation. Great! Now he was going to have to go round and make sure that the old witch hadn't drunk herself into a coma and drowned in her own puke.

Or maybe he wouldn't bother.

Maybe he'd just go back in the morning and see if he'd got lucky.

As well as the toothbrush they had originally set out for, Angel had a new dress, a couple of tops, a pair of jeans, a nightie and her first-ever pair of high-heeled shoes in her bags by the time they got back to Lisa's that evening.

318

Too tired to cook after all the walking around, Lisa ordered a Chinese takeaway. Then, later, she opened a bottle of wine and gave Angel a glass as they cuddled up on the couch to watch a film together.

Unused to alcohol, Angel was more than ready for her bed by the time the film had finished. When Lisa checked on her a short time later and saw that she was fast asleep, she smiled and quietly closed the door. Then she ran herself a sweet-smelling bubble bath, and started getting ready for Johnny.

Johnny didn't arrive until two in the morning — and Lisa was lucky he'd come at all.

He'd spent the afternoon and most of the evening playing hardball with a Dutch buyer called Arjen, who had seemed to think that Johnny would agree to pick up luxury cars to order and then ship them over to Amsterdam for a much lower rate than he charged his other buyers. In need of food and fun by the time he had finally managed to talk the man around to his way of thinking, Johnny had treated them all to dinner at The Hilton to seal the deal.

Reformed-character Dave had boringly opted to go home to his wife after the meal, but their new friend was still raring to go, so Johnny took him to a nightclub and introduced him to the delights of Manchester by chucking a load of booze down his neck, powder up his nose, and girls into his lap.

They ended the night in a Chinatown casino, where Johnny won fifteen grand at the poker table — and promptly lost it again on the roulette wheel. Up for an orgy by the time they left, Arjen invited Johnny and the girls back to his hotel to carry on the party. But Johnny wasn't into other blokes watching him at it, so he declined politely and hailed a cab for himself and his bird, who had already suggested that they go to her place for a private party of their own.

And she'd been as fit as fuck, so Johnny had been well up for it. But after a couple of minutes in the back of the cab, with nowhere for her rank breath to go but up his nose, his stomach had started churning and he'd ordered the driver to pull over.

"Where are we going?" the girl asked, trying to follow him when he climbed out.

"We're going nowhere, darlin'," Johnny said, pushing her back in and closing the door before handing the driver a couple of twenties.

"What's wrong?" she persisted, opening the window now and giving him a fresh blast.

"Jeezus, love, you need to see a dentist," he told her, grimacing as he took a few more notes out of his wallet and thrust them through the window at her. "Here, go and buy some mouthwash."

"Fuck you!" she snarled, snatching them.

Quipping "Not with breath like that, you won't," Johnny walked away in search of another cab.

He found Lisa fast asleep on the couch with a sheet draped lightly over her. Grinning when he lifted the corner and saw the red satin basque and black silk stockings she was wearing, he squatted down beside her and put his lips to her ear.

"Hey, sleeping beauty . . . wakey, wakey."

Lisa opened her eyes and smiled sleepily up at him. "I thought you weren't coming," she said, sliding her arms around his neck.

"And miss out on my surprise? No chance."

"Do you like it?" she asked, pushing the sheet off so that he could see the whole of her outfit.

"Love it," Johnny said. "Go and make sure Angel's asleep."

Lisa wrapped the sheet around herself, tiptoed upstairs and peeped into the spare room. Angel was curled up on her side, her hair fanned out on the pillow around her pretty face, her breathing slow and deep.

"Sleeping like a baby," Lisa assured Johnny when she came back down. "I think the wine must have really gone to her head."

"Wine?" On the couch by now, Johnny frowned up at her. "What did you give her wine for? She's too young."

"Oh, come on, she's a big girl now," Lisa argued, sitting astride him. "One little glass of wine isn't going to hurt her, is it?"

"I suppose not," Johnny conceded, pulling her towards him.

Lisa closed her eyes when he kissed her, and ran her fingers through his hair before reaching down between her legs to unzip his fly.

"Oh, that's hard," she moaned. "Oh, yeah, baby, you can give me some of that . . ."

"*Ssshhh*," Johnny hissed.

Determined to keep his mind on the job at hand, Lisa grabbed his face in her hands and sucked his tongue into her mouth as she lowered herself slowly onto his cock.

"Oh, Jeezus," he groaned when she started riding him in a circular motion, gradually increasing the speed until he thought his balls were going to explode.

"*Ssshhh*," she mimicked, sinking her teeth into his neck.

"Bitch," Johnny muttered, both loving and hating the pain. When he could take no more, he flipped Lisa onto her back and gave her what she was asking for.

"Wow, where did *that* come from?" she gasped, clinging to him when he'd finished. "I won't be able to walk in the morning."

"You always get me going, darlin'," he told her, grinning as he sat up.

"Yeah, 'cos I'm the best," Lisa said huskily.

"Sure are," Johnny confirmed, winking as he zipped himself back up. "Right, I'd best get going."

"You're *going*?" Lisa echoed, a look of disbelief replacing the smile of satisfaction. "I thought you were staying the night?"

"Angel's here," he said, as if he thought she'd forgotten.

"She's fast asleep," Lisa reminded him. "And I'll set the alarm to make sure we're up before her in the morning. She'll never even know you were here."

"Nah, can't risk it." Johnny took his cigarettes out of his pocket and lit up.

"Where are you going?" Lisa demanded, her eyes flashing with suspicion. "I know you're not going back to yours, 'cos there's no way you'd stay with Rita on your own. You're going to see some other woman, aren't you?"

"You reckon I've got the energy for another woman after what we've just done?" Johnny laughed. "I'm not fucking superman."

"I don't believe you," Lisa argued, tears sparkling in her eyes.

"Look, I'm going home," Johnny told her truthfully. "I need to check that the old bitch is still alive, for starters. And the nurse told me to put together a bag for Ruth, so I've got to sort that."

"Do it in the morning," Lisa implored, clutching at his hand. "Please, Johnny, it's been ages since you've stayed the night, and I just want to go to sleep with your arms around me."

"You know I would if I could," he crooned, pulling her against him and hugging her. "But I can't."

"I hate this," she complained, resting her head on his chest. "Ruth's had you for years, and even now she's in hospital she's *still* pulling all the strings."

"Don't start," Johnny muttered, pulling away. "You knew I was married when we got into this, so there's no point moaning about it."

"Yeah, and you said you wished you'd picked me instead of her."

"I do." Johnny sighed. "But I've got to put Angel first."

323

"She won't be a child for much longer," Lisa pointed out. "Anyway, she loves me, so she'd come to terms with it pretty fast if she found out about us. It wouldn't hurt her half as much if she knew you'd left her mum for *me* rather than some random slag she'd never clapped eyes on in her life."

"I'm not leaving Ruth for anyone," said Johnny. "Not right now, anyway."

"But you're still going to do it when Angel's old enough?" Lisa asked, hope sparking in her heart that these years she'd spent pining for him hadn't been wasted after all.

"I'm too tired for this," Johnny said with finality. "We've had fun tonight, so let's just leave it at that, eh?"

Lisa drew back her head and gaped at him. "Are you finishing with me?"

"Did I say that?" Johnny asked. Smiling slyly when she shook her head and he saw the relief in her eyes, he said, "I'll try and come round in the morning before I go to work. But if I can't make it, take her out again. Go to the pictures, or something."

"So, you mean you *won't* be coming."

"No, I mean I'm definitely going to try. But anything could happen between now and then. The yard could go up in flames, or Ruth could take a turn for the worse."

Lisa sighed resignedly. "Okay, I'll see you when I see you."

Johnny grinned and gave her a slow kiss before leaving.

Cold when he'd gone, Lisa snatched the sheet off the floor and wrapped it around her shoulders before making her way up to the bedroom. All the effort she'd made to look sexy for him, and it had been all over in a flash. She didn't know why she bothered.

CHAPTER
TWENTY-FIVE

Angel overslept for the first time in years. She wasn't quite sure where she was when she first opened her eyes but, when she remembered, she smiled and stretched her arms out above her head.

Revelling in the freedom of being able to get up in her own time, without her mum or nan barking at her to hurry up, she had a wash and got dressed, and then went downstairs to make Lisa some breakfast. But Lisa had already gone out and had left twenty quid, a key and a note on the kitchen table.

Angel picked the note up and read that Lisa had gone to the dentist and would be going straight to her mum's from there so probably wouldn't be back until late afternoon. Angel was to help herself to anything she wanted, and use the money to go shopping if she got bored. Oh, and PS: her dad had rung while she was asleep to say that something had cropped up, but he would come round to see her after he'd finished work tonight.

Disappointed to have missed her dad's call, but not overly surprised that he'd put work before her, Angel made herself a cup of tea and a piece of toast, and then phoned Vicky to see if she fancied going into town. Fed up when Vicky's mum informed her that Vicky had just gone swimming with some of her friends, Angel gazed out of the window at the lovely blue sky. It was boring walking around town by yourself, but too nice a day to waste sitting inside. So she went to the shops and bought herself a couple of magazines, and then went to the park at the end of the road.

Even in the blazing sunshine, the park looked dismal. There was a tiny playground to the left of the path as she entered, comprising a set of seatless swings, a see-saw, and a lopsided roundabout. Beyond that, a bricked-up toilet block squatted beside an old tennis court that had long ago lost its net. But it was still better than being stuck in the house all day by herself, so Angel found herself a nice patch of grass and settled down to read the magazines.

She'd read one and had just started on the other when she heard the sound of a child crying out in pain. She shielded her eyes with her hand and peered around. A group of young girls were huddled together in the doorway of the toilet block on the other side of the park. Concerned that one of them might have had an accident, Angel got up and strolled towards them.

As she got closer, one of the girls glanced around and, eyes widening, legged it towards the gate at the far side of the park. Angry when she saw that the two girls who were left behind were kneeling on top of another smaller one, pulling her hair and punching her, Angel yelled, "Hey! Pack that in!"

The girls stopped what they were doing at the sound of her voice and raced after their friend, and Angel rushed to their victim. The little girl was sitting up by now, crying as she examined her bloodied knees.

"Are you all right?" Angel asked, squatting down beside her.

The girl nodded, but it was obvious to Angel that she was hurt. Her bushy hair was standing out in clumps around her head, and her tear-streaked face was covered in welts from where the girls had raked her with their nails before setting about her with their fists.

"Do you know them?" Angel asked, peering angrily around to see if the girls were still in sight.

"Yeah, but it don't matter," the little one said, sniffing and making little gulping sobbing noises. "I just wanna go h-home."

"I'll walk with you," Angel told her, helping her to her feet. "Do you live near here?"

The girl nodded and pointed towards the gate. The scent of urine wafted up from her, and Angel suspected that she had probably pissed herself with fear. But she quickly realised that it might not be that recent when she noticed the child's dirty dress, and the streaks staining both of her skinny legs. Angel felt sorry for her. As badly as her own mother had treated her over the years, at least she had been always been fed and her clothes had been washed. But this skinny little thing looked like she hadn't eaten in weeks, and she stank to high heaven.

Angel felt a little thrill of revulsion when the child reached for her hand, but she swallowed it and walked her out of the park. The girl led her past Lisa's house and around two corners, but as they were approaching the house that she'd pointed out as being hers the front door opened and a woman with an equally skinny face and wild hair came out carrying a bulging bin bag.

"Oi!" she yelled when she clocked her child walking hand in hand with a stranger. "What's going on?" She dropped the bag and ran out onto the pavement. "What's she supposed to have done?" she demanded, snatching the girl away and glaring at Angel.

Shocked by her aggressiveness, Angel took a step back. "She'd not done anything," she said. "Some kids were beating her up in the park, so I walked her home."

"What kids?" the woman demanded, glaring at her daughter now.

The girl winced and raised her arms as if she was expecting to get hit. "Kerry, Simone and Danielle," she stuttered.

"And you just stood there and let them?" Her mother clumped her across the side of her head. "How many times have I told you to stand up for yourself, you stupid little cow?"

"Hey, there's no need for that," Angel protested. "There were three of them, and they looked a lot bigger than her."

"What's it got to do with you?" the woman spat, sneering as she looked Angel up and down. "Standing there in your fancy clothes, with your posh voice, making out like you've got a clue what it's like to bring kids up round here."

"I'm sorry, I didn't mean to offend you," Angel murmured, feeling more awkward than she'd ever felt in her life before. "But I don't think you should be taking it out on your daughter. It wasn't her fault."

"What's going on?" a man asked just then.

Angel glanced around, and her heart sank when Ryan came striding out of the house. And he didn't look any less shocked than her as he stopped in his tracks and stared at her.

"This posh bitch making out like I don't know how to look after my own kid, that's what," the woman snarled.

"I'm sorry," Angel stammered. "I was only trying to help." She cast an apologetic glance at Ryan and then walked away.

"Yeah, that's right, piss off," the woman yelled after her. "And keep your nose out of my family's business in future, you stuck-up little bitch."

"Mam, just shut your mouth and get back in the house," Ryan hissed. Then, jumping the fence, he called, "Angel . . . wait!"

She had tears in her eyes when he caught up with her at the corner. "Oh, Christ, what did she do?" he groaned. "She didn't hit you or anything, did she?"

"No." Angel shook her head and tried to step around him.

"Well, what happened? Did you catch my sister shoplifting or something?"

"No, I found her getting beaten up," Angel told him, wondering why both he and his mother had automatically thought that his sister had been up to no good.

330

"Shit, not again." Ryan gritted his teeth and raked his fingers through his short hair. "Those little bitches are always picking on her. It does my head in."

"So do something about it," Angel said coolly.

"It's not that easy," he replied. "I don't expect you to understand, because you've probably never been hit in your life, but it's never going to stop if she doesn't start sticking up for herself."

Angel raised her chin. "For your information, I *have* been hit — loads of times. And it's terrifying when you're a defenceless little girl."

"*You?*" Ryan frowned. "Who'd hit you?"

Angel kicked herself for opening her mouth and lowered her gaze. "No one — forget I said it."

"Not your dad?" Ryan's voice was filled with disbelief.

"Course not," she shot back indignantly. "My dad would never lay a finger on me."

Ryan was truly glad to hear that, because he liked and respected Johnny Conroy and would have hated to think that he was the kind of bastard who would abuse his own kid.

"Look, I'm sorry about my mam kicking off," he apologised. "She doesn't mean to be so hard on our Cherise, but she's forever telling her not to go to the park on her own, and she just keeps sneaking round there, even though she knows them girls are going to be waiting for her. *I* can't do anything about it, 'cos I'd end up getting nicked. And there's no point telling their mams and dads to sort them out, 'cos

331

that just makes them hate Cherise even more than they already do."

Angel saw the sincerity in his eyes and realised how difficult this must be for him. "It's all right," she said kindly. "I shouldn't have interfered."

"No, I'm glad you helped her out," said Ryan. "I'm not saying you did anything wrong, I'm just trying to explain why my mam reacted like that."

"Well, there's no hard feelings on my part," Angel assured him.

"Thanks," he murmured. "Anyhow, I suppose I'd best get back — make sure she's okay."

"Hope she is." Angel smiled.

"She's tougher than she looks." Ryan smiled back.

They looked at each other for a few more seconds, but there was really nothing left to say, so Angel said goodbye and walked away.

Ryan chewed on his lip as he watched her go, and reminded himself of all the reasons why he shouldn't even think about trying to take this any further. She was the boss's daughter . . . she was still at school . . . she was way too gorgeous to look twice at a broke-arse bloke like him.

It didn't work.

"Angel! *Wait!*"

Almost halfway down the street by now, Angel stopped and turned around.

"Do you fancy going out sometime?" Ryan asked when he reached her. "To the pictures, or something?"

Angel dropped her gaze. "I'd like to, but I'm not sure if I can."

"Sorry, I shouldn't have asked." Ryan held up his hands and took a step back. "Stupid, really — me working for your dad, and that. Anyhow, you've probably already got a boyfriend?"

"No, I haven't," Angel said quickly. "And it's got nothing to do with my dad. It's just . . ." She trailed off, too embarrassed to tell him that the real reason she couldn't say yes to a date was because she wasn't allowed to go out with boys.

A knowing look came into Ryan's eyes and he said, "Look, just forget I asked, yeah? See you around sometime."

Angel frowned when he started walking away. He thought she was being a snob because he worked for her dad.

"Ryan, wait!"

"What?" he said flatly, turning and looking back at her.

"I *would* like to go out with you," she told him, blushing furiously because this was the first time she had ever spoken to a lad like this.

"But you can't, because I'm black," he said, stating rather than asking.

"God, no, that's got nothing to do with it."

"So what is it, then?"

Angel bit her lip. This was really hard, and she had no idea how she was going to make it happen, but if she didn't do it now she might not get another chance.

"When do you want to go?" she asked. "To the pictures, I mean. If you still want to?" she added nervously.

"For real?" Ryan gave her a questioning look. Grinning when she nodded, he said, "How about tomorrow? We could meet here at seven?"

Angel nodded again, her heart already beating ten to the dozen in her chest.

"Cool." He smiled, and Angel's stomach flipped when she noticed the dimple in his left cheek.

"Hang on — what's your name?" she asked when he started to walk away again.

"Ryan," he told her, still grinning.

Angel was worried as she made her way back to Lisa's. Ryan was the most gorgeous lad she'd ever seen in her life, with his beautiful soft brown eyes, that stunning smile, and that little-boy dimple. But if she couldn't make it tomorrow, that would be it. He would never want to see her again.

"I am *wiped*," Lisa said when she came home a few hours later.

"Do you want a coffee?" Angel offered, jumping up from the couch.

"Oh, God, yeah," Lisa moaned, dropping her handbag and kicking off her shoes. "I had to go to the dentist this morning and I'm only just starting to feel my lips again." She slipped her jacket off and hung it on a hook behind the door before following Angel into the kitchen. "Two fillings — can you believe that?"

"Did it hurt?" Angel asked, aware that her hands were shaking as she filled the kettle.

334

"Not as much as the toothache would have done if I'd left it," Lisa said, flopping onto a chair. "Then I went to my mum's, and she had me running round after her like a blue-arsed fly all day. I told her . . . I said, you've only twisted your ankle, Mam, not snapped the bleedin' thing off, so stop acting like a cripple. But she's been like, *get me this, get me that*, all day. I could have bloody throttled her."

"Ah, well, you can put your feet up now," Angel murmured.

"Oh, I intend to. I'm going to park myself in front of the telly, and I'm not moving again for the rest of the night," said Lisa, reaching down to rub her aching feet. "So, what have you been up to? Hope you haven't been too bored?"

"I bought some magazines and went to the park," Angel told her, fetching Lisa's coffee to the table and sitting across from her. "But I saw some girls beating another one up, so I —"

"Oh, you didn't get involved, did you?" Lisa cut in with a groan. "They're a right load of rough bitches round here. Hope they didn't follow you back to the house or I'm going to have murder!"

"They were only little. I just chased them off and walked the girl home."

"Oh, well, good for you. But you've got to watch your back round here, 'cos you never know who's watching you. Don't suppose your dad's been round while I was out?"

"No." Angel shook her head and gazed down at her fingers linked together on the tabletop.

Lisa noticed the way she was chewing on her lip, and asked, "Is something on your mind, babe?"

"I was just wondering . . ." Angel said tentatively. "Would it be okay if I stayed a few more nights?"

"Fine by me," Lisa said. "But your dad's the one you need to be asking, not me."

"Will *you* ask him?" Angel gave her a pleading look. "He might say yes to you."

Lisa narrowed her eyes. "What's going on, babe? Is there some reason why you don't want to go home? It's not your nan, is it?"

"No." Angel shook her head. "I just want to stay. I hardly ever see you these days, and I thought it'd be nice to spend a bit of time with you while my mum's in hospital."

Lisa started laughing and shook her head. "God, you're a terrible liar. You couldn't sound any more sincere if you poured honey on it."

"I'm not lying," Angel insisted, her cheeks turning pink.

"Babe, I know when I'm being buttered up," Lisa told her. "Just tell me what's really going on. Have you made plans to go to a party, or something?"

"Not a party," Angel muttered, too guilty to look at her. "The pictures."

"With?"

"A boy."

"Really?" Lisa raised an eyebrow. "Wow, you kept that one quiet. I never knew you had a boyfriend. Does he go to your school?"

"No, he works for my dad."

"You're kidding me!" Lisa drew her head back. "Does your dad know?"

"God, no," Angel gasped. "He'd go mad." She gazed up worriedly at Lisa now. "You won't tell him, will you?"

Lisa's heart went out to her. Almost sixteen, and she'd never ever been out on a date. This was the time when she was supposed to be learning how to kiss, falling in and out of love, having a laugh, getting her heart broken — all the things that taught a girl how to be a woman. But that prissy cousin and sour-faced old bat of an aunt of Lisa's had got the poor thing locked up so tight that she was in danger of turning into a replica of them if she wasn't allowed to start spreading her wings.

"I won't breathe a word," Lisa promised. "But I hope you're being sensible?"

"It's not like that," Angel said, blushing all over again, because she knew exactly what Lisa was getting at. "I've never been out with him before. I just saw him earlier and he asked me to go to the pictures — that's all."

"Yeah, well, don't let him pressure you into doing anything you don't want to do," Lisa advised. "He's obviously older than you if he works, and men can be buggers for that."

"Ryan's not like that," Angel insisted, unable to stop herself from smiling.

"Ryan, eh?" Lisa grinned. "So what's he like, this *Ryan?*"

"Oh, he's lovely," Angel gushed. "He's not cocky or anything, he's just really, really nice. And he's got a gorgeous smile, and this little dimple just here." She put her finger to her cheek.

Lisa saw the unmistakable signs of first love developing before her eyes, and it made her nervous. It was all very well letting Angel stay over for a couple of nights so that she could enjoy a rare bit of freedom. But a couple of nights was more than enough time for a young girl to fall in love and it would break her heart when she had to go home again, because there was no way her mum was going to let her go out dating.

"Babe, I think we might be running before we can walk here," Lisa cautioned. "We don't even know if your dad's going to let you stay yet. And even if he does, what if he comes round while you're out? Where am I supposed to tell him you've gone?"

"I hadn't thought about that," Angel murmured, her shoulders drooping. "What should I do? I told Ryan I'd meet him on the corner at seven."

Lisa gazed at the girl's miserable face and sighed. "Look, no promises, but let me talk to your dad. You still won't be able to go out even if he says yes," she reiterated thoughtfully. "But that doesn't mean you can't see Ryan. You can go and meet him, and fetch him round here — if you want? That way you get to spend a bit of time with him, and I get to check him out and make sure he's good enough for you."

"Really?" Angel gasped. She jumped up when Lisa nodded and then she rushed around the table with a massive smile on her lips. "Oh, thank you, thank you!"

338

she gushed, hugging her. "You know you've always been my favourite auntie, don't you?"

"I should bloody hope so," Lisa chuckled. "Seeing as I'm the only one who hasn't got a beard. It's no wonder the rest of 'em hate me so much."

"Well, I think you're great," said Angel, kissing her on the cheek before going back to her own seat.

"I am, aren't I?" Lisa grinned and reached for her cigarettes.

"Yeah. And you'd make a really great mum, too," Angel said.

Smile slipping, Lisa lit her smoke and shifted in her seat. "Christ, is that the time? I'd best start thinking about what we're going to have for dinner. And then I'll give your dad a ring — find out if there's any news on your mum."

A little wave of guilt washed over Angel. She'd been so wrapped up in thoughts of Ryan that her mum hadn't even crossed her mind.

"Don't worry." Lisa reached across the table and squeezed her hand. "She'll be fine, or we'd have heard by now. And don't worry about the other stuff, either. I'll square it with your dad — I promise."

CHAPTER
TWENTY-SIX

Ryan was a bag of nerves as he got ready to meet Angel the next evening. And that was a weird feeling, because he'd been out with loads of girls and had never felt this jittery over any of them. But there was something about Angel that set her apart from the rest, something special and untouchable. She made him want to be a better man — richer, funnier, bigger, more handsome. But he wasn't fooling himself that this date was going to turn into anything. As soon as she realised what a loser he was, she'd be bound to lose interest and go back to her rich boys.

"What are you all ponced up for?" his dad sneered when he walked into the living room at quarter to seven to get his jacket.

"I'm not," Ryan muttered, secretly wondering if he might have gone a bit overboard. His G-star jeans and Adidas trainers were brand new and he already felt a bit uncomfortable, because he didn't want Angel to think that he was the kind of guy who cared more about his own appearance than hers. And his Versace T-shirt looked mint. But she had money, so what if she sussed that it was a fake?

But it was too late to change now.

"You look lovely," Zeta said quietly as he passed her in the hallway on his way out. "Really handsome."

"Cheers, mam." He smiled. "See you later."

Angel was nowhere in sight when Ryan reached the corner where they had arranged to meet. The palms of his hands felt clammy, and he caught himself whistling through his teeth — a sure sign that he was nervous. He lit a cigarette and leaned back against the wall.

She's changed her mind, the voice in his head piped up. *She only agreed to go out with you to shut you up. She never really intended to go through with it. You're not good enough — you know it, and so does she.*

"Sorry I'm late," Angel apologised when she walked around the corner a couple of minutes later.

Ryan straightened up when he saw her. "Wow, you look fantastic."

Self-conscious, because she hadn't quite mastered the heels yet and was terrified of falling flat on her face, Angel smiled shyly. "Thanks."

"Ready to get going?" He flicked the cigarette away.

"I can't," she admitted. "Not because I don't want to," she added quickly. "It's just that my mum's in hospital, and I'm staying at my aunt's, and she doesn't really want me to go out for too long in case my dad rings."

Ryan was disappointed, but he tried not to show it. It was only what he'd been expecting, after all. He just hadn't expected her to come and tell him in person. He'd thought that she would just not bother turning up.

341

"It's okay," he said. "Hope it's nothing serious with your mum?"

Touched that he'd asked, Angel said, "My dad hasn't really said much, but he reckoned she looked a bit better when he went to visit her earlier."

"That's good," said Ryan. Then, "Right, well, I'll get going, leave you to get back to your aunt."

"Actually, she was wondering if you'd like to come for a brew?" Angel asked. "It's only round the corner, and she'd really like to meet you."

"Yeah?" Ryan gave her a disbelieving look. Most of the white girls he'd been out with hadn't been too keen on taking him home to meet the folks.

Which reminded him of something that had been niggling him.

"What about your dad? Only, I've been thinking, I probably should have asked him if it was all right to take you out before I went ahead and asked you."

"No, don't do that," Angel blurted out. "He, er, doesn't actually know I've seen you since that day at the yard."

"Oh, right." Ryan read between the lines and guessed that she didn't think her dad would approve. "Maybe we'd best just leave it then?"

"Okay," Angel murmured, disappointment threatening to bring tears to her eyes. "If that's what you want."

"Course it's not," Ryan told her. "I just don't want to cause any trouble. I like you, Angel. I mean, like, *really* like you."

"I like you, too," she admitted, her voice little more than a whisper.

342

Ryan's stomach flipped, and he inhaled deeply. No other girl had ever had this effect on him. Angel had been on his mind ever since their eyes had met through the office window back at the yard, and he'd been dying to see her again. She was so pretty, and sweet, and he wanted to stroke her hair and hold her and kiss her.

Angel was looking at him, waiting for him to say something. There was fear in her eyes. When Ryan saw it and realised that she was even more scared than he was he cupped her face in his hands and kissed her gently.

"Sorry," he muttered, pulling away after a moment. "I shouldn't have done that."

"I liked it," she gasped, her heart thudding in her chest.

"Me, too, but —"

Angel raised up onto her tiptoes and kissed him again to shut him up. Lost in the moment, Ryan pulled her into his arms and held her close.

Lisa came around the corner and stopped in her tracks when she saw them.

"Oi!" she hissed. "What d'ya think you're playing at, you idiots?"

Ryan jerked back with a guilty look on his face. "Christ, I'm sorry . . . it was totally my fault."

Lisa looked him up and down, and then turned to Angel, her eyebrows raised in approval. "I see what you meant."

Angel gave her a pleading look, begging her not to say anything else. But Lisa hadn't come to embarrass her or tell them off; she'd come to see what was keeping them, because the longer they stood on the street the more chance there was of Johnny driving around the corner and catching them. At least if they were in the house she could get the boy out of the back door if Johnny turned up, so he'd be none the wiser.

"You don't have to worry about me," she assured Ryan. "But it's not exactly smart to snog in the middle of the street if you're trying to stay undercover."

"Sorry," Ryan said again. "I'll go."

Lisa saw the look of despair on Angel's face, and said, "You bloody won't. I've been waiting half an hour to meet you, and I got a cake out and everything. And there's no way me and her can eat it all, so you'd better just get moving."

"Leave him," Angel said quietly. "Let him go if he wants to."

"He doesn't," Lisa said knowingly. "He just thinks he should. Am I right, Ryan?"

"I, er, guess so." He shrugged.

"See?" Lisa smiled at Angel. "Now stop messing about and get inside before your dad turns up. Come on . . ." She summoned Ryan with a jerk of her head.

He looked at Angel to see what she wanted him to do.

"You don't have to," she said. "It's totally up to you."

A slow smile lit up Ryan's face. "Suppose I better had," he said, reaching for her hand. "Don't want you eating all that cake and getting fat."

"He's lovely," Lisa said when Ryan left her house a couple of hours later. "I can see why you fell for him."

344

"I haven't fallen for him," Angel lied.

"Oh, well, you won't mind if I have a crack at him, then, will you?" Lisa teased. Laughing when Angel's face fell, she said, "Chill out, babe, he's about twenty years too young. Anyway, he wouldn't look twice at an old boot like me when he's got a gorgeous young thing like you to keep him happy. He couldn't keep his eyes off you."

"Really?"

"Girl, if he ain't crazy into you, I'm the queen."

Angel went to bed happy that night. Lisa was convinced that Ryan really liked her, and she hoped that she was right, because she really liked him — a lot. More than a lot, in fact.

Lisa talked Johnny into letting Angel stay for a few more days, and it was the best time of Angel's entire life. She had always liked Lisa, but the more time they spent together, the closer she felt to her. The age difference seemed to get smaller and smaller, so she now felt more like Lisa's friend than her niece — or second cousin, as she really was. And it was bliss to wake up in the morning and not have someone nag her the instant she stepped out of her bedroom. Fantastic to eat dinner with another person, instead of sitting on her own in the kitchen. Brilliant to stay up late and watch TV with someone who could limit themselves to a couple of glasses of wine instead of swilling a whole bottle of spirits, and who laughed when she got tipsy, instead of getting argumentative and nasty. And, best of all, she got to spend a lot of time with Ryan.

He had taken to calling round in the early afternoon and staying until he had to go home to get ready for work at night. Which pleased Lisa, because he had turned out to be pretty handy with a screwdriver, so she finally had someone to do all the little "man" jobs that had been building up over the years. And he refused to let her pay him when he fixed something, as if, Angel thought, he already considered himself part of the family.

But as lovely as the dream had been, it came to an abrupt end when her dad came round one morning and told her to get her stuff together.

"Sorry, darlin', I know you've been enjoying yourself," he apologised. "But your mum's insisting she wants to come home, and your nan's got the place in a right mess, so you're going to have to sort it out."

"Is the hospital all right with her coming home?" Angel asked. She felt petty even saying it, but she didn't want to go yet.

"They reckon she's healing well," Johnny told her. "They've persuaded her to stay another couple of days, but they think she'll be okay after that."

"Can't I just come home when she does?"

"Sorry, love, but it's going to take that long to get the place clean. And I've got some meetings this morning, so I need to get moving. Go get your stuff so I can drop you off, eh?"

Angel did as she'd been told, but it pissed her off that it fell to her to clean up her nan's mess, and she didn't speak all the way home. She kissed her dad goodbye when they arrived at the house and then she traipsed up the path, carrying her bags.

She was shocked when she let herself into the house. She hadn't even been gone a full week, but everything was already coated with dust. And her nan had obviously spent the entire time drinking, because there were empty bottles everywhere. And the whole house reeked of urine, which made Angel wonder if her nan had been pissing on the carpets.

But shocked as she was by the mess, she was even more shocked when she saw her nan. The woman had always been skinny but now she was thinner than ever, and there were deep hollows under her dull eyes as if she hadn't slept a wink all week. But, most worryingly of all, she was still wearing the same dress that she'd been wearing the last time Angel had seen her at the hospital. And it was so dirty that Angel suspected she'd been wearing it the whole time Angel had been gone. In which case, she'd probably been wearing the same underwear as well.

Ashamed of herself for not even having wondered how her nan had been getting on by herself, Angel put her bags in her bedroom and then went from room to room opening all of the windows to air out the house. That done, she got cracking on the cleaning — in the hope that it would distract her from thinking about Ryan. But it didn't work, and he was all she could think about as she dusted the furniture, hoovered the carpets, scrubbed the ledges and polished the windows.

He was her first-ever boyfriend, but she already knew that she wanted to be with him for ever, so it was killing her not knowing when she would see him again. And she'd left the paper he'd written his number down on in the drawer at Lisa's, so she couldn't even call him to tell him that she'd had to come home.

But there was nothing she could do about it right now, so she pushed him firmly out of her mind and tried to concentrate on the house instead.

When the cleaning was done she went into the parlour. Her nan was sitting in her chair with a vacant look in her eyes, and she looked so old and lonely that Angel felt bad all over again for having left her on her own for so long — and for having practically ignored her since she'd come home.

She squatted beside her and said gently, "Why don't I run you a bath, nan? Then you can have a nice soak while I make dinner. And I'll see if there's anything on telly for us to watch together later, if you want?"

Rita turned her gaze on her and, for a second, it seemed as if she didn't know who she was looking at. But the confusion quickly cleared and the old glint of meanness was back.

"Piss off. I don't want nowt from you."

"I'm only trying to help."

"Are you deaf as well as stupid?"

"Suit yourself." Angel sighed and pushed herself back up to her feet.

After dinner, which she ate on her own in the kitchen while her nan ignored the plate she'd taken into the parlour for her, Angel went to bed and cried herself to sleep.

CHAPTER
TWENTY-SEVEN

It was 2a.m. when Ryan and Tommy dropped the pickup car at the garage. They usually shared a cab home but Ryan wanted to be alone tonight, so he decided to walk.

There had been a cloud hanging over him since he'd gone round to Lisa's the other day only to discover that Angel had gone home, and he'd been wondering when — or even *if* — he was ever going to see her again.

He was still thinking about her as he turned the corner onto Lisa's street when his gaze was drawn to the headlights of a car turning in at the other end. As it pulled up outside her house, the front door opened and light spilled out onto the pavement. Lisa came out onto the step just as Johnny climbed out of the car, and when he walked up to her she grabbed him by the front of his jacket and kissed him before pulling him inside.

Shocked, Ryan stood and stared at the now closed front door. No way had he just seen that. No way.

When the downstairs light went out and, moments later, the bedroom light came on, he shook his head in disgust and walked back out to the main road. His brain was fried. Johnny was a married man — how could he do something like that? And with Lisa of all people. And how could *she* do it to Angel, when she knew how much the girl adored her dad? It was just plain wrong on so many levels.

Ryan hadn't intended to go to Angel's house but that was where he found himself twenty minutes later. He'd never been there before and he felt conspicuous as he walked up the avenue. It was one of those posh neighbourhoods where everyone had a flash motor, and matching net curtains upstairs and down. He doubted that they saw too many black faces around here, so he kept his head down and walked quickly along to Angel's house.

He stopped at the end of her drive and gazed helplessly up at the windows. He didn't even know what he was doing here. There was no way he could tell her what he'd just seen, because it would break her heart. And that was if she even believed him — which she probably wouldn't, because he still didn't believe it himself.

A noise from across the road shook Ryan out of his thoughts. Scared that he'd been spotted, he ducked into the shadows and made his way down the side of the house into the dark back garden. A light was on at the downstairs window, and he held his breath and edged up to it to peep into the room. The TV was on in the corner, and an old lady who he guessed to be Angel's nan was sprawled on the couch with her eyes closed and her mouth wide open.

Ryan stepped back and peered up at the windows. The master bedroom was usually at the front of the house, so the chances were that one of these two windows belonged to Angel's room. He picked up a small clump of soil from the flower bed and tossed it at the smaller of the two, then waited a few seconds and did it again. After a moment, the curtain twitched and Angel's sleepy face appeared. Her eyes widened when she peered down and saw him. She pushed the window open.

"Oh, my God, what are you doing here?" she hissed. "You've got to go before someone sees you."

"It's all right, your nan's flat out," Ryan whispered back. "And your dad's busy," he added, trying to keep his voice even so that she wouldn't pick up on anything being wrong.

"How do you know?" Angel asked.

"I just saw him when I left work," he lied. "Come down for a minute — I want to see you."

"Wait there." She closed the window quietly.

A few seconds later, Ryan heard the sound of a key being carefully turned in the back door, and then Angel was in his arms.

"I've missed you so much," she whispered, kissing him greedily.

"Missed you too, baby girl," he murmured, holding her close and stroking her hair.

"Come with me." She took his hand and led him up the garden to a shed at the far end.

"What are you doing?" he asked when she opened the door and pulled him inside.

Hushing him, Angel rooted through the pile of junk that was heaped in the corner until she found the rolled-up rug she was looking for. She laid it out on the floor and sat down.

"We shouldn't be in here," Ryan said, feeling suddenly nervous.

"I just want to be alone with you," Angel told him, reaching for his hand and tugging him down beside her.

He kissed her, but pulled back when she slid her hand down to his crotch. "Don't," he groaned.

"I want to," she told him huskily. "I love you, Ryan."

"We shouldn't do this," he murmured. "You're too young."

"Don't you love me?" She gazed into his eyes.

"Yeah, course, but —"

"Sshhh." She put her finger on his lips. "Don't say anything, just do it. *Please* . . . I want you to."

When Angel moved her hand back down and slowly unzipped his fly, Ryan closed his eyes. He knew it was wrong, but he'd been dreaming about this since the very first moment he'd laid eyes on her — and he wasn't strong enough to resist.

"I haven't got anything on me," he gasped at the last minute.

"I don't care," she whispered, pulling him into her.

When it was over, Ryan pushed himself up onto his elbow and gazed down at her.

"Oh, God, did I hurt you?" he asked when he saw a tear slide from her eye and roll down into her hair.

"No, I'm just happy," Angel said, putting her arms around his neck and pulling his head down. "Let's run away, then no one can stop us being together."

"We can't," Ryan told her gently. "If we're going to make this work, we've got to do it right."

"You mean tell my dad?"

"Yeah." He nodded. "I know you're scared, and he'll probably be mad. But I reckon he'd come round if he knew how serious we are."

"Are we serious?" Angel probed, needing to know that it wasn't just her who felt like this.

"As serious as it gets," Ryan told her.

"I don't want you to go," she moaned when he sat up. "Let's just sleep in here. No one will notice I'm not in my room."

"I've got to," he insisted, kissing her softly. "And you need to go back inside. It's too cold out here."

Angel sighed, and reluctantly let him help her to her feet. "Will you come back tomorrow night?"

"For sure, baby girl."

Hand in hand they left the shed and darted across the grass. Ryan kissed her one last time and started to back away down the path. Angel was smiling, but when she saw a movement in the shadows behind him her eyes widened in horror.

"What's wrong?" Ryan whispered, giving her a questioning look. When she didn't answer, he turned his head to see what she was staring at. A thrill of terror ran through his body when he saw Johnny standing right behind him.

"This ain't what it looks like, Mr C . . ." he spluttered, holding his hands out, palms up. "We weren't doing nothing, I swear."

Johnny seized him by the throat and slammed him up against the wall. "Shut your fucking mouth, you dirty little bastard," he growled. Then he punched him in the gut.

"Dad, don't!" Angel cried, her knees turning to water as Ryan's face contorted in pain. "You're hurting him!"

"Get in the house," Johnny ordered.

"It's not her fault," Ryan gasped, struggling to breathe as the pain seared through his body. "Take it out on me, not her."

"Oh, I'm going to," Johnny told him quietly.

"Who's there?" Rita stumbled into the doorway just then, wielding an empty whisky bottle above her head. "Oh, Jeezus!" she squawked when she saw Johnny with his hand around the boy's throat. "We're being burgled! Someone call the police!"

"Shut it!" Johnny hissed. "Get back inside — and take her with you." He jerked his chin at Angel.

"Nan, stop him," Angel sobbed, tears rolling down her cheeks. "He's going to kill him."

Rita gazed confusedly from Angel to Johnny. Then a light switched on in her eyes, and her lip curled back in disgust.

"You filthy little whore," she hissed. "How could you let one of *them* put their hands on you? Your grandad will be turning in his grave."

"I love him!" Angel cried. "And he loves me!"

"Get inside, you dirty little bitch!" Rita yelled, grabbing her by the hair and tugging her over the step. "Just wait till your mother wakes up and hears about this — she'll skin you alive!"

When she had closed the door, Johnny headbutted Ryan and then laid into him with his fists and feet, only stopping when he could barely see the boy's face for blood. Breathing heavily, he stared down at him lying in a heap on the floor at his feet.

"If you ever come near my daughter again, I'll kill you — you got that?" he growled. "Now get the fuck away from my house before I change my mind about letting you go."

"I'm sorry," Ryan croaked, coughing as blood trickled down his throat. "But I love her. And I was going to come and see you . . . ask your permission."

"One more word and you'll be leaving in the boot of my car," Johnny warned, reaching down and hauling him to his feet. "Now fuckin' *move*." He hurled him up the path.

Angel was sitting at the kitchen table sobbing hysterically when her dad walked in after seeing Ryan off. She looked up at him accusingly and wailed, "I love him! You had no right!"

The slap was so hard and swift that it knocked her off her chair and sent her sprawling across the floor. She came to rest against the sink-cupboard door and stared up at Johnny in mute shock. In her entire life, her dad had never so much as smacked her hand. And he had never *ever* looked at her the way he was looking at her right now: a mixture of disgust, fury, and disappointment — but mainly disgust.

Even Rita was shocked as she watched from the doorway. "Go easy," she cautioned.

"Shut your mouth," Johnny growled. "This has got nothing to do with you, so fuck off."

Rita didn't need telling twice. As bad as her Frankie had been, she had never once seen as murderous a look in his eye as the one that was in Johnny's now. She flicked one last pitying look at Angel, then scuttled into her parlour and shoved a chair up against the door to keep him out.

"Go to your room," Johnny told Angel, his voice so quiet that she almost didn't hear what he'd said. "And don't come out again until I tell you to."

Angel scrambled to her feet and edged past her father with terror in her eyes before fleeing up the stairs.

Alone, Johnny yanked the cupboard open and took out a bottle of whisky. He twisted the cap off and drank a long mouthful straight from the bottle, then got a glass and sat down at the table to finish it off.

He could easily have killed Ryan just now, and he wished he had, because then the situation would have been dead and buried along with the boy's body. He felt sick to his stomach at the thought of his beautiful girl being mauled. All he'd ever done was try to protect her, and he was furious that a boy he'd trusted and liked had come creeping round to his house behind his back to take advantage of her.

The devious bastard had fed her the oldest line in the book by telling her that he loved her, and she'd fallen for it, like the naive little girl that she was. She didn't have a clue how men operated. But Johnny did, because

356

he'd done the exact same thing to her mother — and look where that had landed him.

But it wasn't happening again. The boy had been warned, and if he chanced his hand he'd lose it — along with his head, his legs, and his dick.

From now on, Angel wouldn't be leaving this house except to go to school. And to make sure that she didn't try to pull a fast one, Johnny would be dropping her off in the morning and picking her back up in the afternoon. And then she would be locked in her room with the windows nailed shut, until she got over whatever she thought she felt for the prick.

Ryan limped his way out of the avenue and around to the main road. He saw a taxi in the distance, and leaned against a lamp-post for support as he waited for the vehicle to pull alongside. When it did, he waved, but the driver took one look at his battered face and put his foot down. So he staggered on, feeling with every step as if he'd been stabbed with a red-hot poker.

His mobile rang just as he reached Hulme. Hoping against hope that it was Angel, he gritted his teeth against the pain and pulled the phone out of his pocket. But it wasn't Angel — it was Lisa.

"Johnny's found out about you and Angel," she blurted out before he could speak.

"I know," Ryan muttered.

"Oh, God, I'm so sorry," she groaned, hearing the pain in his voice and guessing that she was too late. "It's my fault. He came round earlier to drop something off, and we got chatting and I let it slip. I would have warned you earlier, but it took me ages to find your number."

Ryan closed his eyes and inhaled deeply. *So they'd only been chatting, had they? Up in the bedroom, after kissing on the step. Yeah, right!*

"It doesn't matter," he murmured. "Just make sure Angel's okay."

"Johnny would *never* hurt Angel." Lisa was adamant. "He loves her too much."

"Hope you're right," Ryan said quietly.

He cut the call and continued on home.

"Where have you been?" Ryan's mum demanded, rushing out into the hall with a wild look in her eyes when she heard the door opening. "Some men came round and tried to kick the door in, and —" Zeta stopped mid-sentence when she noticed the state of her son's face. She flicked the overhead light on to get a better look. "Oh, my God, what happened?" gasped, her hands flying to her mouth.

"Nothing," Ryan muttered. "I'm going to bed."

"Son, you're hurt," she cried, stepping in front of him as he made for the stairs. "You need to go to hospital."

"Just leave it," he groaned.

"Leave what?" his dad asked, lurching into the living-room doorway. He'd been asleep in his chair and his face was heavily creased. But it brightened up when he saw the state of his son. "Fuckin' hell, what've you done to deserve that? Been dipping your wick in some other fucker's bird, have you?"

358

"Shut up, Gary," Zeta snapped, too concerned about Ryan to worry how he might react to her speaking to him so sharply. "This is serious. He could have internal bleeding for all we know."

"I'm okay," Ryan insisted, gripping the banister rail and hauling himself up the stairs.

"If this is owt to do with them blokes who came round earlier, you'd best hope this is an end to it, 'cos there'll be a fuckin' bloodbath if they try it again," his dad called after him. "They caught me kipping this time, but they won't get that lucky again."

Ryan ignored him and went into his bedroom. When the door had closed behind him, he took off his jacket and T-shirt and gingerly examined his ribs. He was covered in bruises, and one of his ribs was jutting out a little further than the rest. But it wasn't the first time he'd had his ribs broken, because his dad had already been there and done that. So, knowing that the doctor would only bandage it if he went to hospital, he tore up an old T-shirt and used it as strapping, then took some painkillers and climbed carefully into bed.

He didn't blame Johnny. Any man would have done the same if they had caught some little piece of shit like Ryan putting his hands on their daughter. He just wished he'd been a better man and stopped Angel when she got started tonight, and then they might have stood a chance. But Johnny was never going to let him anywhere near Angel after this. And that hurt way more than the physical pain.

CHAPTER
TWENTY-EIGHT

Angel's heart was broken, and she felt as if her life was over. Her dad still wasn't talking to her beyond issuing instructions, and her mum had been gloating ever since it happened, making snide comments whenever her dad was home — probably, Angel suspected, to make sure that he didn't forget what his daughter had done and soften towards her.

Her days had become one long tedious round of being watched like a hawk. She couldn't move at home without her mum and her nan demanding to know where she was going and what she was doing, and if she stayed too long in the bathroom they'd be banging at the door in seconds, demanding that she unlock it.

And it was just as bad at school. Her dad would drive her there in silence, and watch until she'd entered the building. But there was no escape even then, because he'd spoken with the head, who had subsequently ordered the teachers to check on Angel's whereabouts throughout the day, so she couldn't even have a chat with her friends at break without one of them popping up. And then, at hometime, her dad, or one of his trusted employees, would be waiting at the gate to take her home again.

When Angel started to feel sick and went off her food a few weeks into her sentence, she put it down to the stress of not being allowed even to breathe without asking permission first. But her mum thought otherwise.

"Go and do this," she ordered, coming home from the shops one afternoon and dropping a pregnancy test onto the kitchen table where Angel was doing her homework while her nan watched over her.

Angel blushed and shoved it away. "No. I don't need it."

Ruth looked at her mother. "Has she been sick again while I've been out?" She pursed her lips when Rita nodded, then put her hands on her hips and glared at Angel. "I'm not going to tell you again, lady. Go to the bathroom and do it — now."

"Fine, I'll do it." Angel snatched up the box and shoved her chair back. "But you're wrong."

"Yes, well, we'll soon find out, won't we?" said Ruth, following her out of the door and up the stairs.

Angel stopped in the bathroom doorway and raised her eyebrows. "You're not coming in with me."

"Oh, yes, I am," Ruth told her. "There's no way I'm trusting you to do it on your own. You'll probably shove it under the tap or something."

The thought hadn't even crossed Angel's mind. But she still didn't want her mum standing there watching her. That was just disgusting.

"I won't be able to do it if you're there," she said, standing her ground. "You can't force me to wee."

Ruth exhaled loudly with irritation. "Right, I'll wait out here. But you can leave the door open so I can hear if you run the tap."

Aware that it was the best she was going to get, Angel reluctantly did the deed, even though she was sure that it was a waste of time. She and Ryan had only slept together that one time in the shed, and she'd had her period straight after, so there was no way she could be pregnant. Although she kind of hoped that she was, because then they would have to let her see him.

And that was all she wanted: to see him, and ask if he still felt the same about her as she did about him. He'd said he loved her, but he'd made no effort to contact her since her dad had caught them and she was beginning to think that he'd changed his mind.

Back in the kitchen after Angel came out of the bathroom, Ruth drummed her fingers on the table and stared at the little stick. A couple of minutes that felt more like hours later, the display popped up in the little window: *Pregnant . . . 4–5 weeks.*

"You stupid idiot!" she yelled, jumping up and smacking Angel hard across the face. "Why couldn't you just keep your knickers on? You're not even sixteen — what the hell were you playing at."

"She's a liar, an' all," Rita chipped in. "She sat there and barefaced lied to my face that all they'd done was have a kiss that night."

"Well, you're not keeping it," Ruth went on, marching out into the hall and bringing back the phone book.

362

"Too flaming right she's not," Rita agreed, huffing. "I'm not having no black baby in *my* house."

"Shut up, Mother," Ruth snapped. "I don't care what colour it is — she's not old enough to have a baby, full stop." She turned to Angel now and gave her an ominous look as she flipped through the phone book. "You wait till your dad hears about this."

Tears were already rolling down Angel's cheeks, and her whole body was shaking.

"Cry as much as you like," Ruth went on unsympathetically, "but it won't work this time. Your dad's going to see you for what you really are." She clicked her fingers at Rita. "Pass me the phone."

Angel cradled her stomach with her hands as she listened to her mum make an appointment at the family planning clinic for the following week.

When that was done, Ruth rang Johnny and told him to come home — and why. Then she and Rita sat and waited, their stares fixed firmly on Angel in case she got any ideas about trying to do a runner.

Johnny strode in half an hour later and slammed his keys down on the ledge. Angel was huddled in her chair with her arms wrapped around herself, her face streaked and blotchy. She looked so young and scared that he would normally have pulled her into his arms and told her that everything was going to be all right — that he would *make* it all right. But this was too serious, and he was too mad.

"What have you got to say for yourself?" he demanded.

"I'm sorry," Angel croaked, unable to look at him. "I didn't mean for it to happen."

"Famous last words," snorted Rita.

"I've made an appointment at the clinic next week," Ruth told him. "They'll examine her and talk to her, then book her in for an abortion."

"Sooner the better," Rita chipped in again.

"No," Angel sobbed, shaking her head. "I don't want an abortion. Please, Daddy . . ."

Ruth slammed her hands down on the table. "You'll do as you're told — and keep your mouth shut while you're at it! You haven't got a clue what you've done, have you?"

"This isn't about you any more," Rita joined in. "We're the ones who'd have to bring the little bastard up; feed it, and clothe it."

"I can do it myself," Angel argued tearfully. "I'll do everything."

"You haven't even left school yet," Ruth reminded her angrily. "How are you going to support it when you can't even support yourself? And how do you think it'd look, you waddling into your exams with a fat belly on you? You want everyone to know what a whore you've been?"

"And with a black lad, an' all," Rita reminded them, sneering. "I'll never be able to set foot out of the door for the shame of it."

"Will you just stop going on about that?" Ruth hissed through gritted teeth.

"Both of you shut up," Johnny ordered, already sick of hearing their voices. "And you get to your room." He jerked his thumb at Angel. "I'll deal with you later."

"Daddy, please . . ." she implored, giving him a heart-wreching look as she stood up. "Don't make me get rid of it. I can look after it. I'll be a really good mum."

"You've lost the right to say what you do and don't want," Ruth barked, clenching her fists on the tabletop. "It's going, and that's final."

"No!" Angel cried, desperation loosening her tongue. "I love Ryan, and he loves me — and we haven't done anything that you and my dad didn't do first."

Ruth leapt to her feet. "How *dare* you try and make out that this is anything like me and your dad! I was nearly twenty when I had you, and we'd been married for three years. We were *respectable*!"

"Only 'cos you lost the first one," Angel countered defiantly. "That's why you got married — 'cos my grandad *made* you. My dad never loved you like Ryan loves me."

Ruth's face had gone as white as a sheet, and foam had gathered at the corners of her tightly drawn lips.

"You little *bitch*," she snarled, flying at Angel and laying into her. "How dare you talk to me like that! How *dare* you!"

"Pack it in," Johnny bellowed, dragging her off.

Chest heaving, her hands coated in the hair that she'd just pulled from Angel's scalp, Ruth glared at him. "Don't tell me you're defending her after what

365

she's done! You heard what she said; are you just going to let her get away with it?"

"*Go!*" Johnny barked at Angel.

Still sobbing, she fled from the kitchen and ran up the stairs to lock herself in her room.

Johnny turned on Ruth when she'd gone, and warned, "Don't you ever put your hands on her like that again."

"She asked for it," Ruth hissed, her nostrils flaring.

"Why? For telling the truth?" Johnny challenged her. He shook his head in disgust when she pursed her lips. "Don't make out like she's a whore when you did the exact same thing."

"I wasn't as young as her," Ruth shot back defensively.

"You were only a year older," Johnny reminded her.

"Well, she didn't know that, so she had no right to say it," Ruth argued. "But I can guess who told her," she added, with a knowing sneer. "And that was exactly why I didn't want her getting too close to my cousin, 'cos she's a poisonous big-mouthed bitch. But you had to go and let your precious daughter stay with her as soon as my back was turned. So this is your fault, not mine."

"It doesn't matter whose fault it is," Johnny replied coldly. "It's going to get sorted, that's all that matters. But if you lay one finger on her in the meantime, you're gonna know about it. And the same goes for you, old woman." He turned on Rita. "The pair of you just leave her alone until her appointment comes up, or you'll have me to answer to. You both got that?"

Ruth and Rita simultaneously screwed their lips into tight knots and folded their arms. Satisfied that they wouldn't dare to go against him, Johnny snatched up his keys and walked out.

Everything that could be done right now had been done, and he had better things to do than listen to those witches go on about who was to blame. They *all* were, in his opinion. Angel had been brought up to be a decent, truthful young lady, so she should have known better. But if Ruth had been more open and honest from the start, her own experience would have served as a valuable warning to their daughter about the consequences of letting boys sweet-talk you out of your knickers. And Johnny wasn't entirely blameless, either. If he'd paid more attention to Angel instead of leaving it all to her mother and nan, he might have noticed that she was starting to take an interest in boys and could have nipped it in the bud before it got to this.

But hindsight was a wonderful thing, and it *had* happened, so there was no point raking over the shoulds and shouldn'ts of it. They just had to wait for the clinic appointment, and hope that nothing happened to delay or prevent the abortion.

All cried out, Angel began to formulate a plan as she sat in her room for the rest of the afternoon. But to have any chance of making it work she realised that she would have to act repentant, make them believe that she had seen the error of her ways. So at teatime she went downstairs and ate her meal in chastened silence. Then, after dutifully cleaning up when they had finished, she went back to her room and waited and listened.

It was gone ten before she heard her mum and nan start one of their drink-fuelled arguments. She knew that they wouldn't be able to hear anything outside the parlour as their dispute grew progressively more heated inside, so she pulled out from under the bed the little rucksack that she'd packed and crept down the stairs. She held her breath when she reached the hall and eased the front door open before sliding out into the darkness.

It was cold outside, and Angel shivered when the wind slapped her face. But she didn't stop; she just pulled her collar up around her ears and ran head down to the end of the avenue. She'd taken forty pounds out of the tin her mum kept in the bedside cabinet. She used some of that now to take a bus into Hulme.

Zeta Johnson's eyes narrowed when she opened the door and saw who was standing on the step.

"What do you want?" she demanded.

"I'm sorry to disturb you," Angel said nervously, "but I was wondering if Ryan was in?"

"No, he's not," Zeta snapped. "And don't ever call round here at this time of night again. I'm trying to get the baby to sleep, and you've disturbed him."

"Sorry," Angel murmured, touching her stomach reflexively at the mention of babies. Then, licking her lips, she said, "I, er, don't suppose you know where he's gone, or when he'll be back?"

Zeta didn't even bother answering; she just slammed the door in Angel's face. Ryan had enough problems without some stuck-up girl complicating his life.

Angel blinked back her tears and walked back down the path. What was she going to do now? She couldn't just hang around on the off chance that Ryan might come back soon, because he might stay out all night and she would freeze to death. Anyway, she couldn't be seen out on the street. Once her mum realised that she'd gone, she'd tell her dad and this would be the first place he'd come looking for her.

Wishing that she'd thought to bring a hat, or at least a hooded jacket, Angel put her head down and walked around to Lisa's. She knew that she wouldn't be able to stay there for long because her dad would check there, too. She just needed to get Ryan's number so she could at least call him and tell him what was going on.

She stopped in her tracks when she turned the corner and saw her dad's car parked outside Lisa's place. Terrified that he was already on the hunt for her, she turned and fled back through the maze of streets until she found an alley to hide in. She squatted down between two stinking wheelie bins, hugged her knees to her chest and swiped at her tears. She couldn't stay out all night in the cold but she couldn't go home, either. Her baby's life was hanging in the balance, and she was the only one who could protect it.

As Angel sat there trying to gather her thoughts, a memory sparked in her mind and she pushed herself back up to her feet. There *was* somewhere she could go — somewhere her mum and dad would never dream of looking for her. She just hoped she could remember the way.

CHAPTER
TWENTY-NINE

Cathy frowned and glanced at the clock when she heard the doorbell. It was almost midnight. Who the hell would come calling on her in the middle of the night?

The police.

Worried as it occurred to her that if it *was* the police it could only be bad news, she took a last drag of her cigarette and stubbed it out in the overflowing ashtray. She glanced around the living room, dismayed by the heaps of newspapers that were strewn around Les's chair, the thick coating of dust on the glass TV table, the dead plants adorning the windowsill, the cups and ashtrays littered all over the floor and coffee table. The coppers would think she was a right tramp if she had to bring them in, but there was nothing she could do about it now.

The bell rang again.

Cathy pulled her jumper down and patted her hair into place as she made her way to the door. But it wasn't a uniform that greeted her when she opened it; it was a young girl with a rucksack.

"Are you Cathy?" the girl asked quietly.

"Who wants to know?" Cathy pushed the door to until it was open just an inch and peered out warily through the crack. A few months back there had been a spate of breakins on the estate, where a woman had knocked on the door and gained the householders' trust by pretending to be in labour and asking if she could use the phone, only for two men to rush in as soon as the door was open and ransack the place.

But the girl had no bump, and she had called her by name, which made Cathy curious enough not to slam the door in her face.

"I'm Angel," the girl told her.

"Am I supposed to know you?" Cathy asked, still eyeing her with suspicion.

"I'm Johnny's daughter," Angel elaborated. Then, frowning, she said, "Sorry, I thought this was Cathy Conroy's house. I must have got the wrong number."

Cathy felt a jolt, as if she'd been kicked in the stomach. "Wait!" She pulled the door open and peered at the girl. "Why are you here? Has something happened to Johnny? Has he been hurt?"

"No, he's fine," Angel assured her.

"Has he sent you?"

"No. He doesn't know I'm here."

"How old are you?" Cathy asked. It was dangerous for a full-grown man to be out alone around these parts at night, never mind a slip of a girl.

"Fifteen," Angel told her. She felt suddenly tearful again, and bit down hard on her lip. But it didn't work.

"Hey . . ." Cathy reached out and patted Angel on the arm when she burst into tears. "What's up?"

"Can I come in?" Angel sobbed. "I just — just need to s-sit down."

Cathy cast a nervous glance out over the girl's shoulder. Les had been out drinking all day and he could come back at any time. He didn't like people coming round but he especially wouldn't like it if he knew that the girl was connected with Johnny. He'd been furious when Cathy had questioned him about the alleged beatings after Johnny's last visit and had banned her from ever mentioning his name again.

But, if this really was her grandchild, she couldn't just leave her on the step in this state. So, against her better judgement, she said, "Come on in and have a cup of tea, love. But it'll have to be quick, and then you'll have to go. Okay?"

Angel nodded, and sniffed back her tears as she followed her grandmother inside. She didn't know why she'd come, or what she'd expected this woman who had never laid eyes on her in her life before to say; but it had been the only place she could think of. And it had taken her ages to find it, because she'd only ever been to this area once before, when she'd been ten and her dad had driven her through the estate. He'd told her that this was where he had grown up, and had pointed out his old school and the houses of his old mates — and the block of flats where he and his mum had lived.

"Can we go and see her?" Angel had asked, curious to know about his side of the family because he never, ever talked about them. But he'd just said, "Maybe one day," and carried on driving.

She'd asked a few times after that, but he'd always said he was too busy, or too tired. Until, finally, he'd snapped, and said, "Look, we're not going — not now, not ever. She didn't give a toss about me when I needed her, and that's all you need to know, so drop it."

He'd never mentioned his mother since, and Angel hadn't either. But she hadn't forgotten and had sometimes toyed with the idea of coming to see this other grandmother. Now that she was actually here, it was nothing like she'd imagined. In her childish fantasies, her dad's mum was a chubby, kind nan, with white hair, twinkly eyes and a loving smile, who welcomed Angel with open arms. But the reality couldn't have been more different. This nan looked younger than the other one, but she was just as scrawny. Her jeans looked baggy on her stick-like legs, and the vertebrae of her spine stood out through the back of her jumper like a string of beads.

"Sorry about the mess," Cathy apologised as she led Angel into the kitchen. "I've not been too well lately, so things have got a bit on top of me.

A bit?

Angel's gaze flitted from the dirty plates heaped in the sink, to the foul-smelling bin, to the ledges covered in discarded microwave-meal boxes.

"Sit down," Cathy said when she'd finished making the tea a couple of minutes later and turned back to find the girl still standing in the doorway.

"Thanks," Angel murmured. She perched on the edge of one of the chairs.

374

Cathy put the cups down and went to the living room to get her cigarettes. "Smoke?" she asked, offering one to Angel when she came back. She lit one for herself when the girl shook her head and said, "How did you find me?"

"My dad drove me round here once," Angel told her. She rubbed her nose on the back of her hand. "When I was little."

"What, he brought you round to visit me?" Cathy was shocked. It had been some twenty-odd years since she'd last seen him, and she still thought about him. But after their last argument she hadn't heard from him — or of him — so it was sickening to think that he might have tried to build bridges and she had missed him.

"No, he was just driving past and he pointed the block out to me," Angel told her.

"Oh." Deflated, Cathy took another drag on her cigarette. "Is he all right, though?"

"Yeah, fine."

"Still married?"

Angel nodded.

"Working?"

Another nod. "He owns a car lot. It's really nice."

Cathy raised an eyebrow. So her son had done well for himself — that was good to hear. She'd always thought he had it in him, but there had been times when she'd despaired of him ever putting his talents to good use. Especially when he'd gone off the rails as a teenager. He could be so extreme: she'd thought that he would either end up running a bank or doing life for robbing one.

"I hope you don't mind me calling round like this," Angel asked. "I wasn't sure I'd find you, but I asked a woman downstairs and she told me which number you lived at."

"Did she now?" Cathy muttered, mentally cursing her big-mouthed neighbours for blabbing her private business to all and sundry. The girl could have been sent by a debt collector to track her down, for all they knew.

"I'm sorry," Angel apologised, sensing that it wasn't such a pleasant surprise. "I shouldn't have come, but I had nowhere else to go."

Cathy looked at her thoughtfully. If she'd had nowhere else to go before she came, where was she planning to go when she left?

"You haven't run away, have you?" she asked.

Angel nodded, and lowered her gaze. "I'm pregnant," she murmured. "And my mum and dad want me to get rid of it."

"Pregnant?" Cathy's brow furrowed deeply. "I thought you said you were only fifteen?"

"I'll be sixteen in a few weeks," Angel told her, swiping at a fresh tear that was trickling down her cheek.

"Oh, Jeezus, what a mess." Cathy sighed. "More kids having kids. Like there's not enough neglected babies in the world."

"I'd never neglect my baby." Angel was indignant. "I'm going to be a really good mum."

"I'm sure you think so, love," Cathy said gently, "but it's nowhere near as easy as you kids seem to think it is. Maybe you'd be better off going home, eh? Your mum and dad are obviously trying to do their best by you."

"My dad might be," Angel conceded. "But my mum and my nan just don't want me to have it because they think they'll have to pay for it. And my nan doesn't want a black baby in the house," she added angrily.

"I didn't bring your dad up to be a racist," Cathy said disapprovingly.

"He's not," sniffed Angel. "It's just her. She's horrible. But I don't care what she thinks. It's who you are on the inside that counts, and Ryan's lovely."

Cathy smiled. This granddaughter of hers was a pretty girl, and obviously every bit as passionate as her dad had been when he was little. Cathy remembered how vehemently he'd defended his friends when she'd warned him off hanging around with them. She'd been right, because the buggers had deserted him without a second thought when he'd landed in trouble, but he'd refused to hear a word said against them.

Her smile slipped when she heard the sound of a key turning in the front door.

"You'll have to go," she told Angel quietly, stubbing out her cigarette in the ashtray.

But it was too late. Les was already walking into the kitchen.

"What you doing in here?" he demanded, a churlish edge to his voice, his breath ripe with alcohol. "Don't tell me you've decided to clean up?" He looked at the sink and sneered. "Shoulda known that'd be too much to ask." He lumbered over to the fridge and took out a can of beer, but just as he was about to tear off the tab he spotted Angel and a leering grin lifted his miserable lips.

"Oh, hello . . . and who are you?"

"She's just going," Cathy told him, gesturing at Angel to get up.

"What's the rush?" Les's eyes were trawling over Angel's body. "We haven't even been introduced yet. I'm Les . . ." He held out his hand.

Angel took it and gave him a nervous smile. It hadn't occurred to her that she had a grandfather as well. Her dad had never mentioned him.

"I'm Angel," she told him. "Your granddaughter."

"You what?" Les snorted, drawing his head back and giving her a quizzical smile. "I don't think so, sweetheart. I've got no kids, and if anyone's trying to say different they're lying."

Cathy inhaled deeply. "She's Johnny's girl, Les. She's in a spot of trouble and thought I might be able to help her. But I can't, so she's going."

Les's smirk had turned into a sneer at the mention of *that* name. But he didn't blow up as Cathy had expected, he just looked Angel up and down and said, "Well, well, so the little bastard wasn't completely useless, after all."

"Les, don't," Cathy said quietly. "The past has got nothing to do with her. She's just a kid."

"Sorry . . ." Les held up his hands and staggered towards a chair. "You haven't finished your tea," he said, glancing into Angel's cup as he flopped down.

"No, 'cos she's going," Cathy said again. Les being this nice was almost as scary as him being nasty, and she didn't like the way he was looking at the girl.

But Angel didn't know him, so she just presumed it was the drink talking.

"So, you're Johnny's girl?" Les stared at her. "Well, well. Pretty, ain't you? Take after your mam, do you, pet?"

"Not really," Angel murmured, flicking a curious glance at her grandmother who was hovering behind him, wringing her hands.

"Les, she really needs to go," Cathy said. "You've got a bus to catch, haven't you, love?"

Les saw the gleam of fresh tears flooding the girl's eyes and narrowed his own. "Is something going on here that youse are not telling me?" he asked. "The buses don't run round here at this time of night."

"No, she's going to have to walk down to the quadrant," Cathy lied. "That's why she needs to get going."

"Sounds to me like you're trying to get rid of her," Les said perceptively. "Hope that ain't because of me? 'Cos if it is, there's no need. I've got no problem with her."

"It's all right," Angel told them, sensing that her grandmother didn't really want her here. "I should go."

Cathy looked at her guiltily. "Will you be okay?"

"Woman, it's twelve in the morning," Les berated her. "You can't send her out there on her own — she could get raped, or anything. Let her stop here for the night." He looked at Angel now. "You wanna stop here for the night, pet?"

"I, er, should probably go," she murmured.

"Where?" he asked. "Thought you were in trouble?"

"A bit," Angel admitted, squirming in her seat. She knew the man was drunk, but there was something about the way he was looking at her that was making her feel uncomfortable.

"She's pregnant," Cathy told him, hoping that information would be enough to take the leer out of his eyes. "And she's only fifteen."

"And your dad's letting you walk around at this time of night on your own?" Les gave a disapproving shake of his head. "Well, don't you worry about a thing, pet. Me and your gran will look after you. There's a spare bed, and you're welcome to it."

"Really?" Angel looked from him to Cathy. "I'll go first thing in the morning."

"You stop as long as you like, pet." Les gave her a sly grin. "Been a long time since I've had a pretty little thing like you to keep me company over breakfast."

CHAPTER
THIRTY

Ryan arrived home at half past midnight. After losing his job with Johnny, he'd been forced to take a part-time job collecting glasses at a bar in town, and he absolutely hated it. The pay was shit, and the work was dirty. Not to mention dangerous when the idiot students got bladdered and started chucking glasses around and fighting among themselves. But his dad had started making noises about sending his mum back out on the streets after his savings had run out, so he had no choice but to stick it out.

Exhausted now, having been run off his feet all night, he groaned when he glanced out of the kitchen window as he was pouring himself a glass of water and saw Johnny's car pulling up outside.

Johnny was already out of the car and banging on the door with his fist by the time Ryan reached it. Ryan guessed that he was in for another going-over and steeled himself for a kicking before opening up. But Johnny didn't go for him, he just barged past and marched into the kitchen.

"What are you looking for?" Ryan asked when Johnny saw that nobody was in there and headed for the living room.

"Where is she?" Johnny demanded, flicking the light on.

"Who?" Ryan whispered as he followed him back out into the hall. "Johnny — Mr Conroy . . . my mum and dad are in bed. You'll wake them up."

"Tell me where she is, then," Johnny ordered as he set off up the stairs.

"That's my kid brother and sister's room," Ryan hissed when Johnny reached the first bedroom.

Johnny ignored him and pushed the door open. He jerked his head back when the smell of warm piss assailed his nostrils. He peered into the room. A small girl was sleeping in a single bed, and a baby was flat out in a cot, but there was no one else in there.

He moved to the next room and switched the light on. The bed looked empty, but he pulled the quilt off to make absolutely sure and felt the mattress to see if it was still warm. It was cold, but Johnny still wasn't convinced that nobody had been in it. So he looked under it and then checked the wardrobe before yanking the curtains open and peering down into the dark back garden.

"Where is she?" he demanded again, turning back to Ryan who was watching from the doorway. "And don't fuck around with me, son, 'cos she's not at Lisa's, so she must be here."

"If you're talking about Angel, I haven't seen her," Ryan told him truthfully.

"Don't fucking lie to me!" Johnny seized him by the throat and pushed him out onto the landing, forcing him back against the banister rail. "You've got two seconds to tell me where she is, or I'm going to shoot you," he growled as he rammed the muzzle of a gun into his stomach.

"On my life," Ryan gasped, his eyes widening with fear. "I swear she ain't here, Mr C . . ."

The noise had woken Zeta and she opened her bedroom door. "Oh, sweet Jesus!" she shrieked when she saw what was happening. *"GARY . . . GARRRYYYY!"*

"Mum, just go back to bed," Ryan told her, trying to keep his voice even. "I can handle this."

His dad had woken up by now and he lumbered out onto the landing, rubbing sleep from his eyes. "What's going on?"

"Get the fuck back in there before I shoot the lot of you," Johnny warned through gritted teeth without looking around.

"Just go," Ryan told his parents urgently. "Everything's all right . . . there's been a misunderstanding, that's all. But I'll sort it."

Gary didn't need telling twice. He was a fist merchant, not a bullet dodger, so he grabbed Zeta and hauled her, still screaming, back into their bedroom. He slammed the door shut behind them.

"Where is she?" Johnny asked again.

"She's not here," Ryan repeated truthfully. "I haven't seen her since you told me to stay away from her that night."

"You're lying." Johnny jabbed him with the gun.

Ryan winced as pain flared in his still-bruised ribs. He gritted his teeth. "I'm not, I swear. You can shoot me if you want, but please don't hurt my mam or the kids. And don't do it here," he begged. "If you're gonna do it, take me somewhere where they don't have to watch me die. *Please*."

Johnny heard the sincerity in Ryan's voice and knew instinctively that he was telling the truth. If he was brave enough to offer up his life to protect his family, he was brave enough to front up to Johnny about Angel. But he was still saying that she wasn't here.

"If she comes, you'd better ring me," Johnny said. He stuck the gun back into his waistband and headed for the stairs.

Unaware that Angel *had* been round tonight and that his mum had seen her off, Ryan followed Johnny outside.

"I know you hate me," he said, "and I don't blame you, 'cos I was bang out of order for going round to your place like that. But I love her, Mr Conroy, and if she's missing I want to help find her."

Johnny could tell that he meant what he'd said, and he had to admire his guts for coming after him after having had a gun pulled on him. But if he hadn't crossed the line and put his filthy hands on Angel in the first place, none of this would be happening. Johnny wasn't about to let him think that it was all forgiven and forgotten.

Lisa came around the corner just as Johnny unlocked his car. "Any luck?" she asked as she ran up to them.

Johnny shook his head.

"How long's she been gone now?"

"An hour, maybe more," Johnny told her, ashamed that he couldn't be more accurate. But Ruth had only realised an hour ago that Angel had gone and she'd delayed telling him because she'd been scared that he would blame her.

"Well, I've rung everyone in the family, but no one's seen her," said Lisa.

"I know — Ruth's already tried."

"What about *your* family?" Ryan ventured. "I know she doesn't really know anyone from your side," he went on, feeling disloyal, because this was stuff that Angel had trusted him to keep to himself. "But it might be worth a try."

Lisa looked at Johnny and shrugged. "She has asked me about your mum a few times in the past. I've never met her, so I couldn't tell her anything. But she's definitely curious."

Johnny pursed his lips and thought about it, but quickly ruled it out. "Nah. She wouldn't know where to find her. Ring me if she turns up." He climbed into the car and pulled away from the kerb with a squeal of tyre rubber.

Ryan ran his hands through his hair as he watched Johnny go, and Lisa saw the worry in his eyes.

"Don't worry, he'll find her," she said quietly. "She won't have gone far."

"Why did she run away, though?" Ryan wanted to know. "That's what's worrying me. I haven't seen or heard from her in weeks, and Johnny was really mad when he caught us that night. You don't think he's done something to her, do you?"

"Johnny's *never* laid a finger on that girl in anger," Lisa told him emphatically. "She'll just be scared 'cos . . ." She caught herself and trailed off without finishing the sentence.

"Scared 'cos what?" Ryan demanded, sensing that she'd been about to say something significant. Irritated when she shook her head, he said, "Come on, Lisa, she's fifteen, and she's out there on her own in the dark. If you know what's going on, just tell me."

"I can't," she replied guiltily. "It's not my place."

"Neither's screwing her dad, but that didn't stop you."

Lisa's mouth dropped open. "How dare you!"

"Don't do this," Ryan groaned. "I saw you, okay? But I didn't tell Angel, so I don't think it's got anything to do with her running away."

"No, it has not," Lisa said indignantly, determined to front it out. "And what do you mean, you saw us?"

"That night when Johnny caught me and Angel," Ryan told her, sighing. "I was walking home from work and I saw him pull up outside yours."

"That's nothing," Lisa said dismissively. "He pops round all the time to check I'm okay. We're family — it's perfectly normal."

"And is sticking your tongue down your relatives' throats normal?" Ryan gave her a knowing look.

Lisa blushed and folded her arms. "I hope you haven't told anyone what you *think* you saw, 'cos Johnny won't be too pleased if it gets back to him."

Ryan was fed up with playing games. "Look, I'm not even arsed what you and Johnny get up to," he told her bluntly. "I just want to know why Angel's run away. I'm worried about her."

Lisa narrowed her eyes and stared at him for several long moments. Johnny had only just told her about the baby but he obviously didn't want Ryan to know or he'd have told him when he was here just now. But that was half the trouble with this family: they were too fond of keeping secrets. They were all so busy trying to hide what they were feeling and thinking that they were strangling themselves and each other. Ryan was better off out of it, in her opinion. But he had the right to make that decision for himself. Whereas Johnny and Ruth — and especially Rita — did *not* have the right to decide if his child lived or died.

"Angel's pregnant," Lisa told Ryan. "But you didn't hear that from me."

Ryan gaped at her. "You're kidding me!"

She shook her head and gazed back sadly at him. "And I've only just found out myself, so don't think I've been keeping it from you."

"I can't believe it," he croaked. "Why didn't she tell me?"

"She didn't know till this afternoon," Lisa said. "When Johnny came to mine, looking for her, he said her mum had made her do a pregnancy test and when it came back positive she made an appointment to get it aborted."

"Angel wants to abort my baby?" Ryan looked hurt and confused all at once. "Without even telling me?"

"No, *she* wants to keep it," said Lisa. "But *they* won't let her. That's why she's run away. I'm so sorry."

"It's not your fault," Ryan said quietly. "Thanks for telling me. I know it can't have been easy."

"You won't tell Johnny, will you?" Lisa's eyes were filled with worry. "He really is trying to do his best by Angel and none of this is to spite you — you do know that, don't you? It's just hard for him to accept that his child's growing up. Must be hard for any parent," she added wistfully.

"I wouldn't know," Ryan said bitterly. "Seeing as they didn't even want me to find out about it. Christ, why didn't she come to me? We could have talked to them. Together."

"It probably wouldn't have got you anywhere," Lisa told him sadly. "They're not exactly big on letting people interfere in family business."

"This is my family as well," Ryan reminded her. "*My* baby."

"I'm sorry," Lisa said again. "If there was anything I could do . . ."

"It's not your fault." Ryan exhaled wearily. "And, don't worry, I won't tell Johnny you told me. I just hope he finds her, 'cos now there's not just her to worry about."

Lisa gave him a regretful smile and apologised yet again. Then, biting her lip, she said goodbye and went home. She felt terrible, and wondered if she'd done the wrong thing by telling him. He wasn't going to have any say in what happened, so maybe he'd have been better off not knowing.

Ryan's head felt like it was imploding as he walked miserably back into his house. He couldn't believe that the Hyneses were just going to kill his baby without even telling him about it. That was so wrong. But there was absolutely nothing he could do about it. Johnny had already proved that he was capable of doing just about anything to keep Ryan and Angel apart.

His dad was waiting behind the front door. The punch caught Ryan completely off guard and knocked him flat on his back.

"Pleased with yourself, you little bastard?" Gary loomed over him with his teeth bared and his fists clenched. "Bringing twats like that round to my door and scaring the fucking life out of your mother?"

"It was a misunderstanding," Ryan told him again, holding a hand to his bleeding mouth as he gazed up at his father.

"*Misunderstanding?*" Gary roared as he kicked him in the ribs. "I'll give you fucking misunderstanding!"

Johnny drove around the area for a good thirty minutes without seeing a soul. The streets were deserted, and his heart was growing heavier by the minute. There was just no place he could think of where Angel might have gone, other than to Lisa's or Ryan's. She was really upset — but was she upset enough to do something stupid? That was what was worrying him now. They had backed her into a corner when she'd been at her most vulnerable, and it had pushed her over the edge. And he was as much to blame for that as Ruth was. She might have made the decision to arrange the abortion, but he'd gone along with it without giving a second thought to what Angel might have wanted. They were treating her like a child who had no right to make her own decisions. But, like Lisa had said, Angel was a young woman now. She would be sixteen in a matter of weeks, and that wasn't so much younger than Ruth had been when she and Johnny had got married. And Ryan seemed genuinely to care about her, whereas Johnny hadn't given a toss about Ruth.

Deep in thought, he didn't realise he was heading towards his mum's estate until he pulled up outside the flats. He switched the engine off and peered up to the third floor. It was a long shot — a *really* long shot — but he was here now.

Cathy had made up the spare bed and given Angel an old nightie to wear. Then, after making sure that the girl was settled, she'd gone to bed.

Angel had been on the verge of falling asleep when the door creaked open. Her heart gave a painful lurch when she squinted at the silhouette outlined in the dim light and realised that it was Les. His leering smiles in the kitchen had unnerved her, and when her grandmother had left them alone while she made the bed he'd put his hand on her leg and stroked it up and down. She'd wanted to run out of there but she'd been too scared. Then her grandmother had come back and brought her to this room, so she'd thought she would be okay.

"You awake?" Les whispered as he crept towards the bed.

Angel held her breath. She could smell alcohol and the rancid scent of sweat. He sat down heavily, and her body bounced as his weight bore down on the mattress.

"I've never seen anyone as pretty as you," Les crooned, reaching out and stroking her shoulder as she lay hunched under the quilt. "You remind me of a girl I used to know. She was my girlfriend. Her name was Jillian. She said I was the best boyfriend she ever had 'cos I treated her real good . . . Do you want me to treat *you* good, an' all?"

His breath was coming in short, wheezy little bursts as his stroking continued.

Angel bit her lip to keep from crying out. She just wanted him to think that she was asleep and go away.

"I can show you a good time," Les whispered as his fingers found the edge of the quilt and peeled it down slowly. "You and me could have some real good fun. And I've got lots of money, so if you play nice I'll buy you anything you want."

The doorbell rang. Les jumped, and Angel heard him breathe in sharply.

The bell rang again, and then the caller started hammering with the knocker. The noise woke Cathy and she wandered out into the dark hall.

"Les . . . ?" she hissed. "Les, where are you?"

Les got up and tiptoed to the door. "I'm in the bathroom," he called through the crack, trying to throw his voice to make it sound as if he was on the other side of the corridor. "See who it is and go back to bed."

Cathy put the chain across and opened the door a crack. Her jaw dropped when she saw Johnny standing there.

"All right, Mum?" he said quietly, his stomach churning at the sight of her. It had been a long, long time. "Sorry to disturb you, but I don't suppose my daughter's been here, has she? Her name's Angel."

"I know," Cathy murmured, her eyes glittering with tears as she gazed at him. Her lovely boy had become a really handsome man.

"Is she here?" Johnny asked, surprised, because he hadn't actually expected her to be. He'd half expected to find that his *mother* wasn't even here, that she had moved out years ago, or died, or something. But she *was* here, and so was Angel. "I need to see her."

"She's asleep," Cathy told him. "Why don't you come back in the morning? It'll give her time to think, and then we can all sit down and talk."

"What are you talking about?" Johnny frowned. "This has got nothing to do with you. You don't even know her."

"She's scared, son. She came and found me, so I've got a duty to look after her."

"Are you having a laugh?" Johnny gazed at her in disbelief.

Back in the spare room, Les had no idea who was at the door. And he didn't care. He and Cathy hadn't slept together in years, and the drink had made him horny.

"*NO!*" Angel screamed when he slid his hand under the quilt and tried to work his way under the nightie. "Leave me alone!"

Johnny heard her. He looked at his mother, and then barged his shoulder against the door, over and over until the flimsy chain snapped.

"What the fuck . . .?" Les yelled, running out into the hall with the tip of his hard-on poking out through the flap in his pyjama bottoms.

"Les!" Cathy squawked when she saw it. "What the hell are you doing?"

"If you've fucking touched her . . ." Johnny roared as he rushed Les and knocked him to the floor. "I'll kill you, you cunt!"

"Daddy," Angel sobbed, running out into the hall and throwing herself into Johnny's arms as he stood over Les.

"Did he touch you?" Johnny asked, his breathing heavy.

She shook her head and burst into tears, scared that her father would go crazy if she told him the truth and end up in prison.

"Go outside," Johnny told her, staring down at the man on the floor.

"I want to stay with you," Angel cried, clinging to him.

"*GO!*" he ordered.

"Come on, love," Cathy grabbed her hand and tugged her away from her dad.

"I didn't do anything," Les whimpered, his hands shaking in front of his face.

"You beat the shit out of me for years," Johnny snarled. "And you told my mum I was a liar. Now tell her the truth."

"I never meant to hurt you," Les cried, tears rolling down his fat cheeks as a pool of piss started to spread out on the lino around him. "Honest to God, I didn't. I was just trying to be your dad."

"What would an evil cunt like you know about being a dad?" Johnny spat. "And what were you doing to my girl?"

"I never laid a finger on her," Les squeaked. "I swear to God."

"So what were you doing in that room with her?" Johnny demanded. "And why was she screaming?"

"She came on to me," Les blubbered. "I was telling her to leave it out."

"Daddy, I didn't," Angel sobbed. "I didn't want him in there. I told him to leave me alone."

Johnny turned and glared at his mother. "Still think I was lying about him?"

Cathy looked back at him mutely and wrung her hands nervously.

A light came on in Johnny's head.

"You knew . . ." he gasped. "You fucking *knew* and did nothing about it. And now you've let him get at my girl as well."

"Johnny, I didn't," Cathy croaked. "I love you — I would never have let anyone hurt you."

"Save it," he hissed, marching over and snatching Angel away from her. "And *you* . . ." He turned back to Les. "Come near me or mine again, and you're dead."

He pushed Angel out of the door and took her down to the car.

"I'm sorry, Daddy," she cried, clinging to him again when they were safely locked inside. "But I swear I didn't do what he said."

"Ssshhh," Johnny soothed, holding her close. "Everything's going to be okay. I won't let anyone hurt you again." He swallowed hard now and said, "I know you're scared, darlin', but I need to know if you were telling the truth back there. Did he — you know?"

Angel shook her head and buried her face in her dad's chest. She felt dirty and ashamed, but she knew that he would go back if he knew that the horrible man had touched her, so she couldn't tell him. Not now, not ever.

Johnny exhaled shakily, relieved, and at the same time angry that he had played a part in pushing Angel into the grips of that monster. If Ryan hadn't mentioned Johnny's mother tonight, he would never have thought of coming here — and God only knew what Les would have done to the girl. But he had got here in time, so he had to just be thankful for that.

"Let's get you home." Johnny started the engine. "Your mum's worried sick."

"I want to see Ryan," Angel sobbed. "Please, Daddy. I need to see him and tell him about our baby."

"Sweetheart, it's late," Johnny said quietly, setting off. "Let's just leave it till morning and then we'll sit down and talk about it."

"No, you'll lock me in and make me have an abortion," she cried, tears streaming down her cheeks.

"I won't," he promised. But she didn't believe him. "What are you doing?" he asked, slamming the brakes on when she started tugging at the door handle.

"Getting out," she wept. "I'm going to see Ryan. And if you don't let me I'll just run away again."

"All right, just stop it." Johnny grabbed Angel and pulled her into his arms. "You can't go running around in a nightdress at this time of night."

"I need to see him," Angel wailed.

Johnny sighed. "All right, I'll take you round there," he conceded. "But we're only staying a few minutes, then I'm taking you home and you're going to get some rest. We'll work out what we're going to do about this in the morning. Okay?"

Too tired to carry on fighting, Angel nodded.

Johnny drove back into Hulme. The lights were on in Ryan's house when he pulled up outside, and several of the neighbours were standing on their steps staring at the door. Johnny heard the sound of muffled screaming coming from inside the house when he opened his door, and he told Angel to stay put before running up the path.

He squatted down and lifted the letterbox flap. Ryan was lying on the floor, and his father was standing over him with a baseball bat raised above his head. The boy's mother was screaming at her husband to leave their son alone, and a small girl was hopping up and down in distress on the stairs, a look of absolute terror on her face.

Johnny kicked the door, and was about to do it again when Zeta yanked it open.

"Stop him!" she cried. "He's going to kill h —"

The word died on her tongue when she saw who she was talking to. She'd assumed that it would be the police, or a brave neighbour who'd had enough of the regular disturbances coming from this house and had come to tell them to pack it in.

Johnny saw the shock in her eyes and guessed that she recognised him from earlier, although he'd been pretty sure that she hadn't seen his face at the time. But there was no time to stop and talk, so he pushed past her and ran down the hall, kicking the man in the back of his knees and sending him crashing down.

The bat flew out of Gary's hand and went skidding along the lino, coming to rest in the living-room doorway. He groped for it, but Johnny stamped down hard on his hand before kneeling down and ramming the muzzle of the gun against his throat.

"Don't fucking move," he warned, his voice a hiss. Then, looking back at the woman — who was still standing there, her eyes wide with shock — he jerked his head towards the girl and said, "Close the door and take her upstairs."

"Do it, Mam," Ryan groaned, pulling himself up painfully when she didn't move. "He's my boss — everything's cool."

"You all right?" Johnny asked Ryan when the woman snapped out of her trance and hustled the child away.

"Yeah," Ryan gasped as he hauled himself to his feet. "I've had worse."

"Angel's in the car," Johnny told him. "Go and sit with her. But try not to get blood on my leather, eh?"

Aware that he was trying to be kind, Ryan gave him a tiny pained smile and hobbled out.

"I've got no argument with you," Gary bleated, his scared eyes swivelling up to Johnny. "I don't even know you, so just go, and we'll forget all about this, yeah?"

Johnny shifted the barrel of the gun slightly and jabbed the muzzle into his flabby cheek. "Big man, ain't you? Kicking the fuck out of a kid."

"*You* did it," Gary muttered nervously.

"I had my reasons," Johnny replied coolly. "But it seems to me that you do it just for kicks. Those black eyes and bust lip your wife's got — walk into a door, did she?"

"She winds me up," Gary wheezed. "Any man'd do the same if they had to put up with her."

"You ain't a man," Johnny spat, disgust in his voice. "You're scum and, if you ask me, they'd be better off without you."

"You're not going to shoot me, are you?" Gary squeaked, panic in his voice and eyes. "Please, mate, I ain't done nothing to you."

A siren in the near distance broke the spell. Johnny guessed that one of the neighbours had probably called the cops after hearing the commotion. He clicked back the safety catch on the gun.

"Aw, no . . ." Tears of terror spurted from Gary's eyes. "I don't wanna die . . . please don't kill me."

"I wonder how many times your wife and kids have felt exactly the same as you're feeling right now when you've been kicking the shit out of them," Johnny mused.

"I won't do it again," Gary sobbed. "I swear on my life!"

Johnny didn't believe him for one minute, but he didn't have time to argue about it.

"If I find out you've opened your mouth about this, I'll be back," he warned. "And there'll be no talking next time. Got that?"

Gary nodded his agreement. "Yeah . . . anything you say."

Johnny pushed himself up and went quickly back out to the car. Angel was sitting in the back seat with Ryan. She'd ripped a strip off the bottom of the nightie and was dabbing at the blood on his face.

"He's hurt, Daddy. Really hurt."

"He'll be all right," Johnny reassured her, setting off smoothly. He turned the corner just as the police car came in at the other end of the road.

CHAPTER
THIRTY-ONE

Dave and Hannah lived in a neat little semi in a quiet cul-de-sac in Stretford, not too far from Johnny's place. Johnny had rung on the way, so Dave was waiting, and he opened the door when his friend's car pulled up behind his in the drive.

Johnny jumped out and went to help Ryan out of the back. "Wait there," he told Angel. "I'll be back in a minute."

"I want to stay with him," she sobbed, still distressed about Ryan's injuries.

"Darlin', just trust me on this," Johnny insisted. "You can see him tomorrow, but I need to get him inside so Hannah can see to him."

Angel nodded and hugged herself as Johnny took Ryan into the house.

"Jeezus," Dave said quietly when he saw the state of the boy. "Tell me you didn't do this."

"Not this time," Johnny admitted. "This is his dad's handiwork."

Hannah came bustling out from the kitchen. A look of pity came into her eyes when she saw Ryan and she beckoned them on in. "Bring him in here."

400

She was a health visitor, and that was as close to a medical person as Johnny dared to take Ryan right now.

"He doesn't reckon anything's broken," he told Hannah as he helped Ryan into the kitchen and sat him down gently in a chair. "But there are a few nasty cuts that need looking at."

"Leave it to me," Hannah said calmly. She was already filling a bowl with warm water.

"Thanks." Johnny kissed her on the cheek. "And I'm really sorry to bring this to you, but there was no one else I'd trust to look after him properly."

"It's not a problem," Hannah assured him. "I've got the spare bed ready, so I'll patch him up and give him something to help him sleep. He'll be right as rain in the morning."

Johnny thanked her and told Ryan that he would come back tomorrow.

"I'm sorry," Ryan said sincerely. "I didn't mean for any of this to happen. But I do love her — you've got to believe that."

"We'll talk tomorrow," Johnny replied quietly, letting him know with a few discreet gestures that he didn't want him to tell Hannah and Dave anything that they didn't need to know.

Ryan got the message and nodded.

Johnny went out into the hall and pulled the door to.

"What's going on?" Dave wanted to know.

"I haven't got time to explain right now," Johnny told him. "I just need to get Angel home. Can you do us a favour and stash this somewhere?" He pulled the gun from his waistband.

Dave looked at it and then back up at Johnny. Disappointment clouded his eyes. The gun had been Frankie's, and Johnny had said that he was going to get rid of it ages ago. But Dave figured this probably wasn't the best of times to start having a go at him about it, so he nodded and took the weapon.

"Are the police likely to come here?" he asked, sliding it into his dressing-gown pocket.

"No." Johnny shook his head and headed for the door.

He figured that Ryan's dad was too shit-scared to grass him up. And he doubted whether the mother would say anything after what she'd seen him do to her son. But, just in case, he didn't need to be caught with the gun.

"We'll look after Ryan," Dave assured Johnny as he showed him out. "You just take it easy, yeah?"

Johnny nodded, waved, and climbed into his car.

Ruth and Rita were sitting in the kitchen when Johnny and Angel walked in a short time later. The ever-present bottle of whisky was on the table between the two women.

"Oh, so he found you, did he?" Rita started as soon as she saw her granddaughter. "And I hope he gave you what for, you selfish little cow. Have you any idea how worried your mother's been?"

"Shut it," Johnny snapped, glaring at her. "And if you're going to start" — he turned on Ruth — "don't, 'cos I've had enough shit for one night."

402

"Is everything all right?" Ruth asked, wisely keeping her own angry words to herself. "Where was she?"

"She'd best not have been with that black boy again," Rita said scathingly. "You can't trust them an inch."

Johnny glared at her and she held up her hands and made a zipping gesture across her mouth before reaching for the whisky to refill her glass.

"Where was she?" Ruth asked again. "She wasn't with him, was she?"

"No, she was at my mother's," Johnny told her.

"What?" Ruth gaped at him in confusion. "*How?* She's never even met her. Has she?" she asked now, suspicion sparking in her eyes. "You haven't been taking her round there behind my back all this time, have you?"

"Have I hell," Johnny snapped. "I haven't seen my mum in years, you know that."

"So how did she know where to go?" Ruth turned to Angel now. "Well? How long have you been sneaking round there?"

"It was the first time," Angel told her truthfully. "And the last," she added plaintively.

"Too right." Johnny put his arm around her.

"What's going on?" Ruth demanded. "Has something happened?"

"Later," said Johnny. "Let's just go to bed. It's been a long day, and we're all wiped."

"Oh, I see, so she gets off scot-free again, does she?" Rita scowled in disapproval. "Gets herself knocked up at fifteen, then runs off like a dirty little tearaway, leaving me and her mum's nerves in tatters. But she gets to go to bed like nothing's happened? What kind of punishment is that?"

"What do you want me to do to her?" Johnny demanded. "Beat the shit out of her? Would that make you happy?"

"No, I'm not saying that," Rita grumbled. "But, if you ask me, you're to blame for this. If you'd been harder on her from the start instead of treating her like a precious little baby she'd have known to behave herself."

"Like anyone would take parenting advice from *you*, after the mess you made of bringing up *your* daughter."

"Ex*cuse* me . . . I'll have you know there's nothing wrong with our Ruth."

"Oh yeah? So how come she was so desperate to get away from you if you're such a good mother?"

"She's lived with me her entire life."

"Only 'cos she can't shake you off. Even when we had our own place we couldn't get away from you. You were there all the time, sticking your beak in, trying to control her."

"That's rich, coming from you. The man who can't stand to spend time with his own wife."

"Stop it," Angel begged. "Everyone's always arguing in this house, and I'm sick of it."

"Me, too," Johnny agreed. "Come on — bed. We've got a lot to talk about tomorrow."

"With Ryan?" Angel asked, gazing up at him. "You're still going to let me see him, aren't you? You promised."

"What's this?" Ruth frowned.

404

"I'm keeping the baby," Angel told her, her chin raised.

"Oh no, you're not," Ruth shot back. "Have you told her she can?" she asked Johnny now.

"I've said we'll talk about it," he told her.

"See!" Rita piped up scornfully. "Soft as shit. She blubs, he crumbles."

"This has got nothing to do with you," Johnny said angrily. "This is *my* family, and I'll decide what's best for them — so keep your nose out and your nasty opinions to yourself."

"Johnny, I want to talk to you." Ruth rushed after him when he led Angel out of the room. "You can't just decide something like this without consulting me. I'm her mother."

"You decided to arrange the abortion without consulting me," Johnny reminded her as he gestured at Angel to go up the stairs. "And she doesn't want to do it, so we're not forcing her."

"She's *fifteen*," Ruth squawked. "She can't have a baby at fifteen."

"She'll be sixteen by the time she has it," Johnny said calmly. "*If* she has it," he added. "Nothing's decided yet, so stop freaking out. We'll talk about it tomorrow."

He walked up the stairs now, leaving Ruth angrily grinding her teeth in the hall below.

CHAPTER
THIRTY-TWO

Ryan's face was a mess and he was aching all over when Johnny picked him up in the morning. He climbed slowly out of the car when they reached Johnny's house and held his ribs gingerly as he followed him inside.

Angel was sitting in the kitchen with her mum and nan. She leapt up when she saw Ryan and ran to him.

"Are you all right? You look terrible."

"I'm cool," he told her, moving his arm to hug her but thinking better of it when he saw that the women were already glaring at him. "Hello." He nodded at them politely.

"This is Ryan." Johnny introduced him. "Put the kettle on, Ruth. He needs to take some painkillers."

"Did you do that?" Rita asked, nodding towards the boy.

"No." Johnny shook his head and shrugged his jacket off.

"Should have," she muttered. "My Frankie would have. But he was a *real* man."

"Your Frankie barely touched me when I was in this same situation," Johnny reminded her. "And if you're going to start opening your big gob before we've even started, you can piss off out of it."

Ruth made a pot of tea and carried it and five cups over to the table on a tray. She laid it down, took her seat and poured, taking a surreptitious peek at Ryan from under her lashes as she did so. This was the first time she'd actually clapped eyes on the boy, but even with the terrible bruising and swelling marring his face she could see that he was very good-looking. He also had good manners and a pleasant air about him, so she could see why Angel had fallen for him. And it was easy to see from the way the boy was looking at Angel that he felt the same. But Ruth was determined that they still couldn't have this baby.

Johnny lit a cigarette and offered one to Ryan.

"Oh, well, that says it all, doesn't it?" Rita said scornfully. "Right pair of old pals, aren't you? Why don't you just go the whole hog and ask him to move in?"

Johnny ignored her and turned to Ryan.

"Right, son, let's kick off by laying our cards on the table. I take it Angel told you what was going on when you and her were in the car last night?"

"Yeah." Ryan nodded. He wanted to add that he was absolutely ecstatic, but he thought it wiser to keep his feelings under wraps for the time being, and hear what the Hyneses had to say.

"Here's the problem," Johnny went on. "She's only fifteen, and we think that's too young."

"I'm not," Angel blurted out. "I'll be a really good mum." She stroked her stomach. "I already love it."

Ruth inhaled sharply and gazed down at her cup. Those were almost the exact words that she had said in

407

this same room twenty years ago. But it had been Johnny in the firing line that time and her dad holding the metaphorical shotgun to his head.

"I said we'll talk about it, and we will," Johnny told Angel. "But that doesn't mean we're just going to say yes because you want us to. There are loads of things to take into consideration before we make any kind of decision."

"I've already decided." Angel raised her chin. "And your mum said the doctor won't do it if I tell them I don't want to, so you can't make me."

"My mother had no right to get involved," Johnny replied through gritted teeth. "And I don't want to hear her name in this house again. You got that?"

Angel was sorry that she'd mentioned her other nan, because she hadn't wanted to upset her dad. But this was her baby they were talking about, and she *would* have her say — whether they liked it or not.

"I'm sorry," she told Johnny repentantly. "I know you're trying to do your best by me, but I'd never forgive myself if I let you hurt my baby. And I'd never forgive you, either. If you try to force me, I'll run away and you'll never see me again."

"Stop being such a drama queen," Rita scoffed.

"I mean it," Angel said quietly.

Johnny gazed into his daughter's eyes and knew that she did.

"Can I say something?" Ryan asked.

Johnny jerked his chin up at him. "Go ahead."

"I totally get why you're so against this," Ryan started nervously, "'cos *I* wouldn't want someone like me anywhere near my daughter. I've already told you how sorry I am, and if I could turn back time it wouldn't have happened."

"I don't regret it," Angel interrupted, pain in her eyes as she stared at him. "I love you, and I thought you loved me."

"I do," Ryan assured her. "And I'm not saying I regret it — not the way you think I mean it, anyhow. I just went about it the wrong way." He looked Johnny in the eye now. "I should have come to you first, Mr C; asked if it was all right to take her out. But I messed up, and I'm sorry."

"Too right you messed up," Rita chipped in sharply. "But you can save your apologies, 'cos we ain't interested."

"Mother, keep out of it," Ruth said quietly. "This is between Johnny and the boy."

"Not what you said when it was him and your dad," Rita grumbled. "You had plenty to say back then, as I remember."

Ruth could have reminded her mother that she hadn't even been in the room when Ruth, her dad and Johnny had had this same conversation, and had only come in at the very end. But she couldn't be bothered, so she gave a dismissive wave of her hand instead.

"I *am* sorry," Ryan repeated sincerely. "But I'm not sorry I met Angel, because she's the most special girl in the whole world, and I love her."

Johnny sighed. "I know you think you do, son, but you're both too young to know what love is really about."

"Trust me, I know," Ryan told him with certainty. "But I still get why you're not happy about it, so I'm not going to sit here and say it's going to be easy, 'cos I know it won't. All I want is a chance to prove that I can be a good dad to my kid. I'm not earning a lot right now, but I can get more hours. Or I'll get another job — whatever it takes."

As Johnny listened, he remembered what *he* had said when Ruth had got pregnant that first time. He'd sat at this table and offered to hand over whatever was left over from his dole money after he'd sorted himself out, as if a couple of piddling quid a week was sufficient. And if Frankie had let him, he'd have walked away without looking back. But here was the boy, talking about taking on an extra job to pay for his baby, and that put him to shame.

"I'll take care of Angel, as well," Ryan said now. "When you think she'd old enough."

Johnny frowned. "I hope you haven't got any stupid ideas about moving her into that house of yours, 'cos I'm telling you now, it ain't happening."

"God, no, of course not," Ryan agreed. "I'm gonna save up and get us a decent place."

"Don't be so ridiculous," Rita butted in. "You've only known each other a few weeks, and her grandad would turn in his grave if he thought she was living in sin. No." She shook her head and folded her arms. "If they're going to be stupid enough to let her have this baby, you'll make an honest woman of her or sling your hook."

410

"Will you just keep your nose out?" Ruth snapped. "She's too young to get married."

"She'll be old enough in a couple of weeks, so long as you give your consent," Rita pointed out. "Or do you *want* her bringing shame on us with a bastard baby?"

"No one's marrying anyone," Johnny said quietly, remembering how suicidal he'd felt when he'd been forced to marry Ruth.

"I'd love to marry Angel," Ryan told him. "I just didn't think you'd want me to."

Johnny looked at him closely. "You mean that, don't you?"

"More than I've ever meant anything," Ryan answered sincerely. "I know it's going to take time for you to trust me, but I'll wait however long I have to."

Angel looked at Ryan with tears in her eyes. "You don't have to go that far. I'd never try and force you to do something like that."

"I *want* to," he insisted. "It's all I've been thinking about since I heard about the baby."

"I need to go to work." Johnny stood up. "We'll talk about this again when we've all had a chance to get our heads around it." He jerked his chin at Ryan. "Do you want dropping back at Dave's? They said you're welcome to stay a few more nights."

"Nah, I'd best go home."

"Are you sure that's a good idea?"

"Don't worry, I won't be staying," Ryan assured him as he got up carefully. "I'm just going to grab some stuff and go to my mate's till I get somewhere else sorted."

Johnny nodded and slipped his jacket back on.

Ryan held out his hand. "Thanks, Mr C. I really appreciate you letting me come round to talk. I know how hard it must have been after I disrespected you like that."

"It's not over yet," Johnny told him, picking up his keys. "There's loads still needs sorting out. But in the meantime you'd best hurry up and get better so you can come back to work."

"For real?"

Johnny shrugged. "If she's as dead set on keeping the baby as I reckon she is, you're going to need every penny you can get. It's not cheap being a dad, you know."

Ryan grinned widely and said goodbye to a disapproving Ruth and Rita before he followed Johnny out.

Angel went after him, and put her arms around him on the doorstep. "Sorry," she apologised when he winced. "I just love you so much."

Ryan smiled his special dimply smile and whispered, "Love you, too, baby girl."

CHAPTER
THIRTY-THREE

Ryan was walking on air. He'd moved in with his mate Tommy the morning after the fight with his dad and life was just getting better and better.

After a few more talks round at their house, Johnny had decided to let Angel have the baby and he'd then given his blessing for them to get married. So, when they invited him round for dinner on Angel's sixteenth birthday, Ryan had got down on one knee and proposed properly.

Johnny had known that he was going to do it and had offered to help him buy the ring, but Ryan had insisted on using the money he had earned and saved — which wasn't much, so it was the tiniest diamond in the world that he presented to Angel. But she loved it nonetheless.

Now that they had Johnny's blessing, and Ruth's reluctant acceptance, the wedding was booked for three weeks later — almost the exact same length of time as it had taken for Ruth and Johnny to get married after their wedding date had been decided. But, unlike their glitzy ceremony and celebration, Angel and Ryan had decided on a low-key affair in the registry office, with just close family and friends in attendance. And they'd opted to come back to the house for the reception instead of splashing out on a fancy venue, despite Johnny having assured them that he would be picking up the tab so they could have whatever they wanted.

"It's about us being together and making our vows," they had told Johnny. "And we don't need to put on a show for the rest of the world to do that."

As preparations got under way back at the house, Johnny kept Ryan busy down at the yard. Like Frankie before him, he was determined to include the boy in the day-to-day running of the business — not only to give him and therefore Angel and their unborn child a good financial start in life but also to ensure that Ryan would be equipped to pick up the reins when the time eventually came for Johnny to hand them over.

Ryan was more than up for the challenge. No job was too big, too small or too dirty for him, which impressed both Johnny and Dave. And his good manners and amiable personality made him a natural for sales, so it wasn't long before Johnny set him to work alongside Tony, their only other regular salesman.

Ryan threw himself into his new career with a vengeance, not only to repay Johnny's faith in him but also because it kept him from fretting about his mam. It killed him not being able to see her and the kids, but his dad had banned him from going anywhere near them or the house and he knew that it would only make matters worse for them if he ignored the order. They still had to live with the bastard, after all.

In the back of his mind he couldn't help but wonder why his mam hadn't come looking for him during this time. She was a grown woman, so she could have if she'd wanted to. But she hadn't, so she obviously didn't. And that hurt. But there was nothing to gain by letting it eat him up, because, no matter what his dad did to her or the kids, she stuck blindly by him.

Still, despite all that, Ryan couldn't bring himself to get married without at least telling her and giving her the option of coming along. So, a week before the big day, he swallowed his pride and rang her.

"Where have you been?" Zeta hissed when she heard her son's voice. "I've been worried sick."

"At Tommy's," Ryan told her, warmed by the thought that she hadn't turned her back on him after all. "You should have come round."

"I have," Zeta told him. "A few times, but no one's ever there."

"Oh, sorry," he apologised. "I've been really busy at work. But anyway, listen — I've got something to tell you."

"What is it?" she asked, turning and glancing nervously at the living-room door when she heard a noise.

"I'm getting married," he announced, his voice as joyful as she ever remembered hearing it.

"Really?" She frowned. "Who to?"

"Her name's Angel," Ryan told her. "You've already met her," he went on with a smile in his voice. "Gorgeous blonde girl who rescued our Cherise from them girls in the park — remember her? You should do,

415

'cos you had a right go at her. But you'll love her when you get to know her."

Something clicked in Zeta's mind and a thrill of dread ran through her. That girl had come round to the house that night, and a couple of hours later the man Ryan had called his boss had barged in and started flashing a gun around.

She breathed in shakily and asked, "Is she anything to do with that man who came round that night?"

"Yeah, she's his daughter," said Ryan, chuckling softly as he added, "Yeah, and I know what you're thinking, but you're wrong. I'm not interested in his money. I just love her and want to spend the rest of my life with her. And not just her." He paused and took a deep breath before delivering the next bit of news. "We're having a baby."

"No . . ." The blood drained from Zeta's face.

"Christ, Mam, you don't have to sound so happy about it." Ryan laughed. "I know it's a shock, but the registry office is booked for next Friday, so —"

Zeta didn't hear the rest. Gary had come storming out of the living room, and his eyes were so wild that she dropped the phone in fright.

"Give me that," he bellowed, shoving her out of the way and snatching the phone up off the floor. "That you, you little prick?" he barked into it. "Well, fuck off, and don't ever ring here again, 'cos you died to me the day you brought a fucking maniac into my house and nearly got me killed. And the same goes for your mam. Contact her again, and it'll be on your head what happens!"

416

He slammed the receiver back onto its cradle and backhanded Zeta across the face, sending her flying down the hall.

"You ever go behind my back and talk to him again, I'll fuckin' kill you," he hissed. He rushed at her where she'd landed against the bottom step of the stairs and put his hands around her throat. "And then I'll kill him and them other two brats, an' all. This is *my* family, and I can do whatever the fuck I want to it. And no cunt's gonna tell me different — gun or no gun. D'ya hear me, bitch?"

On the brink of passing out, Zeta clutched at his wrists and nodded.

"Good job an' all," Gary snarled, tossing her aside and going back to his beer.

Zeta stayed where she was, her whole body quivering, her heart thudding so loudly that it sounded like bombs going off in her head. Gary was more than capable of carrying out his threat, she had absolutely no doubt about that. But she couldn't just sit back and let her son marry that girl, because it would ruin his life. She had to put a stop to this wedding before it was too late.

CHAPTER
THIRTY-FOUR

The sky was a brilliant azure blue when Angel opened the curtains on the morning of her wedding. There wasn't a cloud in sight, and the sun was already shining brightly despite it being only six o'clock. It was the best omen she could have wished for, and she was certain that God was smiling down on her, Ryan and their baby. Nothing and nobody could spoil this day. Not her mum with her mumbled misgivings, or her nan with her nasty under-the-breath remarks. *Nothing*. At eleven o'clock today she would officially be Mrs Angel Johnson. And, sad as she felt that she would never again be called by her father's surname, she couldn't wait.

The rest of the morning rushed by in a blur. The hairdresser arrived at seven and did Angel's, Ruth's and Rita's hair and make-up. Then the girl from the dress shop arrived, followed by the florist with the bouquet, the buttonholes and the posies for her mum, nan, Lisa, the two aunts she'd invited, and her sole bridesmaid, her schoolfriend Vicky.

Angel would have liked Ryan's little sister Cherise to have been a bridesmaid as well. But none of his family were coming, which was kind of sad. But it was his business, not hers, and Angel didn't want to quiz him because it was obvious that he didn't really want to talk about it.

Johnny stayed in his bedroom while all the woman stuff went on throughout the morning. He read the papers and watched a bit of telly, trying to pretend that he was cool about what lay ahead.

Ready by ten, he went downstairs and paced the front-room floor, smoking cigarette after cigarette and staring out of the window, waiting for the cars.

"Here . . ." Ruth came in and shoved a glass of neat whisky into his hand. "Drink that, and calm down. You're going to wear a hole in that carpet if you don't stop walking up and down on it."

"Cheers." Johnny took a grateful swig.

"You look very handsome." Ruth smiled up at him as she straightened his tie. "You know, this is where I found my dad on the morning of *our* big day," she said, a wistful glow in her eyes. "He was doing exactly what you're doing — pacing and smoking." She laughed softly. "He was a right hard bugger, but his heart was soft as anything when it came to me."

"I know," Johnny agreed, giving her a rare hug. "He was a good dad. I modelled myself on him."

"Really?" Ruth gazed up at him as she savoured the hug.

"Yeah." Johnny took another swig of his drink. "I never told you what really happened when I went to tell my mum about you and the baby, but we had a massive falling-out, and when I left her flat I remember vowing that I was never going to treat my kid like she'd treated me. I was going to be the best dad ever — like your dad was with you."

"And you have been," Ruth said softly. "Angel couldn't have asked for better."

I haven't been the best husband, though, have I? Johnny thought guiltily. But he didn't say it.

The doorbell rang.

"I'll get it," Rita called, already on her way up the hall, her heels clicking on the laminate flooring.

A couple of seconds later, Lisa popped her head around the door. She was smiling, but the smile slipped when she saw Johnny and Ruth embracing.

"Sorry." Ruth detached herself. "We were just reminiscing about our big day." She dabbed at her eyes with the back of her little finger so as not to smudge her make-up. "It seems like only yesterday. And now our little girl's about to take the same step." She smiled lovingly up at Johnny. "Hope they're as happy as we've been over the years."

Lisa couldn't take any more. She already felt sick to her stomach, and she flashed an accusatory look at Johnny from under her lashes as she said, "Hope you've got the wine open, Ruth? I really need a drink."

"I'll get you one," Ruth said. "I could do with a quick brew myself. My nerves are shot. You look very pretty, by the way."

"Thanks." Lisa smiled tightly. "So do you."

Angel was coming slowly down the stairs when Ruth and Lisa went out into the hall, and they stopped in their tracks and stared at her.

Suddenly misty-eyed, Lisa said, "Oh, babe, you look beautiful."

"Stunning," Ruth agreed. "Absolutely stunning."

Angel smiled, but her gaze drifted over their shoulders to her dad who was standing in the front-room doorway.

"What do you think, Daddy?"

Johnny shook his head and stared at his daughter in wonder. The dress was far simpler than her mother's had been. It was pure white satin with a lacy overdress and a slimline skirt that flowed softly to the floor. It had a sweetheart neckline and elbow-length sleeves, and the bodice was adorned with tiny pearls and subtle diamanté chips, which matched Angel's simple pearl earrings and the delicate tiara that was perched in her upswept hair.

"I can't even speak, darlin'," he murmured. "You look . . . incredible."

Ruth sighed softly and took Lisa's arm. "Come on — let's leave Daddy and his princess alone for a minute."

Lisa suddenly got it, and she smiled to herself as Ruth led her into the kitchen. *That* was why Ruth was being so nice: because Johnny was about to hand his daughter over to another man, and Ruth thought that she would be the only woman in her husband's life at long last. But she was wrong: because Johnny loved Lisa, and as soon as Angel and Ryan were settled he would do what he'd been promising to do for so long and take his rightful place in Lisa's bed — permanently.

★   ★   ★

Ryan had been on a knife-edge all morning, even though everything had been running like clockwork so far. He'd woken up on time — and without a hangover; the carnations had arrived in perfect condition; and the suit hadn't shrunk, fallen apart, or succumbed to moths. Nor had any of the other nightmare scenarios he'd been imagining come to pass.

Tommy had been great. He'd kept the beer flowing and the cigs coming, and he'd been chattering away non-stop to keep Ryan's mind off what lay ahead.

When the car arrived, Ryan's nerves jumped up a notch. Not because he was having second thoughts, but because he couldn't believe that this was really happening.

Dave and Hannah were already at the registry office.

"You look smashing," Hannah said, hugging Ryan. "Angel's a lucky girl."

"He's the lucky one," Dave corrected her, winking at Ryan. "But I don't suppose I have to tell you that, do I, lad?"

"No." Ryan shook his head and rubbed his hands together.

"Let's go wait on the steps and have a fag," Dave suggested, sensing that the lad's nerves were frazzled.

"I'll stop here." Hannah reached into her tiny handbag for her compact mirror. "Need to touch up my lippy."

"Nowt wrong with it." Dave kissed her. "You look gorgeous."

"Go and have your fag," Hannah said, smiling as she shoved him away. "And don't go walkabout."

422

Dave winked at her and followed the lads outside. He passed cigarettes to Ryan and Tommy and lit one for himself.

"Nervous?" he asked Ryan.

"A bit," Ryan admitted.

"Don't be. It'll all be over before you know it."

"Can't wait."

"Do us a favour." Dave jerked his chin at Tommy. "Just nip down to the corner and keep your eye out for the cars. Wave when you see them coming, so I can get soft lad inside."

Dave drew on his cigarette and waited until Tommy had gone. Then, turning to Ryan, he said, "You know I think you're a good lad, don't you?"

"Mmm." Ryan nodded, wondering where this was going.

"And you know I think the world of Angel, an' all," Dave went on. "So I want you to look after her, yeah? Marriage ain't always easy, and even the best ones have hiccups. But if you hit a low point, don't fall into the trap of thinking there's something better over the hill. Every girl's got a pussy, but they haven't all got the full package, and when you find one that has, you do right by her. D'ya get me?"

"I get you." Ryan nodded. "And you've got no worries, 'cos Angel's the one."

Dave peered into his eyes. Satisfied by what he saw there, he clapped him on the back.

"They're coming," Tommy yelled, waving to attract their attention.

Dave gave him the thumbs-up and took a last drag on his cigarette before hustling Ryan back inside.

In the ceremony room a few minutes later, Ryan breathed in deeply when the registrar's assistant pressed play on the CD machine and Angel's chosen song floated softly out of the speakers.

He turned his head when he heard the swish of material, and his stomach did a somersault when he saw Angel gliding towards him on her father's arm.

"You look beautiful," he whispered when she reached him.

"So do you," she whispered back.

"Are we ready to proceed?" the registrar asked. Smiling when they both nodded, he said, "We are gathered here today, to witness the joining together in matrimony of Ryan Lewis Johnson and Angel Rebecca Conroy . . ."

When he asked who would be giving this woman to this man, Johnny stepped forward and took Angel's hand in his. Their gazes met, and his heart filled up with a conflicting mix of pride and sadness. He raised her hand and kissed it softly, then placed it in Ryan's and stepped back.

It was done. Angel was no longer his.

When the ceremony was over and the couple went to sign the register, Johnny walked briskly to the door.

"Where are you going?" Ruth hissed.

"Need some air," he told her. "Won't be a minute."

He rushed outside, lit a cigarette and leaned back against the wall.

424

"Excuse me . . ."

He glanced around at the sound of the voice and squinted at the woman who was staring up at him from the foot of the steps.

"You're Angel's dad, aren't you?"

"Yeah." He nodded. Then, straightening up when he realised who it was, he said, "Sorry, love, didn't recognise you."

"Is — is it . . ."

She trailed off, but Johnny guessed that she was asking if she'd missed it. He nodded.

"'Fraid so, love. You should have rung — we'd have held it up for five minutes if we'd known you were on your way."

"Oh, no," she said quietly, her face crumpling.

"Hey, don't get upset," Johnny said, trotting down the stairs. "You're here now, so it's not a total disaster. Ryan will be made up to see you."

"He won't," she croaked, her eyes filled with pain as she looked up into his. "Not when he hears what I've got to tell him."

"Has something happened?" Johnny asked, getting a horrible feeling that she was about to say that one of Ryan's relatives had died. He just prayed it wasn't the kid sister or baby brother, because that would destroy him.

"I'm so sorry." Zeta's tears had started to fall. "I couldn't get hold of him, and it's been really difficult to get out 'cos Gary's been watching me like a hawk."

"What are you trying to say, love?" Johnny frowned.

"Only they'll be out in a minute, and I don't want

anything to spoil their day. Tell me what's up and I might be able to soften the blow."

"You won't." Zeta shook her head. "No one can. It's terrible, really terrible. And now it's too late."

"What is?"

"I can't tell you. I shouldn't even be here. Gary's going to kill me if he finds out."

"Hey, you're part of this family now," Johnny told her reassuringly. "And we look after our own, so don't you worry about Gary. I'll sort him out."

"You don't understand," Zeta sobbed. "This is bad. Really, really bad."

"Come on, love, nothing's so bad that it can't be sorted." Johnny put his arm around her as she cried. "I can help. Just tell me what's wrong."

"You're his dad," Zeta mumbled.

Johnny jerked back, his face screwed up in disbelief. "Don't be so ridiculous. Why would you say a thing like that?"

"Because it's true."

Johnny felt the anger churn in his gut. The kids would come walking out at any minute, and their marriage would be damaged before it had even started if they were confronted by this crazy bitch spouting shit. He grabbed her arm and marched her away from the entrance.

"Listen, love, I don't know what kind of sick game you're trying to play here, but it ain't on. Your son and my daughter have just got married, and they're about to have a baby. Have you any idea what it would do to them if they heard what you were saying?"

426

"It's true," Zeta insisted. "I wish it wasn't, but it is, and there's nothing I can do to change it. That boy's my life. Don't you think I know how much this will hurt him?"

"So fuckin' pack it in before he hears it," Johnny ordered. "I wouldn't mind, but I'd never even seen you before I came round to yours a few weeks back."

"It was a long time ago," Zeta sobbed. "You've forgotten."

"I'm not being rude," Johnny said, "but I have *never* slept with a black woman in my life. If I had, believe me, I'd remember."

"I used to work at LA Ladeez," she told him.

"*And?*" He shrugged. "I don't even know what that is." Then, glancing nervously back at the door, he said, "Look, love, it's your problem if you screwed around behind your old man's back, but don't try and drag me into your mess."

"Ryan is yours." Zeta was adamant.

Johnny's patience snapped. "Just fuck off back to your crack pipe, or whatever you've been taking that's got your head all twisted up," he snarled. "And keep your whacked-out fantasies to yourself."

"Johnny . . .?" Ruth called out just then. "Are you out here? Where are you? They're about to come out."

"Coming," Johnny called back. Then, giving Zeta one last warning look, he shook his head and ran back up the steps.

Dave and Hannah followed the wedding party back to the house in their own car. There had been no chance

427

to talk back at the registry office, but Dave had something on his mind.

"I want a word with you," he said quietly, pulling Johnny out into the back garden.

"What's up?" Johnny asked, taking out of his pocket the spliff he'd made earlier and walking around to the bushes to light up.

"Who was that woman you was talking to?" Dave demanded. "And don't say you wasn't, 'cos I saw you. And if it was one of your tarts, you're bang out of order for fetching her near Angel's wedding."

A grin spread over Johnny's face as his friend told him off. "Finished?" he asked when he stopped. "First off, no, it was *not* one of my tarts — as you put it. And second, I'd never do anything to upset Angel, and you should know that."

"I do," Dave conceded, taking the spliff when Johnny offered it to him. "But you've got to think about how it would have looked to her if she'd walked out and seen you. Who was it, anyhow? And why was she crying? Is it someone you've dumped?"

"Will you be told? She's nothing to do with me," Johnny reiterated sounding amused. "If you must know, it was Ryan's mam, and she's mad as a fuckin' hatter, so I was telling her to clear off."

"Why, what happened?" Dave sucked deeply on the smoke and glanced back to make sure that Hannah wasn't watching through the parlour window. She didn't mind him having the occasional smoke, but she wouldn't approve on a day like this.

428

Johnny rolled his eyes. "You're not going to believe it, but she only tried to tell me I'm his dad. Now is that crazy, or is that crazy?"

"You're kidding?" Dave snorted. "You're not even black. Like, *hello!*"

"Neither's his dad," said Johnny. "But that's not the point."

"So what did you say?"

"I said, I don't know what sick game you're playing, but you'd best quit it before someone hears you and starts spreading it about. Can you imagine the shit *that*'d cause?"

"Volcanic." Dave shook his head. "Is she a crackhead or something?"

"That's what I thought, so I told her to get back to her pipe and leave me out of her fantasies."

"Too right." Dave chuckled and passed the spliff back.

Johnny drew on it. "I told her, I said I'm not being rude, love, but I've never slept with a black woman in my life. But — see how fucked her head is? — she goes, I used to work at LA Ladeez. Like that was supposed to mean something."

"Eh?" Dave narrowed his eyes. "Say again?"

"LA Ladeez," Johnny repeated, frowning. "Do you know what it is?"

"Oh, mate." Dave ran a hand over his suddenly sweaty face. "That's the club where we took you on your stag night."

"And . . .?" Johnny's mouth had gone dry.

"And the lads put to, and we kind of paid for you to have some private entertainment," Dave admitted. "But you were totally kaylied, so there's no way you could have got it up."

Johnny gaped at him for several long moments. Then, grinning again, he threw a playful punch at his arm.

"Nice one, mate, you had me going for a minute there."

But Dave didn't smile. He just held Johnny's gaze with a guilty one of his own, and Johnny's heart sank like a brick.

"You're not kidding, are you?"

Dave shook his head.

A terrible flashback leapt into Johnny's mind, and he was back in the hotel bar with Frankie.

"Forget about the slags . . . I've decided to let it slide this time . . ."

Then he was in bed with Ruth in the honeymoon suite, his eyes closed, a hazy vision of a woman . . . his cock in her mouth.

"Who did you set me up with?" he demanded. "What colour?"

"There were two of 'em," Dave told him. He sounded sick. "One black, one white."

Johnny turned and stared through the parlour window at Ryan, who was making his way around the room offering sandwiches to the guests. No way . . . there was no way the boy could be his son. No way on Earth. It just wasn't possible.

430

"You'd best talk to his mam again," Dave suggested quietly. "At least you'd know, one way or the other."

"Nah, it's bollocks." Johnny shook his head. "Look at him. He looks nothing like me."

"But you can't know that for sure," Dave said gravely.

"I can't." Johnny gritted his teeth. "What if it turns out he *is* mine? What am I supposed to tell Angel? That she's just married her brother, and is about to have his baby? It'll destroy her."

What was left of the colour in his cheeks drained completely when another thought occurred to him.

"What the fuck am I supposed to tell Ruth? She's put up with a lot, but there's no way she'd stand for this. And I'll lose everything if she divorces me. I signed a contract — I'll be out on my arse." He looked at Dave with dread in his eyes. "I'm finished."

"No point thinking that far ahead," Dave said calmly. "Let's just take it one step at a time. Talk to Ryan's mam, and we'll take it from there. Yeah?"

"Yeah." Johnny nodded and sighed heavily. One of the best days of his life had just become the absolute worst.

CHAPTER
THIRTY-FIVE

Angel and Ryan had insisted that they wanted to go to Blackpool for their honeymoon. Johnny had tried to persuade them to choose somewhere more exotic, somewhere at least *sunny*. But they just wanted to have fun, and there was nothing more attractive to a couple of kids than a massive funfair and an endless row of slot-machine arcades. And the beach was just across the road, so it was heaven on all counts.

They were so excited when they came downstairs with their suitcase after the somewhat subdued party that Johnny had to force himself to smile, even though his heart felt like it had a lead weight in it.

"Ready?" he asked, reaching for his car keys.

They nodded, their faces beaming as they clutched at each other's hands.

"Can you give me a lift?" Lisa asked as they headed for the door.

"Yeah, sure," Johnny murmured, waving her out.

"You'll come straight back, won't you?" Ruth asked as she came out onto the step to wave them off.

"I just need to nip down to the yard and do a bit of paperwork," Johnny lied. "But I'll try not to be too late."

432

"Can't Dave do it?" she asked, standing close and stroking his lapels. "I thought we could have an early night."

"I'll try," he said unenthusiastically. Then, remembering that he was going to have his work cut out to keep her if Ryan's mother turned out to be telling the truth, he kissed her and winked. "See you in a bit."

Lisa stayed in the car when Johnny got out to walk Angel and Ryan into the train station. When he came back she had her arms folded, her legs crossed, and a furious scowl on her face.

"What's going on, Johnny?"

"What do you mean?" he asked as he set off.

"You know what I mean, so don't act stupid," she snapped. "All that kissy-kissy shit with Ruth. Angel's gone now, there's no reason to keep up the act."

"Not now," Johnny groaned. "I've got shit to deal with, and my head's already mashed."

"What shit?"

"Nothing that concerns you."

"Don't you dare try and fob me off with that old line." Lisa bristled. "I'm not Ruth. You can't just pat me on the head and tell me to keep my nose out of man stuff. I've wasted the past twenty years of my life waiting for you."

"Wasted?" Johnny repeated, with a dry smile. "Like that, is it? Well, sorry for wasting your time, darlin'. Maybe you'd best stop holding out for something you're never gonna get, then, eh?"

"You bastard," Lisa hissed, tears flooding her eyes. "You're not dropping me like that. I'm worth more than that, and you know it."

Johnny sighed heavily. "Yeah, I know, and I didn't mean to upset you. But you know the score. If I walk, I lose the lot."

"You'd still have me," Lisa reminded him.

"And you'd get bored without the money," Johnny told her. "And don't lie and say it doesn't mean anything, 'cos we both know you'd hate it if I was skint. We'd be at each other's throats in no time. Then *you'd* probably chuck *me* out, and that'd be it. I'd have lost everything. The business, Angel — and you."

"I'd never chuck you out," she insisted. "You still don't get it, do you, Johnny? I *love* you."

"And I love you, too." He sighed. "But we've got to be realistic."

"That's all I've ever been," Lisa replied resignedly. "Dreams are for kids like Angel," she added wistfully. She'd envied her cousin for getting married before her, and now even her cousin's *kid* had beaten her up the aisle. A few more years and no man would look twice at her, never mind ask her to marry him.

"I'm sorry," Johnny said. "This isn't how I planned for things to turn out, but it is what it is. And it's not *that* bad, is it?" He reached over and gave her thigh a squeeze. "We've still got this."

"Yeah, but I'm still sharing this with Ruth," Lisa muttered.

"I spend more time with you than I do with her," Johnny pointed out.

"But you don't sleep in my bed," Lisa said quietly, swiping a rogue tear off her cheek. "I never get to wake up next to you. I never got to have a kid with you, or call you my husband. And I never will, will I?"

She gazed at him, but Johnny kept his eyes firmly on the road. There was no point saying anything when she got like this. He just had to let her pour it all out, and then make it all better with a bit of loving.

Lisa exhaled loudly and stared out of the window as they drove on.

When they reached Hulme, Johnny turned off Chester Road a couple of streets back from hers.

"What are you doing?" Lisa asked as he drove slowly down the road towards Ryan's parents' house.

"Just need to check something out," he murmured.

"Like what? Ryan's not even here. You've just seen them off on the train — remember?"

Johnny stared at the house as they passed, and Lisa frowned. "What's wrong, Johnny? Have you got some kind of beef with them? Is that why they weren't at the wedding?"

"Jeezus, will you quit with the questions?" he snapped, putting his foot down and screeching around the corner.

"Go easy, Speedy Gonzales," Lisa complained, clinging to the sides of her seat.

"Sorry." He pulled up sharply at her door. "See you tomorrow."

"You're not even coming in?" Lisa's brow creased with disappointment. "I thought that was why you told Ruth you were going to the yard."

"There's something I've got to do," Johnny told her.

"Like what?"

"I can't tell you."

"Oh, I see." Fury sparked in Lisa's eyes. "Got someone else lined up, have you? Younger and prettier is she? Like I used to be before you stole half of my life. Well, fine . . ." She unbuckled her seat belt. "You go for it. But don't bother creeping back round here when you get fed up, 'cos I've had it with you."

"It's got nothing to do with another woman," Johnny lied. "Just trust me on this."

"Why should I?"

"Because I'm asking you to."

Lisa's chest was heaving. Johnny looked at her breasts moving up and down inside her tight top and grinned.

"All right, I'll come in for a bit."

"Don't put yourself out on my account," she huffed as she pushed the door open and climbed out.

Johnny switched off the engine and followed her into the house.

After they'd made love Lisa lit a cigarette while Johnny went to the toilet. As soon as he'd gone his mobile phone began to ring on the bedside cabinet. She reached for it without stopping to think that it wasn't hers. Before she had a chance to speak, Dave started talking.

436

"Have you seen her yet?" he whispered. "What do you think? Is he your kid, or what?"

Lisa hung up.

Johnny was still naked when he walked back into the room five minutes later. He was rubbing his wet hair with a towel.

"Hopped in the shower," he explained. Then, tilting his head to one side when he saw Lisa sitting in Ruth's old wicker chair, with her dressing gown on, a moody look on her face and her foot bouncing up and down like it was on a spring, he gave her a questioning smile. "What's up with you?"

"Dave rang," she spat, her teeth clamped angrily together. "Wanted to know if you'd seen *her* yet. Oh, and is the kid yours?"

"Jeezus," Johnny groaned. "Tell me you didn't speak to him!"

"I didn't get a chance," Lisa yelled. "He just came right out with it. But is that all you care about? Him finding out about us and telling your precious fucking *wife?* Maybe I'll save him the trouble, hmmm?" She jumped up and snatched her own phone off the ledge. "I'll just call her and tell her all about it," she hissed, scrolling through her numbers. "And maybe I'd best tell her about your other kid while I'm at it? What d'ya think, *stud?*"

"Lisa, stop," Johnny yelped, running around the bed and snatching the phone out of her hand.

"Give it back," Lisa demanded as she tried to grab it. "I hate you!" she cried, smashing her fist down on his chest when he moved the phone out of reach.

"You're a bastard! You've been stringing me along for years, and all the time you've been having kids with other women. Well, you've crossed the line this time. I'm going to tell Ruth everything!"

"Just listen to me," Johnny pleaded, grabbing her wrists as she made for the door. "It's not what it sounds like."

"Fuck off!" Lisa spat as tears streamed down her face. "I know what I heard, and don't you dare try and twist it round and make out like I'm stupid. You've got another kid. What's his name, huh? How old is he? Does he fuckin' *look* like you?"

Johnny pulled her into his arms as her heart broke. She struggled, but he held on tight.

"I swear to God, it's not like that," he told her. "Just calm down and I'll tell you the truth."

Lisa sobbed for a while longer. Then she pulled herself together, swiped at her puffy eyes and wrenched away from him.

"All right, talk. I'm listening."

Johnny sat down on the bed and patted the mattress, gesturing for her to join him. But she went back to the chair and lit a fresh cigarette with shaking hands.

"All right, it's like this," he said. "A woman's claiming that she had my kid."

"I *knew* it!" Lisa's nostrils flared as she struggled to keep the tears at bay.

"Nearly twenty years ago," Johnny went on. "Way before you and me got started."

A flicker of confusion came into her eyes. "Does Ruth know?"

"No." Johnny shook his head. "And neither did I till today. That's why Dave was asking if I'd seen her yet, because he said I should go and talk to her — find out if she's lying."

"Are you still seeing her?"

"No, and I didn't even know I'd slept with her. It was supposed to have happened on my stag do, but I knew nothing about it."

"Now I know you're lying," Lisa said scathingly. "You can't have sex and not know about it."

"On Angel's life." Johnny crossed himself.

Sure now that he was telling the truth, because she knew how much Angel meant to him, Lisa frowned.

"She came to the registry office," Johnny went on. "She was outside when I went for a fag, and she just came right out and told me."

"But if you don't know her, how did she know who you are?"

"Fuck knows." Johnny shrugged. "I mean, I know who she is *now*, but I only met her for the first time a few weeks back."

"So you *have* been seeing her?"

"No."

"You must have — or how else would she have known where to find you today?"

Johnny closed his eyes and sighed. "She's Ryan's mam."

"*What?*" Lisa's mouth dropped open. "You don't mean . . . she's not saying it's *him*?"

Johnny nodded.

"Bullshit," said Lisa, the word hissing out of her as if she'd been deflated. "No way. That would mean . . ."

"Yep." Johnny's voice was grim. "Angel's just married her brother."

"No." Lisa shook her head. "This isn't happening. Oh my God. What are you going to do?"

"You tell me." Johnny wrung his hands in a gesture of helplessness. "I hoped I might see her when I drove round there. But I don't even know what I'm going to say if I *do* see her. And I was pretty nasty back there at the registry office, so she might not even want to talk to me again."

"She can't drop something like this on you and then refuse to talk about it," Lisa said indignantly. "And if she tries to, I'll *make* her talk."

Johnny gave her a grateful little smile. "Guess this isn't quite how you expected to end the day, is it?"

"*Nothing's* ever quite what I expect with you," she replied dryly. "Anyway, why don't you just go and knock on the door? Then she'll have to talk."

"I can't. Her husband's a bit of a beast."

Lisa drew her head back and gave him an incredulous look. "Since when has Johnny Conroy been scared of beasts?"

"I'm not," he told her. "But *she* is. And she's the one who'd cop for it if he found out why I was there. I'm pissed off, but not enough to do something like that to her."

Lisa nodded. "Okay, I see your point," she said, standing up. "I'll go and pour us a drink. Get dressed, then we'll work out what to do about this."

440

Johnny reached for her hand as she headed for the door and said, "Thanks, Lisa. It's good to know I've got you on my side."

"You always have had," she said softly.

CHAPTER
THIRTY-SIX

The following afternoon Zeta had just made a bottle for the baby and was drying her hands on a tea towel when the doorbell rang. She glanced out through the kitchen window and tutted when she saw a blonde woman on the step.

She opened the door. "Yes?"

"Oh, hiya, sorry for disturbing you." Lisa smiled. "Are you Zeta Johnson?"

"Who wants to know?" Zeta narrowed her eyes and took a step back. If the woman was a bailiff or a summons server, the door was going to be slammed right in her face.

"Aw, sorry, love, I've given you a turn, haven't I?" Lisa chuckled, deliberately roughening up her tone so that the woman would know that she was from around here. "I'm like that, an' all. Number of times I've hid behind the sofa when the debt collectors come calling, or the TV detector van's on the street."

Zeta gave a little upward jerk of her chin and said, marginally less aggressively, "It's all right, I was just busy. What d'ya want?"

"I've got a parcel for you," Lisa lied. "Looks like it might be from a catalogue," she added, praying that the

442

woman actually used catalogues. But then, most of the women round here did — Lisa included.

Zeta peered at Lisa's hands, and then at the ground around her feet. "So where is it, then?"

"Oh, yeah, sorry . . . it's round at my place." Lisa grinned. "Don't know why they brought it to mine, 'cos it's not even the same number, never mind the same street. But they're a right load of cowboys, them delivery drivers. I went out with one once, and he reckons they just bung stuff out anywhere when it starts getting late and they've still got a load on."

"Why didn't you bring it?" Zeta asked, thinking it must be true what they said about blondes being as thick as pig shit.

"I was going to," Lisa told her. "But I had to rush out this morning and couldn't take it with me. Then I got off the bus and realised I'd have to pass yours to get back to mine, so I thought I might as well let you know about it so you can come and get it — save me having to walk back round with it."

"I can't come right now," said Zeta.

"No probs — whenever you're ready." Lisa tried not to look too disappointed. "But if you're coming tonight it'll have to be in the next half hour or so, 'cos I've got a date. And I don't know when — or *if* — I'll be coming home," she added with a conspiratorial smile.

"Where is it?" Zeta asked, wanting rid of her.

Lisa told her the address. Zeta thanked her, said she'd come as soon as she could and closed the door.

★　★　★

"Well?" Johnny looked up from the couch when Lisa walked in. "Did you have any luck?"

"She's coming," Lisa told him. "Not sure when, though."

Twenty minutes later there was a knock at the door. Lisa was lying on top of Johnny, but she quickly peeled herself off him and shooed him into the kitchen. Then, after patting her hair down, she answered the door.

"Oh, hiya, love. Come in a minute, I'll just get it for you. It's in the back room."

"I'll wait here." Zeta stayed put.

"Aw, please don't," Lisa said quietly. "There's someone I'm trying to avoid, and if they see you standing out here they'll know I'm in."

Zeta sighed, but relented and stepped inside.

"Sit down." Lisa waved her towards the couch. "Won't be a minute, but there's a load of junk in the back and it might have got covered."

She went through to the dining room and jerked her head at Johnny.

Zeta had just sat down when Johnny walked in. Her eyes widened and she jumped straight back up to her feet.

"Not so fast!" He ran to the door before she could get there.

Zeta turned to go out the back way instead, but Lisa was blocking the dining-room door.

"What do you want?" Zeta asked.

"The truth," said Johnny.

"I've already told you. But you made it clear that you didn't believe me, so what's the point?" Zeta folded her arms and gave him a defiant look.

"Tell me again," Johnny ordered. "And you might as well sit back down, 'cos you're not going anywhere till we sort this out."

Zeta scowled with irritation. "You do know Gary's going to come looking for me if I don't go back in a minute, don't you?"

"Let him." Johnny shrugged. "You're the one who doesn't want him to know about this. It makes no odds to me."

Zeta sensed that he was going to stand his ground. She didn't have time to argue, so she sat down sulkily.

"What do you want to know?"

"First off, how can you be so sure it was me?" Johnny asked. "Not being funny, love, but if you were working in that kind of club and getting paid for extras you must have had hundreds of blokes."

Zeta's cheeks reddened. It had been years since she'd sold herself, thanks to Ryan's wages keeping them afloat. And she hadn't wanted to do it when she *had* been doing it, so it was shameful to have to talk about it. But this was too serious for modesty.

"It was you," she told him, her gaze lowered. "It was a club rule to make the punters wear joeys, but we'd run out that night. I wasn't going to do it, but your mate paid well over the odds and I was broke, so . . ." She trailed off and shrugged, her cheeks still flaming. "A few weeks later I realised I was pregnant."

"Were you with your husband back then?"

Zeta nodded.

"So it could be his."

She shook her head now. "He was locked up when I got caught. There's no way Ryan could be his."

"So how come *he* thinks he is?"

"'Cos he's not too bright when it comes to dates. I made out like Ryan was premature, and Gary's not interested in that sort of stuff, so he didn't ask questions. But *I* knew."

"That still doesn't explain why you think it was me," said Johnny, clutching at straws. "You couldn't have known my name, and there's no way you would have recognised me."

Zeta's cheeks flared afresh. "I had your wallet away," she admitted. "There was a signing-on card in it with your name on it, and a little photo of you and a girl out of one of those machines. I've still got it. The photo, I mean, not the wallet or the other stuff."

"Why?" Lisa couldn't hold her tongue any longer.

"I don't know." Zeta's shoulders drooped in shame. "I just thought you were really nice-looking." She flicked an embarrassed glance at Johnny. "And then Ryan came out so gorgeous and I guess I had some kind of romantic notion that one day . . ." She flapped her hands and sighed. "One day, Gary might — I don't know — leave, or *die*, or something."

There was as edge of longing in her voice when she said this, and Johnny and Lisa exchanged a *what the fuck?* glance.

446

"And what then?" Lisa asked. "This fantasy of yours . . . Gary dies, or pisses off, and then what? You and Johnny get together and bring your son up together, happy ever after, la la la?"

"I know it was stupid," Zeta answered defensively. "But when you've got sod all to hang onto, anything's better than nothing. Anyway, now you know, so I'll go."

"You can't just walk away from this," Johnny said incredulously. "If it's true — and I'm not saying I believe it — but *if* it is, then there's a great big mess that needs sorting out. Ryan and Angel are married, and that's against the law."

"So are a lot of things," Zeta said pointedly. "I might be black, and I might have done stuff that I'm not proud of, but I'm not as stupid as people seem to think. I know my son's been working for you, and there's no job that pays as much as he's been coming home with for a couple of hours' work of a night. No legal one, anyhow."

"Stop trying to change the subject," Lisa chipped in. "Marrying your own brother is major. Have you any idea how much trouble they'd get into if anyone found out? And they're having a *baby*. What if it comes out with two heads, or something?"

"Jeezus, Lisa, do you have to?" Johnny groaned.

"I'm sorry, but it needs saying," Lisa replied.

"There's no point talking about it," Zeta said wearily. "I tried to stop it, but I was too late, so we might as well just forget it. They're married, and they're having a baby, and I know he loves her, so what's the point of wrecking their lives?"

"They can't stay married now we know," Johnny gasped. "It's not right."

"What's the difference?" Zeta asked. "Seriously. They've already done it, and that can't be undone. Anyhow, it's not like they grew up with each other and knew what they were doing. That *would* be wrong. But they haven't got a clue. They just met and fell in love. They're innocent."

"*We* know," Johnny reminded her. "Shit, they're supposed to be living in my house when they get back off their honeymoon — but how can I let them share a bed like a normal married couple now?"

"If you love them, you'll just have to try," Zeta said simply.

"Are you for real?" Johnny's expression was a study in utter disbelief. "It's *sick*. I'm not having my daughter screwing her own brother."

"If they don't know, it won't hurt them," Zeta argued.

"But what if they find out further down the line?" Lisa asked. "Or should I say *when* they find out, 'cos they're bound to. The kid will probably be deformed in some way, and it might end up needing all sorts of operations. So what happens when the hospital do blood tests and put two and two together?" She stared from Zeta to Johnny. "Sorry for being so blunt about it, but this isn't going to go away. They need to be told, and this marriage needs to be annulled asap."

Johnny closed his eyes and lowered his head into his hands. Lisa was right, but it was going to absolutely break Angel's heart. And the baby was something else they were going to have to deal with. Knowing Angel, she might still refuse to have an abortion, and what then . . .? They'd be stuck with it for life.

CHAPTER
THIRTY-SEVEN

Ruth was in bed, reading a book by the light of the lamp, when Johnny got home that night. He knew she'd been waiting up for him when he saw that she was wearing a negligee instead of her usual flannelette cover-all nightie. She had on eyeliner and lipstick, and she'd brushed her hair and left it loose so that it lay softly around her shoulders.

Johnny had always liked her hair. It was thick and glossy and always smelled sweet, and the fact that she was wearing it down was a clear signal that she was up for sex. But he doubted she'd still want it when she heard what he had to say.

He desperately didn't want to tell her, because he knew that it would turn their entire world on its head. If she let him stay — and it was a very big *if* — she would be in total control, and she would make sure that he knew it. And he wouldn't blame her after the way he'd treated her over the years. But she could just as easily kick him out on his arse. So, either way, his life was going to be shit from here on in. But he had to tell her because he had to tell Angel and Ryan, and there was no way of doing that without Ruth finding out.

"You look tired," Ruth said, looking up at him and noticing the lines etched on his face. "I told you to leave that paperwork for Dave. You'd already had a stressful day, what with the wedding and everything." She smiled now, and closed her book. "Angel rang while you were out, by the way. They've booked into the hotel and were just about to have dinner. Then they were going to wander down to the arcades for the last hour. She sounded that excited, I was a bit jealous."

"Ruth," Johnny said quietly. "There's something I need to tell you . . ."

"No!" Ruth gaped at him as if he'd just admitted to murdering the pope. "No, you're lying."

"I'm so sorry," Johnny murmured, his shoulders drooping as he sat miserably on the edge of the bed. "I didn't believe it. Still don't want to. But it all fits."

"How could you?" Ruth was crying now. "How could you do this to me? I've given my whole life to you."

"I know," Johnny said, reaching for her hand.

"Don't!" she hissed, slapping his hand away. "Don't you dare touch me. You disgust me. I'm not stupid," she went on through gritted teeth. "I know you've had other women. But this . . ." She trailed off and shook her head, the pain of his betrayal shining out through the tears. "You've had a baby with someone else."

"I didn't know," Johnny reminded her. "It wasn't like I've been playing Daddy to him behind your back.

Angel's my only child — always has been, always will be."

"But she's not, though, is she?" Ruth spat. "Not if what you're saying is true. And I can't imagine why you'd tell me if it wasn't. After everything I've been through, that was the only thing I had that no one else could give you. Your first child. Except she's not."

"She is to me," Johnny insisted. "In my heart, where it counts."

"Oh, Johnny, what have you done?" Ruth asked plaintively.

"I didn't know," he said again, shaking his head. "I honestly didn't know."

He looked so miserable, Ruth knew that he was telling the truth. She pushed the guilt aside and got up onto her knees, pulling him into her arms. He was her man, and good women supported their men through thick and thin. If they stuck together, they would get through this.

"We'll have to tell them," Johnny said quietly. "And we're going to have to stop them from having this baby as well. It's not too late, is it?"

"I don't know." Ruth sighed. "I'll make an appointment at the clinic." She inhaled sharply. "Do you think we'd best ring Angel before they — you know?"

"They've probably already done it," Johnny said resignedly. "They're on honeymoon. Anyway, it's too late to worry about that now. It's not like they haven't done it before."

"Only once."

452

"Once, twice, a thousand times — what difference does it make? No." Johnny exhaled loudly. "Might as well let them enjoy the next few days, 'cos God knows they won't be enjoying themselves after they get back."

CHAPTER
THIRTY-EIGHT

Angel was glowing when she stepped off the train, and Johnny felt sick to his heart when she ran into his arms.

"Did you have a good time?" he asked, holding her tighter than he'd ever held her before.

"Oh, Daddy, it was amazing," she gushed. "The best time of my life." Detaching herself when Ryan walked up with their case and several carrier bags, she linked arms with him and laid her head on his shoulder. "Ryan's been treating me like a queen."

"Good," Johnny muttered, shaking the boy's hand.

"It's been fantastic," Ryan told him. "Had to force her out of the arcades, though, or we'd have been broke on the first day. You've raised a right little gambler."

Johnny groaned inwardly when the pair gazed lovingly into each other's eyes. They were absolutely crazy about each other, but in twenty short minutes their world would be torn apart irreparably. And it was all his fault.

"So, have you missed me?" Angel teased as they walked out to the car.

"Course I have," Johnny told her. He held the back door open for her.

"I've missed you, too," she told him, giggling as she climbed inside. "Ryan had to tell me off because I kept wanting to ring you."

"At two and three in the morning," Ryan said. "I told her you wouldn't be interested in what was going on outside our bedroom window, but she wanted to ring every time anyone laughed out there, she was that excited."

Johnny smiled tightly, and closed the door when Ryan had climbed in beside Angel.

He was quiet on the drive home, but Angel didn't notice because she was too busy gushing about the fantastic hotel, their lovely room, the brilliant rides on the fair, the money she'd lost in the arcades . . .

Ruth had been waiting nervously. When she saw the car, she ran to the door.

"Hi, Mum," Angel trilled, jumping out and giving her a hug.

They had never been as close as a mother and daughter were supposed to be, and Ruth was taken aback by the overt show of affection.

"Come in," she said, unsure how to deal with it. "I'll put the kettle on."

Rita wandered out of the parlour.

"Hiya, nan." Angel waved. "I've brought you back some rock."

Rita raised an eyebrow and looked at Ruth. When Ruth gave her a warning look and mouthed *Not yet*, she shook her head and went back into her room.

"Put the case in our room," Angel told Ryan when he came in behind her dad with the bags. Giggling, she said, "Sounds funny, that, doesn't it? *Our* room." She gave a happy sigh and took the carrier bags off him. "I'll wait till you come down, then we can give them their presents."

Ruth and Johnny exchanged a hooded glance and traipsed into the kitchen.

Ruth put the kettle on and made a pot of tea.

"This is for you," Angel said, her eyes glowing as she took a small, neatly wrapped present out of one of the carrier bags and handed it to her mum. "I love it — hope you do too."

Ruth peeled the paper off and smiled when she saw the necklace. It was a tiny silver rose pendant on a delicate silver chain.

"It's beautiful," she said.

Angel smiled and took another present out of the bag. "This is yours." She handed it to her dad. "I let Ryan pick it, so don't blame me if you hate it."

Johnny opened it and raised an eyebrow when he saw the matching cigarette lighter and keyring.

"It's great. Thanks. I'm always losing my lighters, but I'll look after this one. And I needed a new keyring."

"See, I told you he'd like it," Ryan told Angel proudly.

"Men," she scoffed. "There's a load of rock as well," she went on, reaching back into the bag. "They're all different flavours, so you'll have to have a root and decide which ones you want."

Ruth looked at Johnny and gave a surreptitious nod. He took a deep breath and said, "Angel, hush for a

456

minute, darlin' . . . there's something we need to tell you."

"Nooooo . . ." Angel wailed. "No, I don't believe you! You're lying!"

"I wish we were, baby," Johnny put his arms around her. "I swear to God I had no idea, or I'd have told you."

Ryan's face was a mask of shock and disbelief. "This ain't real," he mumbled. "This ain't real . . ."

"I'm so sorry." Ruth reached over and patted his hand. "We both are."

"You're lying," Angel said again, dragging herself free of her father's arms. "You've been planning this all along to punish us."

"Don't be ridiculous," said Ruth.

"Shut up!" Angel yelled, slamming her fist down on the tabletop. "*You* probably came up with it, 'cos that's the kind of twisted thing you'd do."

"Angel, this is my doing, it's got nothing to do with your mum," Johnny told her firmly. "She only found out a couple of days ago — same as me."

"Don't talk to me," Angel spat, glaring at him with the grief of betrayal in her eyes. "You're my dad — you're supposed to look after me."

"I have," Johnny said helplessly. "I *will*. But we had to tell you — you understand that, don't you?"

"No," she sobbed, shaking her head and clutching at her stomach. "No, I don't understand. Me and Ryan love each other, and you just want to destroy us because your marriage is a joke. But you can't. No one can. 'Cos we're too strong for that."

"You're brother and sister," Johnny told her.

"I don't care," Angel hissed. "That's your problem, not ours. We're married, and there's nothing you can do about it."

"Angel, get real," Johnny groaned. "What do you think's going to happen when the baby's born? There's every chance it'll be deformed."

"I . . . don't . . . care," Angel said slowly and angrily. "It's *our* baby, and we'll love it whatever it looks like."

"It's not just what it looks like that you've got to worry about," Johnny told her. "It could have brain damage, or be blind, or deaf. *Anything* could be wrong with it."

"I've made an appointment at the clinic," Ruth chipped in. "The sooner we get it taken care of, the sooner we'll be able to sort out the rest of this mess."

"How dare you?" Angel snarled. "You've got no right, and I won't go. I am having my baby, and if you try to stop me I'll go to the police. And I *mean* it. You're not murdering my baby."

Rita had wandered in. She tutted loudly when she heard this, and said, "Don't you come marching in here shouting the odds like you're the queen bee, lady, 'cos you've had your own flaming way for too damn long. This is *our* house." She pointed from herself to Ruth. "And we'll decide what happens in it."

"Stick your house," Angel yelled at her. "And stick you. I've never liked it here, anyway. Come on, Ryan, we'll go to your mum's."

458

"We can't," he said, the shock still evident in his voice.

"Fine, then we'll got to my Aunt Lisa's. She won't turn us away."

"You're going nowhere," Johnny said firmly. "Just sit down, 'cos we're going to talk about this whether you like it or not."

He stared at his daughter, and she stared stubbornly back.

"Don't make me say it again," he warned her quietly.

Lips closed tight, nostrils flaring, Angel grabbed her chair and dragged it right up next to Ryan's before sitting down.

"Go on, then," she said icily. "Talk. But it won't make any difference. We're still going to be married, and I'm still going to have this baby."

CHAPTER
THIRTY-NINE

The next few months were hell on earth for Johnny. Angel wouldn't budge, and he knew that she would follow through with her threat to leave home if they pressurised her — and there would be nothing they could do to stop her.

Nothing legal, anyway.

Angel loved Ryan too much to let him go, and no matter how many times Johnny and Ruth reminded her that he was her half-brother she just didn't care. Echoing what Ryan's mother had already said, she argued that they hadn't grown up together, so therefore there was nothing dirty or weird about it.

Ryan, on the other hand, just couldn't get his head around it at all. He was still too shell-shocked to really deal with any of it.

Ruth and Rita wanted Johnny to send him home to his mother. But Johnny knew exactly what would be waiting for Ryan there, so he couldn't bring himself to do it. And he argued that at least if Ryan was here where they could see him, they had a chance of keeping this awful secret contained. Anyway, if Ryan left Angel would follow him, so it was better to let him stay — for now.

Angel's last month was especially difficult. Her stomach was enormous, and her ankles were so swollen that she could barely walk. But she couldn't visit the doctor because she was terrified of somebody in authority finding out and taking the baby off her — as her mum and her nan had ominously told her would happen. And that was why she agreed to a home birth when they suggested it, even though she knew that something could go wrong and she would have no pain relief. But she decided that she would sooner take the pain than risk losing the baby.

Drained by the stress of it all, Angel spent the last few days of her pregnancy in bed. The pain started as soon as she woke up on the final day, but it was several hours before her waters finally broke and her labour really got under way.

Ruth and Rita were ready. They shoved Ryan out of the room, telling him that it was no place for men, and then they watched and waited as Angel writhed in agony.

"I want my dad," she cried, thrashing from side to side as the pain tore through her.

"He's at work," her mum told her.

"Ring him," Angel begged.

"I have," her mum said. "He's busy. He promised to come as soon as he can."

Angel had never before felt such agonising pain and there were moments as the next few hours ticked by when she thought that she was going to die. But there was no such escape, and the pain just kept on coming.

Miraculously, she fell asleep for a few minutes in the early evening, but when she woke she heard her mum and her nan whispering on the other side of the room.

"I'm getting a bit worried," her mum said. "Maybe we should call an ambulance."

"And ruin the plan?" her nan hissed. "We've come this far, so don't go panicking now."

"I know, but it's going to be so hard."

"Shut up! Or do you *want* her to cotton on?"

"No, of course not,"

"Well, button it, then. And go and check on the blackie. Make sure he doesn't come bursting in."

"Ryan," Angel murmured. "I want Ryan."

"Not now, love," Ruth said soothingly. "Men don't belong at births. He's happier downstairs watching telly."

"My dad . . .?"

"Still no word. I'll ring him again in a bit."

Rita yanked Ruth's arm and jerked her head at her, gesturing for her to do as she'd been told.

Angel was gripped by fear now as well as pain. She didn't know what they had been talking about, but her instincts told her that they were up to something. They were keeping Ryan away from her and she suspected that they hadn't rung her dad at all, because he would have come straight home if he'd known.

Between contractions, she looked around for her mobile and was believed when she saw it on the bedside table. She licked her dry lips.

"I need a drink, nan. Can you get me some water?"

462

"In a minute," Rita told her. "I don't want to leave you on your own, so just wait till your mum comes back up, eh?"

Angel nodded as if she was willing to wait. Then she coughed. And coughed again.

"All right, calm down," Rita said when she started making choking sounds. "I'll get the flaming water."

When her nan left the room, Angel grabbed her phone and rang her dad. She sobbed when she got the busy tone and dialled Lisa's number instead.

"Help me," she whispered when Lisa answered. "The baby's coming and — *aagggghhh!*"

The fiercest contraction yet washed over her, and she gripped the phone so hard that she disconnected the call before dropping it.

"Okay, love, we're here." Ruth bustled back in with her mother on her heels. Rita was carrying a glass of water that she plonked down before raising the sheet to have a look at what was happening down below.

"I can see the head."

"Soon be over," Ruth told Angel.

Angel's mobile started to ring. Rita spotted it on the floor and snatched it up. Seeing Lisa's name on the screen, she sneered and switched it off.

The house phone immediately began to ring. Rita ran out onto the landing in time to see Ryan come out of the front room and go to answer it.

"Leave it," she ordered, rushing down the stairs. "It's for me, I'm expecting a call."

"How's Angel doing?" Ryan asked, his worry clearly visible in his shining eyes.

"Fine," Rita told him. "Shouldn't be long now. Why don't you make yourself useful and go get the washing out of the machine, eh? You can hang it on the line for me — give you something to do while you're waiting."

Ryan nodded, and went off into the kitchen as Rita answered the phone.

"Is Angel okay?" Lisa asked.

"Absolutely fine, nothing for you to worry about," Rita told her.

"She just rang and said the baby was coming."

"Yes, well, me and her mum are with her, so it's all under control," Rita assured her. "Anyway, got to go. We'll ring you when it's over."

"Is Johnny there?"

"Not yet. Bye."

Rita slammed the phone down and rushed back upstairs.

"Lisa," she whispered when Ruth gave her a questioning look. "She rang her." She nodded at Angel. "Told her it was on its way. I said we'd ring her to let her know when it's done, but you'd best hope it's fast, 'cos I wouldn't put it past nosy-knickers to come round."

Ruth nodded and looked down at Angel.

"Just a few more pushes, love."

464

CHAPTER
FORTY

Dave was on his way home from work when Lisa rang him.

"Johnny's not with you, is he?" she asked before he could speak. "I've been trying to ring him, but his phone's engaged."

"He's probably got it in his pocket and sat on it again," Dave told her, chuckling softly. "He's always doing that — ends up ringing random numbers. Have you tried the yard line?" he asked. "He was still there checking out some new motors when I left. Mind you, he probably won't hear it if he's outside, and it might have already switched over to answer-phone mode."

"Damn it," Lisa hissed. "I'll just have to keep trying."

"Something up?" Dave asked.

"Yeah, Angel rang to tell me she was in labour, and she said she needed help. But it got cut off, and she didn't answer when I rang her back."

"Try the house phone," Dave suggested. "Her credit might have gone."

"I rang the house and Rita answered," Lisa told him. "She said her and Ruth have got everything under control, but I've got a funny feeling so I'm going to go round there."

"You might be best leaving them to it," Dave advised. "You know what they're like — they won't appreciate the interference if they've got it sorted."

"I know what you mean," Lisa agreed. "But I can't just sit here. She sounded really scared, Dave. If something goes wrong . . ."

"Look, I'm not too far away," Dave told her. "I'll call in and see what's happening, and let you know. Okay?"

"Thanks," she murmured gratefully. "I'll try Johnny again, then I'll catch a cab over."

Angel was screaming his name, and Ryan couldn't bear it. He wanted to go up to her so bad, but Ruth and Rita had made it clear that he wasn't welcome. And, under the circumstances, he thought it was probably best to stay out of the way.

He and Angel might be legally married, and they might have slept together, but that was before they had found out that they were related. He still loved her, and she loved him just as deeply, but he just couldn't behave the way she wanted him to. She wanted to carry on as if nothing had changed, but it had, so he hadn't been able to do it.

And he definitely didn't want to go into that room right now and see her privates — especially not in front of her mum and nan, who would probably call him a pervert.

So Ryan stayed in the hall and listened as the girl he loved but could no longer have went through agonies upstairs.

He saw the shadow through the glass in the front door and yanked it open just as Dave was about to knock.

"All right, son?" Dave asked, patting him on the arm when he saw the worried look on his face. "Everything going okay up there?" He winced when Angel immediately screamed, and said, "Guess it won't be long now, eh?"

Ryan shook his head. "Hope not."

Johnny's car pulled into the drive. He jumped out when he saw Dave and Ryan in the doorway.

"What's going on?" he asked.

They all raised their eyes to the ceiling at the sound of a baby crying.

"Looks like you're a dad," Dave said, extending his hand to Ryan.

Shocked and relieved, Ryan shook it.

"Congratulations," Johnny added, clapping him on the back. "But how come you're down here? You should be up there with Angel."

"They didn't want me in there," Ryan croaked. "And I didn't think it was right," he added quietly.

Johnny knew what he meant. Angel was determined to carry on their relationship, but Ryan's conscience wouldn't allow him to get intimate with her. He'd stayed to support her through the pregnancy but he hadn't touched her, and Johnny truly respected him for that.

When the crying stopped abruptly, all three men looked at each other. Then Johnny headed for the stairs and ran up to the bedroom.

★ ★ ★

Ruth had the child wrapped in a towel, her back turned to Angel.

"What's happening?" Angel cried, desperate to see her baby. "Why's she stopped crying?"

"Nothing for you to worry about," Rita told her, pushing her back down. "Your mum knows what she's doing."

When Johnny burst through the door his gaze landed on Angel but slid quickly to Rita, who was staring at him open-mouthed, a look of pure guilt on her gaunt face. He snapped his head around and looked at Ruth. She had an intense look on her face, and his stare shot down to the baby in her arms.

"Oh, my God!" he yelled when he saw that she had her hand pressed down firmly over the baby's mouth and nose. "What the hell are you doing? Ruth! *STOP IT!*"

"Leave her!" Rita blurted out urgently. "It's for the best."

"What's going on?" Dave rushed up the stairs, alarmed by his friend's shouting. "Is everything okay?"

"She's trying to fucking kill it," Johnny yelped, wrenching the child out of Ruth's arms.

The baby girl lay floppy in his hands, her tiny mouth — through which she had drawn her first breath just a couple of minutes earlier and cried her first cry — now slack and turning grey.

"Oh, Jeezus, what have you done?" Johnny cried, tears splashing down onto the lifeless little body as Angel screamed hysterically in the bed behind him.

"It's for the best," Ruth said coolly, echoing Rita. "All I've done is put it out of its misery — and us out of ours."

"It's a baby," Johnny sobbed. "An innocent baby."

"It's deformed," Ruth shot back. "And it would have been a burden on Angel for the rest of its life. They're brother and sister — they can't have babies. It's sick."

Dave looked at Ruth with shock and disgust in his eyes. "You evil bitch," he gasped. "You evil, evil bitch."

"This has got nothing to do with you," she screeched. "Get out of my house!"

"No." Dave shook his head as a feeling of deadly calm settled over him. "This has gone way too far. It's time to put an end to it once and for all."

Johnny had laid the baby on the bed and was frantically blowing into her mouth, saying, "Come on, sweetheart" between puffs. "Don't do this to me. Breathe, baby, breathe."

Ryan came in and stood helplessly by the door. "I've called an ambulance," he said quietly.

"No!" Angel screamed. "They'll take her off me."

"They won't," Dave said with chilling certainty. "Because you and Ryan are not related."

"What are you talking about?" Johnny asked, his gaze still fixed on the baby as he gently compressed her chest with his thumbs. "You *know* they are."

"You might be Ryan's dad," Dave told him quietly. "But you're not Angel's. So there's nothing wrong with the baby, and no reason why her and Ryan can't be together."

"What?" Johnny gasped. "Of course Angel's mine. Don't talk fucking stupid, man."

"Mate, I'm so sorry," Dave murmured guiltily.

"Don't you dare!" Ruth screamed, flying at him and tearing at his hair. "Don't you *DARE!*"

He flung her aside and said, "It should never have happened, and I've regretted it ever since. But it *did*, and I knew as soon as I set eyes on Angel that she was mine. I should have told you then, Johnny, but I was too much of a coward."

"You're saying you slept with Ruth?" Johnny demanded. "When? *Where?*"

"It was at your place," Dave admitted. "After Ruth lost the baby and tried to kill herself. I'm so sorry, man. We got stoned, and you weren't there, and . . ." He trailed off and wrung his hands. "It shouldn't have happened, but it did. Angel's my daughter."

"Why didn't you tell me back then?" Johnny's eyes were bright with betrayal. "Why leave it till now?"

"Because I didn't want to lose you," Dave told him shamefacedly. "*She* begged me not to tell you, and I went along with it because I knew you'd never forgive me. But enough's enough. It's one thing breaking up a couple to keep the secret, but it's totally something else to kill a baby. That's just evil."

Before Johnny could say anything, the baby's body jerked and she took a gulping breath.

"Oh, thank God!" he cried, lifting her gently and holding her against his chest. "Thank God, thank God."

The ambulance pulled up outside just then.

"Paramedics," a voice called through the open front door.

"Up here," Johnny yelled.

"She seems absolutely fine," the paramedic assured them after checking the baby over. "But we'll take mum and baby in, just to be on the safe side."

Johnny nodded and ran his hands over his face. He stepped back and watched as they helped Angel into a chair and strapped her in.

"I'm so sorry, darlin'," he murmured.

"It's not your fault," she whispered, tears streaking her face as the baby was at last placed in her arms. "Look, Ryan," she gasped as the paramedics carried her and her child out onto the landing. "She's smiling. And she's got a dimple in the same place as yours!"

Johnny started to follow, but stopped when he realised that Ruth was right behind him.

"Where the fuck d'ya think you're going?" he demanded.

"To the hospital with my daughter," she told him, raising her chin defiantly.

"*NO!*" Angel cried. "I don't want her anywhere near me or my baby. Don't let her come, Daddy — *PLEASE.*"

"You heard her," Johnny growled, shoving Ruth back into the bedroom.

"Johnny, don't go," Ruth begged, rushing after him and clutching at his arm as he made to follow the group down the stairs. "We need to talk about this."

"Get your fucking hands off me," he snarled. He flashed her a warning glare filled with hatred and disgust.

"*Johnnnyyy!*" she wailed, sinking to her knees. "Don't leave me . . ."

EPILOGUE

Zeta smiled when she opened the door and saw Johnny on the step.

"Angel's in the back room with the kids," she said as she stepped back to let him in. "Ryan's poncing about in the bathroom — as usual. I'll give him a shout."

"Cheers," Johnny said, heading up the hall.

"Dad, look!" Angel cried when he walked into the living room. "Heaven's standing up all on her own."

Johnny smiled and squatted down to watch as his granddaughter teetered in the middle of the room. Heaven saw him and gave him a two-toothed dimply grin, and Johnny instinctively held out his hands when she lurched towards him. She managed to stay on her feet and took a couple of tiny stumbling steps into his arms.

"Clever girl," he said softly, sweeping her up and kissing her. He beamed with pure joy.

"Ryan!" Angel yelled. "She took her first steps!"

"Aw, and I missed it," Ryan groaned, rushing down the stairs.

"Look at me," said his little brother Luke as he stood up and took a couple of staggering steps before falling onto his bottom.

"Stop showing off," Cherise scolded, clucking her tongue at him like a little mother hen.

Angel smiled and gave the girl's cheek a gentle pinch. Then, sniffing her fingers, she said, "Ooh, that smells nice. What is it?"

"Just cocoa butter," Cherise said before going back to her book.

"Fancy a brew, Johnny?" Zeta popped her head through the door.

"Not really got time," he told her. "I've come to take Ryan out. And the rest of you can come, an' all, if you hurry up and get your coats on."

"Oh, I'm not really dressed for going out." Zeta self-consciously touched her hair.

"Don't be daft," Angel said, smiling at her. "You look lovely. Doesn't she, Ryan?"

"Gorgeous," he agreed, kissing his mum on the cheek as he went out into the hall to get his jacket. "Where we going, JC?"

"It's a surprise," Johnny told him, winking at Angel. "Come on, you lot — hurry up."

When they were all ready, Angel carried Heaven out and put her into her seat in the back of Ryan's Mondeo. Cherise sat beside the giggling tot and made sure that her straps were secure, before turning and doing the same for her little brother.

Zeta blew them a kiss before climbing into the back of Johnny's BMW. A couple of the neighbours who were standing on their steps waved as the car passed, and Zeta waved back. It still felt weird to be acknowledged after years of being avoided like the

476

plague, but a whole lot of things had changed in the months since Gary had disappeared after a night out on the lash, only to turn up dead the next morning with his face in a pool of slime down by the canal. The kids had never been happier, and neither had Zeta. And it had been fantastic to have Ryan move back home with his lovely wife and baby. Although there had been a little period of sadness after the DNA test had come back negative. Zeta had been truly shocked by that, because she'd been positive that Johnny was Ryan's father. But while any other man would have been furious at having been put through such an ordeal, Johnny had said that he would be there for Ryan regardless.

Johnny had turned onto Lisa's road by now.

"Won't be a sec," he said, pulling up outside her house.

Lisa was upstairs when he let himself in. "Aren't you ready yet?" he yelled up the stairs. "Everyone's waiting."

"All right, all right, no need to shout," Lisa yelled back. She dashed out of the bedroom and clumped down the stairs. "Just had to change."

"Why? What was wrong with what you had on?" Johnny asked, kissing her when she reached the bottom.

"I looked fat," she complained, stroking her bump. "Junior's getting a bit too big for my liking. I'm going to have to go on a serious diet."

"Don't you dare," Johnny warned. He copped a quick feel of her boobs. "I like you like this."

"Yeah, well make the most of these babies while you can." Lisa laughed. "'Cos they're gone when this one pops out and I hit the gym."

"Shut up and get in the car," Johnny ordered, slapping her on the bum as she passed him.

"All right, Zeet?" Lisa said as she hopped into the front seat. "How's the course going?"

"Great." Zeta smiled. "I passed my first two modules, so now I've just got to get through the next eight and I'll be flying."

"Good for you, girl." Lisa winked at her.

Ryan followed as Johnny set off again, but when they had driven around almost every back street in Hulme, only to end up on City Road just over the other side of the park, he said, "What's he doing? Doesn't he know where he's going?"

"Oh, he knows," Angel said, smiling secretively.

Johnny pulled up suddenly, and Ryan had to brake hard to avoid slamming into the back of him.

"Come on, kids," Angel said as she unbuckled her seat belt.

"Are we there?" Ryan asked, frowning.

Angel just smiled again and got out to join her dad, Lisa and Zeta, who were already out of their car and waiting on the corner.

"What's going on?" Ryan asked. "I thought we were going to Pizza Hut or something."

"Come with me," Johnny said, putting an arm around his shoulder and walking him around the corner. He stopped a few feet down and turned Ryan around.

Ryan was confused, wondering why Johnny had brought him here when they were supposed to be going out. But then his gaze landed on the sign that had been erected above the old garage on the opposite side, and his jaw dropped.

CONROY & SON AUTOS

"For real?" he gasped.

"For real." Johnny squeezed his shoulder. "I got the lease last week. We open in the morning."

"But . . ."

"Just shut up and enjoy it," Johnny told him. Then, leaning closer, he whispered, "And keep your fingers crossed that Lisa has a girl, 'cos it'll cost us a bleedin' fortune if we have to get the bloke out to paint an extra 's' on."

"Oi, I heard that," said Lisa.

"We were talking *about* you, not *to* you." Johnny chuckled. "And this is man stuff, so keep your nose out."

ISIS publish a wide range of books in large print, from fiction to biography. Any suggestions for books you would like to see in large print or audio are always welcome. Please send to the Editorial Department at:

ISIS Publishing Limited
7 Centremead
Osney Mead
Oxford OX2 0ES

A full list of titles is available free of charge from:

Ulverscroft Large Print Books Limited

(UK)
The Green
Bradgate Road, Anstey
Leicester LE7 7FU
Tel: (0116) 236 4325

(Australia)
P.O. Box 314
St Leonards
NSW 1590
Tel: (02) 9436 2622

(USA)
P.O. Box 1230
West Seneca
N.Y. 14224-1230
Tel: (716) 674 4270

(Canada)
P.O. Box 80038
Burlington
Ontario L7L 6B1
Tel: (905) 637 8734

(New Zealand)
P.O. Box 456
Feilding
Tel: (06) 323 6828

Details of **ISIS** complete and unabridged audio books are also available from these offices. Alternatively, contact your local library for details of their collection of **ISIS** large print and unabridged audio books.